Praise fo[illegible]ue

"Words cannot express how much fun I had while reading Come True. It's clear that once again, Brindi Quinn has created a highly entertaining masterpiece, and I am in love."

—Liz Wyatt
Quirky Cat's Fat Stacks

"Wishes really do Come True! I guarantee you'll finish this book with a big, shit-eating grin on your face. I certainly did!"

—Stephanie E. Donohue
Author of Windsong

"Come True takes you on an entrancing and magical adventure. Quinn's writing is captivating from start to finish."

—Adina Chiles
Author of Secrets of a Rose

"A true joy to read: delightfully fun, sassy, and snarky with a fantastical flair. Brindi Quinn makes a mark on the book community with a story that's sure to please, and characters that are definitely ones to remember."

—Nicole Northwood
Author of The Devil You Know

Come True

Come True

A BOMB-ASS GENIE ROMANCE

BRINDI QUINN

Come True: A Bomb-Ass Genie Romance
Copyright © 2022 by Brindi Quinn

Published by Midnight Tide Publishing | www.midnighttidepublishing.com
Edited by Meg Dailey | www.thedaileyeditor.wordpress.com
Cover artwork by Em Ryn Art | www.instagram.com/emryn_art
Cover typography by Victoria Cooper Art | www.facebook.com/victoriacooperart

This is a work of fiction. Names, characters, brands, trademarks, places, and incidents either are the products of the author's imagination or are used fictitiously. Any resemblance to actual events, locales, organizations, or persons, living or dead, is entirely coincidental and beyond the intent of either the author or the publisher.

All rights reserved, which includes the right to reproduce this book or portions thereof in any form whatsoever except as provided by U.S. Copyright Law.

ISBN: 978-1-953238-80-1
Original publication date: April 27, 2022

Contents

This book contains sexual content and drug use inappropriate for a younger audience. This book also contains a hearty dose of F-bombs and other adult language that may be offensive to some readers. Triggers include: swearing, fantasy racism, cheating, attempted sexual assault, depression, blood, smoking, drinking, and fantasy violence.

To the failed relationships that made me decent at writing romance.
So long, effers.

CHAPTER 1

Dolly

I've noticed a change in the clientele of this place over the last few years. Used to be it was all thirty-somethings sniffing around for old records. Now, it's just skinny bitches holding up oversized pairs of jeans.

That isn't fair. I'm sure not all of them are bitches.

But some of them are.

This place is a wonderland of abandonment, painted in a film of aged light and reeking of that same sticky smell that always makes me wonder whose past it is I'm breathing—whose stains, whose dust—as I browse the shelves of fancy glassware mingling with dated ceramics, in search of something special.

Definitely not this plate someone made for their mother. It must have been from said mother's least favorite child to have ended up in a place like this.

My fingers trail over knobbed glass and textured pottery, mixing my smudges with all the other smudges that have come before, until landing on one piece that stands out among the rest. It's practically begging for attention, with that fat little bottom and that slender *neck*. And walls dark enough to keep whatever secrets might be plugged up inside. It isn't a vase. But it could very well become a vase. It's a glass bottle, and it looks like something that may have stored precious oils in biblical times.

Yeah. That wouldn't look half bad with daisies stemming from the top. The flowers it holds will keep the darkness at bay. Another living thing to occupy my space. Someday, maybe, I'll get a cat, but for now, all I have are flowers.

If I want to buy anything else here, it will have to wait. I'm not the sort of person allowed to be splurging. In fact, I'm not the sort of person allowed to buy anything. My year of atonement is quickly coming to an end, but for today, I must obey the rules.

No treats. No rewards. No needless purchases.

This vase is a replacement for the one I broke last week.

Nothing more.

I grasp the bottle around the neck and escort it all the way to the counter, ignoring the vintage jewelry and well-sniffed books I would have rummaged through a year ago at this time. The worn reusable sack dangling from my shoulder pats against my thigh in expectation. It's the same one I've had since college. A memory, maybe, of better days. I was a much different person when these threads were strong. Now, it seems like most of what I own is becoming . . . papery.

The bag. My sneakers. My soul.

The bottle doesn't care about the state of my bag. It slides in nicely, settling in like it owns the place, as I butt my way through the doors of the thrift shop and to a world where the birds are up to their normal fuckery under a sky that can't decide what it wants. The daylight is hard at work, fending off the chill lurking in the shadows, while below, decaying petals drench the sidewalks like a springtime plague. Molted pink and dirtied white cling to my soles, desperate for another chance at life.

Shame. They were once something beautiful. This street was like the lure of a siren when the cherry trees were full. People came to gawk.

Last year at this time, I may have been one of them, meeting up with friends, slipping on cheap heels for the sake of cheap tacos at that flossy little place down the street. But my days of salted rims are long behind me. After what I did, I have few friends left.

My apartment comes into sight at the top of the hill—charming, if I can brag a bit, with a weathered brick front and an iron gate that no longer creaks after being well oiled last month. It's a place with history. With character. Marking the people who live here as people worth knowing. That's why James and I chose it. Three aching years ago.

The trees were full then.

Well, I made it a whole two minutes without talking about my ex, so that's great. That's what we call progress.

I stand at the gate and miss the creak of it. The creak started shortly before James moved out, and now that it's gone, this gate, like the flowers, like the bag over my shoulder, is just one more reminder of a time that will never come back.

I regret what I did. That truth resonates through the universe so strongly that it no longer needs to be said. And over these last fifty weeks of atonement, the truth of it has grown no dimmer. It's here. In everything I touch.

Two more weeks.

Two more weeks until I'll let myself move on.

The building smells old. Not as thickly as the thrift shop, but *old*. The wood is stained with the breath of a hundred people who have walked through these halls since the 1920s. Without question, at least a few ghosts roam this place after dark, treading over the same scratched wooden floors they did while they were alive. The super covers the smell with scented plug-ins. One thing I've learned while living here is that lavender does not mix well with must.

My unit is on the third floor, which is great for avoiding window burglars but not so great for fires. Let's hope that whatever comes for me, it isn't a fire. And something is sure to come for me. I feel it constantly lurking over my shoulder, waiting to take a bite. Can I withstand a bite? I'm not so sure.

One good thing about these old buildings is that the doors are solid. Even if the chic brass knob was replaced long before James and I moved in, the door is original, heavy, safe. The heft of it closes behind me as I lock myself in for the night. My apartment is . . . fine. About what you'd expect for a place missing half its stuff. I didn't replace most of what James took, so there are awkward blank spaces on the walls. He kept the loveseat; I got the couch. I have a bunch of movies but nothing to play them in.

In two weeks, I'll begin rebranding the place.

If I'm up to it.

For now, at least I have this vase.

I tell the speaker on the table to turn on and play a mix from my music subscription. It doesn't hear me correctly and tries to schedule an appointment. It's . . . not the best. A knockoff James's mom got me for Christmas the year before last. James took the good one.

James. James, James, James, James. Can I have a single freaking thought without my ex-boyfriend butting in?!

The vase is the real hero of the day. I welcome it to the apartment, introduce it to my coat rack, my video game cartridges, my potted plants—not really. I take it out of the sack and dip it into a bath I've prepared for it in the sink. It needs a good rinse before it can live here. I pick the tacky sticker off the base with nails that haven't seen polish in god knows how long and then move on to the plug. Obviously, cleaning the inside is as important as cleaning the outside, but the little bugger is reluctant to comply. Come on now, we need to get behind your ears. I pull and pry and lube it up with extra soap, but that thing is lodged in there good. Maybe it's glued. Just a thought, but that might have been a good thing to check before I bought it.

If I can't use it as a vase, it no longer counts as a necessity, which means I must go back tomorrow to donate it. And now I'm out a whopping two-ninety-nine. I blanket the outside of it in my nicest towel—only the best for visitors—and then set it onto the counter where it mocks me in that deep, mysterious way it has. It's a shame. I do like the color of it, so dark it's almost black but with hidden pigment when held to the sun.

"You can stay the night," I tell it. "But no free breakfast."

Yes, I've resorted to speaking to things that will never speak back. Is that the true mark of loneliness? Lucky my mom calls every couple of days. Wow. Waiting with bated breath by the phone for one's own mother.

In two weeks.

In two weeks, I can start living again.

"Maybe I'll come back for you in two weeks, if you're still there," I tell the bottle that will never become a vase. "Sorry I made you a promise I couldn't keep. It's kind of my MO."

And then I do something . . . strange. No judgment, I'm in a weird headspace. As I eye the mysterious newcomer of unknown origin, I suddenly feel compelled to . . .

I lift the bottle from the counter and set my lips against it.

Kissing bottles is certainly a new low.

After, I feel silly. Silly may actually be too polite. I feel stupid as hell that I've just kissed a reused bottle I got from the least sanitary of places.

And it seems the feeling is warranted. The moment I return the bottle to the laminate is the moment it all goes dark.

I've been poisoned? I've had an allergic reaction? There are toxins held within that ancient turquoise glass?

These are the thoughts racing through me as I blink open my eyes and find my face planted on the kitchen floor. Never a good idea to get eye-level with your kitchen floor. One finds all sorts of treasures hiding out under crannies and betwixt nooks. I see an eraser, a spill mark, a hair cluster and . . . feet.

FEET?

There are most certainly bare feet standing on the other side of my open fridge door! At least I got my wish. A burglar came for me instead of fire. I reach for a gun, but I have no gun. I don't even like guns. So what do I grab? A fucking *glue gun* from the craft bin beside my kitchen table. And I hold it with all the confidence it hasn't earned.

"L-Larry?" I venture. "Is that you?"

Larry's the name of the super. The only one that should have keys to my apartment.

The fridge door slams, and feet much too tan to be Larry's begin closing in on me. Not to mention, Larry always, always, *always* wears socks. One time, I saw him wear them under flip-flops. That toe-separator was working overtime.

I digress, and the feet are nearly upon me, soon accompanied by a head dropping into frame; the intruder has just crouched. Definitely not Larry. Larry's incapable of smirking like that.

WHAT THE FUCK?

It's a guy and, let's be real, it's a guy of higher than average features, with dusk-blue hair tossed effortlessly with product and eyes a paler shade of blue than I thought possible on a person. Sharp, the centers pierce like turrets through a blizzard while the corners taper with smug amusement.

Oh, yeah, and did I mention he's NAKED? All but for a pair of gray sweatpants low around his waist and rolled up at the ankles.

"Hello, *Master*," he says with undue familiarity. "Sorry for invading your refrigerator. You were taking your time, and I was getting hungry." He makes a chomping noise with his teeth.

"Stay back!" I scamper into a sitting position and steadily crab crawl away from him, holding the glue gun like it might fool him into thinking I'm armed.

"No use pulling the trigger," he counters, straightening to reveal a body that's *lean*. "Your bullets will miss me every time."

He . . . thinks it's a real gun?

But it has a cord!

No matter.

"I have a very steady hand," I assert, knowing my hand is anything but. "You have three seconds to get out of here or I'll shoot!" It sounds like something someone would say in a movie—from what I remember of movies.

"I don't doubt your hand, Master," he says and takes a step

closer. "But you're incapable of hurting me physically. It won't work, even if you try."

Again, this is *clearly* a glue gun.

"How did you get in here?" I demand. "We're on the third floor, and I know I locked the door."

He tips his head. "Really? You're the one that brought me in. You said I could spend the night. And then you sealed it with a kiss."

Blinks befall me—One. Two. Three.

"You were in my apartment the whole time?!" I jab the glue gun in his direction and notice for the first time that it has a half-used stick of glue butting out the ass of it. "You were watching when I kissed that—that vase?!"

And, oh, dear lord, now we've admitted to another living person that we kissed a vase.

"Vase?" He shakes his head comically as though this is all a big misunderstanding. "No, no. That's not a vase. It is my *holding* vessel. I'd invite you in for a tour, but it's a bit cramped."

"Your *holding* vessel? As in something that *contains* you?" I look between the shirtless, blue-haired guy, eyes trailing over the tight chest of him before flicking to the bottle on the counter in all its arcane wonder. "As in, you expect me to believe you came out of it? Like you're a . . . a *genie* or something?"

"To be honest, genie is kind of a derogatory term where I come from, but—"

"Get out." I prod the glue gun at him with new vigor. "Get out, get out, get out!"

For a moment, it's as if a shadow settles over his brow as a shimmer from some nonexistent light source catches his eye. "Is that a wish?"

"No, it's not a fucking WISH! It's a demand. Get out of my apartment or I'm calling the cops!"

His face falls, disappointed by my answer, and he shrugs. "They won't be able to see me."

And it seems he has no intention of budging. I scoot from the safety of the linoleum, which has the audacity to cover beautiful hardwood floors, and into the living room, which looks like someone's in the middle of moving out of it, and search for something that might make for an actual weapon.

Dumb move. All the knives are back in the kitchen.

"You don't need to be afraid of me, Master," the intruder says in a dark tone that betrays the contrary. "Just like you can't hurt me, I can't hurt you. It won't work. See?" In a flash, he cops a pen from the holder on the counter and spears it at me with the aim of someone who's spent too many nights playing bar darts. Dexterity has never been my strong suit. Before I can react, the makeshift javelin heads for my throat—but pivots at the last second and hits the wall with an anticlimactic *thunk*.

Blinks ensue. "How did you do that?!" I cry. "It turned, like, ninety degrees!"

"Like I said, I can't hurt you." He stretches long, with his arms cracked over his head, before releasing them and beginning to peruse the area like he really has been welcomed in, poking at a ceramic pot I got from a flea market. "Hmph. Mine's better."

"I-if you're a genie," I stammer, hand clutched around the pen I've captured from the floor. "Prove it."

"Make a wish," he says with the smile of a devil.

"No."

His smile shatters. "Fine." Then he sticks his arm out—which is a rather nice arm, if I'm allowed to comment—and opens his hand stiffly. The bottle, his *holding vessel*, flies off the counter and into his hand as though it's been summoned.

And now I'm really worried. Because this means he isn't an intruder at all.

It means it's all in my head.

"Oh my god." I drop the pen. "You aren't real."

"Ha!" His head falls back in one hard laugh. "That's a fun one. I mean, I am real. Touch me if you want." And as he says it, he grazes his hand over his own abdomen—which, if I'm allowed to comment, is a rather nice abdomen.

Not the time.

"You insist you're real," I say, slow to let it sink in, "and yet the police wouldn't be able to see you because . . . ?"

Awful flippant, his shoulders rise. "You're the only one that can see me."

Real things cannot only be seen by one person!

"I'm having a mental breakdown," I conclude. I know it. He knows it. The vase knows it.

"Eh." He settles into my old dorm-room armchair with little regard for social normalcy. "You'll come around. They allllways do. So—" He circles his finger in my direction. "What's your deal? Why are you so sad?"

Sad?

"I'm not sad," I say, offense apparent.

"Well, your dwelling is pretty sad." He eyes up one dusky space on the wall where used to hang a picture of a mountain James took in Colorado, the outline now a sorry indication that something is missing.

"I like it this way," I say. Which may be the world's biggest lie. I look away from him because lies are most often exposed by the eyes. Not to mention it's been a long, *long* time since I've seen another person's *flesh*, and I'm trying to avoid his at all costs. "If you really are a genie—or whatever the PC term is—can't you at least summon a shirt or something?"

That same dark look from before passes over his face. "Is that a wish?"

"It's a request," I say.

He rolls the icecaps kept in his face and gives a sigh like it's of terrible effort for him to comply. "Fine," he says, "but you'll run out of freebies soon." And then, in the time it takes me to blink, he's wearing a white V-neck T-shirt that looks straight out of a fresh multipack. "Come on over. Let's have a chat." He pats the cushion beside his thigh.

"I'm not a dog, and that chair's hardly large enough for two!"

"Pffft. I know you're not a canine," he says like I'm daft. "You're a human . . . right?"

WHAT ELSE WOULD I BE?

He sniggers over whatever expression I'm wearing. "Just get over here, would you? I'll grant you some wishes, fill my quota, and we can be on our way." Muttering, he takes in another helping of my apartment. "Seems you've got lots to wish for. This should go quick."

Quick? I wouldn't have taken a year-long pledge of atonement if I wanted a *quick* solution to my problems, and I certainly don't need some hot hallucination with intentionally messy hair conjured by my subconscious to fix said problems for me.

"Excuse *you*." I march over and snatch the sketchbook he's just picked up off the table. "I don't need anything from you. I told you, I like my apartment the way it is."

Cynicism sweeps over him. "Sure you do." He straightens as if to cover it. "Fine. But you don't like your life the way it is. *Clearly*. I mean, you were talking to my vessel like it was your only friend."

He isn't wrong, but to have someone else acknowledge it?

I've been feeling papery for so long that anger seems a foreign invader under my skin. "That may be true," I lash, "but I'm perfectly capable of fixing my own life, and I intend to do so . . . eventually."

He lifts a brow that is frustratingly high.

"In two weeks," I add.

"Look, Master, I don't know what kind of game you're playing here, but I know you have wishes. All humans do. I'm the real deal, so just ask to be made into an influencer like eeeeveryone else, and I can be on my merry way, okay? Okay."

Well, he's a snide little fucker, isn't he.

"By the way," he adds, "you don't happen to have a hidden cache of food somewhere, do you? I didn't see much in your refrigerator or your cupboards. Is there another place humans store food?" He lifts the cushion under his own sweat-panted leg to take a peek.

First of all, he snooped that much?!

Secondly—"I have plenty of food," I defend.

"If by plenty you mean plain saltines, vegetables, and instant gruel," he mumbles, foul.

It's true. I haven't eaten anything too exotic in the last fifty weeks.

He rubs the fresh T-shirt over his stomach. "I can't work like this. Let's get some real food, and you can tell me more about how you love your crappy dwelling and don't need my help to fix your depressing life, yeah?"

"Well, when you ask like that," I say, cross.

"Excellent!" He bounces from the chair, loops his arm through mine, and begins dragging me toward the door.

"That. Was. Sarcasm!" I dig my feet hard into the dingy carpet, but he isn't listening; instead, he glances longingly over his shoulder to where his vase is resting on a nicked-up end table.

"It's safe here, isn't it?" he says. "No one's going to break in?"

"The only person who has ever broken in here is YOU."

As his gaze of ice shifts from the vase to my reddened face, the corner of his mouth cocks. "Guess you aren't as blah as I initially thought."

Excuse me, *blah*?

His mouth ticks higher over my lack of response. "What's your name, anyway? I mean your real name."

"You don't need to know that," I snub him. "You're a figment."

"Fine, fine." He heaves another of those lengthy, *weighty* sighs. "Guess I'll just have to make one up then. How abouuut—" He scans over the entry area as if looking for inspiration, settling on a broken lamp in the corner.

"Dolly," I tell him, teeth tight. "My name is Dolly."

CHAPTER 2

Substantial Amounts of Ranch

Dolly. It's such a perky sounding name. People expect things. The genie is no different.

"Aw." He clicks his tongue with patronization incarnate as he lugs me down the creaky hallway. "As in a toy babes play with? Cute."

"I've heard them all." I shrug him off. "And just what *superior* name were you bequeathed with?"

"Velis," he says. "Oop, watch out, Master." He pulls me out of the way just as Larry, the sock-wearing super, rounds the corner with a stack of boxes tucked in his pudgy arms.

"You can call me Dolly," I whisper, flat.

"No, I can't," he counters. "Rules are rules."

"*Then why did you need to know my name*?!"

"Miss Jones? You say something?" Larry peers around the boxes at me carefully.

And now my full name is out in the open for all mythical creatures to hear.

Dolly Jones.

A bit porn-starish, no? Thank my mother.

And it seems *Velis* was telling the truth. Larry doesn't notice him, even as he snaps rudely in the super's face. "See?" the genie croons. "I told you. It's just you and me, babe."

"So, you can call me 'babe,' but you can't call me by my name?" I say dryly.

Velis taps his mouth. "That was a slip."

"Oh! I, uh, didn't call you 'babe,' Miss Jones." And now poor balding Larry is backing away like he's afraid of being accused of sexual harassment.

And by those sinister vibes oozing off Velis, it was no accident.

"Sorry, Larry!" I cup my own ear, lying, "Earbuds. I'm on a call."

"Oh!" He gives a chuckle and relaxes the boxes in his arms. "Didn't mean to disturb ya, Miss Jones."

I take the genie's wrist and yank him after me before Larry can get a good look at my non-earbudded ears. However long I was out earlier, it was enough for the sky to turn overcast. Darkening gray blankets the horizon as we push into the world beyond my brick-fronted abode. It isn't enough to perk up the streetlights quite yet, but it is enough to quiet the sidewalks as pedestrians hunker down in wait for whatever spring storm the sky is promising. The grass out front is almost offensively green, having soaked off the last one.

I hurl Velis to a stop at the precipice of the creak-less gate. "What do you want to eat?"

Smirky darkness wraps around him. "So, you believe I'm real now?"

"No. But I don't know what else to do with you."

"Works for me." He shoves his hands in his pockets and leans around me for a view down the street. "Is there a tavern around here?"

"You want a drink?" The *genie* wants a drink?

"Um, yeah. I've been stuck in my vessel for over two weeks." He says it like I should know better. "I want a scotch."

Ooh, and he thinks he's a fancy genie, does he?

"And a burger," he adds.

I eye his bare arms and feet. I, myself, am wrapped in the

same homely sweater I throw on nearly every day. It didn't come with thumbholes, but I've since burrowed some of my own.

"Aren't you going to get cold like that?"

But in less than a blink, Velis has donned dark jeans and a trendy little jacket. "I'm good," he says. "But cute of you to worry about me, *Master*."

"Okay, you keep saying 'Master' like it's obligatory. You can stop calling me that at any time, you know."

"I can't," he retorts.

We're walking now, down the mass grave of petals, toward a main street impossibly quaint for our century.

"It's not like there's anyone here to rat you out. Assuming you really are a genie and you really have a genie code or something," I scoff. "Er, what? Why are you staring at me?"

"What happened to your hair?" he says.

"What *happened* to it? Rude. Nothing happened to it. It's always been like this." I bundle myself further into my sweater as a little of that spring chill whizzes by on the wings of a bicyclist.

"Lie to me if you want, Master, but I saw a picture of you in your dwelling. It used to be long."

That's—!

Fine. Whatever. Really, what's the point of lying to a figment of my own creation? Might as well dive headfirst into this rabbit hole if I'm going to be shoved down it anyway.

"I . . . buzzed it," I admit. "About a year ago."

And I can't say I regret it. It's easy, feels nice when the wind pulls through, and I like the way it pairs with a set of suede booties.

Not that I really wear booties anymore. A bit too bougie for someone in my situation.

"Good choice," he says, admiring my choppy, grown-out hair in a way that makes me tuck it around my ear. "Looks better now. You've got a good chin for it." He seems to lose himself in thought. "My former masters all had long hair. I don't know if they could have pulled it off . . ." His sneakers tap enough to echo. The petals he whisks up feel as real as the ones I do. The crisp air tosses his slate blue hair as though it exists.

If I hadn't seen the way Larry ignored him, I would swear he were a real physical being.

"I can't believe I made you up," I tell him. "Not bad."

"Not bad?" His lips are well-formed. The corner of them springs. "What's that mean?"

"I mean, I'm not usually this creative." Is this what a year of total abstinence does to a person? What's the backstory here? Does he come with one, or did I stop with those abs? "How long have you been a genie?" I probe.

"Mm, about four months?" he says, nonchalant.

"You're . . . a baby genie?"

He halts, and the petals halt with him. "Okay, enough of that. I told you, 'genie' is derogatory. We are called djinn, and not all of us grant wishes. I had a different job before I started this."

So the genies have a whole society, then?

Maybe, once this mental break is over, I should focus my efforts on writing a book.

"And there's, like, a fantasy world that you come from?" I ask next.

"Ha!" Velis tucks his head backward. "Yours is the fantasy world, babe." He beckons to a streetlight just flickering awake for the night. "You use magic to light your houses and television cubes, don't you?"

He's getting awful comfortable throwing that 'babe' around.

"You mean *electricity*?"

Velis holds his forehead, muttering, "WHY do I have to explain this to every human I meet?" He digs at me with his stare. "Your world runs on an unseen energy source—that's the definition of magic. They write stories about your world in mine."

I mean, I guess.

At the end of the street, we pass a house with a garden of vibrant craft-fair yard pieces, rebellious against its well-trimmed neighbors.

"This way." I tip my head to steer him toward a bar I

haven't been to in over a year. A place from my old life. One sure to dredge up unwelcome memories, and not just about James.

Do any of them . . . go there still?

With any other ex, I would have stalked the shit out of him on social media for a month or two and then called it good, but because deleting my profiles was part of this hell I've committed to, I have no idea what James is up to, nor any of our old friends. I ran into one of them at the pharmacy once, but she acted like I wasn't there and tapped at her phone like a little gremlin, alerting the troops of an enemy sighting.

"W . . . what?" I say, reserved, because the djinn has crouched to my level and is studying me without shame.

"Regret," he says. "That's what I've been feeling from you, isn't it? We can use that, you know. Turn it into a wish." His eyes shine at the word.

It would be very much like my own imagination to confront me about my inner demons.

"So, how many wishes do I get?" I deflect, nestling further into my sweater.

He straightens, distracted by the *magic* of a traffic light directing a sole car. "That depends on what you wish for. Each human soul has a specific amount of value tied to it. And each wish is worth a fraction of that value. The more grandiose the wishes, the fewer you get. People tend to blow through 'em pretty fast. I think the longest I was bonded to someone was maybe six hours? Man, your kind really don't have much in the way of control, do they? It's like, the minute you give them the means, they . . ."

He's rambling about the folly of humans, but I'm stuck elsewhere.

"Did you say *soul*?"

"Oh, yeah, gotta give something to get something," he answers offhand. "Did I not mention that before?"

No, he didn't mention it!

"You aren't imaginary," I realize, eyes waxing as I steadily inch away from him. "You're a *demon*. I give you my soul, and you grant my wishes."

For whatever reason, accepting the existence of demons is much easier than accepting the existence of genies. Blame my upbringing. Some things can't be conditioned away, and rigorous Sunday school is one of them.

He sighs low and drapes his head forward. "Oh no," he groans, "one of *these*. No, I'm not a demon. No, you won't be eternally damned by giving me your soul. Souls are like virginity. You don't really need it, and then once you lose it, can you even really tell?"

Based on my felt storyboard days, I don't think that's accurate.

"Oh look, we're here," he chirps as though forgetting I've just mislabeled him as a fiend from hell. He sniffs at the air in front of a bar boasting the state's best ranch and three-dollar drafts. "Smells oily." He doesn't say that like it's a bad thing as he starts for the door. "Er, Master? You coming?"

My feet have rooted desperately into the gravel out front, for they remember this place, that fried smell, that delicious, delicious ranch that makes you order a side of fries just for the dip of it.

Velis frowns at me. "Ugh. What's wrong with you? It's like you just sucked yourself into your . . . self."

"I'm . . . working through some issues," I hesitantly admit.

"Clearly." He elongates his neck and taps at his chin. "You know, if you're avoiding someone, I could alter your appearance. Of course, that would count as a wish."

"No," I say, resolute. "No wishes. I'm going in, and I'm doing it on my own."

"No wishes?" Crestfallen is the right word for the look he bears as I push past him into the bar.

The other side is a world from memory. I brace myself and search the shadows for familiar faces as I take in the ambiance of it all, the clink of glass and the squeak of vinyl reluctant to let its occupants leave. Small-town bars all have that same smell: a worn, dingy smell that lets a person know it's okay to relax. If only I could heed it. Each chuckle from the bar pulls my attention, each swing of the kitchen door makes me jerk. That corner booth is the one I've sat in the most—I can almost feel the seat pulling at my thighs to get me to stay as I try to slide away to the bathroom.

I hate booths. They gross me out. You never know what kind of human residue or food crumbs may be wedged between the seats. That never stopped our friends from requesting them. They liked to be the loudest, biggest group in the bar.

Relief exits through my nose when I realize there's no one here from my past life. A few business folks with their ties loose and blouses untucked. A pair of girls pouring over a binder, planning something. A few other randos searching for solace in fuzzy foam and amber ale.

"Table for two?" A girl as perky as my name approaches the front. Unfamiliar. Must be a new hire over the last fifty weeks.

"Just one," I correct, holding up a finger.

But my single finger is closed in on by other *imaginary* fingers stemming from an imaginary hand. "Two," Velis says, poking his head around me. "Not a booth. The boss wants a table."

By 'boss,' he means me.

And how did he know I wanted a table?!

"Sure thing," the hostess responds, and the djinn begins to follow her, leaving me dumbstruck at the door.

"Huh?" I look at her. "Huh?!" I look at Velis, prompting him to throw a wink at me over his shoulder. "*I thought you said I was the only one that could see you*!" I accuse through my teeth, hustling to catch up as he pulls out a high-top chair for me.

"You are." He slides my chair in more forcefully than is necessary, dropping his mouth close to my ear. "When I want you to be."

Dick!

Judging by the way the waitress is dead set on him as she hands him a menu, she finds the djinn attractive. Well, you can't blame her there. Some people are all looks. And by the way she's just flicked that stare of hers in my direction, she's wondering what on earth someone like him is doing with someone like me—makeup-less, baggy-sweatered me.

Velis orders himself a scotch before turning to me expectantly.

"Water," I say.

"Boooring."

That's me. Boring. By choice. There are worse things.

With the hostess shuffled away, a million memories overtake me—of shared appetizers and spilled drinks—as the overhead lights cast judgment on the back of my neck.

"What happened to you?" Ice-eyed Velis is watching me reminisce like I'm a fascinating museum piece, with his elbow resting on the table and his cheek smooshed against the curl of his fist. "Those pictures in your bedroom nightstand are like a completely different person."

"You were in my bedroom?!"

"Uhh." The hostess—now taking on the role of a waitress—stands at the table's edge holding a water in one hand and something that looks like piss in the other. "Do you want to wait to order food until he's back?" she asks as she sets down the glasses.

"Until he's back?"

"From the bathroom?" she says, eyeing me like I'm unstable.

Meanwhile, Velis is smiling wickedly over my reaction to his sudden invisibility.

"Yes," I say, jaw tight and glare settled on a face only I can see. "We'll wait until he gets back."

The waitress is glad to be rid of me.

"*What the hell*?!" I seethe. "Why do you keep messing with me?! I brought you out for your freaking scotch despite all my better instincts telling me not to indulge in whatever the heck is going—"

"*Indulge*." He lets off a visible shiver. "Say it again."

A bit pervy, no?

"I'll pass."

He grumbles, pats the table with both hands, and then swoops in for his fancy little glass of scotch. "I'm messing with you, Master, because I like my wardens to be lively. It seems this is the only way to make your blood move. I felt it the moment you picked me off that shelf: you're stagnant. We can't have any fun if you're stagnant."

"What makes you think I'd want to have any fun with you? I happen to be abstaining from fun at the moment," I tell him.

"Why the fuck would you do that? You know, you really shouldn't have engaged with a genie if you weren't looking to have a little fun," he says.

NOT LIKE I KNEW WHAT I WAS DOING WHEN I PICKED UP THAT VASE!

"I thought you didn't like the term 'genie,'" I say, spending all efforts on remaining calm.

"Only we can say it. You can't." He takes a swig of his drink.

Oh my god.

I feel like slamming my head against the high-top. Instead, I set it down with the dullest of thuds. Apparently, Velis hasn't made himself visible yet; the waitress has yet to return.

"You might as well just tell me," he says, sliding his glass of scotch from hand to hand so that it sloshes. "I'm not going to quit bugging you until you do."

"Tell you what?" The words contort against my squished cheek.

"Why your dwelling looks so depressing. Why you're 'abstaining from fun at the moment.' Why you don't own anything nice even though your bank statement says you have plenty of money."

"*You looked at my finances?*"

Meaning he knew my full name all along. Little shit.

He downs the rest of his glass and loosens his neck. "Goddamn it feels good to be out of that lamp." Visible again, apparently, he motions the waitress over for a refill and orders himself a burger.

"And for you?" The perky girl holds the pad of paper in her palm expectantly.

"I don't want anything," I say. A lie. Truthfully, I want an overflowing basket of salty, crispy fries, golden like Aztecan treasure, and a generous portion of that soupy, savory ranch that's perfectly drinkable on its own.

The waitress waits a moment for me to change my mind—or

maybe she just wants a fresh ogle at Velis. Velis, meanwhile, is ogling me, eyes narrow and mouth contemplative.

"No," he says after a moment. "She'll have your largest bucket of fries and substantial amounts of ranch dressing. Whatever that is."

The waitress doesn't give me a chance to object before scribbling it down and sauntering away, ponytail swaying.

"How did you . . . ?"

"I'm a genie," he says simply. "It's my job to figure out what you desire."

"You can read *minds*?" A scary, scary thought.

"Not minds. More like moods," he says. "Which is how I know you're super sad and super regretful. It's like you're suppressing yourself. Am I right?"

Eerily.

He lifts an eyebrow as if I'm as transparent as the empty glass in his hand. "I mean, if you think about it, I'm the best person you could tell," he says. "I don't know anyone you know. I have no real interest in your life. Whatever it is, it's impeding me from doing my job and moving on, so you might as well just get it over with."

So the sooner I tell him, the sooner he'll go away?

"Fine," I say as the waitress returns with Velis's second scotch. "I'll tell you if you promise to leave me alone after."

I've already had to admit this so many times. To James. To our friends. To my mother, who wants to know why I haven't returned home all year. One more time. I'll admit it one more time and then I'll move on with my life.

"I . . . did something bad," I start.

He keeps his gaze shrewdly on me. "Mmhmm."

At first, it's hard to muster because it isn't a thing I ever thought I would have to say, and when it finally comes out of me, it feels like sickness the morning after a night of mistakes:

"I . . . cheated on my boyfriend. We were together for three years prior."

That straightens him up. "Yowch. You don't seem the type." He sizes me up with new interest.

"I know. I mean, I'm not."

"Then why'd you do it?" he asks bluntly.

My throat protests. That's more detail than I wanted to share. Just in time, the waitress returns with Velis's greasy-bunned burger, gleaming beneath the dimmed lighting, and my barrel of fries and that succulent, drippy ranch I've tasted so many times in my dreams.

Torture.

Of all the difficult moments over the last fifty weeks, this is the most brutal. The smell of it wafts into me, more tempting than a harlot. Velis watches me darkly, shivering.

"*Nice.*"

Does he get off on seeing me drool over fries?!

I swallow it away. "I didn't mean to cheat." I wince because, even after a year, it all feels like it happened to someone else. "It happened when my boyfriend was out of town for work last spring. The rest of our friends went to a local music festival and then to a party at a duplex a few of them rent. That place was so gawdy." I look back on it fondly. "Decorated with all kinds of shit they stole from hotels and restaurants, and crap they picked up at flea markets. It was the perfect place to just chill out. No expectations—" I realize I'm stalling. "Anyway. I drank too much and blacked out, but apparently, somewhere in there, I came on to my boyfriend's friend. His best friend, actually."

"Sticky," Velis says, biting into his burger. Grease drips down his wrists in response.

"It gets worse. The guy I slept with was dating another girl in the group at the time, and I was pretty close with her, and after it happened, she turned vicious. We all went to college together, but the rest of them knew each other from high school. I was a transfer student from out of state. They were basically the only friends I had here, aside from fake work friends, so after it happened . . ." I collect myself via a lengthy sigh. "I don't blame them for cutting me out, but the shitty part is that they're all still friends with Gabe —the guy I slept with."

"Wait, what?" Velis sets his burger down.

"I guess it was easier to forgive him because they knew him a lot longer . . . and because I'm the one that initiated it."

Velis is quiet a moment, judging me like all the rest.

"But you don't remember initiating it," he says slowly.

Or maybe he isn't judging me after all.

"No. But I do get a little *frisky* when I drink, and apparently, there's a picture of us looking pretty chummy from that night, so it's not like I think Gabe's lying about what happened."

Besides, the alternative is something much worse. Something I'm not willing to entertain. I've often wondered whether it makes me strong or weak to deny the possibility that I was a victim in all this.

"Anyway, you're right about my life being shitty," I carry on, "but it's by choice. After what happened, I made a year-long pledge to abstain from . . . well, everything. The rut I'm in is a rut I dug myself, and I'm perfectly capable of getting myself out. But not until after I finish atoning for what I did. And I only have two weeks left, so really not an optimal time for a genie-demon to appear."

Velis reaches for one of my fries, which I still haven't caved over, and takes an obvious bite. "So, you've been atoning for something you don't remember, for the sake of people who don't even know you're doing it?"

Wrong.

"I'm not doing it for them. I'm doing it for myself," I clarify. "To prove to myself that I can control my urges. And to prove I'm not a bad person."

"Oh, you're not a bad person," he says, cavalier.

"You don't know me."

"Yeeeah, but I do know that bad people can't see my vessel. It ensures wishes can't be made to do harm." He stops to think about it. "You know, if I were you, I'd make a wish to go back and watch what happened that night."

"*No.*" I feel myself jerk away. That night isn't something I ever want to revisit. "And no wishes, period. I'm fifty weeks in, and I'm not wasting it all on something as indulgent as a wish. To wish for something without earning it goes against everything I've worked for. You may as well find someone else's life to invade because this tap is empty. That waitress seems interested, though. Look at her over there, perking around."

He isn't listening. He's caught on a word—

"*Indulgent.*" He draws a hot breath through his nostrils before shaking it away. "Sorry, as fun as that waitress seems, I can't. The thing is, I'm stuck to you, Master, until I grant your wishes."

"But I said I'd tell you what I did if you promised to leave."

"But did I ever verbally agree to that, though?" He wrinkles his face as if pretending to replay our conversation.

He's right.

"Fucker."

"Heh." He accepts it like a badge of honor.

"Can't I just wish for something inconsequential then?" I bargain.

"Well, you can, but it won't count. Wishes only tick away at your soul if they're meaningful to you. It has to be things you actually desire." His eyes shine seductively. "Like these fries." He tosses another into his mouth with eyes locked on mine the entire way.

I choke down the scowl wrestling its way out. "Then what happens if someone refuses to give up their soul to you?"

He shrugs. "Hasn't happened yet. Like I said, all humans have wishes. They're one of the most indulgent races. That's why I'm hunting here and not in one of the other realms."

"*Hunting*?"

A very predatorial thing to say.

"Did I say hunting?" He fans a hand at me. "I meant soliciting."

I scooch back my chair. "Demon. You are most certainly a demon."

He laughs. "I'm not. I'll prove it." He glances around the table as if searching for something to argue his case. "Here, open your mouth."

"My *mouth*?"

"Just open it."

I do so with the opposite of haste. If he touches my mouth, I'm going to bite off his finger.

But I've forgotten about that incident with the pen. With reflexes sharper than any human's, Velis plucks the best fry of the basket, drenched in a holy shroud of ranch, and shoots it between my lips.

Even if I want to spit it out, I'm incapable. The heavens sing as my mouth clamps down and begins to digest the delicacy riding my tongue.

"What you're doing is stupid," he says. "Everyone makes mistakes—human, djinn, waterhorse. And in your case, if you were too intoxicated to remember it, then you sure as hell weren't sober enough to be responsible for it. If it were me, I'd be pointing fingers at the guy who *does* remember it. Just my two dirham—er, cents. My two cents." He tosses his hands behind his head and leans back. "Dang, this is the most personally I've ever conversed with a human. Who knew your lives could be so dramatic?"

Dramatic? He clearly doesn't understand the gravity of the sin he's just committed. I'll give him dramatic.

"*What have you done*?" My words shake, and I grip the edge of my chair, nails sinking into stubborn wood as that little piece of heaven slips down my throat. "I . . . I couldn't resist it. I knew it. I knew I would break." The chair gives a reluctant squeal against the cement floor as I push it from the table, throwing a wad of cash beside a driblet of ranch before storming away from the high-top, past the ever-more-casual business folk and to the door.

"M-Master?! Wait!" Visible or invisible, I hear Velis scampering after me, but I'm already through the door, where those darkened skies have started giving way to promised rain. It's as though it's been waiting for me to reemerge. The drops start light into my hair but soon begin to pellet down, bouncing off my cheeks and absorbing into my sweater as, overhead, the roars of thunder beckon in the distance like the mightiest of heralds. "Master, wait!" Velis the temptress jogs up beside me. "Wish for an umbrella! You're going to get soaked!"

"NO!" I shout at him through the coming sheets. "I told you, no fucking wishes!"

It's hard to tell now which droplets were produced from the skies and which are falling from my eyes as frustration squirms out of me.

"Goddamn, Dolly," Velis says my real name for the first time, "it was one flipping fry."

"Leave me alone!" I storm away from him, as determined as the storms rolling in over the flowered streets, pulling into my lungs cool, heavy air laden with the horizon's intentions.

It may not seem like much. But to me, it's everything. I've put so much effort, so much weight into this agreement I've made with myself, as if surviving it means I can survive what I did.

The truth is, I didn't black out on that night. Not entirely.

I remember kissing Gabe. I don't remember who started it, but I remember the tiniest moment where I should have pulled away. Instead, I kissed him. I *wanted* to kiss him. And though I've strained my memory into the reaches of oblivion trying to figure out how it started and how it ended, one thing is clear—that one moment. That's the moment I was tested.

I failed the fry.

Just like I failed the kiss.

Starkly, the rain above me stops. Velis has caught up to me, clutching a blue-and-white striped umbrella concocted out of thin air. "I mean it, Master. This is your last freebie. Next time, you have to wish—"

"You know what I wish?!" I smear the wet from my face. "I wish that you would—"

"Don't." His hand is firmly over my mouth, and that stare piercing through an icy sea is set on me without remorse. "Don't wish for that. It would be problematic. I'll play nicer, okay? I can be nice if that's what you want."

I don't know if I believe that. He's been kind of a dick since I met him.

"I'm sorry about the fry. I was just trying to help. Don't make the wish you were about to make, okay?"

He's desperate. I was about to wish he'd leave me the fuck alone, and it seems he fears a wish like that. For the first time since appearing in my kitchen, he shows a semblance of vulnerability in those penetrating eyes of his.

And, goddamn, he's got a jaw that could cut glass. I must look like a Muppet next to him. Whatever the circumstance, it feels nice to have another person touch me after so long. Nice to have someone in my near vicinity interested in conversing.

Dangerous thoughts for a person committed to a pledge like mine. A pledge that has dictated my every waking breath for the last 350 days—enough to make me feel guilty about being touched by another living person.

Maybe that fry wasn't a symbol of my lack of restraint. Maybe it was a symbol of how consumed I've become with all this. If I'm strong enough to withstand temptation for an entire year, then I'm strong enough not to be defined by a slice of fried potato.

"I overreacted," I say into his hand, feeling my panic subside. "I'm cool now."

"Wait, really? Just like that?" He checks me twice before lowering his hand timidly. "I don't get you."

He doesn't need to. What he needs to do is get out of my life so that I can rebuild it.

"You can't move on to your next master until I use all my wishes?" I say.

"I can't."

"And by making wishes, I'm giving you my soul?" I ask.

"You are."

"But it won't affect me in this life or the next?"

"It won't."

But of course I can't believe something like that without proof. From what I've heard, souls are kind of an important piece of the human equation. "Is there some way to verify all that?" I ask.

"Not really." His stare doesn't falter. "Just . . . I can't lie. I mean, I can lie, but not to you."

"Aha! But what about when you said you were going to prove

you weren't a demon and then you shoved a fry into my mouth? By my calculation, *that* was a lie."

"Nope. A demon wouldn't have done that. It was an act of kindness. Like I said, I was trying to help—specifically, to help you remember what it's like to indulge so that we could move on to the fun stuff. This deal is mutually beneficial." Water drips down his neck. "You get to live your best life, and I get a keepsake."

A keepsake. "What do you do with the souls once you have them?" I pry.

The corner of his mouth kicks into a dimple of amusement. "That's a secret," he says.

"So, you can't lie, but you can withhold the truth?"

"Oh, trust me, doll, if there's a loophole out there, I've found it."

These pet names of his are getting old. It's like he knows he can get away with it because he's cute. I should wish to make him old and fugly.

"Don't you fucking dare."

So, he really can sense what I desire.

Muscles that haven't been used in a very long time fight for control of my face, and the moment they win is the moment Velis's look of warning melts into something else. Something that's a little like seeing the first snowfall of the year and wondering if it will last.

"Wow," he says. "Those pictures weren't kidding. You really are pretty when you smile."

I thought he said he couldn't lie.

Beyond the curtain of shower forged by one steadfast umbrella, gravel ricochets the pelting rain in every direction, pealing constant enough to dull out everything else. Within this cocoon, a smile rises and falls as quickly as the life of a moth.

"Look, Master, I can't stay here and mess around with you for two more weeks. I'm on a tight schedule, and I was locked in my vessel for waaaay longer than I meant to be. You're going to have to get over your shit and make a wish. Ideally tonight. By the way . . ." Velis glances over his shoulder. "How long have we been together?"

There's something in the way he asks it.

"Including the time I was knocked out? Four or five hours."

"Crap. That long?" He sets his hand to the small of my back to push me forward. "Come on. Let's go back to your dwelling. Think about what you're going to wish for along the way."

Sneakers soaked, Velis ushers me through puddles flush with pastel petals like miniature boats, the petrichor of it all splashing us through misty air, the rumble of the skies vowing more to come. And all the way up the hill, I can't help noticing the way he keeps checking the shadows behind us.

"Velis, are you on the run from something?"

"What?" He gives a patronizing chortle, shaking his head as if I'm crazy to think so. "N-yes." He clasps his own mouth. "Fuck."

It seems he was telling the truth about being unable to lie to me. It's clear he meant to say no.

I cement myself in place. "Who?"

"Make a wish and you won't have to find out," he growls, bitter over the slip. Then, he and the striped umbrella move on without me. I sprint after to regain cover, tucking close to him as he marches on in silence until reaching the squeak-less gate of my lovely, haunted apartment.

As with every other time I lay hand to those iron bars, I wince at the conjuring of what was lost. Unlike every other time, there's someone here to see it. Watching me carefully to understand the emotion driving the change in my expression, Velis wrinkles his nose. "*That's* what you want? Weird, but okay." The magical genie touches his pointer and middle fingertips to the gate's hinge before lowering his voice to my ear. "This is the sort of stuff I can do for you, Master. Think outside the box, yeah?"

When he presses the gate, it gives an angsty screech in return.

And just like that, it's no longer a symbol of better days lost. It squeaks now, just like it squeaked a year ago.

Relief escapes me in the form of an involuntary breath, and Velis, still observing me from the corner of his eye, gives a nod of approval. "Good. What you just felt, you can feel it tenfold. I can make it happen for you. All you have to do is make a wish."

I'm silent all the way through the faux-lavender halls because I'm finally coming to terms with the fact that the person beside me is a mythical creature here to win my soul.

And that's a bit much.

CHAPTER 3

Bottled

"LET'S GO OVER THE RULES," says the genie, returned to those rolled gray sweatpants and crisp white T-shirt while settled forward in my apartment's best and only armchair, elbows rested lax and hands dangling between his knees. "I can't change the past. I can't change anyone else's destiny but your own. And some wishes are worth more than your soul would allow. For instance, I can't make you a ruler of your country or anything like that. But it never hurts to ask. Ask away, and I'll let you know if it's something I can make happen."

"Velis . . ." Because I'm not a magical being, I'm forced to wring out my hair the old-fashioned way. "Soul stealer or not, I appreciate what you're trying to do, but I'm not the kind of person that wants something for nothing. And especially not now—"

"You've got to. You've got to make a wish. No is not an option." He quickly scans the balcony's sliding door where flecks of rain spray off nearby trees and stick to the glass.

Maybe I can read moods too. He's obviously growing more and more anxious as the day lengthens.

"First, tell me why you're so dodgy all of a sudden," I barter. "What's after you? And why does it matter how long we've been together? I know you said you're on a tight schedule, but—"

"Nothing you just asked me matters for your purposes. All you need to focus on is what you want to wish for," he cuts me off.

Not good enough, and he knows it.

"How about this?" he continues, fidgeting. "Make some future-dated wishes. If you refuse to enjoy yourself now, set them forward two weeks when your pledge or whatever is over. Like, 'I wish that in two weeks, I'll become a famous influencer with five hundred thousand subscribers and five paid sponsorships.'"

Again with the influencer crap?!

"Why the hell would I want to become an influencer?" I ask as I disappear into my bedroom to retrieve dry clothes.

"Isn't that what all human girls want?" he calls after me. "That's all the last ones have wished for. That and money. And to grow their lips and their butts."

"Um, no." I poke my head out of the bedroom. "Becoming an influencer is the last thing I would want. You couldn't pay me to— What kind of girls are you sticking your bottle around?"

"Don't blame me. I don't choose the mark. My vessel does. I've been meaning to ask, why did—" He stops his train of thought as I exit the bedroom holding the lumpy, drippy sweater I've just removed from my chilled, wet skin *because some of us can't get magically dry*.

"What?" I look behind me to see whatever it is that's made him lean forward.

"Damn, Dolly! Why would you cover up a body like that?"

Oh. The thing he's gawking at is *me*. I've changed into black leggings and a black long sleeve. All black is my go-to. It's easy, it helps me stick to the background of any scene, and best, it makes me feel like a cat burglar.

Slinky.

But . . . why is he looking at me that way? I may be small but I'm not thin. I've never *been* thin. It's not that I'm unhealthy or anything, just squishy enough to feel uncomfortable in a bikini.

"I mean, look at your ass! You're a little bombshell!" He shakes his head before situating himself back into the chair. "Er, sorry. I was surprised to see how . . . shapely you are after being covered up by that spinster's smock the whole day. Where were we? Right. Why did it take you so long to come for us in that used goods mercantile? Could you not feel me drawing you in?"

But I'm preoccupied with twisting around to get a look at my own rear.

"Hey, sexpot! Focus." He lobs the remote at me, but at the last minute, it veers to the left and hits the wall of the hallway, releasing half-dead batteries and bits of plastic all over the place. "Whoops, that was harder than I meant it to be," he says, making a face like he's just, I don't know, *broken someone else's remote*.

"What the hell?!" I lurch. "It's not like I have a lot of possessions! You don't need to break the ones I do have."

He hops from his resting cushion. "You'll have plenty when I'm done with you. Let's start small." He hustles over and picks up the murdered remote, dangling it before me with his thumb and pointer. "Wish for it to be repaired."

I'm considering it, actually—eyeing the smashed-in buttons and broken back, wondering if I can twist this into a necessity. But as Velis stands pinching the corpse of plastic and parts like it's a dead mouse, we are both summoned by a loud rapping against lumber older than either of us.

Well, me for sure. I'm not sure how fast genies age.

"Larry?" I start, as he's the only visitor I'm likely to ever get at my door, but the question is quickly absorbed into the warmth of Velis's palm as he takes me from behind and cups my mouth.

"*Shhh*!" His breath is close enough to disrupt the finest hairs of my ear.

I protest a distorted version of his name as he holds my face hostage and slides me along with him to see through the peephole criminally bored through that beautiful, original door.

"*Shit*!" He swears a nearly voiceless swear and begins frantically surveying the apartment, holding a finger to his mouth before releasing mine long enough to retrieve his vessel from the counter. Curvy bottle in one hand, curvy human in the other, he drags us both to my bedroom, where he tears open the bifolds of my closet and shoves me inside, closing the doors firmly behind us so that only slits of light enter the crowded space.

"What the hell, Velis?!" I bristle. "Who's out there? H-hey! I have those organized, you know!"

He ignores me, pawing through stacks of folded clothes and making a mess, going so far as to pull additional blankets from the top shelves to further congest the space before wedging his bottle into the thick of it all.

"Come here." Without waiting for any sort of consent, he moves in on me, and in the aftermath, I'm tucked close to his chest in an almost consoling embrace. His adrenaline speaks of someone who's just suffered a jump scare, the rush of it separated from my coddled cheek only by soft, warm cotton.

"Close your eyes, Master."

They're already closed. Because I haven't been held like this in quite some time. And never by someone who looks like him. And my pulse can't decide whether to calm or race.

Whatever kind of primal reaction that may be, it's overtaken by an overwhelming sensation, like being caught up in the suction of a wind tunnel. Velis cuddles me closer to shield my eyes from the chaos happening around us until the whoosh of air dies, and when he finally allows me the space to open my eyes, we're no longer in my closet. We're in a small, round space with dark, curved walls, scattered with hand-bound books and patchwork pillows and colorful poufs that look like they belong in a bazaar at the edge of a desert. The walls glint in the amber light of a lone iron fixture hanging low from the ceiling.

"You *teleported* us?"

He gives me a dull shrug. "Not really. Technically, we're still in your closet. Here—let me clean up." He circles his finger above his head, and the books stack onto a shelf, the pillows sort into a pile, and the poufs recede against the wall, revealing something the size of a frisbee glowing on the floor. Velis moves to retrieve the disc-like object, which looks to consist only of brilliant blue light, and lifts it to his face as if about to take communion.

"What is this place?" I gander. "Some sort of . . . bohemian love nest?" The whole of it is no larger than my apartment's kitchen.

"*Love* nest?" He tosses me a questionable glance over his shoulder. "What the heck is that?"

"Well, what the heck is *this*?" I gesture.

"It's my vessel. Duh." He returns his attention to the blue light streaming from his hands.

Meaning . . . I'm inside a genie's bottle?!

"You SHRUNK us?"

"Shhh!" he scolds. "Keep it down! There's no guarantee they won't hear us if they get close enough."

"*Who*, Velis? *Who* is outside my apartment?"

He ignores me, eyes lapping up whatever he sees in that sheen of blue. "Aw, hell. It's both of them. Or rather, two of the three." He tosses the disc into the smattering of pillows. "You have to make a wish," he charges, marching over and setting his hands on my shoulders. "Make one with me. Now. Just . . . something. So that I can get a piece of you."

A *piece* of me?

"Well, I wish you would tell me who we're hiding from," I say offhand.

Whether or not I mean to cast it as a real, full-bore wish, it hits Velis differently than anything I've spouted at him so far. The bohemian love nest blazes with a blue glow as a dozen pairs of electric eyes bounce off the glassy luster of the walls, each a reflection of an annoyed genie standing in the middle of it all, eyes searing like a neon bar sign.

"Tch. Seriously?"

He grips his lips together and releases a huff of tight, defiant air through his nostrils, hands pressed to his knees, and gives me a frustrated sort of smile that shakes his mouth as he fights to keep it from opening. I stumble away from him because I don't want to get sprayed by whatever's about to erupt.

"My brothers!" he blurts at last, letting his head fall in release. "My older brothers. Argh! Damn it! You don't need to know that! Are you satisfied, *Master*? Are you—" He stops himself, then rubs his fingers together as if inspecting invisible goo. "What the—? I didn't even get anything off you for that!" Accusation rippling, his face plunges into darkness. "How did you do that? I just granted you a wish—an *actual* wish—without siphoning any of your soul in the process." He takes a foreboding step toward me. "Tell me how you did it."

"Hell if I know! I didn't even mean to make a wish! I was being sarcastic!"

He takes another step closer to dock hands on my upper arms, flicking his eyes up and around us, as if listening for sounds beyond the bottle, before shooting them back to mine. "*Make another one.*"

"Why are your brothers after you?" I settle. "I wish you would tell me."

"Goddamn it!" A second time, his eyes rage blue. This time, though, he doesn't fight the inevitable. His words come rushing out like the legalese at the end of a radio ad: "Because we're in a competition to win lordship over our family's estate, and I'm in the lead, and if they get to your soul before I do, I'll lose."

Oh. Right. Of course. "What?"

He lets his head fall with the heaviest of groans. "I didn't get anything off you that time either."

"You mean to tell me this is all some *game*?" I push him away. "You coming into my life and demanding wishes out of me?! You trying to 'siphon' my everlasting *soul*?!"

I may not be my best, strongest self, but I am sure as hell no one's plaything.

"You know," he says, eyes cast downward, "I'm getting *reeeally* tired of this, Master. I could put you in a compromising position so that you're forced to make a wish. A better one."

The tilt of his mouth is enough to send me back against the thick, opaque wall of glass. "You're *threatening* me now? What happened to not being able to hurt me?!"

"I can't *physically* hurt you. But like I said, loopholes."

So much for 'playing nice.'

Abruptly, though, he groans again, and this time, it seems to be at his own expense. "No, I wouldn't do that," he mutters to no one in particular. "Jeb would. But I wouldn't."

I relax from the wall, for those darker notions have absorbed back into him.

But being threatened like that?

I have been tame for weeks and months, but I wasn't always this way. Once upon a time, I was a girl with *bite*. "Don't threaten me again, Velis," I say in remembrance of an older, fiercer me. "I'm sure I can find some loopholes of my own."

Namely, wishing for him to exile himself inside a peanut shell.

The countenance I give him is enough to make his ego sheath. "I'm sorry, Master," he says. "That was desperation."

"So, I take it Jeb is one of your brothers?" I venture. "One of the ones outside my apartment?"

"Inside your apartment, actually."

"*What?*"

He shrugs. "They're magical. Of course they can get in. The knocking was just an effort to conserve power."

"And they're looking for the lamp—er, vessel—so that they can get to me? Why?"

He's quiet. And saying his name sparks nothing.

All a bit hypocritical for my taste.

"I mean, if you think about it, I'm the best person you could tell," I mimic in a voice deeper than my own. "I don't know anyone you know. I have no real *interest* in your life. Whatever it is, it's impeding me from doing my job and moving on, so you might as well just get it over with."

Sharp, his gaze returns. "Is that supposed to be me?" he says, somewhat put-off. "You . . . have a really good memory."

Only for things that don't matter.

Arms folded, he paces to the opposite side of the vase. "Why do you want to know my business so bad?"

Seriously?

"First of all, it's very much become apparent that it's my business too. Secondly, I spent all afternoon being badgered by you about my past. Clearly, there's more going on here than just a genie—sorry, *djinn*—coming into my miserable life to grant me wishes. Before I give up something like my soul, I want to know the terms of it all."

"But humans never care about that stuff," he alleges.

I give him one of the shrugs he so likes to give out himself. "I do. I don't want to make a wish, so if I do it, I need to know what I'm doing it for. I may have overreacted about that fry, but I'm committed to abstaining from pleasure until my pledge is through. To tell you the truth, I don't even know what I'd wish for if I had to. I don't want some glamorous life I haven't worked for. I'd consider doing something to better the world, but only if I know what it is I'm trading and why."

In the silent aftermath, I'm probed by an impossible stare, both flat and, at the same time, whetted. Like it costs him zero effort to suffer his full intensity onto whatever he looks at. The kind of stare that makes you feel naked; it grades me and decides, maybe, that my honesty is worth something. "Souls don't mean a lot in your world," Velis reveals, "but in ours, souls are like money. They're power."

"Money?" My thoughts on that are apparent in the twinge of my eyebrow. "You plan to milk me for profit like some cow?"

"Sure, if I could get anything off you."

"That's incredibly offensive."

"I don't mean it to be. Like I said, it's a mutually beneficial agreement. You get to have your best human life, and I get paid." He reassesses. "Look, I didn't sign up for this either. I wasn't even meant to be a wish granter—our family's in the ruling class—but our father thought it would be amusing if . . . No, that's more than you need to know. All you need to know is that my brothers are trying to cheat and that my life is going to be a whole lot worse if you don't let me better yours. I wouldn't put it past those two to put you in serious danger if it means milking a strong wish out of you, either. Trust me—I'm the one you want to be dealing with in this situation. So please, Master, make a wish, and this time, don't suppress yourself."

So 'milking' is the term we're sticking with?

And besides that, 'suppress myself'? That's basically all I know how to do.

"Shit!" Eyes spasming upward, Velis reacts to a mountainous creak from the giant world beyond the glassy walls of our love nest. The whine of an upset closet door? Too dark and thick to see through, the bottle's floor rocks beneath my unsteady feet as it's dislodged from the mess of blankets Velis used to cover us.

"*Do something*!" I hiss, talons having involuntarily latched onto him.

"YOU do something!" He stumbles into me as the floor shifts like a funhouse, the bottle victim to the upheaval of blankets in the outside world. "I can't just cast magic willy-nilly! The big stuff has to be for your benefit. So make a friggen' wish, and this time, do it right!"

Wait—it isn't in my benefit for them not to find us?

Velis anticipates what I'm thinking. "It only *technically* benefits me if they don't find us. You could make wishes off any of us. But choose me, Master. I'm the nicest one, I'm the one that found you, and I deserve it the most. *Please*."

A tiny piece of me wants to lap up his desperation, thinking about his blasé attitude over exchanging my everlasting soul for a thing like money. But there's something in the way he frantically searches overhead. What if his brothers are even worse? What if one self-interested genie is more than enough to handle?

"If I wish this, you have to tell me the rest of what I want to know," I negotiate. "No more beating around the bush. Do you promise?"

The wall catches my shoulder hard as we both slide into it, Velis scowling at the ceiling that's putting him in such a precarious situation.

"Velis?"

"Argh! Fine!" he snarls.

"Say it."

This time, his scowl is directed at me. "I promise!"

"I wish your brothers couldn't find your vessel no matter how hard they search my apartment!"

I cling to his side as the ground offers its most unruly motion yet, heaving books from the shelves that coast across the room and land at the bottle's lowest point, while the overhead light thrashes angrily.

Velis, meanwhile, is using unhuman strength to root us in place. "Yes! Excellent wish!" The throb of blue shines bright with Velis absorbing my wish through his eyes, and after, there's space-like gravity defiance as the bottle levels and the world steadies.

"Thank Maka. You've cloaked us." Velis crouches on the hard, smoothed ground in relief, though it is a relief shorter lived than most. "Fuck!" He squints at his fingertips, rubbing them against his thumb. "Why can't I take any of you? That should have been an easy swap! You sure you're human?"

Again, WHAT ELSE WOULD I BE?

A firm hand lands on my shoulder, his face imposingly near. "Open your mouth."

"No. I'm not falling for that again."

"Then spread your legs."

"Hell no!"

"*Then open your mouth.*"

Those are my choices? His hand clenches into me, threatening to pry me open if I don't do so willingly.

"For what?"

But he takes the opportunity to capture my jaw, pressing his fingers into the side of my cheeks that force my mouth to remain open on the word 'what'. I would bite him if his hand weren't so artfully positioned.

"I see it in there." He clicks his tongue. "So why can't I siphon it?"

He cranes down at me like the world's most intrusive dentist, close enough to feel the heat respiring from his nose on my chin. Close enough to get wrapped up in the scent of someone else's musk.

"Your soul." He releases me. "I can't access it."

"Oh no," I muster with the least amount of sincerity. "Guess you'll just have to find a new victim to suckle off."

"*I can't*," he says through tight teeth. "I told you, I can't move on until I'm through with you. But . . . I've never seen anything like it before. Wish for something else."

"I wish you were bald."

"DON'T!" He clutches his own head and turns away from me, scorned like Quasimodo.

But the wish doesn't stick, maybe because I don't truly desire him to be bald.

"Not cool, Master."

"None of this is cool," I say with a commensurate glare to match his own. "Now, tell me the rest. About your brothers—about my soul."

He shuns away again, this time grouchy and grumbling. He owes me the truth. I made him promise, and because he can't lie to his *master*, a promise is binding. I'll admit, it feels nice to be in a position of power.

It's been a long time since I've felt powerful.

With other mythical creatures still out pillaging through my battered belongings, I wait for Velis to live up to his end of the deal, letting it settle that I've either had a full-on mental break or I'm currently inside a genie's bottle. With a genie.

A magic-wielding, wish-granting, kind-of-a-dick genie.

Was he just lounging around in here the last two weeks, shirtless and bored, waiting for me to retrieve him from that stuffy thrift store? If he can't use 'big' magic for his own benefit, does that mean those books were all he had for entertainment?

"What language is this?"

"Huh?" He looks over his shoulder to where I'm examining a scrolling alphabet imprinted on the spine of an antique book with a faded cover. "Oh. Makayen."

Never heard of it.

"It smells like you in here," I observe, returning the tattered book to its shelf while its brothers remain scattered about the floor.

"I have a smell?" Velis asks, arm beginning to lift like he means to take a whiff.

He does have a smell, but it isn't a smell I can describe. It . . . isn't a bad smell. Not that I'd ever tell him that.

"W-what are you doing?" I shrink against the nearly empty bookcase, for a genie's nose has just been stuck deep into the nape of my neck.

"You have a smell too," he says when he comes out for air.

And he leaves it at that.

And I can't help wondering when I last washed my hair.

"Tell me, Velis! What's the deal with your brothers? And this whole game thing that's happening? And why you'll lose it if they find me? You promised you'd tell me, and you can't lie to me, so that means you have to."

"I sure do," he coos. "*Eventually*. Don't blame me if you forgot to make it timebound." And always, he's throwing around those damn shrugs of his.

No! He is not weaseling out of this one. I'm stuck in a freaking bottle in my freaking closet after being jerked around all freaking day. I gather a generous helping of his shirt's collar and scrunch it like a 1950s bully. "Tell me, Velis! Tell me now!"

But for all my heated breath, he's stiff, offering nothing in the tells of his features as he stares down at me over raised cheeks. Until I feel the push of a swallow against my knuckles gripping his shirt. "You know, I've never had a girl in here before."

Somehow, he's taken this all as an invitation to slip a hand to my waist.

I push him away. "Quit."

"What?" he panders, head tipped.

"You know what you're doing."

He says nothing but leaves himself cocked like a confused puppy.

"You're trying to distract me because you know you're . . . you know you look like that."

"Look like what?" he asks.

Like a perfectly formed being?!

"Master, look like what?" he asks again. Steadily creeping, a grin hiding in the corner of his mouth begins to bloom like a timelapse.

I'm in no position to be acknowledging his hotness. Not at the tail end of an abstinence pledge. Not after I ruined my own life because I couldn't keep it in my pants. I'm lonely. I've been lonely. It's easy for paper to get caught in the wind.

"Never mind," I say, mediating my breath and pulse. "Tell me what I want to know, Velis. I wish you would."

Eyes radiating, his expression flatlines. "Why, *Master*, must you keep doing that?"

And then, like word vomit, the truth comes:

"It's not like it's my life's goal to be here in the human world, chasing after souls. I'm here because of my father. He's an overseer of lands, what's known as a govern in our world. Like I said, our family's in the ruling class, so our estate is bigger than most, coveted, actually. Under normal circumstances, the lands and title would go to the firstborn son, but my father had three sons by his first wife, all born on the same day. Our estate can't be split, so our father devised a contest to select an heir. Whoever wins the most soul power in a set span of time will be named his next lord-in-waiting."

"Those two guys out there are your triplet brothers?"

"Yes and no. They are my triplet brothers, but I'm not one of the triplets. I'm my father's last son, born of a different wife than the others and not technically eligible to inherit our lands because my mother was of mixed race."

"Mixed race?"

"My mother was a half-nymph. So I was basically invited into the soul contest as a joke. Since I'm not full djinn, none of them expected much out of me. But joke's on them because I actually took the fucking lead. I've been working my ass off to get there, too, which is why our little situation isn't ideal."

Situation. Making him wait in the thrift store, refusing to make a wish, not allowing him to siphon my soul once I'd made one . . .

"So, you're, like, trying to shatter the status quo?" I guess.

"Not really. I just want to piss them off, and if it comes with a shiny new title, all the better. The thing is that, once they fell too far behind, my brothers stopped trying to find their own masters and started coming after mine. Their goal is to make a deal with you. If they can get you to wish my soul power over to them, I'll be dropped out of the running. Only my master has enough pull to wish something like that."

"They want to use me to steal your 'earnings'?"

"That's the gist." It seems he's talking to me outright now, rather than being compelled by the wish. "I meant what I said earlier. Souls have no bearing in your world. They were once important for your kind, a sort of spectrum to determine your eternal fate, but a few thousand years ago, they lost all significance. I'm not sure why. Once you siphon enough of your soul to me, we'll become tethered, and they won't be able to interfere with us anymore. From everything I know and everything I've seen, that should have started when you made your first wish. I have no idea why it isn't working. Maybe it's the nymph in me."

"So, we aren't tethered yet?" I ask.

"Not quite. But I am bound to you—the reason I've got to use magic in your favor. I can only have one master at a time, and you became mine after you kissed me. There's no breaking that bond until your wishes are fulfilled." Begrudgingly, he admits: "Unless another djinn manages to tether you before I do."

"Kissed your vessel," I correct.

"Oh no, doll. When I'm inside, we're one and the same." He makes a single smack with his lips.

It doesn't count. I am, of course, not allowed to do something so indulgent as kiss another living being. But I kissed a bottle, not a person. I feel no remorse.

"I'm assuming there's a reason I felt compelled to kiss an inanimate object?" I query.

"Because you're a fish."

A *fish*?

"It's like casting a line out to sea. Our vessels are the bait, only there's one specific fish they go after each time. My vessel chose you because you meet specific criteria: first, you're a good person, so you won't cast any evil wishes; second, you've got a heart's desire, something you want more than anything, that I can give you; third, our arrows are aligned—the theory being, it makes it easier for you to trust me and the process."

He pauses at my visible confusion over the word 'arrows.'

"Oh, right. I forget you guys don't have that here. It's, ah . . . What do you call it? Like, a horoscope? Or signs, I think one of my masters said? In our world, the cosmos is like a grid, or a music sheet, and each person from each realm is an arrow on that grid, tipped to varying degrees. If two people's arrows are tipped at the same angle, they're thought to be more compatible."

Do I get it? No, I don't. Velis can tell.

"Think of it like a huge blank sheet of parchment with a trillion dashes on it. Some dashes are like this." He sets his hand flat before his face. "Some are like this." He angles his hand upward diagonally. "And so on. When you think of the tenths and hundredths of a degree people can be tipped on, there are a shit ton of combinations. My vessel seeks out those who are closest to the alignment of my arrow."

My forehead wrinkles with the complexity of a fantasy race's mythos. "There's a big sheet of paper showing that somewhere?"

"Not a real one, but there are some djinn who can see it and read it in the skies. We're all given our arrow alignments at birth. Mine's 4AQ.7. Yours must be something close to that for my vessel to have chosen you."

To be honest, it sounds like a bunch of bullshit. Then again, I've never put much stock in human astrology either.

"Only thing is, once it sets a master as a mark, the master usually comes for me pretty fast. This is the first time it's taken weeks for me to be found. I mean, I had one chick go scuba diving to find me a few hours after we dropped. It's just weird. Firstly, it took you forever to find me. Secondly, we don't seem to be compatible at all from what I can tell. And thirdly, I've yet to siphon even a snippet of your soul away from you." He sheds foulness. "Granting all these free wishes is cutting into my wallet."

Well, *excuse* me. Not like I wanted to cast any of them to begin with. And also . . .

"Um, Master, mind telling me why you're examining my crotch?"

"Psh. Don't flatter yourself," I rally. "I was just checking to see if—" I admit I've been searching his pockets for bulges. "You have a wallet for soul juice?"

"Not literally! Geez. I was just trying to relate it to your terminology." A trace of mirth flexes through his tartness as he scoops down to retrieve his disc of light from its home of pillows. Face bathed in blue glow, he flinches over what he sees therein. "Yikes. Sorry about your dwelling." He's hasty to redirect: "Nothing a few wishes can't fix."

My apartment? What the hell are they doing to it?!

But when I zip to his side to get a look at whatever he's seeing, all I see is a flood of blue light washing out from the disc and spilling into Velis's chilly eyes like some evil fucking genie warlock.

"What is that thing?" I ask. "I see nothing when I look into it."

"That's because you don't have these." He points to his own irises, which swell brilliantly in response. "It's called a Ray. My 'wallet,' if you will. The closest thing I can compare it to would be a tablet in your world. I can see what's going on outside my vessel with it, it keeps track of my soul balance, and the best part? It's got all my favorite shows."

. . . Genie shows?

He frisbees the Ray onto his bookshelf with unhuman precision, upsetting the lone book I placed there. "Okay, enough of the twenty questions, Master. They're going to be at it for a while. Might as well work on tethering while we're stuck in here." He shoots himself into the nest of pillows and pats the well-loved cushions beside him. "Here, girl."

"I told you, *I'm not a dog*."

"Yeah, and I'm starting to suspect you aren't a human either. At least not a full one. Come over here and tell me your family secrets. Got any relatives that float or anything?"

Float?

"My family is completely normal, and I'm completely human," I respond flatly.

"In that case, we may need to try extracting your soul through *other* means."

The way he says it makes me take a step in the opposite direction. "Other means?"

My suspicions are warranted. Arcane darkness befalls him. "Come here, Dolly. I'll make sure it doesn't hurt."

"You realize I haven't agreed to give you my soul? You seem pretty entitled to something you haven't been promised," I say.

The genie retorts, "Naw, you'll give it up. I just have to make you the right offer. Your heart's greatest desire. As soon as I figure out what that is, we'll be in business for sure."

My heart's greatest desire? Sounds fictional.

"Sure, sure," I say, "but first, remind me why I have to lie like this?"

I rest over a mess of quilted bedding that smells like Velis, with my head in Velis's lap and my cheeks saturated in magical glow from the disc he's holding over my face.

"Shh, I can't concentrate with you squawking so much."

"At least tell me what you're doing. I only agreed to this because you said it would help get your ransacking brothers out sooner. That light is obnoxious."

"I'm Googling you."

"Genies have Google?"

The swift push of a hand to my forehead stops me before I can get a better look.

"No. *Obviously*. Like I said, I'm trying to be relatable. If I told you what I'm actually doing, you'd only have more annoying questions. By the way, that doesn't count as a lie. Jokes are allowed so long as they're said with the intent to reveal the truth after. Also, doesn't count as a lie if I genuinely think I'm telling the truth.

Loopholes—lucky you." He pats my head pompously, leaving his hand in my hair when finished.

And then he begins to pet me.

What in the actual hell?!

I don't even know if he knows he's doing it, to be honest. The movement is slight, and his brow remains deeply concentrated on the Ray in one hand, as if unaware the other is gently rubbing my hairline. However inconspicuous, the feel of it sends spider-like tingles down my back.

I can't remember the last time I was caressed.

With that intrusive thought, Velis suddenly halts and leans over to look at what his hand was just doing. "Oh." He catches my eye. "You want more of that, huh?"

Because he can sense what I desire. FUCK.

"Yeah, right! Get off me, you—"

"It's okay, Master. I don't mind." Gaze abnormally soft, he takes to stroking my hair again, muttering under his breath, "*If it will shut you up.*"

That's it!

But when I roll to get away from him, he catches my face. "I'm kidding. Just relax, okay? This is going to take a while." He coaxes me back into place and returns to the motion like he's trying to lull me to sleep.

For how frustrating and cocky and blunt he is, I can't deny the melting sensation of his fingertips through my roots. Skin against skin. Organic matter to organic matter.

I didn't realize how much I missed being touched.

Because the only people in my life who would still offer it are hours away, even by flight. After everything that happened with James and Gabe and all our friends, I considered quitting my job and fleeing to the safety of air that tasted like childhood and arms that would embrace me without judgment. To Mom's weird casseroles and neighbors that would treat me like I'm twelve.

But how could I serve penance in an environment like that?

"Master?"

I didn't notice, but Velis's relentless stare has become fixated on me again, his disc pulled out of the way to get a better look.

"What?"

He tosses the artifact aside to free me from his lap. "Come here."

Oh god. What now?

"I could feel how badly you wanted one of these. It's on the house." Cotton strands woven together have never felt so soft, the hum of a heart never so cadenced as his warmth bleeds through the cloth separating our skin. A hug? Velis has just pulled me in for a hug. And as I heed the rise and fall of his chest and the tightness of his arms around me, I feel once removed from the dark shadows of regret that plague me beyond the confines of a vase that never was.

I love it.

And I hate how much I love it.

There's something to be said about being comforted, even after fifty weeks of delay.

Velis swallows. "You're kind of hard for an empath to be around, you know." And then he stings, "It'll be nice when I can move on from you."

Eyebrow sharp, I kindly dismiss myself from him. I'm well aware I'm something of a mess, but I don't need him saying so during a moment of vulnerability. Ass.

"Yo, where are you going? We aren't done yet." He jiggles the retrieved disc expectantly.

"Argh! No, okay? I'm not lying in your lap and letting you stroke my hair like we're cozy until you tell me what you're doing with that Ray thing."

His turrets graze me. "You're frustrated."

That much is obvious.

"Because you want me to touch you more."

Stupid mind-reading genie.

"Even if that were the slightest bit true, it would have *nothing* to do with you. It's just that I haven't had human contact in a while."

A while. An understatement.

"I'm not a human." He stares at me longer than is socially acceptable, and when I refuse to budge, he lets out a sigh of extraordinary effort. "Fine. If you must know, I'm studying your soul against my former masters' souls to see if there's anything noticeably different about theirs—the clarity, the weight, the scent—so that I can figure out what's wrong with yours. It helps to be close to you for it. I have their souls' data stored inside my Ray, but I can get a better read on yours if we're touching. Even more so if you're relaxed."

So, the hair stroking wasn't absentminded at all.

"I can hug you again if you'd rather we do it that way," he says.

"I'm good."

He narrows his eyes shrewdly because he knows the truth. I narrow mine further, daring him to try touching me again.

But as I try to look menacing, Velis only raises a lip. "Look how bold you've become, *Master*. Used to be I couldn't even take out a pen without you flinching."

If only I had a pen.

"Used to be I couldn't"—I lunge forward to psych him out—"without you flinching."

Only, he doesn't flinch in the least.

Oh my god, how embarrassing!

Unruffled, his gaze permeates me without the slightest tell of emotion for an uncomfortably long time.

"So . . . you're kind of a dork, then?"

"Burn in hell." But secretly, I'm desperately clawing at any remaining street cred leaking through my pores while he continues staring, staring, staring!

"I like it."

Point blank, this is all he says before returning to the disc.

If I didn't already know he was incapable of lying to me, it would be impossible to tell whether or not he means it. That mouth of his keeps shifting from desert flatness to smirking iniquity without warning or recovery. And those crystalline eyes don't help.

The damage a person could do with eyes like those.

It's as if he were built to catch me off guard.

"Why are you staring at me, Master?"

He isn't looking at me, but I'm in his peripherals.

If I'm honest, his face is the sort of face you want to stare at, but he's definitely not the sort of person that should be told so. Before I can waffle for an excuse, his shoulders jerk as though he's just witnessed a grisly car crash through the blue tablet in his palm. "Er, sorry about your television cube."

"My TV?!" The vase offers no hints through its obsidian shell. "How long until they're done destroying my apartment?"

He flicks his eyes to me accusingly. "Yeah, sucks being stuck in here, doesn't it? Try two and a half weeks."

Not my fault his lamp sucks at enticing people. "Can't I just wish that they forget what they're doing and leave?"

"I mean, you could have done that upfront instead of cloaking us. Seems like a waste of soul power at this point—seeing as you've *yet to repay any of what you've taken from me*. They'll leave on their own soon enough. I'm guessing they made a deal with a non-tethered mortal to wish for my location in exchange for a one-off, and they'll need to go back and fulfill their side of the bargain sooner or later. They're really only a threat until we're tethered. After that, you'll be fully mine, so they won't be able to make deals with you." He shoots me a look thick with ulterior motives. "Aren't you excited to be mine, Master?"

"*Thrilled.*"

"That's if I can get any kind of read on you." The genie tablet clangs against the bookshelf, having just been bowled across the floor. "It should be easier than this. I'm starting to think there's something wrong with my vessel. Not like it to lead me to a dud."

Excuse me—*a dud*?

"For now, we'll just have to try more wishes and see if one sticks. Wish us out of here, will you? Make it juicy and wish us somewhere you've always wanted to go. Your shitty dwelling won't miss you."

He may be right about the apartment, but as I've repeatedly

told him, I'm not a person who deserves to go 'somewhere I've always wanted to go.'

"Come *on*, you don't want to be stuck in here any more than I do. Can't you just tack on a few extra days of your pledge after I'm gone?"

I mean, I guess. I did commit to a whole year of abstaining, but I never said it had to be consecutive. And he's right. I'm sick of being stuck in here with him.

"A week," I bargain.

"Geezus."

And if I'm going to wish us anywhere in the world, I might as well pick a place I may never get another chance to go:

"I wish you'd take us to the Uyuni Salt Flats in Bolivia."

Eyes pulsing, Velis takes hold of my arm and frowns. "Salt flats? I should have known you'd pick something boring like—" His complaints are cut off as the wish is enacted. For the briefest of moments, it feels like we no longer exist, as the curved glass walls and floor sprayed in pillows give way to the darkest darkness I've ever seen.

And after?

Velis's tone is unlike any I've heard from him so far: "Woah."

CHAPTER 4

The Endless Stars

"WHAT REALM IS THIS? Is this still Earth?"

I missed it. I had been hoping to see the moment the smugness melted off Velis's frustratingly perfect face, but I am too caught up in the beauty of where we've landed. I saw this in a Nat Geo article once. The pictures didn't do it justice. Pictures never do.

In the day, a thin, glassy layer of water makes this place an effortless reflection of endless blues and puffy whites.

But it isn't day, and the experience is something altogether different at night.

There is no skyline. There is nothing built by man to hint at it. Instead, a world of stars wraps around us, seeming to stretch on for eternity, illusioned by the glossy ground that boasts streaks of pink and blue gasses usually reserved for the highest reaches of the midnight sky. It is skin-prickingly beautiful, otherworldly, a thing of dreams. Cool night air teases at our hair and tastes of places we've never been as silence allows Velis and me to exist, feet wet, in the center of an endless galaxy.

Here, I could run on and on and on, it seems, and end in a place without a name.

"This is Earth," I tell Velis. "Somewhere I've always wanted to see. I figured if I'm going to cheat, I may as well go big."

"But we're standing in the stars!" Velis cries, yet to release my arm. "How can this be Earth?"

"I'll show you on a map when we go back." I slip out of his grip to dip a hand into the shallows. "It's an illusion, see?"

"I didn't know Earth was this . . ." His icy blues are drawn to the inky sky. His Adam's apple bobs. "Are there more places like this here?"

He's taking this all . . . unexpectedly.

"Many. I have a whole bucket list of places I want to go someday. The Arashiyama Bamboo Grove in Japan. The Isle of Skye in Scotland. About a hundred others. That money you saw on my bank statement, that's what I've been saving for. Unfortunately, this is the first place I've gotten around to. My ex was afraid of flying."

"You mean my masters could have been making wishes like this the whole time? Instead of brand ambassadorships and follower counts?!"

I snort. Definitely not the reaction I expected.

"*Brand* ambassadorships? Seriously, given the chance to wish for anything, why wouldn't you wish to experience something like this? This is literally the first thing I thought of. There's so much beauty in the world we never get to see. I want to see it. Even if it's just a little."

I was expecting to feel so much more complacent at seeing him this flush with wonder, but actually . . .

"Did it work?" I rush. "Are we tethered?"

"Huh? Oh, right. No. Doesn't feel like it. But . . ." His eyes find the pool at our feet. "It's worth the price this time."

Damn it. I want to gloat, but he's acting so . . . This is the first time I've seen him stop to breathe. The first time he's shown a shred of vulnerability. Equally vulnerable, I breathe too, letting the initial impact of it all wear off until I'm lost to the feeling of drawing in foreign air in a place that isn't ours.

I'm not a religious person. My Sunday school days are far in my rearview. But it's hard to look at a place like this and not feel something greater pressing down. I allow a smile to exist softly before falling.

"Stunning." A single word escapes Velis's mouth, and when I turn to him, I find he's gazing into the expanse behind me.

"R-right? If only I had a camera."

I should remember to be more careful about what I say around a genie.

This one reaches behind his back to unveil a fancy looking camera I haven't the slightest idea how to use, handing it to me like a macaroni necklace he just crafted. "Here."

"Did you just make that? Sorry. I don't actually know photography well. I meant it more as a hyperbole. I . . . realize that wasn't clear."

"Oh." Velis retreats the gift he's just concocted, and when he brings his hand around from behind his back again, there's no sign of it. "Then instead . . ." He opens his arms. "How about this?"

"What?"

"I can feel it. You're sad because you're not here with the person you thought you'd be here with."

He's right. I did want to come here with James.

But James and I had different ideas of what was worth seeing in life.

"I'm fine. That emotion was fleeting." It isn't a lie.

Eyes tossed to the ground, he casts a scowl. "Just come here, would you? I know you desire an embrace. It'll distract me until it's fulfilled. I won't push you away this time. You can stay as long as you want. As thanks for taking me here."

Maybe it's the fact that my guard is already lowered. Or maybe it's the fact that touch is such a core human need. To be without it for so long . . .

Before I know it, I'm settled against Velis's chest with our feet dipped in the shallow water, his arms a warm defense against the cool onslaught of night.

Is it pathetic that out of anything I could have in the world, this is what I want most? Even if it comes from a stranger. Even if it's out of pity.

With that thought, the genie squeezes tighter.

"You should make more wishes like this once we're tethered." His voice hums deeply through his chest. "I wouldn't mind sticking around a little longer if we get to see more places like this."

Maybe Velis is capable of being something other than an ass. For everything else he would have me believe about him, asses don't comfort people like this. I'm broken. I know I am. And that's why it feels so good to be held together by someone who doesn't care about me enough to hurt me.

There's a rhythm to our pulses and breaths as Velis takes in a landscape painted by something far more infinite than either of us, and I take in his borrowed warmth. I sink into it. Deeper, deeper.

"Son of a bitch!" Velis's displeasure suddenly reverberates into the stars, and I'm shoved violently behind his back by the hands that were just embracing me—as two flawless faces appear in the darkness before us, each harboring a set of blue eyes icy enough to cut through the night.

"Hello, *little brother*."

It's the taller of the two who has just spoken. Taller, only by deceit, for he wears a set of heavy leather boots to boost his stature—a trick I've used plenty.

"Jeb," Velis grumbles, teeth bared.

The person occupying the boots is lean and sports a brightly colored tank top beneath an open sweater, a little preppy, a little punk, with modest gauges, a hoop through his nostril, and hair the same dusky color as Velis's—albeit a shade or two darker—trimmed at the sides and swept back at the front. Jeb. Unarguably, those frosty eyes look coldest on him.

In fact, he looks like the sort of person who has never owned a pet.

It's obvious the person beside Jeb is a twin—or rather, the second in a set of triplets—but while the mold is the same, the two are anything but identical.

"Arrik," snarls Velis.

This one dons an expression of pure fuck-all, with most of his hair buzzed but for a short strip down the middle, and dark tattoos crawling up his neck and out the sleeves of his shirt. If I had to guess, his entire body is painted that way, save his face, which holds only one small symbol stamped into the cheekbone at the corner of his eye. Arrik. A bad boy genie. Or at least that's what he wants you to think.

All of them have mouths meant for mocking. All of them have bodies structured by the gods.

"*Is everyone in your family hot*?!"

Velis ignores me but forces me closer behind his back. "You're too late," he bids his brothers. "We're long tethered."

A lie Jeb immediately sees through. "Dumbass," he says, stony-faced. "If you were, you wouldn't be running from us. I take it this one won't put out like the rest?"

"About fucking time," mutters tattooed Arrik, panning over the endless horizon but showing no trace of awe. Arrik's voice is a gritty one, almost like he was up all night shouting. He *looks* like he was up all night shouting.

"Language!" Jeb snaps at his brother.

"Fuck. Fuck. Fuckity fuck," his brother drawls back.

Jeb narrows his eyes at Arrik's defiantly raised eyebrow before returning to us. "That's unlike you, Vel. Losing your touch? Or is she playing hard to get?" He shifts as if to appraise me. "Not quite as girly as your usual marks. Is that why you can't seal the deal, Vel? Are her desires too complex for a breed like you?"

A . . . breed? Did Velis's own brother really just call him a *breed*?

"Shut up, Jeb," Velis retorts, withholding emotion enough to make his back shake.

Meanwhile, Arrik seems to have summoned an unwrapped popsicle out of Bolivian air.

Um . . . sure?

"Why don't you come play with us for a while, *Dolly Jones*? I can promise we're more fun." He bites the tip off the popsicle with seduction apparent.

Is that supposed to convince me?!

Not to mention, of *course* he knows my name. Because he and his brother ravaged my whole damn apartment, mail and all. Larry's going to kill me if they put holes in the walls.

"Ready to stop playing djinn yet?" Jeb carries on, tone soft and calculated and a little like a librarian on a killing spree. "Even if you win, you know Father will never make you an heir. So why not just give up, hand over your master and your balance, and run off to be with the nymphs?" His expression curls. "Oh yeah, I forgot, they don't want you either."

Wait, so all that stuff Velis said about being invited into the contest as a joke was . . .

"Genies can be racist?" I whisper behind Velis's back.

He says nothing but pushes me further behind him to obstruct me from view.

"What's that, Dolly Jones?" calls Jeb. "You have a wish? I'm happy to grant it for you. You don't want some filthy wannabe touching your soul anyway. These are the hands of a purebred." As he says it, he holds one of them up as if he'd like me to *behold* it.

What a self-important anus. It would be a shame if someone wished those pedigreed hands off his pedigreed body.

Velis stiffens, feeling the pulse of my desire. "Sassy," he says under his breath. "But you can't. It won't work. You can't cause harm, and you can't change destinies. I appreciate the sentiment, though."

"Your plan, then?"

"Wish us out of here and pray it tethers us?"

So we're just supposed to keep transporting around and hoping they don't find us? They found us pretty damn easily this time.

I size up the situation, seeing it all in new light. Those frantic glances Velis kept tossing. His desperation to claim my wishes. The clear cockiness swirling around his two older brothers as they look down on him like he's something lesser, something dirty. I've suffered similar looks from those I once thought friends, but mine were because of something I did and not something I was born into.

And that word. *Breed.* It's so cutting, so ugly, and by the cold pleasure riding Jeb's mouth, that was exactly how he intended it to be. Meanwhile, Arrik's standing over there with that suggestive stare, like he expects me to run into his painted arms at any moment. Like no one's ever told him no.

Trust me—I'm the one you want to be dealing with in this situation.

Maybe I can see what Velis was getting at.

"Actually, I do have a wish for you, Jeb," I announce loudly.

Velis lurches forward to stop me as I step around him. "Master, don't!"

"And you too, Arrik."

The tattooed djinn straightens beside his brother, brow piqued in interest, the naked popsicle stick now tucked into the side of his mouth.

"I wish you wouldn't leave this place until morning. Stay out here and admire the night sky. The dawn too."

With my wish exposed, both djinns' eyes light like stars in the night. And after, Jeb offers a serial killer's smile for but a second, until—

"Hold on, why can't I . . . ?" He snaps his fingers twice before frantically asking, "Arrik?"

But Arrik is already coming to the same conclusion as his brother, failing to detect a hint of soul between the pads of his fingers. "What the shit?"

"Oh, thank Maka." Velis releases the tension he's been holding in his chest. "Not smart, Master! You could have accidentally tethered to them!"

Like I would let either of them near my soul.

"How did you do that? *How did she do that*?!" Jeb seethes in confusion while Arrik sizes me up with new curiosity, lip hanging soft and dark brows bent in focus.

He's quite pretty for a bad boy coated in tattoos.

"How did you do that?!" Jeb charges at us, hand thrust out like he's about to inflict some sort of magical genie retribution, but the moment before he reaches us, Velis spins one-eighty, wraps his arms around me, and pulls me into the abyss.

When I open my eyes, Velis and I are standing in front of my apartment in the black of night with the pavement shining from earlier rain beneath iron streetlamps. Clusters of sickly petals cling to the gutters as the smell of earth and worms rises up from the dirt.

Thanks to the wish I just cast, Velis's brothers are nowhere in sight.

My genie doesn't release me right away. "Oh my god, you had me friggen' worried, Master! The moment you made that wish, I thought I was done for." He pushes me away from himself to arm's length. "How did you keep them from siphoning? Is it something you're consciously doing while making the wishes?"

"Not that I know of. I mean, I'm not super keen on having my soul *milked* out of me, but I'm not really doing anything to prevent it. By the way—your brother Jeb is an asshole. Is that how they all feel about your lineage?"

Water drips off surrounding leaves into puddles waiting to play catch. Velis drops his hands. "Is that really something you need to know?"

Says the person who pried into the darkest part of my past.

I give him blinks until he breaks.

"Ugh." His head falls with the weight of his sigh. "No. Not all of them. Jeb's the worst. Arrik has his moments. My cousins are kind of shits about it, but none of my friends care. Lots of them are mixed too."

"What about the last one?" I say. "You have a third brother, don't you? What's he like?"

"Beckham. He's more reasonable than the other two. Last I heard, he was still trying to win fairly."

'More reasonable' doesn't necessarily mean reasonable, though.

"I'm sorry, Velis. That was frustrating to watch. I get that discrimination exists, but to have it within your own family? Those are the ones that are supposed to support you the most."

"Ha! In what world?"

"In . . . this world?"

This time, it's Velis's turn to blink. And then—"Argh! This is a nightmare. This is the first time they've gotten that close to one of my masters. You're totally Arrik's type too. He likes brunettes."

Does that mean Velis doesn't like brunettes? Not that it matters.

He gives a jolt.

"What?"

"Nothing. I thought I felt something, but it's gone." He studies me before lifting his face to the brick three-story at our side. "I'm sorry, Master, but I don't think I can fix your dwelling just yet. I can't afford to spend that much of my balance until your soul starts replenishing it. We've already spent more than what I would normally give gratis. Can it wait until we figure out what's wrong with you?"

Because he wants to win against those dickheads.

I get it.

"Well, I bought us time, at least," I say. "Let's just hope Larry doesn't need to enter my unit for any reason in the mean—"

Out of nowhere, Velis scoops my chin into his hand and pushes his gaze into mine. "Hey, Dolly, wanna make out?"

"*What?*"

I feel my face flush. Not because I want to take him up on the offer, but because he's looking at me so . . . directly. Not to mention, his mouth very much looks like it was built for making out.

He squints at me, analyzing me for a moment before releasing my chin. "Never mind. I know you can't. I was just trying to get a read on something."

Something that involves asking me if I want to make out?!

"Don't toy with me, Velis. I'm on your side here, but not if you start being a dick again."

He bears the look of someone who's just been shot.

Okay, well, that's an overreaction.

"On my side?" he repeats slowly.

Oh, *that's* the part that hit him?

"Well, yeah," I confirm. "Clearly, those two are horrible."

He studies me like he's looking for a punchline, and finding none, he says, "Oh. Thanks."

Is this a different Velis than the one from before the salt flats? It seems he may have forgotten that dark streak back in my closet.

"Anyway, you're right." He distracts himself with a sky that's nowhere near as clear as the one we just left. "About buying us time. Thanks to you, those two are stuck at that salty place until morning. We should use this time to sleep because they're likely to come after us again tomorrow. I saw what they did to your bed and, ah—is there someplace else we can go tonight?"

Someplace else? I'm not the sort of person with the luxury of friends' couches to crash on.

"Of course, you could stay with me in my vessel, but there's not a lot of room in there."

I am not spending the night in a boho love nest with a ripped dude I barely know.

"Yeah, no. Let's just go to a hotel," I say. "I have plenty of *normal* money, and there's one within walking distance. I just have to go up and grab a few—"

"Yeeeeah, I don't think that's a good idea. I'd rather you not see what they did to the place. Not to mention the door's locked, and it's going to cost me a lot more magic to transfer you inside than it would be to just do myself. I'll run in, just tell me what you want." He pauses. "Or, actually, don't even tell me. Just *desire* it."

"You think you're that good?" I question.

The corner of his mouth sparks with playfulness. "I know I am. Here—" He slips one hand behind my back and presses the other to the center of my chest.

I can get a better read on yours if we're touching. Even more so if you're relaxed.

"Try me. Close your eyes if it helps. And be specific."

He knew about the ranch. And he knew about the hug. But I'm not convinced he'll be able to get an entire shopping list.

With his warm fingers settled against my collarbone, he keeps his eyes locked on mine until I close them, and after, I try to picture what I want from my apartment. Toothbrush, a change of clothes.

I'm distracted by the brush of his fingertips that have just shifted slightly.

"Focus." He pulls me closer by the hand on my back.

I'm trying. It's just . . .

I know he doesn't mean anything by the way he's holding me, but . . .

He smells good. His hands are warm and firm.

And I haven't been touched like this in a very long time.

"Wait," he says, sounding furrowed. "I'm getting something else . . ."

I throw him off me. "You should have enough, right?"

"That's all?" He tips his head. "What about your wallet?"

"Oh, yeah," I say. "That too."

"And your cellular phone?"

"Right," I say. "And that."

"Geez. You are so bad at this." He shakes his head and then—

Poof.

There's no denying he's *desirable*, but I can never, ever, *ever* let him know I think so.

I wait outside under the chill left in the storm's wake, arms folded into myself, exiled from my own apartment, while cars splash by with little regard for spraying water. At least the petals are having a good time.

It's taking Velis awhile to get back here. How long does it take to grab a spare pair of leggings and—

OH MY GOD—underwear! A change of clothes definitely includes undergarments. I didn't specify which pair, did I? Does that mean he gets to pick one? Is that what he's doing right now, looting through my drawer of panties?!

I already know he's a snooper.

"Sorry it took so long." His voice from behind makes me jump. "I had a hell of a time finding this." He tosses a small black zippered pouch at me.

My makeup bag? I haven't worn makeup in months.

"Don't know what's in there, but it pulsed at me from deep down. That's what we call a subconscious desire." Under his breath he adds, "*Don't know why you wanted it so badly if it was buried at the bottom of a friggen' junk drawer*. Here's the rest of it." He swings old faithful—my reusable sack—at me. "See how I did."

I rifle through. It's all here, even the exact pair of leggings I wanted, though I have at least a dozen other pairs. Is it impressive? Yes, but that's not what I'm concerned with.

There. At the bottom of the bag. There they are, in all their black lacy glory.

I haven't worn these in a long time. They were buried *deep*.

"What?" He shoots around me to peer over my shoulder. "Did I get it wrong?"

I shove the panties farther into the bag. "Perv."

"Hey." He holds up his hands. "I took no liberties. Everything in that bag is something you wanted. I can't lie to you, remember?"

Why would I subconsciously want *those*?

"Argh, come on." I hoist those threadbare straps higher onto my shoulder and take off down the sheeny street.

"Judging by your grumpiness, it seems I lived up to my name." He fist-pumps over his own achievement. "I may not be able to siphon you, but I can still get a read on your desires, Master. There may be hope yet."

CHAPTER 5

Checking for Bed Bugs

"Pretty fancy, Master." Velis lets out a whistle and scans the hotel room's interior while sliding his vessel beside the 'television cube.' Not fancy. It's your average mid-budget hotel room with strange generic wall hangings that nobody really loves or hates and foam coffee cups that are far too small for any normal person's morning.

"Check the bed, would you?" I say.

"Check it?"

"Yeah . . . I have a thing about beds. Are the sheets white?"

He tips up the comforter. "Yup."

"Any hair clusters or stains?"

"What the fuck?" He whips the sheets up to get a look at the bottom of the bed. "No? Not that I can see."

"Okay." I take a breath. "Now for the big one. Bed bug check. Look at the mattress cover and see if there's anything unusual going on."

Velis leaps back from the mattress. "Humans have bugs living in their beds?!"

"Ideally, no," I say. "The chances are low. It's just something I have to check for in order to feel comfortable." I kneel into the shaved carpet at the side of the bed, satisfied when I see nothing out of the ordinary. "Okay, we're good." I straighten and give the air a sniff. "Smells nice in here, doesn't it?"

Velis eyes the bed mistrustfully. "There are no bugs?"

"No bugs. I'm gonna go shower, okay? It's been a long day."

I leave him crouched beside the bed, poking at the mattress.

Never has a shower felt more cleansing. I like the water hot. Hot enough that James used to berate me about scalding my skin off. He liked lukewarm showers. He was kind of a wuss that way.

I let the water run through my hair and cry down my face to wash away rain residue and Bolivian air. If I let it keep running, will it wash away everything that's happened? Genies and wishes and teleporting to distant countries?

I wring out my hair, brush my teeth, and study myself in the circle of mirror I've wiped clear. I've put no effort into my appearance in quite a long time. I've been slogging through life, waiting for the passage of restrictions I set for myself. Waiting to feel better about myself and the part I played in ending my relationship and losing all my friends.

I'm strong enough to resist my urges. I'm a good person.

If I say it enough, will I believe it?

Oh, you're not a bad person.

Everyone makes mistakes.

I'd be pointing fingers at the guy who does remember it.

I mean, it's not like I value Velis's opinion. It's just . . . nice to hear someone else say it for once.

Damn, Dolly! Why would you cover up a body like that?!

You're a little bombshell!

You really are pretty when you smile.

I don't need validation from any man—or genie—but I can't deny I felt . . . cuter today than I have in months. The black makeup case sits on the counter, watching me. Is it true I subconsciously wished for it? Did I want a reason to decorate myself?

Maybe. My fingers are, after all, crawling over to it.

Wings. I used to always, always wear winged eyeliner. To the point that my eyes looked weird without it.

Like riding a bike, my fingertips remember how to find the

invisible line connecting the corner of my eye to the tip of my eyebrow and trace it a fraction of an inch. Nothing too crazy but enough to sharpen the eyes.

There, now I really look like a cat burglar.

Velis packed me gray sweat shorts and a dark tank top. My hair is short enough that it waves as it dries. I suck in a breath before opening the door to release the heat I've accumulated.

"Sorry I took so long, I—"

Velis is nowhere to be found.

Oh. Has he retreated into his vessel for the night? That's fine. It's not like I have anything to say to him. I shift onto the bed and curl my knees to my chest, paging through the names on my cellphone. My boss will be happy to hear I'm taking a personal day tomorrow. He's been hounding me to 'use 'em or lose 'em.'

Velis said his Ray can show him everything happening outside his vessel. Is he watching me now? Is that why I feel so awkward doing something as normal as lounging on the edge of a bed? I mean, I guess I expected him to at least say goodnight. Or, like, plan what we're going to do tomorrow? He doesn't want me to cast wishes and tap into his balance, but he still wants to tether to me, so where do we go from here?

Pitiful.

It's pitiful that I've become consumed with this situation all because I've been without true human interaction for so long.

Click!

The tick of a card reader preludes the sounds of someone butting into the door as a blue-haired twenty-something comes shambling into the room holding a plastic ice bucket to his chest.

"Oh! I thought you were inside your vessel."

"Huh? Naw, I wouldn't ghost you like that, Master. Here—" Velis tosses me a can. "Confession time: I *may* have stolen human money from your wallet to buy consumables."

Consumables? He means pop.

Surprising how relieved I am that he hasn't gone to bed yet.

But I'm sure I'd feel the same about anyone who came

waltzing into my life. There's nothing special about him. He's just another living body.

A hot, magical body.

"Woah, you look different," he observes, setting the ice bucket down beside his vessel and cracking open his can of pop.

Makeup, dummy.

His mouth bends at the corner. "You're starting to feel better about yourself, huh? Good. You should. Like I said, you've been way too hard on yourself for something that's not even your fault." He transitions: "So, ah, I'm pretty wired." He gives his can a sloshing shake. "And this isn't going to help. Wanna watch a film or something? I've seen a couple of human ones. They weren't bad."

The genie wants to watch a movie? I'm in a hotel room drinking carbonated beverages with a mythical creature who wants to, what, Netflix and chill?

Speaking of chill. That air conditioner has no reason to be humming like that. It's plenty cold in here as it is.

Weight settles beside me on the edge of the mattress. "Er, is this okay? I get you might feel uneasy after what happened to you."

What *happened* to me?

"I'm not a victim, Velis. I played a part in it."

"Sure." He takes a sip from the can. "Just thought I should check. I don't intend to sleep out here, though. I know you wouldn't be down for that. It's just . . ." He eyes the plush comforter behind us. "It's been, like, four months since I slept in a real bed, so it feels good to take a load off on one. Tell me if you want me to move."

"You mean you don't have pillow nests in your rooms back home?"

I assumed that's how they lived.

"Ha!" His glance harbors amusement. "No, we have beds. Though most of ours hang from the ceiling."

"For real?"

"Oh yeah. Makes for fun—" He stops himself, fighting a smirk. "Never mind."

It should be illegal to say things like that with a mouth like his.

"H-how does one become a wish granter?" I divert. "You said you had a different job before the contest started, so how did you become what you are now?"

He shrugs. "Night classes. Though they do have online programs nowadays."

"Wait, you mean like college? *Genie* college?"

"*Djinn* college," he corrects.

I really have to get better about that.

Velis continues, "Though when I say 'online,' I'm referring to a distance-based communication system that doesn't exist on Earth. 'Online' is just the best way to relate it to what you know . . ." His voice trails, and I suddenly feel the chill of his stare starkly upon me. "Hey, is there a reason you look so sexy right now?"

"*Excuse me?*"

"Yeah. Those shorts clearly hug your ass, and your tits right now are . . . yeah. Not to mention that strap keeps slipping off your shoulder. Are you intentionally looking sexy, or did that just sort of happen?"

I lean away from him. "What, like you think I'm *interested* in you? Like I got all slutted up for some dude I met less than a DAY ago? God, I might be lonely, but I'm not fucking desperate, Velis. These are my pajamas. Get over yourself."

Too far. I've corrected way too far, and I realize it the moment Velis's expression fades. "Geezus, Dolly! Rip my head off, why don't you? That's not what I meant at all, but good to know the only way a girl would be *interested* in me is if she were *desperate* enough." With unhuman precision, he trick-shots his half-empty cola into the waste bin and storms up from the bed. "I'm sorry I'm not a full fucking genie or whatever you females prefer."

Wait, where did *that* come from?

"Apparently, I can only siphon shallow girls' souls anyway. I'm sure I wouldn't be able to handle whatever soul you're hiding in there." Frustrated, he wrangles his vessel by the neck. "I'm going to bed—er, you know what I mean."

He disappears in a blink, and his vessel falls to the floor.

After, I slump to the mattress.

Because I overreacted. Again. Because I'm not over what happened with Gabe. Because I've been wearing baggy sweaters for months to cover up my body. Because I was feeling cute and sexy and because I feel guilty that I don't hate feeling that way.

I feel like I should hate feeling that way.

And Velis overreacted too. Because his mixed lineage impacts him much more than he let on earlier.

I have an impulse to call out to him, to explain myself or apologize, but really, it would be easier if we left things how they are. I don't need to get close to anyone during this stage of my life. Especially not someone as *finely crafted* as him.

I'm lonely. That's the only reason I feel like I want to. I'd be feeling that way no matter who was inside that bottle.

And Velis is stubborn enough that he won't come rushing over to apologize either. Good. This will all go much faster if we aren't *friendly*.

I click off the light, dip under the covers carefully pre-examined by a djinn, and curl onto my side. Through a crack in the curtains, light from the parking lot creeps in like a spotlight of shame.

And the *cold*. Why are hotel rooms always so cold? I don't think those thermostats really control anything. You set it to seventy-five before you leave and come back to a miraculous sixty-eight. And in the middle of the night, it's like it resets to sixty. And this mass-manufactured comforter isn't thick enough to protect me from it.

A chilly minute passes.

Two, three.

I slip out from the covers and start for the thermostat under the window but am intercepted by a burst of smoke that's more like incense and less like fire. It's the first time I've actually seen a djinn emerge from his bottle.

But what's all the smoke for?

I fan it away, noting the way it tastes like Velis smells.

"Wait, let me go first. Before you say anything—" But Velis stops himself, lowering his hands which were in the process of reaching for my shoulders. "Er, why do you look like you weren't expecting me?"

"Because I wasn't expecting you!"

His eyes dart to the bed behind me. "But weren't you on your way over to apologize?"

"No, I was on my way to turn up the heat in here because it feels like an icebox. You were watching me from your vessel?"

"N-*yes*. Goddamn truth oath!" He bares his teeth. "Wait, you weren't going to apologize? You were just going to leave it at that?"

"Uh, yeah."

"What the hell, Dolly?! That was clearly a fight where we were both in the wrong! I was waiting for you to meet me halfway so that I didn't look like the only ass." He clamps his own mouth. "GODDAMN TRUTH OATH!"

Okay, I can't help laughing at that one.

"It's not funny!" But that isn't what his dimples are saying. "Fine. It was funny." He exhales hard. "Look, you aren't a slut. I didn't mean to make you feel like you were. That was shitty wording on my part. What I meant to say is that you look smokin' right now, and that I hoped it wasn't for my sake. It would be inconvenient if you developed feelings for me."

Oh.

Feelings?

Don't flatter yourself, *Vel*.

But, I wonder what would be so inconvenient about it.

Oh shit.

"See?" Velis lurches forward. "It's faint, but I could have sworn . . ."

"I'm not going to develop feelings for you," I say hastily, refusing to entertain the idea. "If you think I look *smokin'*, it isn't anything I did intentionally. I do think I wanted a reason to put effort into myself, and being around someone else gave me a reason. I got upset when you questioned it because I'm having some body issues right now."

"Oh."

If I think he looks disappointed by my answer, it must be my imagination. He thinks it would be *inconvenient* if I developed feelings for him, after all.

"And that stuff I said at the end?" He rubs the back of his head. "That wasn't about you."

I got that much.

"So, are we good?" He stands before me in the near darkness, only one of his eyes lit by the light stealing through the curtains.

"We're good," I say.

The air conditioner has stopped its yapping, and silence feels so much thicker after an argument. His jaw flexes, inviting tension to the party.

No, no. None of that.

"So, what's the plan for tomorrow?" I push past him to finish what I started. "More analysis with that Ray thing?"

"I actually think I want to take you to get your arrow read so that I can confirm it's off-kilter with mine and begin to diagnose why my vessel drew you to me. You're a lot different than the type of girls it usually picks."

"Get my arrow read? There are humans that can do that?"

"Of course not. We're going to Makaya—the djinn realm."

I blink at him slowly. It sounded like he just said—

"We'll go see a djinn reader and find out your alignment. That'll help me figure out what's wrong with you."

Okay, well, that's going to take at least fifteen minutes to sink in.

So now I'm not only accepting that I'm in a hotel room with a hot genie—I'm also accepting that said hot genie is going to take me to the *land* of hot genies to verify that my *arrow* isn't aligned with his *arrow* on a big sheet of *paper* in the *sky*.

"Clarify something for me here, Velis. You said that the girls your vessel typically picks wish for things like lip enhancements and social media status, right? And these are the girls that are supposedly aligned with your arrow? So . . . YOU would wish for that shit if given the chance?"

"Hell no! Their wishes are supposed to be aligned with mine, not the same as. Geez." He holds his forehead like Shakespeare, peeking up at me with a grin. "Do you really think my lips need enhancing?"

"Your lips are massive," I tell him.

Whatever twinkle he's showing grows. "I know. But not, like, freakishly massive, right?"

I should tell him yes.

But he's just tucked his lower one between his teeth to distract me. Now who's making efforts to appear sexy?

"Sorry." He releases his lip and gives a swallow. "I never understood the lip thing. I mean, lips are fun, but there are plenty of other fun bits too."

Bits.

"S-so—" Fucking stutter. "What does it mean that their wishes are aligned with yours? Something like, their wishes are shallow because your intentions are shallow? Because you really just want to grant quick, easy wishes so that you can move on to your next mark?"

"That's exactly it," he says, with a bit of surprise. "You're kind of clever, huh?"

Tch, kind of?

"And because I don't want to make any wishes, let alone quick, easy ones, I'm not the type of person your vessel should have lured," I deduce. "And that's why you said we aren't compatible as djinn and master."

"Yeah, but even so, I should be able to siphon your soul for the wishes you *have* made. The reader will help us figure out why I can't."

Fine by me. Maybe it means I can get out of making wishes altogether.

"Speaking of which," he adds, "scratch that film idea. We should probably turn in if we wanna get an early start in the morning." He scoops down to pick up his vessel. "Where do you want me? Is here okay?" He sets the curvy bottle on the desk in the corner. "I, ah, promise I won't spy on you anymore."

The desk. The floor. The nightstand. Wherever, it seems a little ridiculous to make a grown man sleep in a pile of pillows. I know what I said before about the bohemian love nest, but . . .

"Do . . . you want to sleep in the bed?" I offer with zero confidence in my own question.

"N—" But his mouth won't allow him to lie. "Yes." His teeth become a bear trap: "*That's getting really friggen' old.*"

Thought so.

"I mean, it's a king. It's pretty huge. We could throw a couple of pillows between us," I decide. "And if you try anything, I guess I could just wish your dick removed."

"Ha! If *I* try anything? I can't hurt you, remember? And your dick threats are empty because you can't hurt me either."

I forgot about that.

"I mean, yeah, it would be fucking awesome to sleep in a real bed," he levels. "But are you sure you're okay with me sleeping so close to you?"

Should I be? No. Velis is basically a stranger. Our dozen-plus hours together barely constitute enough time to build any semblance of trust. And yet . . .

"Master? You don't feel sad," he says, "so why do you desire me to hold you right now?" He seems genuine, but with him, I never can tell.

"Your sensors are off." I scoop up a pillow from the bed and push it into his chest. "Touch me and you die."

"So feisty." Wearing a slight ruffian's grin, he begins making his way around the bottom of the bed, where I'm swift to cut him off.

"Wait—I get that side. I don't like sleeping next to nightstands."

He checks to see if I'm kidding. "Why?"

"It's too cramped. I . . . have a thing about beds."

"Seriously? Is that why yours had no headboard?"

That's exactly why.

"Weird. But okay." He pivots and heads for the side near the wall, pouncing atop the covers at the furthest edge. "Oh, faaack yes. Maybe I'll finally get rid of that cramp in my back. Thank you, Master. Really." Clamped around one unlucky pillow, and before I can even wish him to stay on his own side, he quickly falls to heavy breathing.

Meanwhile, my thoughts are swimming too fast for any of that nonsense. Djinn and wishes and piercing blue eyes . . .

I lie as still as can be, ever aware of the body sharing the space with me while my feeble human mind struggles to make sense of this fantasy I've found myself in, until at last, the weight of exhaustion wins.

I wake up to find my pillow has hardened. Groggy, I roll over to a nose-full of linen and pheromone-spiked sweat, as my 'pillow' rises and falls beneath my squashed cheek.

"What the hell?!" I jet up. "Velis! What are you doing over here?!"

"More like what are *you* doing over *here*," he scoffs, shifting his arm tucked around my shoulder.

It seems we've been cuddling. And he's right—I'm well on his side of the bed, our defensive line of pillows chucked all over the ground.

Oh my god, I AM desperate.

And cuddling definitely goes against the stipulations of my pledge.

I scramble to get away from him.

"Hey, it's fine," he reassures me. "It was . . . nice. Kept me warm, at any rate." He sits up into a catlike stretch, stopping to observe: "Wow. You're kind of a mess when you wake up."

Fucking blunt-ass genie. It's not my fault my hair is so thick it sticks to itself and that every time I wake up, it looks like I was in a backyard wrestling match.

"Just so you know, I didn't mean to cuddle you," I tell him.

"Oh, I know," he says simply. "Just like you didn't mean to coo at me in your sleep."

COO?

"Coo, coo, little dove."

I lob a pillow at his face. Or rather, I try to. He catches it well before it hits.

"It's really not a big deal, Master. Not to me. You have the perfect body for snuggling. Ample surface to hold."

See? I knew I was squishy.

"Plus, you smell nice," he adds.

Is he trying to be a walking contradiction? He *clearly* wants to flirt with me, but he also wants to make it clear he doesn't see me as anything more than a means to an end.

And again, this is a mythical creature we're talking about.

"I'm not here for your entertainment," I protest.

"I know you're not," he says in earnest. "You're here to be my master." He bullets the pillow back in my direction with more speed and accuracy than the pillow has ever seen. "And as my master, you should hurry and get ready. Today, I'm taking you home."

CHAPTER 6

Where Arrows Point

"Coo, coo." I don't even care that it's the third time this morning Velis has impersonated a dove in my ear. All this time, an exceptionally long blink was all that separated the world as I know it from something more.

My mortal bones prick with the energy of a thousand tan-skinned people crawling over a city built of the whitest stone and festooned with strings of cobalt flowers slithering over balconies and parapets like party décor. It is a mountain of structures, all constructed of the same pearly rock, where blocky buildings climb over one another, and polished sets of stairs race to the top.

This is a city built on crannies and nooks, with a hundred ways to get to a single destination, and where a single map could never contain it all.

"You live here?" I gawk, eyes painted with the shimmer of a long aquamarine canal feeding through a string of bridges into the heart of the djinn-made mountain.

"Well, not *here* here. That'd be the first place my brothers would look. This is the capital of a neighboring country. Plenty of readers for hire, though. And one of them already knows me. This way."

Velis pulls me in by the shoulder like we're courting before ushering me down an alleyway quieter than the surrounding streets.

Apparently, humans aren't common in these parts. Explains the reason for the oversized hood sheltering my hair and complexion.

"It's your eyes that will be the biggest giveaway," Velis tells me over the hurry of our shoes with his arm tightly tucked around my back. "Remember to look down if we see anyone. I don't need another citation on my record."

"Citation?"

"And a fine. That's what happens if we get caught without paperwork. Unlike other races, humans are only allowed here under certain circumstances."

"Because we're considered *prey*."

"*Actually*, it's because your society is delicate as hell. The introduction of new races into your realm has never gone over well, so prolonged interaction with humans is discouraged. That doesn't just go for djinn, either."

I mean, I can see that. "So then, what circumstances would make it okay for me to be here?"

"Well, if you and I were married, for one. Then it would be okay, but you couldn't go out on your own. You'd have to be accompanied by me at all times and with the proper paperwork."

Aside from humans needing to be registered like dogs here—

"Humans and djinn can marry each other?!"

"It happens, *rarely*. Selfish, though. Their kids would be fucked."

Would being half human in this world be worse than being a quarter nymph? My gut tells me it's too insensitive to ask.

Through branching alleyways stained with stardust, I keep my chin tucked away, barely able to see where we're going, wondering what sorts of people are connected to any feet we pass. The hand on my back is stern and guiding, the pathway meticulously white, until eventually, the connection of passages spits us into an open strip of the city, where I forget myself a moment, tipping my face to revel in the shadow of an enormous set of stone wings positioned high above the square. Bits of sunlight burst through cracks in the marble, making it look like the whole thing is held together by feathers of light.

WOW.

"Master!" My wrist is yanked hard enough to make my fallen hood flap as Velis peels me around the side of a storefront, where he hastily works to return my cover. "Did you not hear me about keeping your face down? There was a watchman over there, and I'm pretty sure he saw your hair!" He sets my shoulders to the wall of pristine stone, listening for the brisk tap of incoming footsteps and letting out a swear when they deliver.

And then—

My chest swells deeper than normal at the feel of his thumb suddenly touching the edge of my lip, and the warmth of his body as it shields me, and the heat of his mouth, deceptively close.

Oh, yeah, sure.

Of course this is how he deems it appropriate to hide me!

To the approaching footsteps, we look like a couple making out.

"Hold still, Master."

As if I have a choice. Sickening to admit it, but I don't think this would fly if he weren't so . . .

If my body weren't so naturally inclined to . . .

He's so fucking hot, okay?

And I hate him even more for it.

I feel his fingers jerk the moment I acknowledge it. His eyes, previously slid to the side to get a peripheral glance at our pursuer, find mine. His throat jumps like it knows something. "Master?"

With a past like mine, I'm not allowed to enjoy a moment like this. After what I've done, it's wrong to indulge in those arctic blues.

His thumb shifts farther onto my bottom lip.

I should push him away. The last time I was in a position like this, I didn't push away. I should . . .

All at once, Velis releases me and turns his back. "Okay, I

think we lost him. Even if he thinks he saw a human, he'll assume we're involved now."

Gee, how ever could he make an assumption like that? Couldn't just dip into a store or use a little magic to obscure us, VEL?!

Without turning to look at me, Velis takes my wrist and leads me after him alongside one of those glistening canals. The air here is warm, like stepping off an airplane into foreign flora after a cold winter. I need a moment to collect myself in it.

I, Dolly Jones, am heavily invested in an abstinence pledge.

I'm in no position to be acknowledging attraction to another living being, and especially not one I met yesterday. I have my own shit to figure out. Besides, the last time I fell to temptation, I ruined my life. Not to mention, Velis is rude, cocky, blunt. He knows he looks like that. He knows what he's doing.

. . . At what point over the last three minutes did his grip move from my wrist to my hand?

"Master?" He doesn't turn to look at me. "Are you sure you aren't trying to seduce me?"

Seriously?! Where the hell is *that* coming from? He's *clearly* the one who has been . . . H-he's the one holding my hand like we're a couple. He's the one that had his arm around me this morning when I woke up. "The answer is no, and why would you think that? You're the one that just cornered me against a wall," I protest, stark.

"You're the one that crawled into my side of the bed," he says quietly.

"That's—!"

"I know, I know. Wasn't intentional. It's just . . ." He flicks his attention over his shoulder. "I've never noticed one of my masters before."

. . . *Noticed*?

"The shape of your body, the curve of your lips. Things like that. You're my master, so how is it that you're making me notice them as though you were a normal girl?"

Ohhh no. Oh no, no, no, no, no.

"First of all, I'm doing *nothing* to seduce you. I have no interest in *being with* you or anyone. Second of all, you've made several objectifying comments about my body since I removed that ratty sweater yesterday. It's not my responsibility to keep you from 'noticing' me. If you're attracted to me, that's your problem."

"Whoa, whoa, whoa. I didn't say I was *attracted* to you. Appreciating something and being attracted to it are two separate things," he says.

I maintain that he knows exactly what he's doing.

"Look, if anyone is guilty of seduction, Velis, it's you. You're the one that keeps finding reasons to touch my back and waist. You're the one that keeps looking at me with that come-hither stare, flexing your unattainably perfect body at every chance."

"Okay, now who's the one objectifying?" he says, unimpressed.

"The first time I met you, you weren't even wearing a shirt!"

"So?" He shrugs. "I hardly ever wear a shirt. You're the one that made me put one on." In a high-pitched voice, he mocks: "It's not my responsibility to keep you from noticing me. If you're attracted to me, that's your problem."

Oh.

He's right.

I may have been doing to him the exact thing I just accused him of doing to me.

"Th . . . that's . . ."

"Wait." He scans me over as if trying to understand a complex algorithm. "ARE you attracted to me, Master?"

"Tch. NO. I merely 'appreciate' your appearance, if that's what we're calling it."

"Good," he says, dropping my hand. "Then we're on the same page. That's the question I should have started with, I guess. And I'm sorry—I didn't mean to disrespect your body. This honesty oath makes it hard to filter, and things tend to come out wrong."

I have no such similar excuse.

"I also admit I've been testing you a little," he says. "Like with that make-out proposition last night. I thought I sensed desire out of the *desert* that is your soul, and I wanted to make sure it wasn't desire for me. Just so you know—" He hits me with an expression devoid of all life. "I would never fall in love with a human. Not even a cute one."

A cute one.

"In case you've forgotten, I have no desire for anything, let alone you," I say. "Let's find this arrow reader and get on with our lives so that I can live out the last two weeks of my atonement pledge in peace."

"Three," he corrects.

"What?"

"You added a week for the salt place."

Thanks for keeping tabs on me, *Vel*.

Flat-mouthed, his eyes search the shadows of my face. "You aren't disappointed." It isn't a question.

"What?"

"You aren't disappointed that I'm not into humans. I just . . . I thought you might be a little disappointed."

Either he's playing games with me, or he's confused about his own 'desires.' Either way—

"Argh, come on!" I take his wrist this time and pull him, though I have no idea which direction to storm off into, so I pick a random one, rounding a corner to find four tall stone columns crawled over by flowering blue vines marking the edge of a wide square.

"Whoa, this looks like something from ancient Greece," I observe, dropping his wrist to run a hand along stone that feels like the smoothest of nail files. It seems like Aphrodite should be there in the center of it all, lounging naked and eating grapes. Instead, there are just a few swoony couples sharing lunch over blankets.

"Well, they were both founded by djinn," Velis notes.

"Really?!"

"No, of course not, *gullible*. I don't even know what 'ancient Greece' is."

Oh. My. GOD.

"They hold concerts here," he says. "My ex and I used to go to them together. They set up food carts all around there." He motions to the perimeter.

His ex? His *genie ex*? He hasn't mentioned an ex before.

Not my business.

"Do you have a girlfriend now?" my mouth asks despite my own resistance. Fuuuck. I don't need to know this. I don't want to know this. I don't want to get to know him any deeper than I already have.

"Do you think I'd be sharing beds with human women if I did?"

"I should hope not," says I, the cheater.

He, the empath, rolls his eyes. "Stop. We don't need those emotions coming back. This way." He nods in the direction opposite of where I was headed.

It's tough to keep my face tucked under a hood when there's so much to see. From what I can tell, the djinn all share that golden skin and those magical eyes, but their hair varies from deepest blue all the way to nearly white. I'm seeing lots of human-esque clothing through my peeks to the surface, the most popular being saggy pants that are tight at the ankle and dropped at the crotch, crafted of rich textiles and decorated with embellishments like beads or sequins. And Velis was right—many of the men are shirtless.

The women too.

"Lots of titties around these parts," I mutter.

"It's great, right?" Velis's mouth is close to my ear. "Look at that one." He points to a particularly enviable specimen with ivy tattoos creeping up her sides.

Yowza. Even I can't deny a great looking breast.

"Do you have any tattoos, Velis?" I ask.

"Do *you* have any tattoos, Master?"

"I do," I say. "Two of them. Bullseyes." I lift my eyebrows.

"For real?!"

"No, *gullible*. And did you forget I've seen most of your body? You left little to the imagination. I know you don't have any tattoos."

"Oh, showing me your tricksy side now, are you? Don't forget there are a few places you haven't seen, *Master*." He stops and scans the street signs marked in that scrolling Makayen language I saw on his bookshelf. "We're almost there. Keep your eyes on the ground or on me, okay?"

I choose the ground.

"So—" He sounds like he's eyeing me over. "Do you have any tattoos for real?"

"I do. Just one. It's personal."

"Meaning you won't show me?"

"I only show my body to guys I've known more than two days, Velis."

"Well, that makes one of us," he counters.

"Hoe."

He lets his amusement shine a little bit longer before stowing it.

"In here."

We slip into a small storefront marked by a long word within the confines of an arrow.

Books. It smells of books. The same way a library or second-hand bookstore smells of books. The fragrance of dusty, well-loved pages and dried glue cracking inside aged spines penetrates the stuffy air. There's comfort in a smell like that.

An old-fashioned entry bell signals our arrival like a nosy little bitch.

The place is cramped. The shelves are packed with paperbacks struggling to fit, and for the ones too fat to make it—those are piled atop the shelves, wedged all the way up to the ceiling. And where that space runs out, the corners form suitable refuge for the remaining stragglers, most of which have pieces of loose-leaf paper shoved here and there.

What a mess. But the best kind of mess, maybe.

"Mayree?" Velis calls down the stacks, peering into the darkness beyond. "You've got a customer here." He speculates, "She's probably out back smoking." And then to the back of the store: "MAYREE?"

"Oh, it's the rich boy." From out of nowhere, the head of an old woman with buggy, almost cartoonish eyes pokes out of a tear in the ceiling. "Surprised you're back," she says with the voice of someone who's either smoked or shouted every day since the day she was born. "Last time you were here, it didn't end so well for you, did it."

Teeth tight, Velis throws me a look.

"Is that a girl with you?" the woman continues, voice weathered enough to squeak, wrinkles deep enough to drive through. "Did you lie to this one too? We all know how well that worked out for you before."

Not all of us, though it does sound like an *intriguing* story.

"Tch!" Frown worsening, Velis grabs the tip of my hood and tosses it backward to reveal my face. "Not a girl. A human."

"Cold. Humans have multiple genders too, you dingbat. But wow. You really did a full one-eighty with this one, huh?"

"We aren't here for that kind of reading, Mayree. She's my master. I need to figure out why I can't tether her."

The woman sizes me up with a spidery stare that would make locusts run. "You don't think that's because of what you are, kiddo?"

"No," he says, dull. "That's . . . never been a problem before."

His less-than-full-blooded lineage, I assume.

"All right, all right. Come on up. Paying with daddy's account again? You know that'll impact the price."

But before he can answer, Mayree's head withdraws into its hole like a prairie dog at the zoo. Velis prods me forward, muttering, "This should be fun."

"So, what's the story?" I pry as he leads me to the back of the store, where a peeling swinging door gives way to a tight staircase. "Something to do with that ex you mentioned?"

"It's not anything you need to know." He sighs, correcting, "It *is* something you need to know—*no* it's not! What the fuck? Why would she need to know that?" He's at odds with his honesty oath. "Argh, come on, I don't like being here, and Jeb and Arrik are far released from that wish you trapped them in by now." He glances behind us before starting up the staircase, the end of which is marked by a dangling curtain of beads. Very boho. Like his bottle.

The upstairs room is lit by stringed lights and accented with cracks of sunny glow coming through paper-covered windows. The air is murky with incense and potpourri, like the store in the strip mall that sells 'other' types of tobacco in the back. Dingy carpet cushions a low table at the center of a messy den, the tabletop already prepped with two clay cups of verdant liquid popping bubbles into the air that smell like something freshly mowed.

Suspicious.

"This isn't like the fairy realm where I'm stuck here forever if I eat something, is it?" I ask as we settle into the moppy carpet.

Mayree, who turns out to be a short, crinkly woman with gaudy bangles up both stick-thin arms, sets her sights sharply on Velis. "She knows about the fairy realm?"

"I think that was sarcasm based on human lore. Most of what she says is sarcasm. Look, we're in a time crunch, Mayree, so we've got to make this quick. My vessel is a family heirloom—" Velis reaches into his pocket to retrieve a tiny version of the orphic vase and sets it on the table.

"You shrunk it?" I gasp, bending down to inspect the relic, which is now no larger than a quarter, and give it a poke with my fingertip.

It's so . . . cute.

Velis ignores me. "This vessel has never steered me wrong before, so why would it suddenly bring me a human I can't siphon? Her desires are totally different from my normal masters too." He pauses to eye me over. "And there are . . . other things."

Other things.

Like how I'm always trying to *seduce* his innocent sensibilities.

A set of invasive eyes probes us from the other side of the table. "Geez louise, do you just go around creating your own drama, rich boy? I thought last time was a doozy." Necklaces dangling, the wrinkled woman nudges me a cup that looks like it was crafted in a beginner's pottery class, still spouting up bits of what is probably poisonous gas into the air. "Drink your tea, girlie. So that we can help this self-absorbed wish granter figure out how to leech off your darling little soul."

"Hey!" Velis cries.

Well, she isn't wrong.

Mayree runs a many-ringed hand through her blue-white hair. "Just want to make sure she knows what she's getting into before we begin."

"Tch! I can't lie to my master. Dolly knows why we're here."

"Oh-ho? First name basis? Naughty, naughty."

Velis flattens his eyes at me to show his annoyance before snatching up his cup and frowning at the festering liquid found therein. "To warn you," he says, "it tastes like shit, but it'll help open our auras so she can do the reading. Pretend it's scotch?"

I take an open sniff. Hints of lawn. And puke. "Scotch wouldn't make it easier."

"We'll work on that."

And he's right, it tastes like actual shit. Greeny, grassy shit.

The things I do for a person I don't care about at all.

I could feel how badly you wanted one of these . . . It's on the house . . .

NO.

I hurry to glug down the rest of the tea before Velis can get a read on my leaking thoughts. Hard to say whether or not he sensed anything; his eyes remain locked on mine through every last chug of his throat, and when he's done, he slams his cup onto a table marked by the rings of other hot cups that have overstayed their welcome. His face disfigures as his tastebuds catch up. "Oh, that is so fucking nasty, every time."

Through all this, Mayree has been watching us like we're a performing art piece.

"I know you said you don't want one of *those* kinds of readings, kiddo, but I think I'd better do both."

"What?" Velis swivels. "Why?"

"You tell me." She simpers, elbows rested on the table and

ancient hands supporting her ancient chin. "What did you mean by 'other things'?"

"Ugh. Fine! Do an arrow reading and a . . . the other kind of reading."

"Excellent." Two wrinkled hands clap together with the energy of someone much younger. "Price just doubled."

"So that's what you're after," Velis says, crusty.

If ever a grandmother could look sinister.

"You remember what you have to do?"

"*Yes, I remember*," Velis says through his teeth. And after, he sighs, flipping eyes to me, but doesn't initiate whatever Mayree expects him to do. "M-Master?"

What's with that stutter?!

Hesitation lingers in the air as particles glide listlessly through a single beam of light hitting the table. A mischievous grandmother waits expectantly, wheezing soft and low.

"Master?" This time, he says my title the same way he did earlier when he faked the kiss.

Only this time, he isn't faking it.

While I become just another inanimate part of the environment, Velis takes my face and leans in. His fingers secure my nape to keep my head from rolling off my neck as that mouth, which has been mocking me ever since I met it, pushes gently against my forehead.

Whatever the 'other' kind of reading is, it involves kissing me?

"Sorry," he apologizes as his fingers slide away, the spiced aroma of the room so thick it's making me dizzy. Then, he turns to Mayree as if he's just filled up a bucket with water or any other menial task. "Was that enough?"

"More than enough. Your turn, girlie. Like he did."

I should probably question what's happening, right? I should be offended that he kissed me without my consent. I should be bothered by these flashes of tenderness where I swear it's almost like he's *into* me. You know, the human he sees as nothing more than a means to an end? The human standing in the way of his lands and title?

I rise up on my knees because he's taller than me and slip my cool hand to the warm side of his neck, and the moment I set my lips to his forehead is the moment I realize:

I'm screwed.

I've sensed it, been pushing it away.

But when I give him my mouth and feel his hands clench my waist in return, my racing adrenaline betrays what I've been denying.

I have a crush on the genie.

And that definitely goes against everything I've worked for. How many weeks will I have to add for allowing myself a crush? And why does it have to be someone like him? I'm worth more than crushing on a hypocritical, self-interested smart-ass.

Maybe it was the way he looked at those stars. Or maybe it was . . .

If you were too intoxicated to remember it, then you sure as hell weren't sober enough to be responsible for it.

Am I really that broken that a morsel of validation is all it takes to set hooks in my chest?

His hands spasm against my waist like he wants to grip me tighter.

Because he likes me too.

I knew it. I've known it. Even if he won't admit it to himself.

Damn, Dolly! Why would you cover up a body like that?!

Just come here, would you? I know you desire an embrace.

I've never noticed one of my masters before.

Velis has a crush on me. He definitely does. And I think he's been fighting his crush even harder than I've been fighting mine.

We met yesterday.

We met yesterday, and these feelings are not normal.

"You two done?" says Mayree's shit-eating grin.

I release my genie, fold myself back into my patch of carpet, and peer into the traces of leaf juice in my cup.

"Good job. You both gave plenty. And would you look at that —" Mayree spreads her hand before us like she's following a horizon we can't see, her eyes ignited with opaline magic that differs from Velis's. "Quite the messy little knot between your lines. Going back all the way to the first time you met."

"You mean yesterday?" Velis scoffs.

"No, I mean *before.* Before she was your master." Mayree lets her hand fall, and the light of her eyes drops with it.

Before I was his master, he was a vase.

"Just as sure as spit is wet, you've met before. And I think it would help you both greatly to recall when that was." The crow's feet at the corner of her eyes deepen with fox-like guile.

"What the hell, Mayree! You're getting our strings crossed with someone else! Dolly and I met yesterday. My first time to the human world was four months ago, and I've had continuous masters ever since!"

Mayree shrugs and her bangles jingle in response. "Don't you have a habit of erasing the minds of humans when you're done with them? Maybe this time you erased your own too."

I don't see it, but I feel it. The dart of his focus hitting my neck.

"Erasing our minds?" I say slowly.

"That's what wish granters do. After they're done with their masters, they erase their memories. Best way to keep the human world from going bonkers. Your kind doesn't do well with foreign magic." Under her breath, Mayree adds, "Though they all just accept electricity or whatever it's called like it's something manmade."

It's my turn to throw my gaze like a dagger. "Seriously, Velis? You plan on erasing my memory when you're through with me? You were just gonna waltz into my life, steal my one and only *soul*, and then wipe my memory?!"

"*That's not something we generally tell our masters.*" And then to Mayree: "Thanks, blabbermouth."

By her energy, not only is she fully aware of the mayhem she's caused, she delights in it. With a flutter of her robes, she hobbles around the table to a nearby bureau. "Arrow time, kids."

From the bureau, grandma devious retrieves a small wooden box that looks like it may have once stored the heart of Snow

White. Stained dark and carved with that same scrolling language, a twist of the latch reveals two iron arrows the length of pencils propped up by a velvet cushion.

"Place it." Mayree offers one of the metal pieces to Velis, but when she drops the arrow into his hand, he yelps in surprise, letting it hit the wood with an angry *thunk!*

"That thing's heavy!"

Yet feeble Mayree was able to handle it with ease.

Suspicious, Velis pokes at the arrow, which has cemented itself so that it's pointing at a long-dead plant in the corner, and no amount of his prodding can get it to budge.

"Your arrow's alignment," says Mayree. "Now, what we would expect of a compatible master-djinn pairing would be for hers to fall parallel to yours, yes?" Even anticipating the weight of the second arrow as she sets it in my palm—

"Umph!"

Velis wasn't kidding. It's like a bowling ball. I use both hands to slip it onto the edge of the table, fingers prepped to push it like the planchette of a Ouija board.

"That won't be necessary, girlie. Go ahead and let go."

She's right. The second I lift my fingers, the arrow rips across the table, pivoting until—

"Oh, *interesting*." Mayree's eyes gleam like ancient pools in the center of a cursed forest, prompting Velis to scramble over the table for a better look. "You were right, kiddo. Your arrows aren't aligned. In fact, they're the furthest two arrows can be from aligned."

Where it should be pointing at the plant in the corner, the tip of my arrow has spun to meet his.

"This human's arrow is pointing directly at yours. To the decimal, I might add."

Velis pushes from the edge. "Why would my vessel pick a master like that?! That's the opposite of what it should do!"

"I wonder." Mayree taps her chin as if humoring a child. "Could be it's broken. Or *could be* it's merely operating under a different set of rules. Too bad there isn't someone around here you could ask . . ."

"*Seriously, Mayree?*"

She shrugs. "My specialty is arrows, not vessels. I'm afraid that's all I got." She begins collecting the heavy pieces of iron from the table like they're nothing before slipping her treasure box back into the shadows. "And in the nick of time too. It seems your brothers are about to arrive."

"What?!" Velis hops to his feet. "Already? How did they—"

Mayree taps her nose. "I'll invoice you."

It's difficult to tell whether Velis is more frustrated that we've solved nothing by coming here or that we'll now have to waste magic to teleport our way out.

"Argh! Come on, Master. Let's go."

"One more thing—" Before he can blink us away, Mayree holds up a hand, tutting around the table to set a wizened palm to my chest: "Whatever you did that's causing you such strife, dear, shame is the least of what you should be feeling. We should never be judged by the worst of what we've done, least of all by ourselves."

I feel Velis's hand squeeze my shoulder just as the downstairs bell gives a snitching ring.

CHAPTER 7

Discotheque

In the center of a rolling field, Velis crouches to the ground and rubs his face, groaning, "What am I supposed to friggen' do with all that?"

Unsure how to answer, I gaze into a distance uninhabited by man- or genie-made structure. I can't even tell which realm we're in anymore. The greenery spread over the hills looks like expensive carpet, like something soft to roll down. And the air is crisp and light and free. Maybe this is that place—the one without a name, where I'd end up if I ever just ran on and on and on.

Why am I going along with all this? Probably the same reason I broke my last vase.

Boredom.

At least, that might have been how it started. But I can feel it, like the pull of a magnet or invisible fishing line. I'm becoming *invested.*

"What was that, Velis?" The cloudless sky draws my eye. "That first test we did?"

"A mating test," Velis says into his hands. "It's something people do when they want to get engaged."

Yeah, I figured it might be something like that.

"And you did it with your ex?" I hazard. "And it . . . didn't go well?"

The look he gives me is dirty. "Yeah, yeah, laugh it up. Joke's on me for thinking I could take a full-blooded girl like—" He stops. "What?"

"*Laugh* it up?" I scoff. "Wow, you really think highly of me, don't you? Yes, I, the brokenhearted cheater, just *love* reveling in the failed relationships of others. Screw you."

Still in a crouch, Velis catches my wrist. "I'm sorry. You're right. You aren't that kind of person." He releases me listlessly to return to his wallowing. "Just so you know, it isn't true, what she said. I've never met you before, and I didn't erase your memory." To himself, he muses: "Maybe in a past life?"

"But you do *intend* to erase my memory," I say quietly.

The breeze kicks up, making the grass around us whisper.

"I mean, I'm supposed to," he says, equally quiet. "That's how we're trained."

"So . . . you could just look at me one minute knowing I'll forget all about you the next?"

Why am I asking this? Even if I acknowledge this stupid crush —even if I suspect he's harboring one too—what good could possibly come of getting him to realize it? We met yesterday. He is a genie. Erasing my memory makes sense.

He doesn't answer me. Probably for the best.

"Where are we, Velis?"

He dismisses the topic with a lazy wave of his hand. "I don't know. In the outlands somewhere."

"The djinn realm still?"

"Mm." He's pouting.

"So, that's it? You're giving up? I mean, if you're already in the lead, you could just camp out in your vessel until the end of your contest, right? How much time is left?"

"Two weeks," he says, flicking his eyes in my direction. "The irony's not lost on me."

Because two weeks is when I would originally have been free to make selfish wishes.

"And no," he says. "I'm not giving up. I want your soul even more now. The payoff's gotta be good for how much work this is. Mayree seemed to be hinting that there's someone around that can help me figure out why my vessel chose you. I think I know who that person is. But . . ." He studies my dark eyes and hair. "You won't be able to get in looking like that. You're going to have to go in my vessel and wait it out."

"Wait it out? For how long?"

"Until this is resolved. I'd say we've spent enough time together for one lifetime, wouldn't you?"

Cold.

If he feels that way, then why was he holding my waist so sensually just moments ago?

You have the perfect body for snuggling. Plus, you smell nice.

Or is he using his loopholes again? Omission. Phrasing. Posing questions as absolutes.

I fold my arms. "If you stuff me in that bottle, it's going to have to be in pieces."

He stares me down, combatting the severity of my brow, until he cracks. "My god, you're something else, Dolly. Authority issues much?"

"Ha! Authority? You're hardly authority, Velis."

His mouth has slipped into something of a schemer's grin, and I can feel my own returning it.

"There is one alternative to going back inside the vessel," he says. "But if we do it, you have to obey me the whole time. Think you can handle that?"

The answer comes quickly: "No."

"Well, try. And another thing—if we do this, it's going to involve seeing me with my shirt off, so try to contain your lust. Now, here's what I need you to wish for . . ."

I stare into a pair of icy eyes that stare back without daring to flinch. The woman before me has short, shaggy hair stained the blue of darkest midnight and skin that looks kissed by a vacation sun. She wears a high-neckline dress shorter than any I would wear in the human world, fitted at the waist and flared at the hip and blue to match her shiny hair.

The only thing we have in common is that winged eyeliner.

Velis stands beside her, chin in his hand. "Yeah. You'll definitely blend in now, Master. I wouldn't know you were human by looking at you."

My reflection is the most gussied up it's been in over a year.

Velis's reflection, meanwhile . . .

His body looks like a god's, uncovered down to the waist, where rests a pair of baggy drop-crotch pants, tight only at the hip and ankles. Damn, that boy is cut. But how? So far, I've only seen him eat burgers and do little to no physical work.

He tucks his hand around my shoulder and appraises us in the mirror. "I think we'd pass for a proper djinn couple, don't you?"

The woman in the mirror is pretty, desirable, confident. Velis's fingertips graze her bare shoulder like he's plucking a petal from a rose.

"You look nice, Master. Too bad we had to mess with your eyes. They look better dark." Taking a final drink of me, he drums his fingers in the space between my shoulders before slipping his hand away.

We stand at the edge of a piazza with a mirrored wall as, overhead, a blue moon hangs low in the sky. The once majestic white skyline of the djinn city is no more. Gone is the sparkling quality that blinded in the afternoon sun. Now, it's all gone soft, drenched in dreamy glow from a host of magically lit lampposts. This can't be real. It must be watercolor. It's impossible that the night air I'm recycling, so misty and cool, is the same air listing through all that flowered ivy dripping over the sleeping stones.

"I think we're even now, Velis."

"Mm?"

"I showed you a beautiful place. This place is just as beautiful."

His eyes, formerly on me, drift to follow my line of sight to the mountainous backdrop of stacked buildings lost to fuzzy hues. "You're right," he says. "I guess I haven't stopped to look at it in a while. I haven't been back to this city since . . ." But the rest fails him.

It has to do with his ex. And a lie he told her.

He flexes his jaw. "Thanks for not wishing it out of me, Master."

It seems unnatural to do so now.

"This way." He motions with his head.

'Romantic' is a suitable word for walking through a fantasy world at this hour of night. To a mortal, it's like a filter has been placed over the city streets. Maybe something called 'fantasy glow.'

And like a knife through a perfect floral cake, the ambiance is interrupted by a place we hear long before we ever see, as the distant thump of party music blares into the night, promising excitement to those bold enough to venture down the next alley. To be honest, it isn't all that different from club music in the human realm. A strong base beat, slightly faster than a human heartbeat, designed to elevate and entice, repetition to make you feel at ease.

"The air tastes fruity," I note as we draw closer.

"Oh, yeah. That's one thing I haven't seen in your world yet. Lots of places here appetize the air. It's like fragrancing but for your mouth." He points at his own mouth and chomps his teeth twice.

He did something similar yesterday.

He's smiling at me unintentionally because I'm unintentionally smiling at him. "What?" he asks.

"I know what eating is. You don't have to pantomime it every time."

"Are you one of those people that hates the sound of chewing?" He clatters his teeth two more times at me, dimples pecked.

"Like I would admit my weaknesses to you."

He pretends to count his fingers. "Booths, runny ranch, beds with bugs in them, my rockin' bod . . ."

"The next time you refer to your own body as rockin', I'll wish your teeth away. Then you'll have nothing to do but gum at me."

"Nice try, but I'm pretty sure that counts as causing me harm. You know, when I met you, I thought you were a masochist, Dolly Jones. Turns out you may be a sadist. So far, you've threatened my teeth, my hair, my *dick* . . ."

"Meh. All things you could technically live without."

"Geezus." Yet, he's still grinning over my callousness. I flash him all the mischief hidden in my teeth, expecting him to build off it, but he doesn't. The drop of his expression is deadening.

"Velis?"

He studies me. "I always flirt with my masters. It helps them feel at ease. They flirt back too. But you . . ."

The sounds of distant excitement reach us. The blue moon shimmers above. The air tells me he's about to say something heavy. I feel it flitting at me, heralding.

The air lies.

"You're mean," he finishes.

I'm hit by the weight of an anvil, and then—

"I like it."

By the look on his face, he doesn't *like* that he likes it, though. "Let's get going, Master."

Ouch.

But why am I disappointed? *I* should be the one putting an end to needless flirting. *I* am the one with no business being attracted to someone. What am I hoping to get out of any of this? Nothing. Not a damn thing. If he proposed we make out again, I would turn him down, *again*. If he held my hand—

He is holding my hand, pulling me through a door that is the apex of the booming music that's been leading us here.

That music intensifies on the other side as we're welcomed by strobing lights and blinking smoke.

"Get ready to see more titties," he whispers in my ear, nodding to the doorman and setting his hand on the small of my back to coax me down a long hallway, which births us into the center of a nightclub that seems to be the wellspring of all the lust contained in the universe.

I've been to plenty of human nightclubs. My friends had some favorites in the city. But never have I been to a nightclub like this.

The dance floor gushes with the pulse of sweaty, half-clothed people dancing in ways that would make a conservative blush as beams of light cut through a swathe of smoke flavored like berry and citrus, while bubble-like orbs of varying size bounce in the air over their heads on beat with the music.

I grip Velis's arm. "Are those two people banging?!"

"Hm?" He looks beyond me to the dance floor, where a couple is going at it with *particular fervor*. He displays humor. "No. But they're close. They've got rooms in the back for things like that."

"*This is a sex club*?"

"No difference here, doll."

Doll. Ugh. He's back to that?

He ventures us away from the R-rated dance floor and to a dim table around the corner of the bar. "The guy I need to speak with is one of the owners. He's upstairs, but I have to get invited up. I'm gonna let the bartenders know I'm here. Do you want anything? My treat."

I'm fairly certain it has to be his treat. I don't have whatever tender this establishment accepts.

I mean, aside from my *soul*.

"I can't," I tell him, desperately wanting something fruity and liquored. "My pledge."

I haven't had a drop to drink in over fifty weeks.

Not since . . .

To be honest, I don't even remember drinking that night. I don't remember the first drop, and I certainly don't remember the last, but as has been proven, I'm definitely not the kind of person who should be drinking in a setting like this.

"I've been meaning to ask, did you have problems with alcohol before that night?"

He sounds genuine.

"Not really. Like I said, I get a little frisky, but that's after, like, *lots* of shots. I haven't overindulged like that since early college. Really, James was the drinker. I usually stop after a beer or two. I'm not sure why last time I . . ."

"*Overindulged*," he repeats, shivering.

"It's . . . really creepy when you do that."

"Sorry." He rubs the back of his head, sheepish. "I can't help it. It's my vessel's bond with you. It's like a sensor going off, saying 'strike now.' It's gonna keep happening until you're no longer my master."

Well, now I know, at least.

"And, okay." He patters his hands on the edge of the table. "I just wanted to make sure I wasn't enabling an alcoholic or anything like that." He straightens and taps his head. "I know what you want."

He turns on heel before I can protest, approaching the bar and leaning over it with his dropped-waist pants that leave so very little to the imagination.

Why, oh why, couldn't I have gotten an ugly genie?

When he returns, he's got a scotch in one hand, and in the other, a tall, thin vial of a mysterious indigo substance with a long bendy straw and several berries I've never seen before skewered on a toothpick. He slides onto the stool next to mine. "Okay, I let them know I'm here." As he skates the tall vial into place before me, he does so with a caveat: "I'm not going to pressure you into drinking this, but if you want it—and I know you do—you'll have no judgment from me. In my opinion, that pledge of yours needn't apply to realms beyond your own. I mean, when else are you going to get to try a djinn classic?"

He watches me contemplate the decision before me.

I do want it. There's no use denying it to a being inclined to read my desires. And it's true I'm curious. And that this will surely be my one and only time in a genie nightclub.

"You're a good person, Master. You deserve a break."

"I'll . . . think about it. Thank you."

"By the way," he says, scratching his jaw, "I know you said you weren't going to show me, but I think I saw a little bit of it from the bar when you were resituating yourself. Your tattoo, I mean. Is it on your thigh?"

Great. Good to know I basically just flashed the whole bar without meaning to.

"Yes, it's on my thigh. And I really don't care all that much about showing you. I was just trying to hold it over you for being an ass. Also, it's kind of a weird spot for what it is. I just wanted it to be somewhere I could cover easily. So don't make fun of me, okay?"

Intrigue lifts his eyebrow. "Do you think I'm the type that would make fun of you for something like that?"

That's exactly the type he is.

I peek behind us to ensure no one is watching, which is stupidly pointless, as the rest of the place is also scantily clad and no one would bat an eye over an uncovered thigh.

"Here—" I set my foot onto the rung in his stool and shift my hip toward him, inching the fabric of my skirt upward to reveal a block of text.

Without shame, he takes my knee to pull my leg closer, edging the rest of the fabric out of the way so that he can read it.

"I know your alphabet, but I'm not familiar with this script," he says.

"It's in cursive," I explain, fighting to ignore the feeling of his hands on my leg, "and my grandfather had terrible writing."

"Your grandfather?" He covers my thigh before releasing my leg.

"Yeah, he was kinda my biggest supporter for most of my life. It's actually his handwriting, taken from a note he wrote me before he died. It says: 'There isn't enough love in the world.' It's what he used to say instead of 'I love you.' Pretty sappy, right? And I realize it's in a pretty scandalous location for something so sentimental."

Velis blinks at me, processing, and then—"I was really close with my grandfather too!" he bursts. "The djinn one on my mom's side. He's the one that went and screwed a nymph and fucked up my bloodline, but he was a good guy otherwise. My vessel was originally his. He left it for me when he passed away, and it's a super valuable one too. Even with my nymph blood, it's never failed me. Until now, I guess."

Well, that's quite the surge of personal information he doesn't usually share. Afterward, he looks embarrassed for it.

"You must have been his favorite for him to have left it to you," I offer.

"Yeah, the other full-blooded grandkids were *pissed*. Anyway, I don't think your tattoo is sappy at all," he says. "I think it's a cool tribute."

"Th-thanks. James thought it was weird. Weirdly sexual or something. I've been a little self-conscious about it ever since he made me show it off at a party."

"Really? Well, that's . . . false. And also, why would you make your girlfriend do that? It's not weird, Dolly. Don't let anyone tell you it is." I think his eyes stay on mine longer than he means them to. When he realizes it, he averts them to the sweaty, lusty entertainment found on the dance floor behind me. "Whoa, look at that one!" He gives my seat a spin. "See him? In the green?"

He's talking about a djinn with spiky hair lying flat in the middle of the room like a starfish, gazing up at the bubbles bouncing in the air above him.

"That dude's living his best life." Velis takes a swig of amber from his glass.

"Oh my god, he looks totally messed up."

"Yeah. If anyone offers you candy, don't take it," he says. He whips out his fingers to count again. "If they offer you something to smoke, you're fine. If they offer you something to drink, you're also fine. We don't have 'roofies,' or whatever you call them, here. That dude? *Definitely* sampled some illicit candy. You don't want any of that stuff."

Noted.

"Of course, if *I* offer you candy, you should take it. You should take whatever *I* offer you," he purrs.

Um, yeah, hard to trust that advice when it comes with such

dark, swimming undertones. "Sketchy genie," I utter. "Er, djinn. Sorry. Why is that so hard to break?"

"Oh yeah, about that . . ." He looks to be deciding something. "Confession: I don't actually care if you use the word genie. I was just messing with you before. It's not offensive to my generation at all. Just don't use it around old people. They're all out of sorts because of some human children's film that mis-portrayed djinn. Apparently, the genie in it sang. And was blue? I don't know. It doesn't bother me."

I know the exact 'film' he's talking about, and it makes me snort.

"Oh my god, you are *nothing* like the genie in that movie."

"Oh yeah?" he jeers, leaning closer. "How am I different?"

That six pack is a rather obvious difference, but I'm not about to feed his ego.

"How am I different, Master?" he asks, softer.

The music in here may be thudding faster than a resting heartbeat, but mine is pretty on par.

For all the strength I thought I'd built, I feel weak.

The air is thick with heat and desire. My dress holds my body tighter than any hands have held me in a long time.

I'm having . . . fun.

Breaking out of the prison I built for myself, being around lights and sounds and people. Being on the arm of someone sexy and complicated, with danger in tow.

I have no right to feel this way.

"Dolly . . ." His pale eyes probe me. "You know, I've never felt someone work so hard for something. This whole time, you've been clenching so tight, resisting your every desire. It's admirable, but . . ." Velis seems about to unleash something. "I can't wait to see your face the moment you release all that tension. It's going to be the most satisfying wish I've ever granted."

Fuuuck.

There's no hiding the desire I feel in this moment, practically bubbling out of me, though I fight against it like it's a door I can force closed. Velis is too close, peering at me like he's trying to see inside my soul, while my fingers bore into the edges of my stool enough to shake.

"Velissimo!"

We've been too engrossed in one another to notice that a topless woman with tattoos covering her shoulders and a golden chain around her middle is standing at the edge of our table.

"R-Rayana!" It's rare of Velis to stutter that hard.

"Get up," she says, hand to hip. "I'm here to escort you to your uncle."

"Wait, your *uncle*?"

"Great-uncle," Velis corrects.

"I didn't know you brought a guest," Rayana says. "Guests aren't allowed upstairs. Friend or girlfriend?"

Velis doesn't answer right away.

"Friend," Rayana determines. "Or it wouldn't be taking so long. Good, you're never as fun when you're cuffed. And you know I'm expecting payment for my services, right? It's been too long since *you* were out *there*." She loops her finger through the waist of his pants in an effort to leash him.

"Wait! Mast—" Velis stops himself. "Dolly, stay right here, okay? Don't move from this spot. I'll be back in ten minutes." He downs the rest of his scotch before letting Rayana pull him away, making efforts to glance back at me every few steps until they're out of sight.

Rayana's leading him in the direction of the dance floor, but my table doesn't allow for the best view. I scoop up the drink Velis bought for me and head for an open seat at the bar. What I see makes me take a lengthy sip of a drink that does indeed taste both fruity and liquored.

I'm a Muppet.

A short, squishy Muppet.

I feel every ounce of that truth when I see the way Velis is dancing with Rayana.

He's behind her, his hands crawling up her flat stomach and down her thighs to pull her closer. And, damn, if she doesn't know how to isolate her hips like a backup dancer from the early 2000s. I can practically taste the salt dripping off them.

The music is sickeningly intrusive, their movement together nauseatingly obtrusive, and I know. I know, I know, I know, I have absolutely zero right to feel jealous.

For all the reasons I've already thought through, I have no reason to feel slighted that he's grinding on another woman in my presence.

That doesn't mean I have to like it.

I'm just taking my second, even longer pull of boozy heaven when Velis stops dead, for he's noticed me sitting at the center of the bar in a cone of fuchsia light.

What the pair of them are doing is actually mild compared to some of the people around them. But Velis's expression is one of guilt. And then it isn't. And then it is. As if he's wrestling with how he should feel about this situation as much as I am.

Rayana doesn't allow time for contemplation. She takes his hand and sets it to her breast.

It's with eyes firmly on me that Velis begins to move once more, feeling her up while setting his mouth to her shoulder.

For an empath magically connected to my emotions, he can surely feel the annoyance I try to hide. The unwarranted jealousy and unwelcome hurt.

I suck the rest of the drink through the straw as the music ends, and Rayana draws him away through the horde and to some door obscured by sweat and smoke.

I need a moment.

"Bathroom?" I ask the muscled bartender.

"Bath?" he says.

"Er, toilet? Toilet room?"

"Back there." He motions to a small hallway on the other side of the bar.

"Thanks." I leave my empty glass on the counter before taking my leave of it all.

Djinn realm bathrooms seem to be no different from human

ones. I stand at the sink a moment, splashing water on my transformed face.

There's no reason to feel this way. He's hot. I've met plenty of hot people in my life. I'm lonely. I've been lonely for months. Now isn't the time to start becoming irrational about it all.

This human's arrow is pointing directly at yours.

Just as sure as spit is wet, you've met before.

And I think it would help you both greatly to recall when that was.

Could there really be more to all this? Some explanation for why I'm so drawn to someone I have nothing in common with?

Or is that just me trying to make excuses for how absurd I'm being?

Semi-collected, I nod to the disguised Muppet in the mirror before venturing out into the muggy club. But the moment I exit, a tattooed arm hooks around my waist.

"Hello, Dolly Jones."

CHAPTER 8

Tattoos and Smoke

I RECOGNIZE THIS ARM, but the last time I saw it, it was capped at the sleeve. This time, there's a whole tattooed body to accompany it.

A body rivaling that of Velis.

My captor is decorated from waist to neck with inky outlines of flowers and weapons and women caught up in smoke. Similar smoke trails from the corner of his mouth, from which dangles a lazy roll of paper resembling a joint but with a much more florid scent than any joint I've ever smelled. He wears only those same baggy pants that seem to be the style here for dudes in their twenties, low on his hips to boast more tattoos hiding beyond.

"You're . . . Arrik?" Velis's older brother.

"You remembered my name? I'm flattered, love."

My danger sensors activate.

"Arrik, I wish you would—"

I'm cut off by the taste of his tattooed finger smooshed against my lips.

"Shh, no need for that, love." His raspy voice is a calm contrast to the muted throb of the club down the hall. "I'm not here to human-nap you."

"You . . . aren't?" I ask as his finger slips away.

He shakes his head and pulls in a deep drag of his joint. "Not if you behave." He exhales a slew of smoke over my head.

Ugh. He's got such a disgustingly cool demeanor, with his chin propped high and his eyes casting silent judgment. He has nothing to prove to me. He has nothing to prove to anyone. He gets whatever he wants without trying.

"I've been watching you since you got here, Dolly Jones. I saw the way you were looking at my little brother."

I fold my arms to protect myself from his implications. "What do you mean *looking*?"

Embers light the ground beside our feet as he gives the joint's ash a flick with his thumb. "Vel might not be able to sense it, being what he is, but I'm full djinn, so to me, it's insipidly obvious that the thing you desire most in this entire establishment is Velis himself."

My folded arms tuck in closer. "You know nothing about me, and you sure as hell don't know what I desire."

A sneer of complacency graces his high-boned face for the smallest of moments. "Thought so." He releases another jet of smoke that spreads and hovers in the air around us. "Which means that, even if we separate you from him, you won't make a wish to transfer his balance over to us, right?"

No. Crush aside, I wouldn't wish Velis's hard-earned soul power over to his brothers based on principle alone.

"Now, my brother Jeb's all in a fuss about how you kept us from siphoning you, but I assume it has something to do with your feelings for Vel." He stamps out a particularly obstinate cinder with the ball of his shoe. "So my thinking is, we just need to get you to break those feelings first."

Wrong. Velis couldn't siphon from me even the first time he tried, and that was well before I developed any sort of . . . Before this CRUSH invaded my life.

"Jeb's plan of attack was to just rush in and grab you, but I prefer to watch things . . . implode. So I've got a new game for us to play, Dolly Jones. And all it takes is a little bit of information. You ready?"

Ready or not, I'm caught in his shadow as his hand suddenly comes flush with the poster-clad wall over my shoulder.

"Vel's lucky he can present as a djinn. Our father's genes are feature-strong, but the truth of the matter is that no one will ever take him seriously with that much nymph blood running through his veins. But his kids? Well, they're a different story. Because anything less than a quarter is considered negligible in our world."

Meaning—

"Mating with a full-blooded djinn is the only way to dilute Vel's bloodline enough to earn his children a spot back into our family's legacy. If he doesn't want them to go through what he's gone through, he needs to marry a pureblood."

I would never fall in love with a human. Not even a cute one.

It happens. Rarely. Selfish, though. Their kids would be fucked.

"Little bastard's gotten close too. His last girlfriend was full-blooded, and shit, if he wasn't crazy for her. Shame she broke it off the minute she found out what he was. But really, who can blame her?"

I'm sorry I'm not a full fucking genie or whatever you females prefer.

Did you lie to this one too? We all know how well that worked out for you before.

"So, there you have it." Arrik thumbs at his joint with that same fuck-all expression. "Even if you look at him that way, and even if he does it back, he'd never let himself fall for you. And I suspect that the moment you believe it is the moment you'll realize you need to rid yourself of him. Be sure to wish for me specifically when that moment comes, love." He lowers his face and voice. "Unlike Velis, I enjoy the company of humans, and I *always* take care of my masters. With a purebred on your arm, you wouldn't even have to wear that tacky disguise. Such a shame to cover such pretty eyes."

I slide around him.

"You've got it wrong, Arrik. I'm not interested in a relationship with anyone, least of all my freaking *genie*. I'm only going along with him so that we can figure out how to break the bond between us. And you? I can't see how I would have any use for someone like you."

If a sixth sense exists, mine is picking up on the energy currently raging beneath his unwavering muscle and stiff, sharp eyes. He snatches my chin, forcing me into his aquamarine stare.

"Unlike my brothers, I have lots of experience with humans, Dolly Jones. Enough to know when they're lying. Enough to know when their *blood* is beginning to *rush*." He shifts his hand to feel the speed of the racing pulse in my throat. "Imagine being with a djinn who knows what you really desire."

My glare should be answer enough on its own.

"Fine. Then maybe you should try telling Vel how you feel." He brings the waning blunt to his full lips. "This should help lower your inhibitions." He takes a hearty drag, then exhales directly into my face. "I'll be waiting in the wreckage."

Smoke burns into my lungs, fragrant like roses and just as thorny. I cough and fan it away, and by the time it clears, Arrik is gone, the lingering haze the only proof he was here.

Seedy-ass genie! Sauntering in here and pinning me against a wall with his stupid, effing perfect body! Staring down at me with those condescending eyes! And what's with blowing smoke directly into someone else's—

Uh-oh.

Oh-ho-ho-no.

I feel it hit, and whatever it is, it isn't a substance that exists in the human realm. Fuck. Getting high definitely, *definitely* goes against my pledge.

The flush of swelled blood pushes through my body. Not just the cheeks and neck but all of me, as a film of rosiest pink begins encroaching over my vision from the outsides in and . . . and . . .

What in the hell?

Little heart-shaped bubbles pop around the edges of my vision. It's another real-life filter. Let's call this one 'kissy poo.'

I've got to find Velis, and it has to be quick. The whole of the club seems to be curving to face me. They can all see me. They can all tell something isn't right.

Like that passing couple, with their eyes larger than should be anatomically possible. And those music notes wafting in from the edge of the hall, bouncing through the air like a kids' sing-along-song. I swim through bent perception that makes the end of the hall seem like it's much closer than it actually is, struggling to make my gait as normal as possible.

In the words of Arrik:

Fuck, fuck, fuckity *fuck*.

Gah! I can't imagine growing up with brothers like those, thinking they're soooo much better than you simply because you've got a teeeensy bit of nymph in you. I mean, who knows, maybe I've got a little bit of leprechaun in me. Maybe I'm part mer.

Oh no. I am definitely getting higher. Velis? Velis! I'm not certain if I'm shouting his name out loud or in my head.

Velis.

I've only met two of the three triplets, but from what I can tell, Velis looks no different from his brothers. And he possesses the same powers as them. You'd never know he was something else by looking at him.

Maybe that's what's made it so hard for him.

Why not just run off to be with the nymphs? Oh yeah, I forgot—they don't want you either.

Shit. This substance is making me feel warm in the heart too. Like I want to *comfort* Velis for the struggles he hasn't even shared with me. Like I want to stick my nose into business that isn't mine and offer him a hug he doesn't want.

Speaking of hugs—

I'm rammed into from the front, hard enough to knock the wind out of me. "Oh, thank Maka! Master, you're here. I came back and you were gone, and the bartender didn't know where you went, and I thought you were mad at me because of Rayana. I've been running around here freaking out, looking for you!"

Velis is holding me to his chest like he'll never let me go as I struggle to regain my lost breath. Harder to reclaim with his ribs pounding with such vitality, his hands gripping with so much intention, his heat permeating my rose-stained nostrils.

"You're a genie. You live in a magic lamp."

He stiffens at the feel of my fingertips digging into his back.

"*Master*? What's wrong with you? Are you—" His hands twitch off me. "Are you HIGH?!"

"No," I lie, smearing my cheek down his fine-ass chest. Dang, that's smooth. And warm. Do djinn not grow body hair?

He holds me at arm's length to inspect me. "Where the hell did you get weed? I was only gone, like, fifteen minutes!"

"Your brother, Arrik."

By the clutch of his talons in the flesh of my arms, it isn't a welcome surprise. "*Arrik's here*?"

"Not anymore. And don't worry, he said he doesn't plan on kidnapping me. I'll recap later." I watch my breath sparkle as it leaves my mouth.

"What?! How can you be so—" Velis's concern shifts as I take his shoulder to steady myself. "Dolly?"

"*Amazing*."

"What is?"

"Hearts. They're sprouting from your skin wherever I touch it." I drag my fingers up his side and watch a trail of bubbly hearts pucker in my wake.

He spasms to avoid my touch. "Shit, that tickles! And crap, that's roseweed. It doesn't do much to us djinn, but to other races, it's . . . You're gonna be all horned up, Master."

Mother-trucker.

"I thought you said if anyone offered me something to smoke, I'd be fine!"

"You will be fine." He shrugs. "Just horny. Before we had high-tech vessels, some djinn used that stuff to lure humans. I guess it's a lot easier to trust in wishes when you see fairies and shit dancing in your peripherals. That's how my family built up most of their wealth, back before there were regulated ethics."

I'm not paying attention to a word he's saying. "Your skin feels nice, Vel."

His jaw tweaks. "Is that . . . what you're calling me now?"

Yes, because every time I say it, a string of glitter spurts from my mouth and settles over his head like a halo.

Vel. Velllll.

"Hey, Vel?" I sparkle. "Back when we were at Mayree's . . ."

His eyes flash.

"When we were doing the mating test—"

"Stop."

"It felt like you—"

"*Stop.*"

"You . . . like me, don't you, Velis."

Uh-oh. I didn't intend to say that.

And yet I had many opportunities to exit along the way.

Vel doesn't respond but looms down at me with eyes that pierce even more than usual, like he's just made a grisly discovery and his mouth doesn't know how to react.

"Velis, do you like me?" I double down.

"Come on, Master. I'll take you somewhere safe." Embrace protective, breathing pronounced, Velis lets his arms circle me through our long blink into darkness.

Somewhere safe. Velis teleports us to the safest place he can think of: the hotel room we stayed in last night.

Only this time, there's a family watching a movie inside.

"Nope!" Velis flickers us to existence for only a second before bouncing us to another, unoccupied room. "Well, those people are going to have a story," he says under his breath.

Hilarious. I unleash my giggles onto a mattress that welcomes me like a stack of pancakes.

"Wait, Master! I haven't checked for bugs yet!"

I've trained Velis well. He busies himself with the mattress's perimeter, while I roll over the comforter, watching bursts of clouds lift in my wake.

"Fuck, you are in the deep of it," Velis observes when finished with his check, giving his head a shake as I try to pluck invisible flowers from my own wrist. "Geez. Come here, Master." Then, he tosses an arm around me on the edge of the bed, wiggling his fingers in front of my face to return my complexion, hair, and eyes to their natural state. "It helps if you just sit and focus on one thing. Stare at that caffeine machine for a while."

Caffeine machine?

"You mean the coffee maker?"

"Is that what it's called? My first master called it a caffeine machine, so that's what I've been going with, and none of the others corrected me . . ."

My takeaway is: "So if I start making up words for human things, you'll adopt them?"

"Ugh. Please don't. It's hard enough navigating the human world as it is. Humanology 101 still has you guys in bonnets, shucking corn."

"Well, to be fair, some people do wear bonnets and shuck corn," I say.

Like that corn-shucking snowman in the corner, for example. But it disappears before I can ask Velis if it's real.

"I saw you fondle someone's boob tonight," I say instead.

His arm around my shoulder tenses. "Y-yeah? How'd that make you feel?"

"I hated it."

"Y . . . yeah. I thought you might. Dolly, look—"

"Do you like me, Velis?" This time, I search him with the eyes I came with, high off my ass, on a bed that feels like it's soaring through the clouds.

"I don't like that you're human," he says, glum.

Of course.

Because everything Arrik said was true.

Why should I care? It's completely asinine to think of a *genie* I met *yesterday* in that way.

And yet, it kind of sucks.

The first adrenaline I've had in me in nearly a year is driven by feelings I don't want, can't control, and that aren't reciprocated.

I fall back onto the bed while Velis remains sitting in place, arm now removed from me.

"Do you think . . ." he starts. "Master, do you think maybe

Mayree was right? That we *have* met before, somehow? I'm not an expert in human interaction, but since the moment I met you, I can't help feeling it all seems so . . ."

He stops himself, but I know what he was going to say:

Natural.

It all seems so natural.

Like we're being pulled together.

"The only way we've met before is if you erased my memory afterward," I postulate.

"I swear I haven't. Try me if you want. Wish for me to tell you the truth."

No, I believe him. No wishes necessary.

So instead, I ask him the question I've been wanting to ask since we teleported here. "Answer me something, and tell me the truth. Am I the only one that can see those snowflakes billowing out of the air conditioner right now?"

He finally allows himself to glance over his shoulder to where I'm intently involved in a staring contest with a dancing snowman he probably can't see.

He looks from me to the conditioner, grin budding. "What do you think?"

"But it looks so real! Then again, my mom says I used to talk about an imaginary alien all the time when I was younger too . . ."

"An *alien*? You are something else, Dolly Jones." His grin now full, he buries it with a sigh. "Go to sleep, Master. I, ah, definitely shouldn't join you tonight."

He's right. His bare skin is glistening like it's all oiled up, the imaginary snow sizzling when it lands on his chest. "You do look really, *really* hot right now," I blurt.

NO. We've discussed this, haven't we? He's not the sort of person that should ever, *ever* be told something like that!

"O-ho?" The bob of his throat is either exceedingly large or is being amplified by my state of mind.

"Yeah . . . I wish I could bite you."

I feel the frost of his gaze just as certainly as the flurry of snow settling all around me. He's taking it in, my bare knees kicked out from below my skirt. My waist, hugged by the dress he fabricated for me. My shoulders, naked.

"You aren't making this easy, Master," his sizeable lips mutter. "If I sleep out here, that makes me a predator, right?"

"Not if you keep your hands to yourself."

"It's not *my* hands I'm worried about, you doink!"

Whose then? *Mine*? "But I don't even have hands anymore." I hold out my stumps, which he cannot see.

This causes him to give his largest snort of all. He scans me over another minute, then seems to reach a decision. He stands from the bed, ambling over to hi-yah the covers from under me.

"Get on that side. You don't like the nightstand, remember?"

I obey, rolling away toward the wall, realizing that as I go, the threads of my dress are quickly unraveling, replaced by—

"H-hey! What the fuck is this, Velis?! An adult onesie?"

"Sure is. That'll keep your *stubs* tucked in nice and tight. Don't try wiggling your way out of it either. There's no zipper. I'll add one in the morning." Satisfied, he pounces onto the free side of the bed. "Nighty night, Master!"

My hands are trapped, my feet are trapped, my entire body is covered up to the cuff of the neck.

"What the hell, you bastard! I'm going to sweat like crazy in this thing!"

His devil's smile disappears into the darkness ushered over the room by his snapped fingers. "Naw. You'll be fine if you quit squirming so much. It's cold in here, remember?"

Colder than ever with all that snow. Grouchy, I thrash about to make a point but am quickly distracted by the absorbing softness of the bed.

The suctioning pillows.

The blanketing dark.

The whir of the air conditioner dies, putting an end to the flurry of drug-induced flakes, and in the leftover silence, Velis's breath persists, shallow enough to betray that he isn't asleep.

I wonder what he found out from his great-uncle.

I wonder if his ex was anything like Rayana.

I wonder if . . .

On the edge of oblivion, I feel him slide closer to me. "Come here, Master." His voice is soft, commanding, sexy.

"Vel?"

Within silence thick as frosting, I hear something ripple. The palp of my heart as his warm mouth finds my forehead and pushes out a secret he doesn't want anyone else to hear:

"I do like you, Dolly. More than I want to. And I'm starting to worry that the next time your heart breaks, it might be because of me."

CHAPTER 9

The Young Laird

REMORSE. Bed-headed, sweaty remorse. That's what I feel for acting such a fool and for leaving most of my cool factor behind in that nightclub. Cool factor I may never be able to regain.

"How ya feeling, sparky?" Velis asks through what sounds like a knowing grin.

"Let me die," I say with a pillow held over my own face. "Just let me die."

"It wasn't that bad," he says with a laugh, adding another pillow to the stack. "It was actually pretty adorable."

I feel my face burn hot enough to slice through these pillows because I do remember the last thing he said to me before we both fell asleep.

And then he cradled me in my full-sized woman's onesie all night until I woke up with my cheek plastered to his chest and my hair glued to my neck from sweat.

I will never, ever, ever sleep in a onesie again.

"You cooled off yet, Master?" he asks both literally and figuratively, now that I'm returned to my sweat shorts and tank top ensemble.

"Be gone with you," I say, muffled.

"Come on, I already knew you were a dork, didn't I?"

"It was mere speculation before," I groan.

He rips the pillows from my hands, simpering down at me with the slightest smirk known to man.

He doesn't bring up what he said last night.

But something is changed in the air around us.

I have a crush on my genie. And he has a crush on me back. And that is ridiculous for so many reasons, yet I can't help returning that smirk stowed in the corner of his mouth as our eyes connect.

But his soon falls because he can't allow it to grow. I understand now, why Velis has been so hot and cold with me. Why it would be selfish for me to pursue the things he whispered in the dark.

I'm not a full person. I'm not a healthy person. I need to stop giving in to things that feel good and recommit to my atonement.

Step one: busy myself with getting ready. I snatch up my naughty little makeup case and head to a bathroom fresh with artificial cleaner.

"So," I call after a few productive minutes, "your great-uncle you met with while I was—"

"Off *toking*?"

"Er, sure. Was it your grandfather's brother? The one you were close with?"

"Yeah, I figured he'd be the most likely to know more about the vessel my grandfather left me. Mayree confirmed our souls aren't compatible, but I have no idea what she meant by 'a different set of rules.' Figured if my vessel's been modified to seek out another kind of—er, sorry—*prey*, he would be the one to know."

"And?"

"Mm, he didn't have much. Mainly said my grandfather went missing for a stretch of time while using it and that he wasn't the same after he came back."

Doesn't seem super helpful.

"He said something else too," Velis continues. "About you."

I poke my head out of the bathroom, one half of my face done and a toothbrush hanging limp in my mouth. "Yeah?"

"He said the only way a human's soul could be kept from tethering is if a wish was made to make it that way."

"Why would someone wish that for me?"

He chews at his cheek in contemplation. "Well, I did the math on how much a wish like that would cost, and really, the only one who could have wished it is you. It would have created a bit of a paradox in that the djinn would be forced to make it but would get no payment in return—a self-fulfilling wish in some regards."

"I've never made a wish like that. I didn't even know djinn were real until I met you. And to be honest, I still go back and forth as to whether this is all in my head."

"It's not," he says with a hearty roll of his eyes. "And I know you didn't make a wish like that, so I'm a bit stumped too. You're sure you're human? Like *for sure*, for sure?"

"As far as I know. Unless there's some huge hidden family secret I don't know about. I do have a cousin with a *lot* of body hair. I mean, like, a lot."

Velis jeers, "Are you implying he's a *werewolf*?"

"It's a she, actually. And probably not. She's also a vegan."

All lies, of course. Judging by those pursed lips, he can easily tell.

"I'm almost wondering if we should get your blood checked," he says on a more serious note. "I do have a vampire friend who could—" He stops when he notices my toothbrush is dangerously on the verge of slipping out of my open mouth. "Kidding. My family's got a hematologist on retainer. Not thrilled about the idea of taking you back to the estate, but . . ."

Okay, but if there's mermaid blood in me, I definitely want to know about it.

"Can't I just wish myself invisible?"

"You could," he says reluctantly, "*but you're turning out to be an expensive little diversion, Master.*"

"Can I just wish the lock on my soul away then, so you can siphon me?"

He shakes his head. "My uncle said that kind of spell only works if it's cast under conditions—meaning certain conditions must be met in order for it to be removed."

"And I can't wish to know what those would be?"

"While I do appreciate your affinity for loopholes, that's another no. I'm not drawing off you right now, and those kinds of wishes are expensive. Messing with the soul costs a lot." He chews his lip. "I suppose I *could* spare making you invisible for a day, though. That's definitely the cheapest option, unless you'll agree to hide inside my vessel. No? Didn't think so."

I sigh. "Always so eager to get me back to your crib."

Oops. That one was an accident.

"I don't sleep in a crib, *Master*. I'm not an infant."

Thank god for cultural misunderstandings.

"Wait a sec—You said your brothers made one-off deals with unbonded humans to find our location, right? Why can't you just do the same so that you don't have to dip into your savings?"

The question strikes Velis disagreeably. "I can't make one-off deals. I can only make them through my vessel. Because . . ."

Because of his nymph blood. Scratch what I said about cultural misunderstandings. More often, they suck.

"By the way, thanks for magically cleaning my clothes for me," I divert. "I'm not sure how much that cost you, but hopefully it was worth the price of not having to smell a seasoned version of me."

"*Seasoned*?" He makes a pew face. "It was nothing. That's just party trick-level shit."

It's with canned humor that he takes the rest of my belongings from me, making them disappear into the vessel, before shrinking the makeshift storage unit down to the size of a coin and sticking it in his pocket.

"Ready, Master?" He moves in to embrace me but pauses at the last second, deeming my elbow the safer option. He takes it as the room melts to pitchest black, and after, we're standing in a flowery courtyard starring lines of shrubs that look to have been planted with rulers. I shield my eyes from the basking sun and my ears from the birds up to their typical fuckery, twitting in and out of perfectly manicured bushes. It's the sort of place that would be featured on a British show set in the 1800s. I expect a gloved queen to come strolling through the emerald rows at any moment.

"Velis!" I whisper, clinging to his toned arm, for there are at least two djinn gardeners staring straight at us.

He ignores me.

"Laird Velis?" An elderly woman in a floppy sunhat and a basket of fresh-picked flowers scuttles toward us. "What're you doing home? Your father don't expect ya for another two weeks!"

The second of the gardeners looks to be in his early twenties, with lighter skin than all the other djinn I've seen and hair that looks more greenish than blue.

"Oy, Vel!" He waves over his head before hopping through a cluster of purple flowers that definitely aren't native to Earth. Earth's flowers don't SPARKLE like that. In fact, all the flowers here seem to be coated in extra-fine glitter, the kind that lines the lungs of art teachers all over the world.

Neither gardener acknowledges the human cowering in their presence.

"I . . . take it they can't see me?" I straighten.

"Mmhm," Velis says under his breath, "but they can hear you, so shut up."

"*A little warning would be nice next time!*"

"I asked if you were ready," he ventriloquizes.

He's enjoying this. Bastard.

And the other two are within whisper-hearing range now, so I'm left to curse at him inside my head.

"Dude, Vel!" The younger gardener pounces toward us with dirt caked on his knees and painted across his forehead. "We missed you around here! Does this mean those other jackasses gave up?"

"Shh!" The elderly woman swats at him. "Don't let the others hear you callin' the young Laird without a title."

"Psh." The green-haired guy waves her away. "Vel doesn't care, do you, Vel?"

"Never," Velis answers with a grin of camaraderie. "I missed you guys too."

"And you don't let yer father hear you calling us 'guys,' my little Laird," says the woman. "Wouldn't want you gettin' scolded again. Ooh—" She grips her apron. "I'd give you a hug right now if we weren't out in the open. We've all been so worried about ya. Is it true yer in the lead?"

So Velis is the sort of rich kid who's friends with all the servants?

Well, that's . . . cute.

"Yeah, but I've run into a bit of a snag. That's why I'm here. Do you know where Ardy is?"

I, the snag, try to keep my breathing silent.

"Let's see," the woman ventures, peeking at the golden sun. "It's forty-four in the afternoon. He should be in the middle library for his lunch, by now."

"Great." Vel gives a nod. "Thanks. I'm in kind of a hurry, though, so—"

"Ooh, yeah, yeah," says the green-haired guy. "Don't let us keep you. But seriously, Vel?"

I matrix out of the way as he lands a dirtied hand on Velis's shoulder.

"We're all rooting for you to win. How sweet would it be if you were our new master?"

"Just as long as it's not young Laird Jeb," mutters the woman, making a crossing motion over her body. "All us halfers are gone if it's him. You'd make an excellent master, Laird Velis. If there's anything we can do to help—"

"You've helped enough. Thanks, guys." Velis makes a small motion with his hand for me to follow him as he cuts around a row of young fruit trees and down a path of short green moss. Ahead lies a pretty white bridge marking the edge of the glittering gardens. Vines twist up its structure and fall over into the pond below. Swans must not exist here, or surely they'd flock to a place like this.

Out of earshot of the gardeners, Velis stops me at the foot of the bridge. "Alright, what is it, Master?"

Judging by where his eyes are pointed—

"You can see me?"

"Of course I can see you! I wouldn't go making you invisible to myself. It would be so like you to wander off and get lost."

"What, because of last night? I *told* you, I was in the bathroom!"

"Yeah, smoking weed with my asshole brother. Look, we don't have time to argue the logistics, so, out with it. What's wrong?"

"Nothing's wrong. I didn't say anything."

"Yeah, but you're *dripping* in guilt, and it's distracting, so you might as well get it off your chest before we get to the manor."

Am I feeling guilt? I guess, if I stop to think about it, that interaction with his servant friends has me . . .

"Nothing's wrong," I insist. "Let's go."

"Don't run away from me, Master. I'm stronger and faster."

Yeah, but I'm *slipperier*.

Definitely not a selling point.

"*Fine*," I land. "I knew you were involved in this soul-gathering competition, but . . . it isn't just a pissing contest between you and your brothers. You really have lands and a title at stake, and people who are depending on you."

He blinks at me. "You knew that."

"I mean, yeah, but I didn't realize the gravity of it until now. And all of this? This running around you've been doing with me?"

Ever since I met him, I've been thinking only of myself. My atonement. My boredom. My reluctant feelings.

"Velis, you said you've never seen anyone work as hard as I have for my pledge, but you've worked just as hard for this. You deserve to win, and all I'm doing right now is holding you back."

The still pond sizzles under the burning sun, much like my neck sears from the burn of his stare.

"God, your emotions are strong. But your guilt isn't necessary. Yes, you are holding me up, but as to the title and the lands and what those two were going on about back there . . ." He frowns into a nearby thistle patch with magenta berries. "Jeb was right about what he said at the salty place. It doesn't really matter if I beat the others. The truth is, they're firstborn purebloods, and I'm not. Even if I win, my father will find a reason for why it doesn't count."

You know Father will never make you an heir, even if you win.

Then, he's been grinding out all those souls these past few months knowing he'll fail either way?

I'm no empath, but I can read the way that affects him.

"Then why are you doing it?" I ask.

His answer is conceived slowly: "There's something you said early on that resonated with me about your pledge. You said, 'I'm not doing it for them. I'm doing it for myself.' I suppose that's true for me too. You've probably guessed by now, but those three—Jeb, Arrik, and Beckham—they've never accepted me as one of their own. For a while, I tried to impress them, but then I thought, why? So, I distanced myself. But they would never leave it alone. In school, a lot of my classmates couldn't tell I wasn't full-blooded, but those three always made sure everyone knew. I couldn't play on any of the sports teams or join the clubs. They made my life hell. Beckham's the only one that really grew out of it. So, when our father proposed this soul-collecting *game*?" Darkness settles over him like a veil. "I'll die before I let them win."

I get it. And his motives are nowhere near as shallow as I originally thought. But the truth of what he's just told me is dulling. The pond no longer seems to glimmer, the sun to bake. And his eyes . . . Eyes as brilliant as those should never look so tarnished.

I shouldn't.

It's a bad idea.

But I can't help myself.

"Dolly?"

This time, I'm the one to initiate the hug. Because I know how healing the act of touch can be. And because I owe him a few by now.

"I don't know shit about the genie world, but I've seen you do some incredible things over the past few days, Vel. You even managed to coax desire out of me, and you know how stubborn I am. If that doesn't speak to your *talents*, then I don't know what does. My two dirham? Your brothers are pricks. Blood is nothing but a substance, and from what I've seen, you're of greater substance than either of them. Any human film will tell you that you're the kind of character that deserves to win." I give him a shake before releasing him. "I'm Team Velis. I'll do whatever I can to help you beat them, okay?"

But his hand around the curve of my back won't let me leave.

Head bent to my shoulder, he pushes me softly against the cool, worn stone supporting the bridge. He stays that way a moment, hand careful on my back, breathing against me, as if on the edge of a cliff, about to take a plunge.

Until he swallows, removes his hand, and pulls away. "Let's go, Master."

He doesn't show me his face the rest of the way along the path.

And, fuck me. Like an unwanted blemish rising on the skin, I feel it coming to a head. This is more than a crush. I'm beginning to care about him. Enough to feel a bit messy.

It's probably best that be our last hug.

Beyond the garden path is a wood of semi-naked trees that look like they've been stricken by a witch's curse. And who knows, in a place like this, maybe they have. Velis charges through the brittle branches reaching after us, his steps crunching with stark intention until the haunted forest ends in a cliff overlooking—

"THAT's your house?! Holy crap! You really ARE rich!"

An enormous estate stretches before us, preluded by more rows of hedged gardens segmented by color. There's a strip of red, of pink, of teal. And the manor itself? It's like something from a fairytale, with spreads of narrow windows and mosaic cupolas and other architecture I'm not smart enough to name.

"There have got to be dozens and dozens of rooms in that thing!"

"Hundreds," says Velis, but he doesn't sound boastful.

"And this garden! It's like . . . I don't even know. So, what was that other smaller one behind the woods? The flowers back there were different. These ones don't sparkle."

"That was my mother's garden," he says, subdued. "Her favorite plants, imported from the nymph realm."

Was. Were.

Come to think of it, he talks about his father in the present but never his mother.

I don't know why I didn't realize sooner.

"My dad died too, you know," I can't help but tell him, soft. "When I was young. Cancer. That's why I was so close with my grandpa."

He slips a look over his shoulder. "Cancer?"

"It's a disease that inflicts humans."

"Oh. Mom's was fairypox." He's silent a moment. "Come on. We'll go in the easy way. I just wanted you to see it from the outside once. Pretty gaudy, huh?"

"You're like a freaking prince or something, Velis. I can't believe you grew up here. My childhood home would look like a peasant's in comparison."

"Your current dwelling looks like a peasant's."

Jerk.

But he's offering a smile for the first time in several minutes. And this time, when I take his hand, he pulls me in for the embrace he withheld back in the hotel room. He doesn't leave right away. Just holds me there, with our shoes in the crispy brush and a curse at our backs and a fairytale at our fronts. The V of his shirt ends at my chin.

Tempting fucking cotton.

"Hold on tight, Master," comes his whisper.

But he's holding on tighter. Tighter than is necessary, holding me in a way that causes my pulse to breed anarchy.

Tempting fucking genie.

The world dissolves as it always does, but when we land on the other side, he doesn't release me straightaway. He brings one of his hands to the back of my hair, humming into my forehead, "I'm sorry about your dad, Dolly."

"I'm sorry about your mom," I say, hands full of his shirt.

I'm not sure if what I'm hearing is my own pulse or a dangerous combination of ours both beating louder and louder until it's disrupted by the reverberating clap of a gong attached to a clock-like device high up on the wall.

Equally high ceilings oversee towers of shelves housing crisp books in neat rows, many accessible only by sliding ladder. The room holds a lovely, set-in scent, like the words in the pages have bled into the dark furniture and mosaic floors. How many of these shelves are actually secret passageways in disguise? And is there a beast lurking somewhere in this castle?

"Forty-five in the afternoon," Velis observes, chin tilted to the clock on the wall.

Whatever their time system here, it makes zero sense to a human. That 'clock' has four hands, with two ticking forward and two whirling back.

"Keep your eyes peeled for a daem in his thirties," Velis instructs.

"A daem?"

"Right. I forget you don't have them in your lore. Uh, black hair, red eyes, horns. Stay close to me and keep quiet. I'd like to avoid running into anyone else if I can help it."

With that, he glissades down a looming aisle of books. Thousands of books, all marked in that Makayen language. I trail my fingertips down the uniform spines that look like they've never even been read.

At the end of that row, Velis skids to a halt, beckoning for us to return the other way. "Cleaning staff."

They're doing a damn good job. I don't see any evidence of dust. Then again, maybe dust only exists on Earth.

Velis steals alongside the rows with quick, quiet steps, tossing glances down each while I trail behind, taking in the wonder of an otherworldly library. The ceiling is domed and decorated with gold paint and mosaic shards. The furniture is solid and velveted, crafted with intention, unlike the cheap mass-produced beginner's furniture cluttering my apartment.

And then . . .

"Oh my god, Velis. Who is that woman?"

The beauty of a large gold-framed portrait hanging over a set of double doors compels me to stop. The person in the frame is one of the most beautiful creatures I have ever seen, with vibrant blue eyes and soft gold hair and the world's most perfect nose.

Velis stops beside me. "That's my mother."

His *mother*? Of course he'd have a mother that looks like that.

"I see where you get your looks. She's stunning."

He tips his head from me to the portrait and back to me. "You think so?"

"Um, yes." It isn't really a matter of 'think.' "Your dad still keeps her picture hung?"

"Oh yeah," he says, "one in every room pretty much. He hasn't remarried yet."

"So, what happened to his first wife, Arrik and Jeb's mom? Did she pass away too?"

"Psh. No. She's still around. My father left her shortly before he got with my mom, but she still waltzes around here like she owns the place. She's . . . kind of a nightmare."

Genies can get divorced. Noted.

And I think I'm starting to understand Velis's situation a little better. "I get it now. Why your brothers are such dicks to you. It's because they're jealous."

It seems obvious to me, but Velis reacts like I'm joking. "*Jealous*? Why the hell would they be jealous of *me*?"

Really?

"Because your dad clearly loved your mother so much. Still does. If he didn't, he wouldn't have these paintings hung all over. I haven't met your father, but if he loved your mother enough to put a giant picture of her in every room, then you've got to be his favorite too, right?"

Velis seems to be waiting for a punchline, and when no punchline comes, he looks away. "You're wrong. My father may have loved my mother, but he never meant to breed with her. He wants nothing to do with me. He has a hard time even looking me in the eye."

The pragmatist in me wants to say it's because those eyes of his look painfully similar to the ones in the portrait. But I know nothing about their situation, and it's really none of my business.

"What about you," Velis changes the subject. "Did your mom ever remarry?"

"Naw. But my grandfather lived with us a lot of the time. Now it's just mom. And our super old, super fat cat named Steve. I plan to go back and visit them." I hesitate. "After my pledge is over."

"Wait, part of your pledge was to not see your mom? After going through a bad breakup and losing all your friends?"

Yes.

And it seems a horrible thing to admit to a person who no longer has a mother.

"It's not like I don't talk to her anymore, but I didn't want to let myself go back home because . . . uh . . ."

Velis finishes for me: "You didn't think you deserved it. Geezus, Dolly! If my mother was still alive when . . . the last time I went through something, she's the first person I would have gone to see. You're too hard on yourself, you know? It's kind of crazy."

I know. I just didn't know how else to function.

"I can't believe someone like you's been locked away for an entire year. With no one to be mean to but yourself," he says.

I roll my eyes. "I'm not that mean."

"Sure, sure, but have you ever considered becoming a dominatrix? You could, like, beat men up and then comfort them after?"

"Oh yeah? Is that what *you'd* want?"

His mouth cracks. "Kinda."

There we go again, twinkling back and forth like any of this is normal.

"You know, I keep forgetting you're invisible. If anyone saw me talking to you right now, they'd think I'd lost it," he says.

"*Yeah,*" I say through clenched teeth, thinking about our interactions with that perky waitress and my confused super, "*wonder what that would be like.*"

"Ha! Oh yeah."

Oh yeah, he says. I take the liberty of moving on without him.

"Smirker," he whispers as he passes, then continues to peruse the aisles in search of a red-eyed man with horns. You know, all the normal stuff.

Argh. We both know this can't continue, so why can't we keep from flirting? He likes when I'm mean. He likes when I'm not. He tries to stop himself from touching me but continues to fail.

Is it possible to combust from sexual tension? Never have my eyes been so often drawn to someone else's *neck*. If given the chance, would I strangle it, bite it, or pucker it between my lips? And how would he react to each?

I want to feel him *gulp*.

Enough.

He can surely feel my desire, and this is helping no one.

A sudden change in his shoulders signifies he's seen something undesirable around the next row of shelves. He stops abruptly enough for me to bang into him, taking my elbow to yank me back the way we came and around the next row of books.

"*Jeb*," he mouths. "Shit! What the hell is he doing here?!" He smooths his hands over his face. "Probably researching why they weren't able to siphon your soul. We have the largest collection of ancient texts in the city."

Of course they do.

Velis chews his cheek, weighing our risk of venturing further. "This might have to wait, Master. If Jeb's here, Arrik's likely not far, and they're on home turf this time."

But I don't want to continue being a hinderance for him.

"Is that Ardy guy the only daem person that would be in the library?" I ask.

"More than likely. Why?"

"Write a note telling him where you want to meet. I'll go deliver it."

He chortles. "Umm, yeah, I don't think so."

"Why not? I'm invisible, so I can move around freely. And if he's the only red-eyed person in here, I'm pretty sure I'll be able to recognize him."

And I've been waiting all my life for a chance to act out my cat burglar fantasies. Black leggings? Check. Black shirt? Check. Black eyeliner? Double check.

"What's with that goony face you're wearing? This is serious! Jeb's a fucking sociopath. Arrik's one thing, but Jeb will literally tie you up and starve you until you give in to him. He'll take you somewhere I won't be able to find you."

"I'm not afraid of him. I can cast wishes, remember?"

"But Dolly, they aren't bonded to you. They don't *have* to grant your wishes the way I do. They only did so last time because they were hoping to siphon off your soul. Now that they know they can't, they have no reason to comply."

Oh. WHAT? Then when I was alone with Arrik and threatened him with a wish . . .

I was in a lot more danger than I realized.

"I won't get caught," I tell him, stretching to show how limber I can be. "We've already checked half of these shelves anyway. There's not that much more ground to cover. I'll do a quick sweep, hand off the note, and be back to you in a few minutes."

He doesn't like it, but a few more limber stretches later, he reluctantly agrees.

"If only I could shrink my vessel while I'm inside it," he mutters, scribbling the note on a scratch piece of paper retrieved from said vessel. "Then I could go with you."

"I'll be fine, Vel. This is a library. It's basically one of the safest places on Earth."

"We aren't on Earth, you tart!"

I clench the paper in my invisible fist, giving him a two-fingered wave before slinking around the corner. Do I understand the gravity of the situation? Yes. But do I still search my brain's database for a spy-themed song to set as my soundtrack? Also yes. I can't remember most of it, though, so a good ten-second loop plays on repeat. Good enough.

Creeping past the second row, I find Jeb in a colorful T-shirt and dark jeans, balancing a half-open book in his palm. All of them have those icy eyes, but his are the only ones that truly feel cold. Bitingly so. He reads the book like he's displeased with it, as though he plans to punish it by pulling the pages from its spine, one by one.

He seems like he'd be a nightmare to date. The kind of person to foster insecurity for the fun of it. Used to be I couldn't pick that kind of person out until it was too late.

My stealth wins. Jeb doesn't so much as flinch as I tiptoe past. The next row is empty, and the next and the next. I see no one else all the way to the back of the library, where a small door leads to a sunlit study alcove with streak-free windows and a mesmerizing view of the gardens. There, a pale man in his early thirties sits reading a book and poking at a bowl of unknown grains with wooden chopsticks.

Velis wasn't lying—the daem does have a set of small horns poking from his tousled black hair, and his eyes are indeed the color of cherries.

Now comes the awkward part.

The note from Velis flutters onto the table, but, engrossed in his book, Ardy doesn't notice. If it were me, I wouldn't want a disembodied voice to appear over my shoulder, so instead, I nudge the torn paper across the glazed wood at him, conjuring a lovely little scraping noise that's sure to alert him.

Still nothing? Fine.

Tucking in my hot breath, I inch dangerously close to the daem, sliding the piece of scrap onto the open page of his book.

A cold hand snatches my wrist.

"Nice try," he purrs, eyes remaining fixed on his book. "I didn't see you, and I didn't feel you, but I'm afraid your shampoo gives you away. In case you're looking for pointers."

His touch is chilled, his pale skin a stark contrast to that charcoal hair and those ruby red eyes.

"Hold on, hold on," he says when I attempt to free myself. "I need to see whether or not you're a threat before I let you go." He uses his free hand to clumsily open the paper. "Velis? Interesting. You're a friend of Velis's? And you smell like a girl." His cherry stare hits my invisible face. "A *human* girl. Why would a boy like Velis be bringing a human girl back *here*? Isn't he supposed to be off participating in some phallus measuring contest? Are we sure this isn't a trap, little mouse? Do you plan on ambushing me once I go to" —he checks the note—"the fifth-floor linen room?"

"No," I attest with his hand still firmly gripping me.

"Ahh, she speaks."

"Velis is still undertaking the contest, but he ran into an issue that requires your blood expertise. He was going to come himself, but that psycho Jeb is out browsing the stacks, so he sent me instead. I'm his current master."

"You're his *master*? And he trusts you enough to deliver this message for him? You did say *Velis*, didn't you? You aren't getting him confused with, say, Arrik?" The daem looks amused. His eyes glint in the afternoon light flooding the small space.

"Um, no. I've met Arrik, and he's kind of a sleaze. Velis and I are friends."

The admission just sort of falls out. But . . . are we friends? Am I allowed to consider him a friend at this point?

"Velis is friends with a human girl?" the daem muses. "Whatever must you look like, I wonder? At any rate, it's worth skipping my lunch for. I'll meet you in the fifth-floor linen room in fifteen minutes, and I'll bring my kit." He releases his hold on me, but before I reach the door—"A word of caution, little mouse. Be careful getting mixed up with young djinn boys. Their society is quite progressive in some respects and quite antiquated in others. I expect it would be difficult to break them of their conditioning." He waves one pale hand over his shoulder before returning to his book. "See you soon."

Progressive like that nightclub. Antiquated like their racism.

I took longer to reach Ardy than I meant to. Velis is likely getting impatient. To make up for lost time, I flit faster past the imposing shelves, feeling confident that the path is unobstructed, rounding the corner where Velis is waiting for me—

And skid to a halt as I nearly barrel into Jeb.

What the hell?!

The meanspirited triplet has moved on to a new tome, flipping disinterestedly through its earliest pages.

It was stupid of us to assume he'd stay in one place the whole time. Especially if he's browsing for answers to the mystery of my impenetrable soul.

He's so creepy. With an aura that's piercing and ominous. Like a flytrap that doesn't try to hide what it is.

I don't risk turning around. Instead, I backpedal away from him. Velis must be freaking out. He knows this is the row I'd return to. He knows his brother has taken up residence. He can't have gone far. Another step backward and I feel comfortable enough to turn away. Only, Jeb is also turning, setting his suspicion directly into my face.

He sniffs the air.

Shit! Is the hotel shampoo really that strong?

Apparently. Jeb takes a step, extending his hand in my direction. Cat burglary tested, I dip away from him and slink away as quietly as possible, but he's more determined now, drawn in by the artificial scent of honey and . . . teakwood? Whatever the hell that is. I'm less concerned about being loud now and more concerned about him not grazing me. With obvious steps, I make a pattering beeline for the end of the shelves, feeling Jeb closing in, refusing to look behind me as I round the next corner—

Where I'm grabbed by a pair of strong, boyish arms.

In the time it takes to blink, the world is gone, replaced by a closet lined floor to ceiling in shelves stuffed with folded sheets that smell like clean laundry.

I spin to face my captor, relief melting over me.

"Velis." I press my forehead to his chest and release all the stress I've been holding. "Why is your brother so scary?"

"I *knew* that was going to happen." Shaking his head disapprovingly, he sets me away from him to look me over. "Nice stealth moves, by the way. Ducking around and creeping backward. Next time do me a favor, Master, and, oh, I don't know, RUN. Gave me a friggen' heart attack."

"So you were *spying*, were you?"

"Yeah, good thing I was, or you'd be in a very different situation right now." He unhands me. "Did you find Ardy?"

"I did. I gave him the note. He'll be here in a few minutes." I lean against a stack of clean blankets to let my adrenaline hush.

Velis watches me, deadpan. "And what are you doing now?"

"Trying to smell my hair." But it's a bit short for that. "Ardy smelled it and found me out, and I think it's what gave me away to Jeb too. Does it smell strong?"

Arms crossed, Vel smiles. "Yeah. I mean, it did. I think I've gotten used to it."

Well, dang. "Next time I go incognito, I need to wash with that soap hunters use. By the way, any idea what teakwood is?"

"Some human nonsense, I'd imagine."

We settle on opposite sides of the room while we wait for Ardy to show, the air in the small space muted by walls of linen padding. Stacks and stacks of bedding surround us, keeping us tucked away from the rest of the world. That's a heck of a lot of sheets. Which makes sense because this place holds a heck of a lot of beds.

"Did you play hide and seek in here when you were a kid?" I ask.

Velis lifts one half of his upper lip. "What's that? A game?"

"Yeah, like, kids go and hide while another one tries to find them? To be fair, it also works with drunk college students." I'm guilty of playing that particular version at least twice. "I imagine a house this size would make for some good hiding spots."

"Humans are weird," he retorts. "They're allllways complaining about being seen as prey and then they make up games where they're essentially prey? What do they expect?"

"What humans have you been around? And why do they feel you're a predator?!"

Velis sprouts a wicked gleam before stuffing it away. "No," he says. "I never played that. But my brothers did lock me in here a few times."

"Oh, wow, I'm so surprised." NOT.

He shrugs. "It's not the worst place they could have picked. At least you can hear yourself think in here."

"I guess."

I've had a lot of time to think over the past year. I'm kind of over it. In two more weeks, I can officially be over it.

Well, plus a week.

Or more.

"Geez, how many weeks am I going to have to add on for all of this?" I mutter.

"Here we go." Velis rolls his neck to let off a satisfying *crack*. "What do you have to atone for now, you little masochist?"

So many things. "Seeing beautiful places, drinking, getting stoned—having fun running around with you."

He straightens from where he's lounging. "You're having fun?"

Oh. Should I not have admitted it?

"I guess, yeah. Compared to coming home alone to my shitty apartment every night eating 'gruel and saltines' and watching the local news. I mean, this is obviously more exciting, right?"

Why do I feel self-conscious for saying so? Because that's one of the lamest things I've ever heard, and it came from my own damn mouth. I tuck my short hair behind my ear in a way only self-conscious people do.

Velis doesn't tease me for it. Instead: "I'm having fun too." But he doesn't sound like he's glad for it. I know this move. This is where he starts to feel too close to me and works to reverse it. "I wouldn't worry about tallying up those weeks, Master. It's not like you'll remember any of this after I get your soul."

Ouch. I knew it was coming, but still.

In sync with my feelings, he gives a jolt, hands out as if about to touch a bomb. "Crap. I didn't mean for that to hurt you."

Invasive empath.

My arms fold themselves as my brow gives a rise of challenge. "Why would that hurt me?"

"Master . . ."

"Why would that hurt me, Velis?" I say again, hating the way it tastes like anger and the unwelcome feeling of moisture starting at the corners of my eyes.

Ohhhh no. We are not allowing that to happen. I make myself stone and divert my attention elsewhere, conjuring bitchy undertones.

"It doesn't hurt me. It's the truth. This is going to end as soon as we figure out what's wrong with my soul, and then I'll never even know I met you. Nothing gained, nothing lost."

Except my fucking soul.

"Okay then," he says, lowering his hands, eyes devoid of life. "If that's how you feel."

Oh, this bitch.

There is a hot spring bubbling in me, swiftly growing hotter the more times he pulls this crap. It feels even hotter amidst the weight of a thousand pressed blankets.

Since when did fresh linen smell so sickening?

"You know that's not how I fucking feel, you jackass! And don't say that like the problem is me!"

Uh-oh. Lock it down, Dolly Jones. Lock. It. DOWN.

"*You're* the one that can't wrap your head around your feelings, Velis! Do you want to snuggle me all night or stuff me in your bottle so you don't have to see me? Freaking pick a lane and stay in it, you stupid genie, because I'm getting whiplash from all this dicking around!"

Not fair. I know why he's doing what he's doing. I know why he can't be with a human. Shouldn't I be glad he isn't just trying to get in my pants knowing it won't lead anywhere?

No, I'm not glad. I'm fed up. And apparently, so is he.

"The problem IS you, Dolly!" He throws out his hand. "I wouldn't have you stuck in my head if you weren't so—if you didn't keep—!"

"What?" I put a hand to my hip. "What am I doing? Oh, am I

seducing you? Am I *tempting* you? Forgive me for having tits and an ass, you hypocritical prick!"

"Wow. You really do think I'm shallow, don't you? It has nothing to do with your ass or your tits. It's the fact that you keep *pretending* to be interested in my life and that you keep baiting me with common ground. Like your grandfather? How the hell did you know that would tug at my heartstrings? And like all that stuff you said earlier, as if you really give a damn about me winning when the cost is your own soul! I don't know what you're playing at, but you have to stop. I told you I'd never fall in love with a human, and I meant it."

Un-be-LIEVABLE!

My anger has reached a level where it's no longer aggressive. It's now the most dangerous kind of anger: a calm one.

This is the implosion Arrik was hoping for.

"Do you really believe all that?" I ask, level tone contrasted by shaking fists. "You believe I'm *trying* to get you to fall in love with me? That I'm just that good at reading people I've never met before—enough to know what to say to make men stray?" Uh-oh. The feelings are melting. The anger is turning into something far, far worse. My voice breaks. "Is it because of . . . It's because of what I did with Gabe. That's why you think that. I'm just a slut to you. Just like I am to the rest of them."

It's a good thing we're surrounded by towels as the sheen of water sets over my eyes, and it's only a matter of time before it begins to slide down my face.

Velis doesn't let it get that far.

In a flash, he's over me, arms around me, tucking me to him protectively. "No. I don't believe any of that. I only said it because I'm an asshole." He squeezes me tighter. "You aren't a slut, Dolly. You're a little smokeshow, but you aren't a slut. I'm sorry I made you feel like one."

This time, I'm sure: that's both our hearts drumming against one another.

He releases me but takes one side of my face to keep me close. "Look, I'm not the kind of guy that fucks around with girls I'm not serious about. If I was, I'd have tried to screw you the night I met you. I'd have taken you out on the dance floor last night and felt you up all over. I'd have kissed you at least five times today. It isn't because I don't want to. It's because I know I can't take this further, and because you're worth more than just being some horny dude's excursion." He slides his hand from my face. "The problem isn't you, Master. It's me. I can't become involved with a human, no matter how . . ." He eyes me over for the right adjective, settling on a safe one: ". . . *mean* that human may be."

I know all of this. I already know it. So what am I doing?

"I know," I tell him. "Arrik told me."

His brow deepens. "What?"

"Arrik told me about why you need to find a full-blooded djinn girl. And I respect it. And for the record, screw your ex. Racist bitch."

Though, to be fair, he's kind of doing the same thing to me.

If he realizes it, he says nothing.

I continue, "I really don't want to become involved with anyone either, least of all a *mythical creature*. I was just frustrated with all the mixed signals. And as much as it sucks, I know you're right about the memory thing too. I really don't need to be sitting in my boring cubicle back home pining over some guy I'll never see again." I force a laugh. "It's like, am I supposed to just hope you'll come popping out of every murky bottle I see at the thrift store from now on?"

He's silent as stone, casting frost on my face.

"Though it's a shame I'll have to forget about the salt flats. Those were . . . they were something, weren't they? Is there any chance you could leave that memory when you take the rest?"

He blinks at me, breathing oddly.

"I'll definitely be happy to be rid of that onesie memory, though. And the time I tried to make you flinch. And when I mooned the whole damn nightclub. Yikes."

Shut up. Shut up, shut up. I'm rambling because I'm trying to keep the moisture from returning to my eyes. The truth? I'm extremely disappointed.

I like him. And I want him. Despite all logic.

And why isn't he saying anything back? He's just standing there, eyes *drilling* at me as if it's the last time we'll ever see one another. Is he . . . He's not going to do it now, is he? Wipe my mind, start fresh?

He sets his hand on my shoulder. "This is the last time."

I sniffle up at him. "What?"

"This is the last time I flipflop, Dolly. I'm sorry for what I've put you through until now." Eyes shrouded, he takes the back of my neck, tips my chin upward and lowers his face.

But the moment I feel the warmth of his mouth is the moment the door to the storage room opens.

CHAPTER 10

Blood Read

"Either you're practicing kissing the air, or that invisible girl of yours is more than a friend," says Ardy the cockblocking daem, toting a toolbox. "If the former, I suggest using an apricot. You'll get a better feel for the process."

Velis still hasn't released me. He swallows before squaring his jaw and flicking his gaze to the door. "*Great timing, Ardy.*"

Meanwhile, my hand is pressed to Velis's chest, feeling his heart race the way mine is racing, lamenting the fact that his kiss was interrupted. I want it even more now. For all my claiming not to be a seductress, I'll admit to the way I'm biting my lip and giving him my doe-iest eyes.

He releases a long, low sound from the back of his throat before reluctantly letting me go.

Was he serious just now? He wants to give in to our crushes? Even though I'm human? Even though I'm his 'master'? Even though he doesn't have time for any of this?

"Well?" says Ardy, kneeling to the ground and opening his case. "Are you going to un-invisiblify her? Or do you like keeping her your secret little friend? I'm dying to find out what she looks like. Sounds like a tomboy based on the voice, but you always go for those fine-china-esque girls, don't you?"

"What the hell is fine china?" Velis grumbles, waving his hand to turn me visible.

Midway through unpacking his tools, Ardy stops to look me over. "Huh."

. . . Just 'huh'?

WHAT THE HECK DOES THAT MEAN?

"Not your type at all," says Ardy, resuming his work. "Hello again, little mouse."

Velis folds his arms. "You have no idea what my type is, Ardy."

"*Velis*." Ardy says his name in a pouting sort of way. "It's okay if your type's changed. At least this one looks healthy."

. . . By healthy, does he mean FAT?

Velis slips his hand around my waist without shame. It's different from the other times. Those were made to feel unnoticeable. This time, he's doing it with as much intention as my blood can handle. "I need you to tell me what she is. Neither I nor Jeb nor Arrik have been able to siphon her soul. Her wishes took, but we didn't get any payment for them."

Ardy is busy screwing what looks to be a magnifying lens onto a handle. "Not smart, letting her around those two. Arrik will gobble her up, and Jeb . . . well, he'd like to dissect her, I'd imagine."

Velis's hand on my waist grips tighter. "I know. It wasn't intentional. We're on the run from them now."

"And Beckham?" hums Ardy.

"Haven't seen him since we started the competition. I heard he was in a land called Afreeka."

"Africa," Ardy corrects. "You really should have taken Earthen geography before setting off on this little adventure, Velis."

"It's not like I had a lot of time to prepare. Our father sprang it on us."

Ardy holds a small vial of clumpy liquid between his thumb and pointer, giving it a shake that sets the fleshy bits spinning in their juice.

That better not be something he expects me to ingest.

"Unlike your father to be spontaneous. I'm sure he's got a reason for it. He always does. Come here, little mouse." The daem pats the ground beside him, where he's borrowed a stack of towels to serve as cushion.

Still eyeing that festering bottle, I slide into position while Velis hangs back, chewing at his nail.

"You'd better come over here too," Ardy beckons him. "In case she needs support during the blood draw."

"I don't mind needles," I assure him.

But what the doctor next removes from his toolkit isn't a needle. It's an obnoxiously long knife that looks like something used to offer sacrifice to a pagan deity, all glinty with forbidden light it hasn't even caught. "We aren't using a needle, little mouse."

"What the hell?!" I leap, basically into Velis's lap.

Velis welcomes it as an excuse to hold me. And because we've left our *relationship* off at a heightened moment, his fingers seem to slow time itself as they slide against the curves of my body, every outside whisper deafened by the stacks of fabric, each dragging exhale of his breath like a bellows against my shoulder.

"Care to craft another onesie?" I mutter. "Maybe two?"

I expect a snort, but what I receive is a chin nestled into the nape of my shoulder and his hands tucking me closer. Cliché, yes, but I feel my cheeks flush from the way his breath is wavering.

Why does it suddenly feel like we're middle schoolers on a date?!

The doctor returns the knife to his toolkit with a loud *clink!* "You're welcome, Velis. Thought you might like getting a little cozy before we start."

"Quit messing around, Ardy! We don't have a lot of time here!"

"But enough time to make out in closets, apparently. Come on, little mouse. This will hurt, but it will be brief, yes?"

With my hand daintily in his, Ardy coaxes me from Velis's lap and waits for me to nod before bringing the back of my knuckles to his mouth and offering me a gentleman's kiss. After, he guides my palm to one of the horns poking from his disheveled hair. "Ready? Three, two—" He plunges downward on two.

OW.

The point of his horn pierces into the plush of my palm, sharp enough to draw blood. "Sorry. I know it is unpleasant." He gives my fingertips a gentle squeeze as crimson begins to leak from the puncture.

A rather *inconvenient* spot for a wound.

Velis brushes a hand across my back. "I'll heal it for you when this is over."

Meanwhile, Ardy has flipped my palm upward and is amplifying the sore via the magnifying glass he previously screwed together. Wouldn't a microscope be a more suitable tool for something like this?

"Okaaay," the daem ruminates, taking a long look. He swaps out the magnifying lens for that vial of murky liquid, unsheathing the glass cork against its neck. The liquid in there almost looks alive. I wouldn't be surprised if it were.

A single drop tips from the mouth of the bottle and mixes in with my blood. And if mixing unknown substances into my bloodstream weren't enough, the red-eyed man next lifts my palm to his face, cradling the back of my fingers between his like they're a valuable piece of jewelry, and takes an ample lick.

V-vampire!

"Ah, very interesting," Ardy says, pushing his tongue over the wound again, intentionally enough to feel skeevy. "Tell me, Velis, do you have feelings for this human?"

A test. Not one either of us expected. And one Velis is sure to weasel his way out of.

Except:

This is the last time I flipflop.

"Yes, I have feelings for Dolly." His gaze is direct and measured, his tone soft and serious. And after, I see the makings of a grin begin to blossom—enough to make me do the same.

"And when did they start?" Ardy presses. "When was the first time you felt a little—boop!" He taps his own chest with his blood-stained fingertips.

A question Velis is less eager to answer.

"Is . . . that really necessary?" he questions.

"If you want to leave here with resolution," Ardy says.

"Ugh. Probably the moment she whipped a crafting gun out at me and pretended it was a real gun, and then just went along with it for a good five minutes."

Wait, *what*?

"Well, now you know," Ardy says to me. "You're welcome."

"You fucking sham!" lashes Velis.

But I'm more concerned with: "You knew that wasn't a real gun all along?!"

"Of course I did," he scoffs. "That's a disarming technique. I told you, I schmooze all my masters. They just don't normally turn out to be so . . ." This time, he settles on a different adjective: "*Spicy*."

Ardy licks my remaining blood from his fingertips like it's gravy. "Well, I think I know the problem. This girl is what's called a magnetium—a special breed of human designed to lure djinn."

He says it unnervingly casually, as if he's telling us his favorite color.

"WHAT?!"

Two shouts ricochet, as I pull my bloodied hand into myself and Velis scuttles away from me accusingly.

"Just kidding!" Ardy unleashes a loud clap, then proceeds to toss his tools back into his bag. "No further tests necessary. She's one-hundred percent human. Just regular, boring old human."

But Velis doesn't look convinced. "Are you sure, Ardy?"

Apparently, me being some magical temptress seems more plausible than him merely catching feels on his own.

"Oh yes. I'm sure. That's human blood. All of it." A momentary flash of darkness shadows him. "I'd know the taste of it anywhere." And just like that, he's back to normal. "All right. Be good, kids. And good luck." He salutes us both before shuffling out of the room, his toolbox hugged to his chest.

Then, Velis and I are alone again in the trampled quiet. "Here, Master." He retrieves my injured hand and forces it closed, and when it opens again, the skin is restored.

"You can quit calling me master, you know. I mean, it was already unnecessary, but now it just feels . . ."

"But you are my master, *Master*. Technically, I'm not supposed to call you anything else. Ever. I've been a bit sacrilegious since I met you."

"Just as long as this isn't you playing out some dominatrix fantasy," I charge.

His dimples are puckered enough that it just might be true. "Well, that was a waste of time. I guess now we know for sure you're human, though. In that case, I think we have to seriously start considering what my uncle said—that you made a wish to protect your soul."

"A wish I don't remember? Doesn't that seem a little coincidental with what Mayree told us? I don't remember making a wish. I don't remember meeting you. Logic suggests the two are related."

"But I don't remember meeting you either. Why would my memory be wiped too?"

That IS the question, isn't it.

I turn over the hand he healed for me, now much silkier than before. "When I first met you, you offered to take me back to the night Gabe and I . . ." I can't bring myself to finish. "Er, what I mean is, you could wish us back in time to when you and I met too, right?"

Velis releases a long, thin sigh. "Yeah, I *kinda* said that hoping to knock out a big chunk of your soul all at once. Time travel wishes are expensive as hell."

"Magic you can't spare," I determine.

"Not if I want to win."

And we for sure want him to win.

"So how does it work, then? The soul balance thing. Your family has a soul *fortune*, right? Can't you just tap into that instead of your contest balance?"

"Not without getting eliminated. We aren't allowed to touch the family account during the duration of the contest. You know—keep it fair."

So much structure to something so ludicrous. "Too bad you can't take out a loan," I sneer, kicking back against a stack of linens.

"Well, that is one option."

Wait, genies can borrow soul juice?

"I'd need collateral, though. Human collateral." He ignores the elephant in the room. "Know any humans we could easily kidnap?"

Predator.

"What? I'd wipe their memory and give them back as soon as we were done with them. I . . . don't like the idea of using you."

Ah yes. The other elephant in the room. Those feelings lingering over us, just above our heads, so abruptly cut off by Ardy's arrival.

I tip my face away from him. "We have to be practical about this, Velis. If you use my soul as collateral, you'll have plenty of power to figure out when I made that wish and why. And once you win my . . . once you win the contest, you can use some of what you've accumulated to repay the loan."

"But if anything goes wrong, the bank will get your soul," he says with a bit of a moue. "I want your soul."

Yes, that much has become apparent.

His gaze sweeps up from the ground. "I want it really, *really* bad."

The words hang, propped up by the stiff silence of the room, as all that tension stored over our heads slowly begins to drop.

"Hey," he murmurs, "let's get out of here, Master. There's one more place I want to show you before we leave."

Who can keep from taking a hand when it's connected to a twinkle like that? The room blinks away, and the first thing to materialize is the scent of foreign air.

"Are we on top of your mansion?!" I cry, gripping a cold steel railing as that same lively sun smiles down from above, the intensity of it broken by wind that's a bit more energetic at these heights.

"No," Velis says, pointing into the distance at a scaled-down version of his sprawling estate. "That's my mansion." He takes my shoulders to turn me. "*This* is the faewood."

The world is split. At our backs, clusters of djinn mansions litter an expanse of lush, velvety green. In front of us, a deep, dense wood of blackest trunks and whitest leaves sparkle like they've been kissed by Jack Frost.

"What do you think?" Velis's mouth is near, his hands on my shoulders.

The dark wood stretches on for miles, scaling over hills and dipping into valleys until it's lost to my imperfect vision. And all through the obsidian stalks, bursts of colorful powder pop into the air and fall to the ground like firework confetti.

Is it better than the salt flats? Unsure. Is it more breathtaking than the glitzy white city? Yet to be determined. All these sights are things that take time to sink in, and once they do, they stay, like tattoo ink. I don't feel worthy of seeing something like this.

"Oh my god, Velis." My skin is raised all over, aroused by the magnitude of what I'm seeing, as blasts of color shoot into the air and sprinkle over the elegant wood.

"I like the way you look at beauty." He sets his cheek to mine. "Most people just look. You absorb. It reminds me to stop and do the same."

I can't answer. My throat is held captive by the shimmer of those leaves, the explosions of colors unknown to the human world, and the rush of exotic breeze through it all as Velis stands behind me, hands on the rail next to mine.

"Before we do this, I need you to know—I have goals, Master, and a human partner doesn't fit into any of them. I don't see any way we can take this very far, and when it's over, I still have to do what I was trained to do. You understand that, right?"

I do.

"I know this goes against your pledge. I know you're still healing from what happened last year. And I know I've been yanking you around these last few days, but . . . I do like you, Dolly. It's fucking ridiculous, and it shouldn't be possible, but I do. I meant it when I said you're worth more than being some rando's excursion, and that's why I feel like such a hypocrite for what I'm about to say. I can't promise you forever, but can I have you for now, Dolly Jones?"

He's right. It's fucking ridiculous.

He's right. I'm worth more than being macked on by some hypocritical, self-interested smart-ass. But . . .

Velis isn't a hypocritical, self-interested smart-ass. Not really.

Wait, Master! I haven't checked for bugs yet!

I was really close with my grandfather too!

I just wanted to make sure I wasn't enabling an alcoholic or anything.

Come on, Master. I'll take you somewhere safe.

Answering immediately seems irresponsible, so I make him wait for it, savoring the way his hands are white-knuckling the steel railing as the wind taunts my hair into his face.

"I don't know, Velis."

I feel every inch of him stiffen.

"I haven't tasted you yet. What if I don't like your flavor?"

His body eases as his aura darkens. "Oh, you're gonna like my flavor, Dolly Jones. I guarantee it."

This is a bad idea. I know it as certainly as I know those are his teeth chewing my ear.

Blame being pent up for months.

Blame chemistry, unseen magic. It sparks between us as he nuzzles his nose along my chin and kisses the weakest part of my neck, summoning a foreign sound from the back of my throat.

"Damn, Dolly," he rumbles, mouth full of me. "You want it as bad as I do. It's freaking *pulsing* out of you."

He isn't wrong. Is there any way to suppress it at this point? Save some semblance of control?

"Don't," he whispers, his shivering fingers weaving up and down my sides. "Leave it. It's so fucking good."

Too much. I don't believe in horoscopes. And I don't believe in arrows spread all over a mystical scroll in the sky. But I have never felt this degree of tension in all my life.

I may be panting, and Velis, a being designed to draw out desire, is feasting on it, probing his hands over me, kissing my shoulder, my neck—

But if he doesn't kiss my mouth soon, I'm going to die.

"Vel," I breathe, "I wish you would—"

He seizes my mouth from behind. "You don't have to wish for a thing like that." He drags his fingers down my lips, peeling them away from my teeth before he spins me and bends me and gathers up my hair to steady my head while his shadow spreads over me.

He kisses my chin, withdrawing to examine my reaction with his perfect, chiseled face and those piercing, probing, delicious eyes.

What a TEASE.

Lapping it up, he moves in to kiss the corner of my mouth while my nails make his shirt pay for the angst he's causing.

We don't have time for this bullshit.

Unable to handle the flushing tension, I snap, forcing him to finish the job with my arms flung around his neck.

God. Damn.

I always knew he had the perfect mouth for kissing, full and soft and grinning naturally between each connection.

He opens it to let me taste him, sliding warm against me, mixing with me, moving in unison with me, leaving me scorching each time his tongue passes mine. And to hear him breathe between each kiss, it's like his breath carries a blueprint for what else he wants to do to me.

I've kissed . . . a fair amount of guys. One girl too.

Never has it felt like this.

With everything in me, I hope it feels the same for him.

He breaks to suck at my collarbone but doesn't stray far, returning to my mouth and bending me over the rail, holding on tight to keep me from flying away. If this is what it's like to kiss him, I can only imagine what the rest of him's like.

I'm worried it's going to ruin me.

I slide a hand to his chest to be sure his pulse is pounding just as hard as mine. To make sure I'm not the only one shivering and goosebumped and two degrees warmer than I should be.

From somewhere deep, he lets out a moan. Or maybe it's a groan. Because he knows, like I do, that we can't stay here and make out forever. That it would be unwise to go further this early in the game.

He needs to stop. I need to stop.

But my hands are holding his cheeks and jaw and finding every excuse to pull him closer and knead through his hair.

With a reluctant noise spawned at the back of his throat, he moves his kiss to a safer place—my forehead. He leaves it there, releasing bull's steam through his nose before finally removing his hands from my squishy body.

He wipes his mouth on his shoulder and turns to hide his face, dropping his head while clutching the rail. "*You have no idea how hard it was for me not to grab your tits just now.*"

About as hard as it is for me to remain standing, I'd bet.

"You're . . . a really good kisser," I swallow.

"I put away my extra tongue for you."

Blink. Blink. Blink.

"Kidding." He manages to toss me a smirk while catching his breath. "Fuuuck." He squeezes the rail. "I was kinda hoping it would be terrible. Make my life easier. But now?" He eyes me over like I'm some unexplained entity. "I mean, you felt that, right? That wasn't normal."

It felt about as good as my first orgasm.

"It was better than most," I admit, leaning against the opposite rail.

"Yeah, but like, *leagues* above. Like magical. And not in the human sense of, 'Ooh it's so magical.'" He mimics a *very* unattractive sounding girl. "I mean, like, *magical* magical. That felt supernatural. Is it because of our arrows? Is that what happens when tips touch?"

"Oh my god, don't talk about *touching tips* in front of me right now."

A smile finds him, crooked and wide.

"Come on, stop looking at me like that and let's go get that loan," I fire. "Figure out why I find you so *palatable*."

"You think that's part of it?" he muses. "Our attraction to one another? Part of why your soul is locked and why Mayree thinks we've met before?"

"It just seems like a lot of peculiarities. Too many to be unrelated."

He hesitates. "And you're sure you're okay with being my collateral?"

Should I be? Probably not.

Are her desires too complex for a breed like you?

It doesn't really matter if I beat the others. The truth is, they're firstborn purebloods, and I'm not.

But seriously, Vel? How sweet would it be if you were our new master?

Ugh. Since when did I become so *altruistic*.

"I'm sure, Velis."

This time, his hand settles on my back quite a bit lower than usual as he prepares to blink us away. "Okay. Put up your hood, and hide your eyes like before. Also, I think you're going to like it in here."

CHAPTER 11
Fool's Errand

I KISSED a genie and I liked it, and there's very little out there that could distract me from replaying the feel of it over and over and over in my head. One would be kissing him again. But two? Well, two would have to be something pretty shiny.

Luckily, we've materialized in just such a place.

Starkly painted walls contrast a floor that is darkest black and embedded with rows of gemstones the size of postcards. The walls dance with the refraction of rubies, emeralds, and sapphires, all lit to be extra sparkly, like the jewelry in a mall display case. The commanding clop of dress shoes brisks past, boasting the hurried importance of the people doing business in a place like this.

It feels like we're in the lair of a dragon, but, like, a *fancy* dragon.

Velis watches me gawk, with pleasure riding his lips, giving me a moment of absorption before escorting me to one of the chest-high counters where stands a young djinn teller with flowing blueberry hair and a brilliantly white smile.

"Young Laird Velis." The pretty girl shines with customer service. "We haven't seen you in months! Here to make a withdrawal from your estate funds?"

She seems to know him well. Maybe we're in his home country this time.

"Hi, Penn. No. I'm actually here for something else." Velis gets right down to business: "I need a loan."

The teller laughs. "A young Laird, needing a loan? Are you sure you aren't just here to ask me out again?"

The flue of my throat coughs.

Apparently, this djinn is a full-blooded one.

"It was one time, *Penn*," Velis parries, sending me a hurried glance. "And we were thirteen."

Ah. Well, that's better.

"And I'm not joking. I need a loan under my personal account. Nothing tied to the estate. I've brought collateral," he says, inching me forward.

I, the collateral, stiffen as the pretty djinn uses the end of her pen to inspect under my hood.

"Hm. Pretty low budget. And I'm guessing you don't have a permit for her, either?" she hums.

Excuse me, LOW BUDGET?

Velis flinches. "No permit. That's why I came to you, Penn. Think you can fudge the paperwork for me?"

"For you, Vel?" Penny bats her lashes sweetly. "NO. I have a reputation to uphold. Maybe one of your purebred brothers could give it a try. I'm sure we could find an accommodation for one of *them*."

Okay, but I'm still stuck on the low budget thing. I mean, I am lower middle class at best, but, what? Can she *smell* it on me?

Skulking darkness flares up around Velis. "Aw, *Penny, darling*, what happened? You didn't seem to mind my dirty blood the last time you invited me out back for a *quick one*."

This time, the flue of my throat clogs.

Penny snarls, "You must have mistaken the word 'trash' for something you identify with, *nymph*. That's the only thing I've ever offered to take out back around here."

"Penn, Penn, Penn. We could do this all day," says Velis,

unfazed. "But the outcome's going to be the same. I'm not asking you to do it for free. I know you better than that."

"Oh," she says, brightening. "Well, that changes things. Let me see what I can do for you, my young Laird."

She bounces away to collect documents from a carved cabinet behind the counter, and the 'young Laird' turns to me for damage control.

"I meant what I said before, Dolly. I don't like to fuck around with girls I'm not serious about. But sometimes they like to fuck around with me. For the record, I turned her down. I think that's part of the problem."

Part of it, but not all of it. "*For the record*, I don't like what's happening here."

Velis watches Penny flip through a stack of folders. "Yeah, me neither."

"There's blatant discrimination going on! How can you stand it? I want to punch that girl in the throat!"

Velis wrinkles his brow. "No, I meant I don't like putting your soul up for collateral. It sounded like an okay idea before, but now it just feels . . . You aren't an object, Dolly. I don't want you to feel like one."

Oh.

He's thinking about me?

And he's right. I may not have felt worth much these last few months, but . . . I know I'm not low budget. I know I'm worth more than being poked at by some bitch's pen.

"I'm not okay with it either. I know what I said, Velis, but—"

"You're allowed to change your mind. Screw all this. I have one more idea." He sweeps me away before Penny the racist can return.

In this world where human souls have a price and our bodies are just a means to an end, Velis has no problem seeing me as a person. Is it because he knows what it's like to be seen as something less?

"Velis? Is that how it is everywhere here? The bigotry?"

"No." He's preoccupied with reading street signs. "So you can stow that budding pity. This city is particularly hoity-toity. The other one I took you to is too. They call places like these the Uppers. Predominantly fullbloods and their kin. But there are plenty of other places in Makaya that are more liberal, where people don't care as much about your blood. It's just this stupid high-society bubble."

Hoity-toity. Explains why both cities were so clean and pretty. This is where the rich folk live.

"Well, I think it's wack. I don't see any difference between you and any other djinn we've met. Do you even share any qualities with your nymph side?"

"Mm, the biggest one is this." He glides his fingers back through his hair, compelling the strands to change.

"You're blond?!"

And damn if he doesn't look even hotter now.

"Surprise." He shows brief joy over my reaction before hurrying to change it back. "There's a constant enchantment on it to keep it that way. My father paid for it as soon as I started school."

"Anything else?"

"Mmm, I don't know, I can do this?" Without lifting his chin, he looks to the sky and lets out a few chirping whistles. A moment later, my cheeks wet with the delicate touch of snow falling directly over us.

"It's real this time, right?" I breathe, watching it kiss my palm and melt.

"It's real." He twinkles. "Nymphs can control the weather, and a lot of them specialize in a specific element like wind or water. All I can do are little party tricks like this." He makes his mouth a circle and shoots out a tiny burst of fire, like a baby dragon.

SICK.

"Well, not to show you up or anything, but look what I can do." I bend my thumb backward really, reeeeally far.

"I win." Smug, he takes a right at the next intersection. This is a different city from the one where we met Mayree, but the only way to tell is that the flowers coating the buildings are yellow instead of blue. An archway to our side drips a curtain of them. Velis tucks the golden strands out of the way with the back of his hand to clear a path for me. "Why don't you tell me about your real hidden talent, Master?"

"Fine," I sigh. "I can also blow smoke rings. Or at least I used to be able to."

"Not that." He gives his eyes a hard roll. "I mean your art."

"*You looked through my sketchbooks*?"

He shrugs. "What else was I supposed to do while I was waiting for you to wake up off the floor? I like to know what I'm getting myself into with a new master. Recon is totally normal by djinn standards."

"But not by human decency standards!"

He points to himself. "Not a human. And you're trying to distract me. I saw your drawings, Master. They were incredible. It seems you like drawing landscapes. You should do the salty place. And the faewood."

"I'm not that good," I mumble. "They're just doodles."

"Psh, who told you that?"

I don't answer him.

He halts. "Master, who told you they're just doodles?"

James did. But I can't bring myself to say it.

Velis frowns. "You know, I haven't heard a single good thing about that guy. He didn't like to travel, he made fun of your tattoo, he didn't support your art, and most importantly, he dumped you over something you don't even remember doing. So either you're skewing him, or he was kind of a tool. Which I don't get because you don't seem like someone that would stand for dating tools. You're so scrappy."

Mean. Spicy. Scrappy.

Easy to say from the outside looking in.

"Yeah, I've always been *scrappy*, but . . . you know how you give an inch and then before you know it, you've given a mile?"

"We use the metric system here, but go on." The end of the alleyway comes, spitting us into a busy thoroughfare.

"With James, it was really great at first. And then I got roped in with all his friends. And then, when it started to not be as great with James, I didn't want to lose what I had with everyone else. We'd fight sometimes, and I can hold my own, but he was the sort to never give in. So, for my own sanity, I just started dropping things. I've done a lot of thinking about it over the past twelve months. My life may have looked pathetic to you when you entered it, but I kind of feel like I was in a cocoon, resting, remembering myself. When I talk about being heartbroken, it's not necessarily for James; it's for all the things that went with him. And there's some guilt there about how I lost myself over the last few years. I feel like I finally have myself back, but there are moments when I don't. You've seen a few of those moments."

Wow. One kiss, huh? One kiss is all it takes to make me bare my soul to him? Suddenly we've gone from genie and master to genie and . . . girl who trusts genie enough to be completely vulnerable with him?

What the hell is wrong with me?

"I'm glad you cheated on him," Velis weighs in. "If that's even what happened."

"How can you think it isn't?"

"Because I've never met a person with so much restraint. Plus, you once threatened to cut my dick off if I touched you, and I think you meant it."

I did.

"Friggen' scary-ass woman," Velis mutters to himself, then politely to me: "In here, Master."

A pull of the heavy golden handles at the top of glistening white stairs takes us into a space where tall, airy curtains flutter against the pleasant breath of open windows, an overhead skybox inviting crisp daylight into the center of the room where a disc of blue light, similar to Velis's Ray, rests on display.

Only this one is the size of a hula hoop.

"What is this place?" I take a quick scan from under my flappy hood.

The blue light from the Ray in the center bounces off Velis's chin. "A message center. My brothers and I have our private messaging turned off on our Rays for the duration of the contest, but these master ones are synced up to all Rays and are allowed to be used for 'emergency purposes.'" He pauses. "It's risky, but I'm going to ask Beckham for help."

Beckham. The third triplet. A person I'm not super keen to meet.

"Are you sure that's a good idea?" I probe.

"Honestly? No. But I like it better than bartering you to the bank like some goat. Beckham and Arrik both worked as wish granters before all this, so they've got their own savings not tied to the estate. Arrik is out for obvious reasons, but I'm going to ask Beckham if he'll lend me some of his."

Okaaay, but—"Why would he do that when you're competing against one another?"

"He's more levelheaded than the other two. He knows I'm not a serious threat, and he's been working on winning the contest fairly, so when my win gets overturned, it'll likely go to him. Really, Arrik and Jeb should be focusing on amassing more souls than him instead of worrying about me, but neither can stand the thought of a breed winning."

"Please don't call yourself that."

His gaze lingers on me, but he says nothing before returning to the disc. Eyes reflecting brightly in the azure glow, his fingers tap rapidly in the air above. "This'll take a minute." He slips me his focus. "How are you holding up?"

I like that he's asking me things like that now.

"What?" he presses, catching my contagious expression. "I take it you're good?"

I want to kiss him again.

"I can feel that, you know." His smile turns roguish. "Of the dozens of masters I've had and all the desires I've pulled out of them, I've never felt one of them *throb* for me like that before. It's yummy."

He shouldn't be allowed to say words like 'yummy.'

He carries on with what he was doing, roguishness seeping.

Gawd, he's magnetic. And that neck. That tan, sinewy, bobbing . . .

"Interesting," he says, low. "It's isolated now, but not on a body part I can do much with. Are you sure that's the one you want?"

What, like I only get one?

"Tch, does your body even really look like that? Or is it all just an illusion like your hair?"

Velis twists fully to face me, head tipped. "Look like what, Master?" He gives it a moment without answer before prodding, "Master, look like what?"

He's such a shit. He knows exactly what he's doing. He's known it all along.

He winks. "This is all me, babe."

"Ugh."

But the 'babe' of it all doesn't seem so bad now. Can I be a feminist and still like the way it's starting to sound?

"Okay." Velis taps his pointer finger in the air over the disc. "It's done. I asked Beck to meet us tomorrow, so we have a little time to spare. Wanna get out of here?"

A rhetorical question, apparently. He doesn't give me a chance to answer before taking my elbow and blinking us somewhere new.

"V-Velis!"

A moment of absolute fear grips my chest as my stomach sinks to my knees, the distance looming below me like I'm walking a tightrope.

"Oh! You aren't afraid of heights, are you? You seemed fine at the faewood watchtower."

Yeah, but that place had a freaking railing!

"Shoot, I forget humans can be afraid of heights since if they fall, that's kind of it for them. Don't worry, if you fall, I'll just undo it." He gives his fingers a snap. "You're safe with me."

If I *fall*. I'd like to avoid *falling* in the first place.

If the cities known as 'Uppers' are formed like mountains, then Velis has transported us to the top of one such mountain.

Below, the stacks of a boxy city rise and fall like building blocks, decorated in sashes of buttercup flowers tossed effortlessly in warm, magical wind.

"It was just a little jarring." I push off him but allow his hand to stay on my hip for support as I remove my hood and let that same tepid wind pull through my hair.

I feel like the king of the mother-freaking mountain up here. Like I must have done something triumphant to have climbed so high.

"It's beautiful, Velis."

Maybe a little more so knowing it costs magic to teleport me around, and that he could have just dropped me into another hotel room like some sleaze.

"Oh." His eyes swim over me like he's trying to read me for deceit. "Good," he exhales. "I thought you might like it. Sorry I freaked you out."

Yellow streamers whip from poles dotted around the city, fighting to escape to the emerald fields beyond. I don't blame them. The world is so much bigger than they know. I would want to break free too.

Velis watches me shamelessly as I absorb a view I will surely never see again.

"You know, it's pretty funny to think of you becoming an influencer after getting to know you," he says, fondly enough to warm my cheeks. "To be honest, I wasn't trying very hard to read you back then. But now, it's fun to find your desires. Like digging through dirt for a speck of gold. Er, not that you're dirt. Just . . . your soul is all wispy and mysterious, and then every once in a while, I can grab a speck of insight."

So that's what it's like for him.

"Master?" Velis's voice is quiet enough that the wind might steal it. "I wanted to apologize for how I treated you early on. We go through training on how to handle certain types. I know I was a little . . ." He stops. "That's not me."

I've gathered that by now.

"You mean, you aren't an asshole?"

"Oh, no, I'm an asshole. Just not *that* big of an asshole."

"Ah." I show him my forgiveness. "That's okay. I'm an asshole too. But just, like, a moderate one."

"I can handle moderate. I kinda like moderate," he purrs.

All right. Based on all that twinkling, this does feel like a good time to make out, doesn't it? It feels like it's already starting. With him stepping closer and claiming my waist, with me pulling out the flirty eyes I've had packed away for some time.

His set jaw nears. My fingers slide.

And then he pounces.

And not in a sexy way.

"Get down!"

I land dangerously near the edge of the ledge, thrust by Velis's sudden tackle. An overcorrection, he quickly scrambles to keep me from losing my footing over the side as a flash of scarlet passes overhead.

A . . . bird?

It looks like a seagull but vibrantly red, circling against the blue sky with wings spread.

"He found a human to make a deal with already?" Velis eyes the bird with disbelief. "But he was just at the estate this morning!"

"Who?" I force myself around his protective grip as the bird makes another pass. "You mean Jeb? THAT's Jeb?! Did he transform himself?"

"What? No. That's his bird."

Even more shocking. "Jeb has a pet? And it's alive?"

"It isn't a pet; it's a device." Thoughts spasm across his brow. "Shit. It must have been Penny. She's so fucking desperate to get in with those guys. I'm sure Jeb's got all his minions on the lookout for us. Sorry, Master. I had a couple more places I wanted to show you, but it looks like we'll have to dip out of Makaya for now. You ready?"

He draws me to him, and the world blinks.

Only this time, it doesn't un-blink.

CHAPTER 12
Wet Swings

The darkness lasts a lot longer than all our previous times teleporting, as if it's gotten stuck.

"Velis?" My voice echoes.

"Hold on, Master," his voice echoes back. "Wait right here for me, okay? I'll be back soon."

What the hell?! He's going to leave me in the space between . . . stuff? Between his realm and mine?

"Don't panic," he says, sounding close and distant at the same time. "I know it's weird here, but you're safe. I'm going to zip back and take care of that bird real quick before we make the journey back to Earth. It will feel like hardly any time to you."

He's serious? But I can't feel anything or see anything. Not even myself.

"That bird is like a . . . what's the thing you have on Earth? A drone? If it caught sight of us teleporting, it will be able to tell where we're headed. I'm going to fake it out by popping into the goblin realm. You, ah, want any souvenirs?"

From the mother-freaking *goblin* world?

"I'm good," I say, curt.

"Yeah, you probably don't want anything from there. It's kinda nasty. It might get cold in here once I leave. Humans aren't meant to travel alone. But I promise I'll be back. Don't let it get to you, okay? The cold, I mean."

The cold?

I understand what he means only after he's gone.

Before, I could feel his presence with me. Now, I feel nothing.

And it's a terrible thing to feel nothing again after feeling something. Cold isn't quite the right word for it. Emptiness. Loneliness. To exist without senses is . . .

This is the most like an actual piece of paper I've ever felt.

Whatever. I can handle a few minutes of anything, right? A few minutes is nothing.

But a few minutes OF nothing?

It's hollowing.

There's something I haven't been able to put my finger on since meeting Velis. A reason I continued to humor all this long after my boredom was quenched. I understand it now, in the absence of everything else.

I feel good when I'm with him. Not just that it feels good to be with him—*I* feel good. I feel good about myself.

And I think he feels good about himself too.

And that feels, at least, like a small, mighty flame against the chill of nothing.

I let it burn in me, pushing away the onset of dark tides until Velis's warmth invades the cold once more. "Okay, Dolly. I'm back. Sorry. I just wanted to make sure we wouldn't be followed. Are you okay?"

"I'm fine."

"I've learned not to trust women when they say those words in that order," says his disembodied voice, suspect.

"I'm not fine?" I try.

"Better."

Like a hiccup, we're back in the human world, at a park not far from my apartment. It feels good to be able to see and touch and . . . smell?

"Oh my god, Velis! You REEK!"

"Yeeeah, goblin realm. Hold on—" He shakes his head. "Better?"

I take a hearty sniff. Yes, his natural scent is much better than whatever piss that was.

"A slight improvement," I tell him. "Did you get the bird thing figured out?"

"Sure did," he says, releasing me. "That device isn't smart enough to follow multiple jumps. It won't know where we ended up. Is this place okay? Figured it might be a little skeevy to just bring you back to the hotel."

"Well, it's no mythical sex club, but it'll do," I say, to his obvious delight.

It smells like it rained again today. The muted river stones bordering the landscaping are glossed over with liquid, and the playground slide pools at the bottom with water. In the human world, it's early evening, though it seems much later, with the sky heavy and infused with tones of green. The rubber swings hang lambent with rainy residue. The air is excited over the quiet of a world gone inside, the atmosphere deep and cool.

It sets chills on my skin.

In truth, this is the sort of setting that invigorates me.

But it's so quiet, still, the wet ground harboring secrets of the day and all the feet passed over it. It feels like a place puppy-love-stricken high schoolers would go for a morsel of privacy.

I find one of the swings, too small for my thighs, wet enough to soak into my leggings, and grasp the cold, slick chain. Velis leans against the swing's post and folds his arms.

"Isn't that device made for children?"

"Children . . . twenty-four-year-olds . . . whomever."

He straightens. "You're twenty-four?"

"As of last month. Why? How old are you?"

"Two hundred and fourteen."

The swing can barely contain me. "Seriously?!"

"No," he says, evil. "I'm twenty-two."

"Oh my gosh, good. Because I always thought it was creepy in supernatural romances when the male specimen is, like, five hundred in the body of a teenager. I am definitely not mature enough for that business." I eye him over. "But you're only twenty-two? Aww, you're a *baybeee*." I pretend to inspect him for flaws. "I don't usually date guys who are younger than me."

"Date?" He tips his head like he doesn't know the meaning of the word.

"Er, court?"

The minute I say it is the minute I wish I could take it back. We've admitted to our crushes. We've given in to tasting one another. But neither of those things means any sort of commitment. And it's ridiculous to think it does. He's a *genie* from a *magic lamp* trying to grant me *wishes* so that he can *steal my soul*. Plus, he's already told me he can't have a future with me. Not to mention that I'm likely rebounding.

"Not that I want to date you," I recover.

Velis's face doesn't so much as spasm. "Oh."

Well, shit! Did he want me to want to date him?!

"Then is *this*"—he motions between the two of us—"all physical for you?"

And he doesn't look like he wants me to answer one way or the other.

"I'm . . . not sure," I say.

"That isn't me fishing for anything. I just want to understand your expectations. Every time I feel your desire for me, it feels so . . ." He shivers: "*Raw*. Besides my rockin' bod—"

"*Pick a different word.*"

His mouth twitches. "Besides my *physique*, are you looking for something more from me? You were so committed to that pact of yours, it didn't seem like anything could break it. I mean, you cried over one friggen' fry. So for you to go all in on that kiss back there, I just want to know if there's more to it, or if this is just you finally deciding to indulge."

It's a bit abnormal for a person who looks like him to be initiating 'the talk' after just one kiss, isn't it?

Or is that my unconscious bias assuming he should act one way because he looks like a fuckboy? It makes sense. That Rayana chick used him for his body at the club. And Penn the bank teller was trying to do the same thing. He lost one girlfriend because he wasn't upfront with her.

It seems he might be trying to protect himself *and* me.

"Velis, I wish you'd go first."

"Not cool, Dolly!" he reproaches, eyes lit.

I mean, if there were ever a time to pull that card . . .

"Ugh, fine. I take it back. Wish revoked. But it may take me a minute to figure it out. To be honest, I haven't had time to consider what I'm doing here myself."

"Take your time," he says quietly. "No judgment."

I dig my shoes into wet gravel and take a deep breath of repose. "I mean, I think it's more for me than just the chemistry between us, Velis. I feel like myself when I'm around you. Like my real self. The one I lost when I moved out here for college. I feel like you've built me up a bit by blabbing out things through that honesty oath you didn't mean to say, and it feels good. It's not that I'm relying on you to hold me up, but you sort of reminded me how to hold myself up. Bantering with you makes me feel sexy and sharp, and I think I needed that to finish healing after all these weeks."

There's more.

"Also . . . I admire you. I admire how hard you're working to beat those assholes, and the fact that you aren't super jaded or broken from the hardships you've been dealt. You just roll with it, and to me, that's a show of strength. The minute I saw how those servants at your estate interacted with you, I knew you were secretly a quality person. You can't force that kind of loyalty. It comes to those who deserve it."

Oh no.

"I like that you have goals, even if I'm literally effing all of them up by being in your life. I like that you can do freaking *magic*. I like that you have been tending to my needs this whole time, knowing you wouldn't get anything in return. That camera you produced at the salt flats, showing me beautiful things because you know I appreciate them, holding me whenever I craved it, taking care of me when I was high as balls . . ."

Yeah. I, um. My like for him is growing.

"That last one's a big one. I went through something in my past that made me feel unsafe in my own body, but you've become mindful of it, acknowledging the times when you were insensitive of it. You even protected me from myself when I couldn't function on my own, and the same can't be said about the last guy I was in a position like that with."

He's stiff, his expression tight.

"I like flirting with you. I like finding out more about you. I am *devastatingly* attracted to your physical appearance. And every time you touched me, grazed me, held me over the past few days, it felt like there was a pulse between us that was something beyond reality. I've never felt so much sexual tension in my whole damn life, and when we finally kissed? It was *majestic*—and I'm *not* an inexperienced person. There's just something about you, Vel. I didn't want to like you, and I kind of hate myself for giving in to it, but I do. I like you, Velis, and I may not have realized how much until just now."

Oh god. I can't look at him. The weight of all that coming out is too much. For how still the air is, it seems a single breath might end up a torrent. Why am I so desperate to fall in love? I'm not. That's the last thing I want.

"I guess I didn't really answer your question, did I?" I say, disturbed by my own feelings.

Velis stares at me, unblinking, through that withholding, blizzard-like gaze, until—

"Dolly." He falls to his knees in the muddy wet below me and wraps his arms around my middle.

"Velis?!"

He nuzzles his head in my chest. "I think you love me."

"NO." I push him off. "I definitely don't love you, Velis."

He's cooing at me. "I think you're starting to."

"Again, no." I wriggle to get away from him. "And quit

distracting me! I just told you sooo many nice things about yourself! You owe me at least a few!"

He shrugs. "You're hot."

"*Not good enough.*" I ramp back on the swing as if I mean to crash into him and hold myself there.

"I'm just giving you shit." He stands and approaches the back of the swing to toss his arms around my neck and set his chin into the nape of my shoulder. "I like you in a courting kind of way too."

Oh, thank christ.

"What can I say? You're a spunky, unapologetic little dork who isn't afraid to stand up for herself and call others out on their bullshit. You're determined and funny. And for how broken you think you are, you still allow yourself to be amazed. Hell, I want to take you places I've visited a million times just to see that stupid, cute look on your face. A person can't experience beauty the way you do without leaving themselves vulnerable, and after what you've been through, that takes a lot of courage." He nuzzles against me, lowering his voice to a volume not meant to leave my hair. "You're adorable, Master, and ever since the first moment I touched you, it's all I've wanted to do. But there's more to it than that. It's refreshing to be around someone who doesn't think to acknowledge my blood. There are plenty of people that like me in spite of it, but you're the only one who seems to like me because of it. You make me feel like I deserve to win this thing, and it's just nice to have the person at my side be *on* my side for once."

I know the feeling.

His tone falls gray as he pulls away, hands directly above mine on the steely chains supporting my weight. "Which is why it sucks that you're human. Admitting my feelings to you doesn't mean my plans have changed. At some point, I need to find a full-blooded girl and convince her to marry me. It's the only hope for my bloodline. But . . ." He sets his forehead to the back of my head. "I can't seem to stop myself. So I guess I also fail at answering the question."

The question as to what we are hoping to get out of this.

"I know you deserve more than what I can give you, and I

don't like putting effort into things that are destined to fail. But I want you, Master. I want you as if you were an actual girl."

"I am an actual girl."

"Crap. I meant like a djinn girl. Biffed it at the end, huh?"

Biffed or not, I'm not used to guys being so honest with me, and I don't think it's necessarily a result of his truth oath.

I tip my head back on the swing to show him my face. "This doesn't have to be hard, genie boy. I was locked in a messy relationship recently enough that I'm not ready to commit to another one. I don't want anything serious, which is why—*and I'll stress this*—I have no intention of falling in love with you. I'm good with like if you are."

There is the quiet dribble of a lonely wind gust blowing old raindrops out of leaves. He eyes me over, a swallow dipping his throat, as his hands support my heavy head. "Yeah," he says. "I'm good with like."

But the moment he sets his mouth to mine, it feels like the cosmos is working against us.

WHY does it feel so good to kiss him?

I twist the swing to meet him face on, pulling my fingertips down his warm cheek and letting him drink me in. To be looked at that way is magical in its own right. It's *awakening*. He's seeing me in new light, as something he can touch and hold, as someone it's okay to be soft with. The earth below us is moist and loamy, the sky above dense and dim. Velis draws his eyes upward, and after, I feel the temperate kiss of spring sunlight. Though the sun is long hidden, Velis has used his nymph side to create a funnel of warmth around me.

"Showoff," I whisper, my eyes locked on his.

The end of this arrangement is going to hurt. If not one of us, it'll be both.

But I've overcome hurt before. And for all the months in solitude I tried to repent and heal, being told I have nothing to repent for may be the stickiest band-aid of all.

I was branded a slut. Told I get too frisky when I drink by a person who always drank more than me. Saddled with all the blame for something I don't remember because I looked the part. Because it had to have been my body's fault. Because everybody likes Gabe.

Velis may not be perfect. He may have had a few things to apologize for over our hours together. But never once has he thought of me as a cheater.

It feels good to have the person at my side be on my side.

For once.

"We have until tomorrow, right?" I say. "Is it okay if we cuddle again tonight?"

Judging by that *gleam* of his, there's nothing he wants more. He sets a hand to my shoulder and removes us from the park with a blip.

"We've kind of done this all out of order, haven't we?" he mentions while crawling onto a bed thoroughly pre-checked for bedbugs. I really, really love that he's just accepted it as a normal part of his nightly routine. The next human he comes to a hotel with is going to think he's a bit of a freak, and I'm here for it. Call it a lasting impact.

"Oh?" I feign surprise. "I assumed this is the way it normally goes when dating mythical creatures."

"I prefer the term *legendary*." He's propped up on one arm, bearing the mien of a conniver. I'm no expert on desire, but it seems like he wants something and like he's considering acting on that something. That something ends up being a kiss to the tip of my nose.

He's actually a sweet genie. Secretly sweet.

"Why are you looking at me like that, Master?" he asks, mouth matching the spread of mine.

"No reason. Go to bed. You aren't getting any," I say and turn away with a hearty reposition of my pillow before I can show him the softness surely betrayed through my eyes.

"H-hey!" he protests, muttering, "I didn't expect any."

"Good."

But I'm grinning enough for it to show in my voice. This is the most schoolgirl crush I've had in a very long time.

"You're so mean, Dolly Jones." He says it like an endearment as he kisses my shoulder goodnight before compelling the lights to darken. And then he slides up behind me and hooks his arms around me to pull me close.

The first time we cuddled, I was unconscious.

The second time, he kept me locked in that sweaty onesie.

This time, though, I feel the shape of his body as it curls around mine protectively like a sentinel. I feel the frisk of his fingertips as they move up my thigh before slipping around my squishy middle. I feel the nuzzle of his mouth against the flat part of my shoulder.

He is secretly a very sweet genie.

Easily, he could move those hands and transition this moment into something else. Easily, he could play off our chemistry to turn the moment carnal.

But he doesn't. He holds me as if he appreciates being able to do so. My ex wasn't a cuddler; he got hot when he slept. But I've always felt safe being held in the night when demons roam free.

I love it. Based on the happy groan Velis allows himself as he settles in, he does too.

How is this the same person that was spearing pens at me just days ago?

He isn't sleeping. I'm not sleeping. And that damn air conditioner is at it again. I suppose I can't complain too much. We aren't official patrons of the hotel, and it gives us an excuse to snuggle closer. He's warm, his arms strong and defined, his skin a bit waxy in a way that makes me think of sex, like if I dug my fingertips into his back, they would have no problem gripping. He's so . . . boyish. Like a lost boy or a pirate rogue.

Or, you know, a twenty-something *genie*.

God, how is any of this real? And how have I come to the point of acceptance? I find his hand around my stomach and weave my fingers through it, to which he flexes his approval and rewards me with another kiss—this one to the neck.

It would be so easy to roll over him, claw at him, hold him

down and move my hips in ways I haven't in months. But, right now, this is what I desire most.

He must feel a pulse from me. He complies by reinforcing his hold around me. The *genie* complies by hugging me tighter.

It isn't difficult to let myself drift into the warmth and safety I feel from him.

Somewhere, in the middle of the night, I feel chill on my back and roll over to find him gone, a thin sliver of light from the bathroom tattling that he's inside.

You know, I never thought to ask how he does that stuff while stowed in his vessel. I've seen him eat and drink too, yet he went two weeks without while locked inside? Maybe he's like a camel. Or maybe his bodily functions turn off while he's dormant. It seemed like his brothers could only locate him once out of that state. A question for tomorrow, maybe.

I hear the sound of the sink shutting off, and I quickly return to my former position, pretending to be asleep.

Why? No idea. It just feels like the proper response. The soft patter of his footsteps takes him to the edge of the bed, where he seems to stop and contemplate the reality of spending yet another night in bed with his human 'master.'

"Fuck, this is crazy," he whispers to himself. "What am I doing?"

Second thoughts? Regrets? Take-backsies?

Apparently not. I feel the weight of him sinking in beside me, skimming his fingers near the strap of my tank top, the warm of his breath letting me know he's about to kiss the edge of my ear.

"Little spitfire," he says with the gentlest chuckle.

We're the same. He doesn't want to like me, but he can't deny it. He knows this is going to hurt us in the end, and he's deemed me worth it.

It will be okay. We're both survivors, and we'll both survive this. At least for a little while, we can allow ourselves the sin of comfort. I wait for his breathing to grow heavy before I allow my own to follow suit.

CHAPTER 13

Companion Hat

The morning comes sharply, like being flung into a cold lake. But if this bed is a lake, that's one hot lifeguard.

"Good morning, *Master*."

Ummm, why is he saying my name like that?

He's hanging over me, his hands pressed into the pillow at either side of my head, looking like he wants to *play*.

"What do you want?" I grouch, knowing I always look a mess when I wake up.

Maybe I spend my nights wrestling demons I bred myself.

"I found out a secret about you," the self-satisfied genie purrs.

"Well, if anyone could, it would be an invasive person like you," I grunt.

"Oh-ho-ho-no, I didn't even have to work for this one. You offered it on your own." His expression vents darkness. "Not only do you coo in your sleep, you also BABBLE. You called me your hottie with a bott-ley."

Velis can't lie to me, so I know it's true. I punish him for hearing it with an angry pillow to the face.

"Look at you, you little pun monger," he muffles against the pillow.

"That wasn't me. It was the vengeful spirit that possesses me on odd nights of the week."

He sets the pillow down morosely. "You shouldn't joke about that, Master. My best mate at university was possessed by a spirit. Made him eat in the middle of the night. Poor dude gained forty pounds by second year."

"I'm waiting," I say, flat.

His mouth begins to pull against his teeth, though he tries to fight it. "For what?"

"You're compelled to say you're kidding, so I'm just waiting for that to happen."

Slowly, he starts to look like someone who's been holding their breath for too long, and when he can no longer stand it: "I'm kidding!" he blurts.

Now it's my turn to be self-satisfied.

The pillow lobs into me. "Ugh, no fair. It's getting harder to mess with you. You're learning too fas—"

He's cut off by another assailing pillow to the jaw. This time, retaliation comes in the form of a pounce, and in the aftermath, his hands are on my shoulders, one of his knees between my legs.

And he's eyeing my mouth like he wants to kiss me.

But *now*? My mouth is less than appetizing.

Is he one of those guys that likes to make out, morning plaque and all? Because I can't get down with that.

And then, akin to a spearmint gum commercial, a blast of icy freshness hits my mouth like I'm standing on top of a minty Mount Everest.

The perks of dating a genie in tune to my desires.

Velis winks, and then he begins his descent, hesitating at the last moment to smile with his eyes closed.

"That's so weird," he whispers. "Good weird. Feeling desire focused on me. I love it, Dolly."

I'm not sure if that counts as narcissism or not. And I find it hard to believe that none of his former 'masters' thought he was hot. But I do know I love the way my desire makes him shiver. I love holding that sort of power over him. Maybe I do have sadist tendencies after all.

I take him captive and pull him down the rest of the way.

Velis was right. It's magical. To feel his hand slide up the side of my ribs. To feel him restraining his body as I bite his lip. It feels good. It feels natural. It feels exciting. And it makes it all too easy to bloom into something more. His fingers nudging at my clothes. My hands inviting his hips closer. The organic progression of two bodies drawn together. I want his sweat. I want to hear his throat whimper. I want to go crazy on him.

Is this what they call magnetism?

If so, it's dangerous. With him, it would be easy for things to move too quickly. But after what I've been through, I need to protect myself. I should *want* to protect myself. My integrity means something.

There's a me inside that is small and vulnerable. It warrants guarding. As things begin to heat, I set a hand against Velis's warm, beating chest and kiss him a kiss that tastes final, hoping his reaction isn't a break-it moment.

"Yeah," he says when he realizes I'm putting a stop to it. "Probably a good idea." His mouth pushes into my cheek with care before he slips off me and to the edge of the bed. "Sorry if I got too . . . Sorry."

"You didn't get too anything," I tell him. "I was worried I might."

"Yeah," he says, glancing back at me. "It's . . ."

Intense. The word he's looking for is *intense*.

"Shit." He smooths his hands over his face and hair. "It's like fuckin' fire, Dolly. I'm worried about crossing your boundaries, so be vocal with me, okay? I may not be able to commit to anything serious, but I'm not a skeeve either."

"I would never let you cross my boundaries," I tell him, and I mean it.

He smiles slightly. "You'd sooner cut off my cock."

Damn straight.

Soon, that smile gives way to musing. "Why IS it like that? Is it because you're human? I know Arrik has a thing for humans, but I just thought it was because they were easy." He's quick to backtrack: "N-not that you're easy."

It's become one of my favorite things—being overtly studied with those unnatural eyes of his. Like I'm a da Vinci or Monet. Like he's trying his hardest to see below my surface, understand what makes me appealing.

I want to get tangled up in that look.

But not today. I kiss him once more to see the way he longs for me afterward, and then—"Come on. Let's get ready to meet your brother."

Am I a tease? I'm not trying to be. This is just me taking what I can without taking too much. Ours will be a short-lived relationship. Best to savor it before it runs out.

When we return to Makaya, the sun is cheerful, the sky unblemished by cloud or haze. According to Velis, he asked Beckham to meet us on the outskirts of their family's property, along the banks of a small lake without a name. Plush moss that pushes like sponge under each step circles the clear, lapping water, which looks like a sheen of crystal covering a floor of polished green gems the size of pebbles.

"You should take one of those." Velis nods. "They turn pink when brought to the human world."

They turn *pink*?

Apparently, in the djinn realm, alexandrite is as common as a river rock.

As I pluck a gem worth more than my mother's house from a basin of purest water, Velis paces, planning out what to say to his brother to convince him to lend us enough power to investigate the lock on my soul.

"The most cost-effective way would be to wish me back in time to observe when the lock was placed, but that's going to take a hefty volt, and Beckham's gonna want interest on whatever he lends me," Velis speculates. "He won't do it for an even exchange."

So even the most reasonable among them would try to take advantage of the situation.

I hold the gemstone to the sky to let the foreign sun breathe life into it, catching my cheek in the shine. "You can't change the past, though, right? That's one of the rules?"

"Not just a rule, an impossibility. The past wouldn't change even if I tried to alter it. It's like watching a film in four dimensions. I can observe, but I can't interact. And I've only done it twice. One of my masters wanted me to go back and find out who started a rumor about her, and another wanted me to take her back to see the concert of a now disbanded music group."

Well, that opens up a world of possibilities. What would I go back in time to see if I could? Or would I rather get a glimpse of what lies ahead?

Velis anticipates it. "Like I said, those kinds of wishes are expensive, and to be honest, not worth it. You get a lot more bang for your buck if you stick to your own time." He taps his temple. "Insider tip."

Noted.

"But what about you?" I ask. "If you wanted, could you use some of your savings to pop into the future for a little peek? I mean, if you've got dozens of souls' worth of power at your disposal."

"First of all, I would never want to look into the future for 'a little peek' because it's terrifying and djinn who have gone into the future usually come back fucked up. Second of all, no. Not sure if you've noticed, but the other djinn we've been around haven't been using much magic. Soul power is precious, so the only time it's really used in excess is for the purpose of getting more—i.e. when being used on humans. Only wish granters or those with special permission are allowed to convert anything but a small allowance to magic. The rest of it is used for essential services like powering our cities and healthcare, or to circulate within our economy."

"So, is it like a trickle-down thing? You get to keep all of what you earn in the human world and then you spend it to disperse it to non-wish granters? Why wouldn't everyone want to become a wish granter in that case?"

Velis breaks his pacing. "You really care about all this,

Master?"

"I mean, if my soul's going to be used for money by some mythical race, I'd at least like to know how it works."

"Of course you would." Amusement piqued, Velis settles onto the moss edged up to the sloshing banks of the water and invites me to do the same. "Lots of people would like to be wish granters, but not everyone can do it. The first reason is that you have to go to school to learn how to read desires, and the training is expensive. The second is that vessels are made of a rare substance called Drake Rock that was mined dry eons ago. New vessels aren't being made, so most of them are family heirlooms passed down from generation to generation. Only those with a family legacy can afford to become a wish granter. My father insisted we all go to school for it, even though Jeb and I don't intend to do it long term." He pauses to run through all the questions I've asked him. "And no, nowadays, wish granters keep very little of what we farm out in the human world. We have to pay super high taxes in order to ensure there's enough to go around. Most people do it to carry on their family legacy, build a bit of wealth, and because it's fun."

Fun. You know, *stealing* human souls.

"Demon."

He points at his own chest. "Not a demon."

His dimples say otherwise.

"So, what were you doing before the contest started, then? That 'other job' you mentioned when I first met you?"

"Stripper."

"You need to start out wearing clothes before you can begin to take them off. Next."

"I'm compelled to tell you that was, indeed, a joke." He grins. "I was a healer's apprentice. That's what I want to be in the future. I've been studying doom diseases, the ones that can't be cured with magic."

So Vel the genie wants to become a doctor?

You know, it would be really nice if I could have ONE wholesome thought without immediately picturing him in a lab coat seductively telling me to say 'ahhh'!

Come to think of it, I had a really, reeeally hot dentist back home, and it was the best motivator for staying on track with my cleanings. Every time I went in, I would lie there, mouth hanging and drool dripping, while he probed around inside my mouth. And when he complimented me on my home care? Oh yes.

Velis sniffs. "Geez, try to contain your desires, would you?"

He can tell that, for once, they aren't directed at him.

"My genie is jealous," I croon to myself.

"Psh." He looks away. "I can look inside your mouth too, if that's what you're into. Humans are weird."

I laugh because *that's* his takeaway.

"By the way, what's *your* occupation, Master? All I know is that it involves a place you don't desire to return to."

Nothing so noble as curing incurable diseases. "I work in an office where I monitor fraud."

"Fraud?"

"Insurance fraud. It's . . . not anything you'd care to hear about. It's extremely boring. We get one or two exciting cases per quarter. Other than that, it's just checking reports, sending emails, and watching the numbers on the clock move backward."

"Time moves backward there?!" he jolts.

I narrow my eyes at him, unsure whether he's being sincere or 'schmoozing.'

Schmoozing, as it turns out. That damn glint in his eye.

I'm beginning to suspect he knows far more about the human world than he lets on.

Little shit.

"Well, is monitoring insurance fraud what you want to do?" he asks, hugging his knees and watching the reeds around the pond sway. "Like, forever?"

No. "It pays the bills."

"Yeah, I saw that," says he, the snooper. "But that's not what I asked. Is that what you went to school for?"

No. "I ended up with a business degree."

"Ended up with? What did you start out with?" he pries.

The otherworldly breeze ripples the water.

"Dolly?" Velis pushes.

For some reason, this answer comes even more reluctantly than when I admitted that I cheated on James.

"Art," I say, eyes downcast. "I moved out west because of their art program."

Velis blinks at me. And then he storms to his feet.

"Fucking hell, Dolly! I knew it! I knew you could draw! Let me guess—your ex told you you were crap, so you dropped out? Why would you do that? You seem so strong and stubborn, so why'd you let a guy like that walk all over you?!"

Walk *all over me*? What kind of battered woman does he think I am?!

It's my turn to bolt up from the ground.

"Fuck you, Velis! And fuck this narrative you're building! I would never drop out of a program I loved because a MAN told me to! How weak do you think I am? Yes, James and I had issues. Yes, he was kind of an unsupportive jerk, but the reason I dropped the art program is because I was struggling financially and I realized I couldn't travel and do all the things I wanted to do with an art degree!"

"Oh."

"Yeah, OH. I got an internship with my current company, and it paid well, and they told me they'd hire me on if I got a suitable degree, so I made the hard decision to do it, and it fucking sucked because all I ever wanted to do was become an illustrator! But you can't just wave a magic wand and make your dreams come true! Life is about hard work and sacrifice, and for me it was travel or art, and I picked travel, okay? The decision was mine, and screw you for thinking it wasn't!"

He doesn't retaliate. He doesn't fire back. He waits for my chest to stop rapidly rising and falling and for red to stop showing in my eyes before he ventures quietly:

"But you haven't traveled at all."

The pressure of the heavens falls on my shoulders.

"N . . . no," I admit to the crushing weight.

"Well, that sucks."

Whatever breeze there was, it's gone silent, listening to our drama.

"Oh my god, I'm sorry." I clutch my mouth. "I'm sorry I freaked out. That wasn't about you, Velis. I clearly have so many issues and shouldn't be getting involved with anyone right now."

Shit. One day into this thing and I'm already screwing it up.

Velis shakes his head. "No, I'm the one that got fired up first. I shouldn't have assumed it had to do with your ex. It's my job to fix people's lives. I keep forgetting you don't need me to fix yours. I need to take off my wish granting hat and put on my companion hat."

That wasn't a deal breaker for him?

"You're allowed to freak out, Dolly. I have issues too. And like I said before, it's nice to have someone on my side for them. I'll try to be better about being on your side too."

Oh my gosh, he's actually really sweet and maybe way too nice for me.

"I gotta say," he continues, "it is cool to see you have that much passion. You really love drawing, huh?"

I know he's an empath, but how is he so *empathetic*? How can such a mischievous little bastard secretly be so . . .

"M-Master? What's wrong?!"

"You're too nice for me."

"Ha!" he blats. "Are you kidding? I'm not *nice*."

"You are! You're looking at me really sweetly right now, and I just feel like a callous rock. This is the third time you've come to meet me halfway after an argument, and I just don't know how to respond to that. It's like I only have two modes now: cave or fight to the death."

"Dolly . . ." His hand is on my shoulder. "You've been sweet to me too. Legit, some of the things you told me last night are things no one has ever said to me before. It may come naturally to you, but most people don't look at me the way you do. I know you're spicy, and I know you have some shit to figure out. I do too. Neither of us is well equipped for what's going on here. But I like you, and I'm all in for as long as this lasts, okay? You remind me of a fire that fights to burn even after being doused, and it's admirable as hell. I want to see you burn brighter. And I want to burn brighter too."

What is happening here? I don't believe in insta-love. In fact, it's one of my least favorite tropes. And I also believe that the things that burn hottest are the first to burn out.

So why does this all just feel so . . .

It's like it hurts.

I settle into him, fit against him like I'm a missing piece, and the rigid edges of me soften as though they have no other choice but to become one with him.

"I'll be better about being on your side too," I promise. "I'll find a balance between sticking up for myself and berating you."

"I'll work harder not to give you a reason to stick up for yourself," he says into my hair.

This isn't an amorous hug. This is a comforting hug. Just two shirts, two chests, two heartbeats pressed together, acknowledging one another.

Maybe arrows are real.

Maybe this feeling is inevitable.

"I like you, Vel," I find myself whispering as though I can't stop it.

He squeezes me tighter as he exhales against me. "I like you too, babe."

Velis kisses my forehead, and I set my ear to his collar, and together, we stand in the squishy moss with calm, glimmering waters at our side and the warmth of day setting into our skin. It's nice to have someone mature enough to know when an argument has run its course. It's nice not to be alone. We're in such a captivating place, with the sun reflecting off the crystalline water as actual crystals shimmer below, and yet I can't keep myself from closing my eyes and cozying up against him.

"Vel?" an amused voice interrupts our peace. "Is that a *human* you're embracing?"

Enter the last of the triplets.

CHAPTER 14

Triple Threat

Velis and I unhand each other and spin to find the person who has been watching us for god knows how long. A person with those same light-colored eyes but with a much more good-natured feel to them than his triplet counterparts. A person with that same shade of dark blue in his hair but with a haircut far more effortless than the others. And he's got a short layer of scruff around his muzzle—just enough to make him look like the rugged star of a cologne commercial. His mouth holds a natural curl, unlike Jeb's cruel jeer, unlike Arrik's seductive simper. He looks like a bit of a trickster.

"Beckham!" Velis exclaims with obvious relief.

Beckham, apparently, laughs. "Why do you sound so surprised, bro? You're the one who told me to meet you here."

. . . Bro?

Well, these two clearly have a much different relationship than the others. And also—

"Dude," says Velis, eyeing him over. "What the hell are you wearing?"

Sheeny pants, a short open vest, and weird booties that curl at the toe.

He's wearing a full-on genie costume?!

"Huh?" Beckham looks down at himself. "Oh! Ha, yeah, I just finished a job. One of my earlier masters ordered it for me on the inner nets, and I decided to keep it. It works great for disarming."

Um, that would be *internet*.

"Woah!" Velis nods his approval. "That's brilliant!"

"Ha, yeah. But no stealing my tricks, bro." Beckham pats Velis on the back before waving his fingers over his chest to morph his outfit into a stretchy denim jacket and loose T-shirt paired with black jeans and a stocking cap. No longer an advert for a Halloween store, he now looks like the front man for an indie band.

"You gonna introduce me to your friend, Vel? She is a human, right?" Beckham offers me his hand and a crooked little smile. "Hey, human, I'm Beck. Vel's oldest brother."

Vel nudges me forward like I'm meeting a mother-in-law. "This is Dolly, my current master."

"Ah, thought she might be." Beck scoops up the hand I give him, bringing it to his mouth and bowing low while keeping his eyes locked on mine the entire time. "Pleased to know you, Master Dolly."

So, he's the charmer of the bunch.

"Wanna tell me what you're doing with her in Makaya, bro? You know, we typically discourage bringing human girls home with us." He shoots me a wink as he releases my hand.

"I know." Velis is adrenalized. "We ran into a bit of a snag, and I don't know who else to ask for help. I need to borrow some of your balance—not your contest balance, obviously, but your savings balance. Dolly has a lock on her soul, and we need to figure out how to break it. She doesn't remember how or when it was placed, but as it stands, none of us can siphon her. Arrik and Jeb tried too."

"You're thinking a time travel wish to figure out how it got there?" Beckham whistles. "That'll be expensive, Vel. I see why you need my help." Taking a minute to decide, his eyes flick between the two of us before ultimately landing on me. "Sure. As long as I can make a little profit off the deal, I don't mind helping you out."

Wait, really?

Maybe he really is more reasonable than the other two. Maybe he doesn't mind giving Velis a little boost because they both know it won't count in the end.

"For real?" Velis's face lights. "Thanks, Beck! That would be a huge help. I considered taking out a loan on her, but Dolly and I have become friendly, and it sort of didn't feel right, you know?"

Friendly.

"Yeah, I saw you were being *friendly* with her. That's . . . interesting. Assuming it's a good story, but that can wait." Beckham scans over the coolly rippling pond like he's checking for fish. "Before we do this, though, I have to ask—are you sure it's what you want? Seems like kind of a lot of effort."

A shiver strikes the back of my neck.

Because there's something in the way he says it. Something that brings me back a year or more. A tone I've heard before, buried under kindness.

"Look, I hear you've been working hard the last few months, but you know Dad's not gonna let you win, right? And you definitely don't want either of those guys to win. So why not just hand your balance over to me right now? Then you won't need to worry about unlocking this human's soul, and you can just enjoy a week or two of freedom before going back to the estate. That's what I'd do."

He says it so off-handedly, like the idea just came to him. Like he's looking out for Vel's best interest.

And yet . . .

Maybe you should be the DD tonight, hon. You know how you get when you drink. And all the guys are going to be there. We don't want to give Fallon a reason to spread more shit about you.

I've heard that tone before, felt it poke and prick and gaslight.

Hey, are you sure you want to enter that contest? You know I believe in your doodles, hon, it's just, this is big-time stuff. I can't stand the thought of seeing you disappointed.

My aching intuition grows as Velis's mood darkens. "I'm sure, Beck. This is what I want. I know it's pointless."

I know it's pointless.

I know it's pointless.

I know it's pointless.

Beckham holds up his hands. "Hey, I get it. Just as long as you know where you stand. I'd hate to see you beaten down after all this. You've been through enough, you know? But if you're sure, mind if I have a quick talk with your human? I'd like to figure out how much this wish is going to cost. Might help to get a fresh pair of eyes on her soul, and I sense you might be clouding her up a bit."

He gives me another of those disarming winks, as if that's all it takes to gain a person's trust.

"Of course. Master, you okay with that?"

Velis shows no fear at the thought of leaving me alone with the last of his brothers. Because this one has done the work to earn his confidence.

"Sure thing," I oblige.

Hands stuffed in his pockets and beaming like the rogue hero of a romantic action movie, Beckham nods to a space a short distance away, where he ushers me into a plastic yard chair he's just conjured, out of place within this setting. He bends down to my eye level, casting a real-life *smolder* at me.

"I'm assuming you want me to take a peek at your soul from the top and not the bottom, Master Dolly?"

"I'm not spreading my legs for you, if that's what you're asking," I respond.

"Oh-ho, *cheeky*. Of course I'd never ask my brother's girl to do something like that for me." He smiles in that sickeningly neutralizing way, hands on his knees like he's speaking to a kindergartener. "But, so we're clear, you are my brother's girl, aren't you? Not just his master?"

I don't think it would be wise to answer.

"It's okay. I saw the way he was holding you before, and hey, I'm glad! Vel deserves to get a little where he can. I'm just surprised he's picked a human to do it with, that's all. It's out of character for him. Unfortunately for you, our vessels aren't allowed to go after people we could become *attached* to, so I'm guessing it's a little one-sided. Let's have a test, shall we?" His tone drops to one of soft seriousness. "What if Velis told you he loved you right now?"

I feel a kick somewhere in the reaches behind my ribcage.

"Yeeeah." Beckham's smile turns smug as he studies my face. "You've got some feelings in there. Good. Then I'm sure you'll want to do what's best for him too. What I mean is, it's going to be pretty hard on Velis when he gets his win revoked. There's no way you could know his story, but the kid's been through blow after blow after blow, what with his mother and his grandfather and his ex-fiancée. As someone that really cares about him, I have to wonder if this would all be easier on him if he just gave it up now, you know?"

And I have to wonder why Beckham would be trying so hard to make Velis drop from a competition he knows he can't win.

Still at my level, Beckham leans in closer. "You can see that, can't you, Dolly Jones?"

There it is. Dolly *Jones*. Velis never told Beckham my last name. Which means that this brother has been in contact with the other two. Which means that the dark streak of intuition I feel every time he talks with such a genuine, *disarming* tone is warranted.

He's a whole other kind of manipulative, trying to appeal to my logic while preying on my feelings for Velis.

But his delivery is crap. Like I would ever fall for that patronizing bullshit.

"Your other brothers are here, aren't they?" I infer.

Beckham freezes, eyes locked on mine because he's been caught. "Cheeky *and* sharp," he says from the corner of his mouth through a plastered smile.

Velis had a lapse in judgment. This isn't a safe situation for him, and I need to stall or divert or get a hint to him as soon as I can. I won't let even the most Machiavellian of the triplets take what is rightfully his.

I am a fire that refuses to die after being doused, after all.

"You're right," I admit to the most dangerous brother. Most dangerous, I determine, because he's managed to swindle Velis's trust. "I do like Velis, and I don't want to see him disappointed."

Beckham views my feelings for Velis as a weakness, but I'm going to use them to my advantage. I'm going to forge them into a shield for both of us.

"But it's more than that," I attest. "I'm not stupid, Beckham. Your brother Arrik already told me that Velis will never reciprocate my feelings because of what I am, and the more I find out about him, the more I understand why. Yes, it would be better on him if this contest were to end now, but it would also be better on me. I realize the deeper into this thing I get, the more it's going to hurt me in the end. I need to forget about him as soon as possible. You can make that happen, right? You can make me forget about him in exchange for helping you?"

Beckham analyzes me for signs of deception before deciding me worthy of striking a deal. "I can," he says, "so long as we become tethered first."

He wants my soul in addition to all the power he's planning to steal from Velis?

Shithead.

"Okay." I give him a look of solemn acceptance. "But I'll only do it if you agree to make it even and share Velis's contest balance with your brothers. I don't want to give either of them a reason to retaliate against him." I take a steadying breath. "Have them reveal themselves. Once you and I are bonded, I'll wish Velis's balance evenly among the three of you. That shouldn't be a big deal to you, right? Because you're in second place right now?"

Beckham lifts his chin. "I see my brother trusts you enough to share the details with you."

Shoot. Is that bad? He assumes Velis is using me as a diversion. He assumes I'm the only one here with feelings. Would his tactics change if he knew we were more couple-y than that?

"I . . . watch him," I lie. "He doesn't notice me a lot of the time, but I always notice him."

The manipulator sets his palm against the center of my chest, holding tight to my stare so as not to let me go. "What if Velis were fucking you right now?" It's like a burst of roseweed to the face. I try to suppress it, keep it tied, but I can't help the acceleration of my pulse as it rears like a wild stallion at the thought of Velis over me, holding me down, sucking my neck.

God, I want him.

Beckham peels his mouth—"You really are a poor, unrequited little lost cause, aren't you? We've got a deal."—and then lets out a sharp whistle between his front teeth and that smug, smug mouth. "Jeb! Arrik! Might as well get out here!"

Beck's summons hits Velis like a spear through the chest, and what starts as confusion quickly shifts to betrayal as Arrik and Jeb both appear against the lake, taking spots on either side of their ringleader brother.

"BECK? What is this?"

"I'm sorry, bro." The traitor drips sympathy. "It's what Dolly wanted. She was ready to give me all of your balance, but I convinced her at least to share it with the others to keep it fair."

WOW. Really? Blatantly throwing me under the bus when I'm RIGHT here? Speaks to his confidence in getting what he wants.

I had it so, so wrong the first time I ever met Vel.

Beckham continues, "Like me, Dolly only wants what's best for you, Vel. She's afraid of seeing you hurt, and I gotta say, she convinced me."

There's no way Velis believes any of that after what we've been through together . . . right? But it's hard to tell. He's preoccupied with scowling at Arrik and Jeb.

Arrik bares his full tattooed chest the way he did at the nightclub, an unlit stick dangling from the side of his lips. He plays with it, toys with it, pushes at it with his tongue while never taking his explicit gaze from me. How many girls has he pulled with that crap?

Jeb, meanwhile, is looking preppy in a bright-colored jacket and clean sneakers, offsetting a face more deadly than should be allowed on a free-walking man. He looks like he's about to hand out punch laced with poison at the school dance for getting kicked off the polo team.

So, we have the fuckboy, the sociopath, and the wolf in sheep's clothing.

And then Velis, scrappy Velis, who is now on high alert and showing his teeth through the pain of deceit. "Dolly! Get over here!"

But Beckham places a hand on my shoulder. "I don't see how that would help things, do you? Her mind is made up. She knows this ends badly for her if she stays with you. But she really likes you, Vel. She wants to make sure you give up this senseless contest before she goes. She's willing to make the hard call in your place. It's too bad she's not a djinn. Sharp girl. Compassionate too."

Again, WOW. He's really selling it. I bet he's gotten away with TONS of shit in his life. Teachers, parents, *women.*

This time, Velis's look of betrayal is directed at me. "Dol . . . ley?"

Oh no. That broken tone is hard to withstand. Because Velis does like me just as much as I like him, and the emotion of it all is getting to him.

I need to get through this before he starts believing it's real.

"Tch, it only took your human three days to turn on you?" Jeb scoffs. "Must be a new record, *breed.*"

"It's because she's decided she'd rather play with a real djinn." Arrik chews at his blunt with a mouth sinfully designed. "Ain't that right, kitten?"

Ew. No. Neither of them is right. And for beings trained to read desire, they sure aren't picking up on the fact that I'd love to slap each of them raw.

I stifle it. It's time to enact phase two of this plan. Stick with me, Velis. I'm going to get us out of here, and it will be worth all those looks you're bleeding at me.

Beck is someone used to being trusted. I offer him as much earnestness as I can manage.

"There is something I haven't told you yet, Beck. Another reason I wanted your brothers to reveal themselves. Velis was lying about why he wanted to borrow your soul juice. It wasn't so that he could go back in time to investigate the lock on my soul. There is no lock on my soul. The truth is, I'm something called a magnetium."

Beckham's tone falls, unimpressed. "Oh yeah?"

He knows I'm trying to play him.

"Yes," I double down. "Velis took me to see a blood expert, and he confirmed it. My soul is more powerful than a normal human's, which is why I can't be tethered by normal means. You won't be able to tether me on your own. It's going to take all three of you."

Arrik waves his hand. "I call bullshit. She's screwing with you, Beck, in order to save *him*. There's no such thing as a magensium or whatever the fuck she said."

"*Language*," hisses Jeb.

"Dolly Jones." Beckham squeezes my shoulder—a threat, though his voice remains jovial. "That can't be true, now, can it? I thought we were starting to see eye to eye. After all, we both want what's best for my little brother, don't we?"

"It's the truth!" I lie with fake gumption. "Velis, I wish you would tell them the truth. What did the hematologist you took me to call me?"

Velis's eyes sear blue, and through his confusion, he spits: "A magnetium?"

Ardy was, of course, joking when he said it, but the triplets don't need to know that.

Because loopholes.

"Wait, for real?" Raspy Arrik removes the roll of sticky paper from his lip and shoots his eyes toward Jeb, but the psycho is too busy glaring at me to notice.

"Velis, I wish you would tell them the truth. What did the hematologist say a magnetium is?"

Another flash of blue zips over Velis's eyes: "A special breed of human designed to lure djinn," he says, almost robotic.

And there, at the end, was that a glimmer of understanding?

"Tch!" Jeb makes a noise of protest. "If something like that exists, then why haven't we ever heard of one?"

"Because they're dangerous," Velis says through his teeth, dropping his head like he's been defeated. "They don't want us going looking for them."

Yes! He's caught on. Because I wasn't the one to ask that question, Velis wasn't compelled to answer it truthfully.

"Well, I'll be damned," mutters Arrik, brow raised with intrigue.

"The truth is, my soul is extra powerful," I persist. "Nothing Velis will ever be able to handle. But according to the reader we saw, the three of you were born under the same star, so the universe sees you as one collective unit. Velis is worried that if you three bond to me, you'll be able to siphon me as one connected entity."

Lies, based on the many fantasy novels I read growing up.

And there is at least one among them who still isn't buying it.

"This all seems extremely far-fetched," Jeb argues, cold.

"Velis," I command, "tell them the truth. Mayree said my arrow isn't even aligned with yours, right? Tell them where it's pointing."

His eyes pulse. "Mayree said it's pointing directly at mine."

Jeb narrows his stare.

"That's why Velis has been working so hard to keep me away from you. The power in my soul is worth more than all that he's collected so far." And now for the grand finale. I muster my most apologetic, heartbroken voice: "I'm sorry, Velis. I have feelings for you. Real feelings. And I know you'll never reciprocate them because of what I am. Beckham's agreed to erase my memory of you if I wish your soul power over to them. I don't trust Arrik, and I don't trust Jeb, but I do believe Beckham when he says he's looking out for you." Boldfaced LIES. "And I do agree it's best for you. Everyone knows that, even if you win, you'll never be made heir. You even said so yourself."

Velis knows I'm playing them. He knows I have a plan. But the hurt on his face is real because he never expected to hear those words from my mouth.

It sucks. It hurts.

But it's his pain that sells it.

"See?" As a person that gets what he wants through false charm, Beckham's ego has been validated. He slips his hand around my shoulder. "We all want what's best for you, bro. You don't have to deal with this hassle anymore, okay? We'll take the magnetium human off your hands, and we'll make sure she's returned safely once we're done with her. Right, *Arrik*?"

Apparently, the tattooed djinn is even less likely to return me in one piece than his sociopath counterpart, who stands beside him like a chunk of ice.

"You promise, right, Beck?" I ask. "That you'll erase my memory of Velis after we're tethered?"

"Of course, Master." When he brushes my cheek with his knuckle, he does so more intimately than any time he's touched me yet because now he sees me as something valuable.

Uncomfortable over his brother's handling of me, Velis lurches forward—

"Velis, I wish you wouldn't interfere!"

"Goddamn it, Dolly!" he cries as his eyes spark.

I ignore Velis's fuming in favor of Beckham, pretending to grow nervous over his touch. "H-how do I do it? Do I have to . . . to kiss your vessels like I did Velis's?"

From behind, I hear Velis make a choking noise, and the corner of *considerate* Beckham's mouth spasms in response. He never grew out of his bullying; he only got better at hiding it.

Fucker.

The hand that had previously caressed my cheek turns to cupping it. "Or you can kiss us directly. That works to seal the bond just as well." He lowers his disgustingly assured face until the scruff of it is nearly close enough to feel. And damn if he isn't slinging his eyes to see Velis's reaction.

Meanwhile, Arrik's cheekbones are forming a chaos-loving smile as he looks on, while Jeb hurries to conjure his shrunken vessel and will it to its normal size.

At least one of them doesn't want to kiss me.

"I'd rather not." I lean away, to Beckham's displeasure, forcing me to cover with: "I've already developed unwanted feelings for one of my djinn. I'm not keen on developing more."

Ego. Fed.

"Of course." Beckham smirks before barking over his shoulder: "Even you, Arrik. Get out your vessel, lech."

While Arrik makes an unenthused show of pulling out his vessel, I appeal to Beckham's ego one last time. "Would it be okay if I go say goodbye to Vel quick? I know this will help him in the long run, but I do feel bad for him. He seems so trampled."

Beckham doesn't answer immediately. With his arm firmly around me, he looks to be thinking of some excuse for why it isn't a good idea.

I'd anticipated that. "If he tries to run off with me, I'll wish us right back here. I'm ready to move on. He already told me we can't be together."

But Beckham still looks wary.

"Velis," I call. "Did you or did you not tell me you can't promise me forever? And that you still intend to find a full-blooded girl to marry? I wish you would tell Beckham the truth."

"I . . . did tell her all that," Velis admits through a hearty frown bathed in the light from his eyes. Arrik's mouth curls; it's exactly what he warned me about back in that club.

Satisfied, Beckham releases me. "Hurry back, Master." He keeps one eye on me as he moves to convene with his brothers. Meanwhile, I'm struggling not to look eager as I make my way over squishy moss to a beaten down version of my favorite genie.

"Velis!" Voice hushed, I swivel him so that his back is turned to the others and so that his body is blocking mine. "Are you okay?"

"What the heck was that, Dolly?" he demands, trying not to let his panic show.

He's not okay.

And we don't have a lot of time to fix it.

"Velis, how do you know your father won't let you win this contest?"

His irritation deepens. "It's common sense."

"But has he actually said anything to make you think it? Or has it all just come from those jerks?" I motion with my eyes to the water's edge, where said jerks are babbling quietly, most likely plotting out what they're going to use my soul for.

"What are you getting at?" Velis asks, cross.

"I don't know squat about your family, and I know I could be way off base and am definitely out of line, but I have a theory. Your father clearly loved your mother a lot. What if he let you in on this contest because he *wants* you to win? Because it was an easy way to get your brothers to give up their birthrights?"

"You don't know my father."

"You're right. I don't. But I saw those servants. I saw the way Ardy and Mayree interacted with you. I saw that portrait in the library. Hell, I've seen *you*. Think about it. Why would those three, even the one pretending to be nice, torment you all these years? With egos like theirs, I have to assume it's jealousy. If they really believed you weren't worthy of becoming an heir to the estate, why not just let you win to see you get crushed in the end? Why would they be so adamant about getting your contest balance if they didn't believe you had a shot at winning? They're *scared* of you, Velis. They're scared of those paintings decorating every room in your manor. They think you can win for real, and so do I." I touch his cheek. "You're worthy of winning, Velis. And everyone knows it."

He swallows as his expression thaws, but the only thing he says in return is, "Dolly."

I may be flawed, and I may be broken, but somewhere along the way, I've become a little bit wholer, fuller, capable of caring for another living being.

The shell of myself I've been carrying around has slowly started to fill out, and now, that blood that used to sit so dormant, that was just a reminder of better times, is searing through me.

"Tell Beckham to fuck off. You're going to win this, Velis. And I'm going to help you. Are you above cheating a little?"

"Cheating?"

"Just to level the playing field, as payback for what they've done to you."

And there, stirring like a corpse flower blooming only once every seven years, bliss begins to overtake him. "You are something else, Dolly fucking Jones. What's your plan?"

"Hold me like you're saying goodbye and close your eyes. I don't want your brothers to see them light up."

Pulse thudding hard enough to feel, he grips me to him, allowing me a soft kiss of parting to the cheek as a way to slip his ear closer to my mouth.

And then I bid him a secret wish.

As I move to pull away from him, his hands keep me captive a moment longer. "I . . . like you, Dolly," he whispers. "I like you so friggen' much."

I like him too. And I tell him so with all the like in my eyes before leaving him to rejoin the enemy.

All I wanted was a new vase for the one I broke.

And now I'm caught up in some genie family feud, wearing the same clothes I wore yesterday, about to fuck over three powerful, magical beings for the sake of a guy who can never love me.

A guy I've known less than a week.

Dolly fucking Jones is right. I'm a mess.

But this is the most fulfilling thing I've done in at least a year, maybe longer. I'm not paper. Today, I am a tree. And all the misogynistic huffing and puffing in the world won't blow me down.

After all the months I spent not fighting for myself, maybe all I needed was a chance to fight for someone else.

Beckham underestimates me, and that will be his downfall.

I approach the three of them, lined up on the shores of a

gemstone-bedded lake, coming first to Beckham, who offers me his vessel—a simple gray cylinder with a rubber stopper. "Is this stainless steel?" I ask, surprised.

"Not all of us use antiques, Dolly Jones," hums Arrik, giving his own stainless-steel-like vessel a shake over my head.

Right. Velis did mention his was a rare heirloom.

I take Beckham's vessel in my palm and move it to my face as he watches on in tepid anticipation. But again, I pause, because a thought has just occurred to me—"I'm not going to faint again, am I?"

"Again?" says Arrik, tossing a look to Beckham. "What the shit?"

Oh. Is that not normal?

"No," says Velis from yonder, mirth riding his breath. "You're the only one I ever made swoon, Master."

Jeb looks sharply from Velis to me, surely taking note of the fondness exchanged between us.

"It's not going to work, you flirt," I scold Velis coldly before finishing what I started and bringing Beckham's vessel to my lips. In the moment after, the manipulative genie's eyes surge bright.

"Bro." Beckham forces kindness and dramatically grips his own chest. "You're killing me. I'll take good care of her, and I'll make sure these two do too. You'll see. We'll go out for a beer when this is all over, yeah?"

So that he can make the bed for future manipulation.

Next is arguably the worst one of all. Pheromone-dripping, sex-mongering Arrik stands with his chin up and his eyes cast down, dangling his vessel by two fingers. I'm eye level with the tattoo of a dagger piercing a kumquat. And oh, look at that. His nipples are pierced. Didn't notice that before.

He is hot, with that joint resting plush against his lips so that the smallest flash of his teeth shows through. But the stench of haughtiness ruins it. He's not worth it. Not by a long shot.

I reach for his vessel, but he lifts it out of the way, making me jump for it and using the moment of distraction to spit out his joint, gather my waist, and land his mouth against mine.

"Fucking hell, Arrik!" lashes Velis, unable to interfere.

"Mm." Arrik smiles against me, arm all the way around my back and fingers collecting my shirt.

He tastes like tobacco and happy hour.

I push him off with all my strength. "I wish you would bite your own lip, Arrik. *Hard*."

"Sorry, love, you can't hurt me now," he rasps, eyes dimming. "But if you want to bite my lip, I won't stop you."

Beckham swats him over the head. "Sorry about him, Master. He's a dog."

They're all dogs.

Two down, one to go. I'm worried about this last one. He still doesn't seem fully on board. He offers me his vessel half-assed and doesn't let it go. He expects me to bend down to kiss it.

Fine. It's a means to an end. And the end will be worth it.

I lower, tipping my head forward, lips nearly to the cool metal of a modern genie lamp when Jeb suddenly seizes my wrist. "I *knew* I recognized that smell!" he hisses shrewdly. "Mind telling me why you were in our library, sneaking around *invisible*? Hey, dumbasses, he likes her more than he's letting on! He brought her HOME with him!"

Freaking hotel shampoo!

I leap for his bottle, pressing my mouth to it just as slit-eyed Jeb tries to yank it away. "Argh!" he yells with a swing that aims to bash me across the face. But he's bonded to me now, and he can't hurt me. The bottle recoils as if it's just made contact with cement, and I stand unscathed.

"Arrik, Jeb, Beckham!" I shout, waiting to see the light of three furious sets of eyes before continuing. "I wish you would transfer all of the soul power you've won during this contest into Velis's balance!"

"I knew it!" scathes Jeb, throwing accusation to his brothers. "You morons!"

"Fuck!" says Arrik, darkening. "Shouldn't have done that, kitten. Now we're going to have to get *mean*."

However venomous the other two are, it's nothing compared

to Beckham, whose composure is broken for the first time since I met him. "You little human bitch!" His voice shakes. "You've made an egregious mistake! We're tied to you now! There's no hiding from us, and we will do whatever it takes to get that—"

"Now, Vel!" I order. "Enact the wish now!"

Velis's eyes blaze brighter than all the rest seconds before the glittering lake, plush green fields, and gemstone shores fall away.

CHAPTER 15

What's in a Name?

"Where are we?" I whisper into the darkness.

There's no response.

"Velis, where are we?"

Warm arms take me and tuck me against an even warmer chest. "I can't believe you just did that. You cunning little fox." By the sound of his flesh, his adrenaline is pounding just as vigorously as mine.

My breath scores the still air. "Did it work?"

"Oh, it worked." I can practically hear his smile. "I've got more power than I know what to do with. Dolly, that was . . . you're a friggen' warrior. And a reeeally good liar." He's buried all up in my shampoo-compromised hair. "You had me worried."

The way he's holding me. It's so . . . tender, like I'm a bouquet of wildflowers he's just gathered up from some sun-drenched prairie at the edge of the world.

"I'm sorry about Beckham. I know firsthand what it's like to be betrayed by people you thought you could trust."

"Y . . . yeah. I think this contest has gotten to him."

I think his personality has gotten to him, but we'll leave it at that.

"Is it true, what Arrik said?" I ask. "They'll be able to find me now that they're bonded to me?"

"Only until you and I are properly tethered. Then your bonds with them will break, and you'll be fully mine. For now, a cloaking wish should suffice."

Fully mine.

"I wish to be cloaked from your brothers." I make Velis's eyes light bright for a brief reveal of his tempting, tempting face.

"Done," he says. "Anything else you want? It's on the house. Everything is on the house from now on. You deserve whatever you'd have me give you."

There isn't anything I want but to be held like this. A hug to make up for fifty weeks without them.

Velis huffs against me in the dark, grip tightening. "No one's ever fought like that for me before, Dolly."

His voice is soft and sexy and vulnerable.

"I meant what I said about you winning," I tell him.

"I know." He sets his mouth to my temple and his hand to the small of my back, pressing into the curve.

"It's hard to look objectively at something when you're in the middle of it, but as an outsider, I see it."

"Like you with your pledge, huh?" he delivers, quiet.

Yes, now that he mentions it. I haven't given much thought to my pledge or my guilt in hours. It all seems so minuscule now, next to fantasy worlds and legacy battles. And James . . . for a while there, I was only remembering the good in him. But saying it all out loud to another person really highlights the bad.

A creak-less gate. Full-flowered trees. A lively bar.

There's pain stored in those memories too. Fights I didn't win. Fights I did win. Words that left scars that only started to heal weeks and months later.

I feel it now. The difference between being nurtured and being oppressed. I feel the difference from a stranger. A sweet, magical, flawed stranger that presses his emotion into me every time he touches me, stronger than words can carry.

It hurts.

And it feels fulfilling all at the same time.

This is what they call a whirlwind romance, and it's set its hooks in me deep, cutting through stone and slabs of recycled metal.

We're two lonely people, filling a need we didn't know we had, mimicking the makings of love.

"You're an incredible person, Dolly. I saw it when I met you, but now, you're starting to shine, and it's so beautiful. I feel like one lucky bastard to be part of it." His lips find my neck. "I like you." They find my jaw. "I wish I could tell you how much."

But those words are forbidden for people who have only known each other a few days. Forbidden for people of different races and worlds. Forbidden for people rebounding. Forbidden for people committed to a short-term fling.

I claim his mouth. Because fighting for him was empowering. Because the longer I spend with him, the more like my true self I'm becoming. Because he's frustratingly imperfect and gives me space to be the same. "I like you too, Vel." I fight to keep my voice steady, but my heart is drumming louder than Viking warships in my ears.

Forbidden. It's forbidden. And insta-love is such a cliché, annoying thing. Such a shallow, impossible thing. We're hopped up on adrenaline and emotion. In a dark, unknown place, where touch is heightened without sight.

I try to peer into that ever-present darkness, which is thick enough to cut. "Where are we?"

"All you wished for was to be taken to someplace safe without needing to touch. So I improvised. We're inside a locked cabinet in my bedroom. And don't freak out, but we're about the height of a can of consumables right now."

"You shrunk us?! *Again*?"

"I said don't freak out! No one will find us here. We're inside a locked cabinet inside a locked closet inside a locked room inside a locked manor. But we can leave now that you've got a cloaking spell on you. Where do you want to go?"

Umm, okay, but we definitely aren't leaving until I find out

—"What's important enough that you put it behind quadruple locks?"

"Oh." His reluctance creates waves through the dark.

"O-or don't tell me if it's too personal. That's fine."

Apparently, it isn't. Not for me.

"It's where I used to keep my vessel," he says. "And also, there's a necklace in here my mother used to wear. The one from the painting you saw. And . . . there's a letter she wrote me before she died. Just some personal crap."

It isn't crap.

And I really, really need to go visit my mom. I was using not seeing her as punishment for myself, knowing it was also punishing her. Knowing there are people out there who don't have a mom. Was my penance really that important to me? Did I really hate myself that much?

"Oh!" Velis gives a jolt. "Do you want to go there now? I can take you."

Because he can read my desires.

"No. That's okay. Thanks. I'll go soon, though. As soon as all this is over. I promise."

All this.

Over.

"Master . . ." His voice trails because he can tell how badly I want to see her, how much I regret not seeing her over the past year.

"Dolly," I insist. "I'm not your master, Velis. I don't want to be your master."

". . . Babe?"

"Babe is fine," I swallow. "I can be your babe."

Oh no. I can feel them both. Both our hearts sending ripples through the air. Like I can feel our connection growing. Because of what I've done for him and what he's done for me.

He presses his forehead to mine and his hands to my waist. Is he shaking? Or is that me?

"I, um . . . Remember what I said about your boundaries, okay? Stop me at any time."

Stop him?

His hands slide down my hips. "I want to fucking devour you, and I don't want to hurt you, because the last time you . . . Just stop me, okay?"

Nope, that's me. I'm definitely the one shaking, trembling, as he uses my hips to pull me flush against him so that I can feel the bend of his zipper.

This time, when he takes my mouth, he does so with hunger, lapping me up, savoring the taste of me, pulling, pressing, breathing.

Oh my god, my body is *throbbing*. There's no air in here. I'm pretty sure this is airtight and unsafe for living things, but whatever air is in here, it's come alive enough to prick my skin as I tug at his hair and taste his sweat. That unholy *neck*. With sinew and blood, swallowing whenever he's nervous, flexing when he's aroused, pumping out pheromones and heat. I could bite him.

"Ah, don't!" He covers it with his hand because he can feel that burst of carnal desire from me.

I can't help laughing at that one. "I don't mean it literally." I am bold enough to lick up his Adam's apple. "You're just so damn hot."

I feel him tense, letting out a stuttering groan of tension when I reach his work-of-art jawline. "How far are we taking this, Dolly?" This time his hands slide upward enough to raise my shirt up my spine.

How far? Only time will tell.

"Change your hair," I request. "Can you make it your natural color?"

Because he looks even hotter that way. He looks like a freakin' Hercules surfer god.

"D-done." Is that stutter of his because I can't contain my overflowing desires? "It's, ah, really intense to be on the receiving end of all that. Just tell me to stop if you need to, okay? I'll do my best."

He plunges, taking my face with pent-up passion. If tension has a tangible form, she's here with us, swelling with each breath, each drop of moisture, each slide of a tongue. He's gripping and pulling, and I'm crawling into him in the still darkness.

And then we're no longer in darkness. We're standing in the middle of a galaxy, with stars reflecting in shallow waters. The salt flats? But by my calculations, it should be light out. Or has he taken us to another time too? The stars melt away, replaced by the top of a tower, where a colorful wood of exploding smoke paints the horizon at our backs. The faewood. A place so striking, it momentarily draws me from the spectacle that is Velis. Another blip later, and we're in the center of a pulsating dance floor amidst sweat and lust. I wear that blue, belled-out dress he made for me, hands sliding over his bare chest and shoulders.

God, *shoulders*. Firm shoulders are a gift from a higher power. And Velis's shoulders? They're in a class all their own.

He spins me around until we're standing in a wet park dripping with the leavings of a storm that gave up as swings creak under ghosts and petrichor fuses into us from wet air.

He's bending me backwards, hands in my hair, mouth to my neck. My knee slides up to his hip to remove any barriers from our bodies drawing closer.

Was I lying this morning when I said I wanted to protect myself? No. I meant it. But I don't feel at risk here. I feel safe.

And women are allowed to change their minds.

We're falling through air now, horizontally, landing on a soft white bed with sterile, bedbug-less sheets.

Our hotel.

His power sets me down gently, one of his hands to my stomach, the other holding my wrist tight to a pillow as he pulls away to study me with that avalanche stare, so piercing, so blue. So sad and yet so laced in gratitude, as though he's living out a dream he didn't know he had.

I get that. I'm the same.

I'm still wearing that blue, high-necked dress. He slips his hand up my knee, up my thigh, to where a pair of illegal black lacy panties reside. He dips a finger into the lace, stare carefully watching mine, and peels them down.

"I more than like you, Dolly. I know it's crazy, but I do."

I more than like him too, but I can't say it, because his hand has found me where I'm most vulnerable, and all I can do is throw my head backward and let out a sound I haven't released in a very long time.

He explores me, even keeled, watching for signs of discomfort, making sure it's okay to progress.

Oh, it's okay to progress. I let him know so by finding his ungodly abdomen and sliding my hand into the reaches.

Holy shit!

His mouth bends when I find him, likely because I'm making the face of someone who's just discovered a dinosaur bone in their garden.

But that soon falls because he's beginning to experience the pleasure I'm already in the throes of. He kisses me wherever he can find me and rolls over me, using his free hand to wave me out of the dress and into the skimpy tank top and shorts that have become my nightly ensemble.

Because he's after my breasts, and that dress didn't allow for easy access. He slides up to take a helping, and my body reacts by hardening. Like he's hardening. But the rest of me feels like a freaking flower opening up to him. Does he want to have a look at my soul? No problem. It's ready for him.

But . . . there is a moment.

One small moment where I remember that the last time I did this—for how fun and exciting and primal it is—last time, it was a thing I didn't want to happen. It was something I don't remember happening. It was something that made me lose control of my body and life.

Velis feels the emotion poking out of me and halts. "Dolly?"

"I'm okay."

"This doesn't need to happen. We can just cuddle like we usually do. I'll be fine with just cuddling."

That must take an extraordinary amount of willpower with my hand around his dinosaur bone.

I say nothing. I'm working through things.

He removes both hands and sets them onto the bed at either side of my face. "You're safe with me. I'm not going to make you do anything you aren't ready for, okay? I didn't even plan on this happening between us, to tell you the truth. It's okay if we don't. Nothing changes."

He means it. He can't lie to me. And besides that, I can tell.

"I want to. I'm sorry. I might be a little awkward with it. But I want to replace the bad with the good. I'm sorry that you're my guinea pig for that."

I refuse to let Gabe define what sex means to me for the rest of my life. Victim or cheater, I won't let this act be ruined by that one night. I'm stronger than that. I'm allowed to move on.

"Guinea pig? Is that a type of pet?" Velis asks, subdued and confused with, yes, my hand still wrapped around him because it's such a lovely fit.

I snort. "Yes. Be my pet?"

"Abso-friggen-lutely." His smirk flares and then settles. "But I mean it, Dolly. We're only doing this if it's for your benefit too. Do you want it?"

Oh, I want it. And he should be able to feel that want rising in me right about now.

That smirk returns. "Okay. Thank Maka." He pants hard and then he begins again. To slide, to probe, to taste, to invite, all the while wearing his sweat like a badge of honor.

He's . . . proud to be the one doing this to me. He's *honored*.

As he pushes over me and slides into me, commanding the position of my hips with a general's poise, I tell myself not to fall for him. These are emotions driven by the physical. Biology is telling me to latch onto him, to mate with him, to become his partner for life.

Because it feels so indescribably good.

He kisses me, touches me, loves me with his body, skimming his thumb over my nipples, taking my ear in his mouth, whispering things in the dark to let me know he likes the way I'm moving, the things I'm doing to him. He handles my back like it's the finest of artifacts, he savors my neck like it's a feast.

And when the best of it hits, he doesn't hold back on how it makes him feel. He cries out, soft and boyish and laden with desire and vulnerability as he pushes against me with all of his might.

And after hours of merging, we lie in the dark, with one bashful sliver of moonlight bold enough to spy through curtains that have probably witnessed dozens of hookups. The sheets are damp and messy—my hair snarled, his flesh sticky—as we lie together, my head in the pit of his arm while he strokes his fingers along my skin and stares up at the ceiling with release and serenity.

That was the best sex I've ever had in my life.

I don't mean to tell him so, but it comes falling out of my mouth.

"Yeah," he admits like it hurts him. "You smell so good. You taste so good. And your tits . . ." They've been sucked by him, bitten by him, squeezed by him. "You're a goddess, Master." He realizes his mistake: "Er, babe."

This discovery is going to make it harder to say goodbye in the end. So we'll just have to fuck and fuck and fuck until it gets old.

Once more for tonight, at least until we run out of fuel. In the midnight hours, the night takes us, though I'm still certain it should be day, and I fall asleep heavier than I ever have before, naked and unashamed, in the clutch of a wish-granting genie in a hotel room neither of us paid for.

That sliver of moonlight eventually transitions to a blast of probing sunlight, calling us from sleep earlier than either of us wants.

But I'm happy because we're holding each other just as securely as when we fell asleep. I slide my hands up the ridges of his abdomen and to the perfectly defined chest he didn't have to work for as he squeezes my nacho-fed ass he somehow thinks is sexy.

"You're going to screw up all my plans, Dolly Jones."

"You've already screwed up all my plans, Velis—" And this is the moment I realize I don't even know his last name. "Djinn."

"Wait—" He shifts onto his elbow. "Do you think my last name is Djinn?" The question comes out extremely dry and extremely flat. "It's not *Djinn*. It's Bolly, you turd."

Dolly . . . Bolly? Dolly fucking *Bolly*?!

He winks. "Kidding. It's Targaryen."

"You've seen *Game of Thrones*?" It's my turn, now, to be both flat and dry.

He shrugs. "One of my ex-masters was obsessed with it." His sigh is drawn out. "Okay, okay, I'm compelled to tell you that was, indeed, a joke. My actual last name is Reilhander. Velis Reilhander. Not quite as sassy as Dolly Jones."

Dolly . . . Reilhander.

No. I need to stop with that shit. What am I, twelve? A fling is one thing, but I'm skipping way, waaay ahead here. Just because we banged doesn't mean we can ever have a life together. Pull the reins, DJ. Pull the reins.

"Not sure what that emotion is," says the empath, stirring, "but I'm glad it isn't regret. In case you're wondering, what we did last night—I loved it."

He loved it.

"I loved it too," I say, small.

I loved it.

I loved.

I love.

Enough.

His fingers flex against my shoulder. "You, ah, wanna guinea pig one more time before we investigate that lock on your soul?"

Not the proper use of guinea pig, but the answer is yes.

This time, I don't even care about my night breath as I roll over him and take his hips between my knees.

CHAPTER 16

The Photograph

I AM NOT in love with a person I met days ago. I am not in love with a person I met days ago. I am not . . . Say it with me. I, Dolly Jones, am NOT in love with a genie, nor will I ever be in love with a genie. Sexual attraction is a powerful thing, and now that it's been fed, it will try to consume everything in its path until it wears off. We just have to wait for it to wear off. Wait it out.

Because I, Dolly Jones, am not in love with a guy I met DAYS AGO.

"Hey, can I make you breakfast?" From the edge of the bed, Velis opens his palm to reveal an uncracked egg. "I feel like you might need sustenance after last night . . . and this morning."

And if that isn't a look resembling love and longing in his eyes, I don't know what is.

Get behind me, Satan.

"Dang, you're like a sugar daddy now that you've got all that stolen soul power," I tell him as I pull my shirt over my newly cleaned body. "I have to wonder, though, whose soul did that egg cost? How many *followers*?"

But Velis is hung up on an earlier part of it: "Sugar daddy?"

"Okay, so you know what *Game of Thrones* is, but you don't know what a sugar daddy is?"

He shrugs. "Do you know what a sky fountain is?"

Nope, I sure don't.

"But you know what a Ray is," he says.

Point taken.

Speaking of Rays—his has taken up residence on the nightstand, pouring out dancing blue light like it's a lava lamp. "I'm just filling out paperwork," he explains. "Time travel is touchy. I need to make sure I follow the rules when I go back."

"When *you* go back?"

"Yeeeah, I wanted to talk to you about that," he says, watching me wiggle into my leggings. "So, technically, I could bring you back with me. As in, it's possible. But it gets a lot more complicated when a human is involved."

I, the human, wait for him to finish.

"You know how wish granters erase our masters' memories at the end of it?"

The end of it.

He's quick to move on.

"Well, you still get to keep anything you wished for. Like, if you become an influencer, that's yours forever because you paid for it. But going back in time for an experience? That's tough to finagle because you aren't allowed to remember your djinn or the fact that it was a wish that got you there, but you get to keep the memory of it. So for the master I took back to see that concert, I had to create a whole reality for her to go along with it, one in which everyone around her remembered her going to the concert. It was kind of a pain in the ass, and I had to get the paperwork approved ahead of time, and I don't think we have time for all that. SO I figured I'd dip back alone, record what I see"—he taps his temple—"and then show it to you once I'm back in the present. Are you okay with that?"

"If that's the way we have to do it," I say. I don't know that I'm all that keen to see an awkward past version of myself anyway. "Just don't go disappearing into the void or anything."

He smiles, wily. "You can call me back to you at any time—you know, if you start to miss me."

Psh. *Miss* him? I think I can spare an hour without him. Hell, it would be good for us to spend some time apart after this rushed . . . whatever this is.

But I can't hide my true desires from a magical empath.

"It's okay," he says softly. "I'm going to miss you too."

He hands me the egg he conjured for me—a raw, uncooked egg—before returning to his light tablet to wiggle his fingers over paperwork I can't see.

"There's two ways we can swing this," he says. "Either wish me back to the first time we met or wish me back to when the lock was placed on your soul. Either should work if we think they're related."

"Well, I still don't believe I met you and forgot about you, so maybe we can start there and get that one out of the way?"

"Sounds good to me." He inputs my response into the air over his glowing Ray. "By the way, I fixed your dwelling last night while you were sleeping. I figured you might want to wait for me there." He looks up with a grin. "Made a few upgrades too. And I put a barrier around it, in case my brothers get bored and decide they want to take out some aggression on your stuff. They may not be able to find you right now, but they still know where you live. With the mods I made, you'll be safe there until I get back."

Sugar. Daddy.

"Thanks, doll," I coo.

"*Doll*?" He says it like it tastes bad. "You know I was calling you that as an abbreviation of your name and not as like a demeaning thing, right?"

Oh.

"And as for 'babe'?" His smarminess grows. "Well, you are a babe. That one just slipped out."

Ugh. Quit looking at me like you want to boink me, *Vel*. We have things to do.

But he won't stop, so I have no choice but to ambush him and take his neck between my teeth.

"Geezus, what is with you and necks?!" He shrugs me off. "Little friggen' vampire."

"Just your neck, Velis. Just yours."

"Good." Though he returns to his paperwork, the smirk hangs.

Hard to believe that *genies* require *paperwork* to travel back in time. Hard to believe this genie is about to step into my past.

I must admit, I still don't buy into much of it. Us meeting before. Our arrows pointing at one another. Me wishing a lock onto my own soul.

"So . . ." I watch the focus in his eyes, set there by the blue glow of his genie tablet. "After we figure out why my lock was placed and how to remove it, you'll finally be able to siphon my soul?"

"And we'll become tethered." A little distracted, he tosses out a smile like it's candy at a parade. "Can't wait."

I let it fall, uncollected, at my feet: ". . . And then?"

This time, I get his full attention.

Why am I asking this? We both already know the answer. It's the reason his brow is dipping to reflect my own.

"You can take your time making your wishes, Dolly. You don't have to make them all at once. We have time."

"But I will have to make them," I affirm, "so that you can move on to a new master."

Stop it, Dolly.

"And after, I'll no longer have a soul or any memory of you."

So that's why I'm not eager for him to visit the past. Aren't there a few more hurdles for us to climb first? Another unannounced enemy waiting in the wings? It's like all the adrenaline we've been running on is about to be spent. Like we're about to come to a screeching halt.

"Don't think about that," he says, capturing my shoulder to draw me into his chest. "We still have time."

His contest ends in a week.

The same time my pledge was supposed to end.

We have a very small amount of time.

Velis rests his chin on my head through the remainder of his paperwork, his hand refusing to relinquish my shoulder.

"All right, babe," he says when he's finished. "I'm ready." Yet he doesn't make an effort to move, even after the light from his Ray dims. Jaw tight, he releases heavy air through his nostrils. "Look, can we just . . ."

"Yes, forget I said anything." Vacations always end sooner when you count them down. "I'm fine. I'm a bitch-hearted realist. Let's go see the damage you did to my apartment, *meddler*."

He hesitates, trying to get a read on the truth behind my hardened chest until—

"Oh," he scoffs, glad to have a distraction. "Just you wait."

I stand, gawking, in the entryway of an apartment that looks nothing like how I left it. "Velis . . . how did you . . . ?"

"Your desires are easiest to read when you're asleep. It's when you open up the most. Do you like it? If it's weird, I can change it. I wasn't a hundred percent sure how you'd feel about it. I took a chance."

It IS weird. But that doesn't mean I love it any less.

It's a replica of my home, the way it was growing up. The shape is different, fitted into a small one-bedroom apartment, but that's the seasoned living room furniture where my grandpa and I would sit watching cheesy paranormal investigator shows on Thursdays, and the shaker-style kitchen table my mom had custom made for our small, non-traditional family, and our bookshelf of collective, dog-eared fiction picked up at library sales after church. Even the smell of it is the same, like baked-in potpourri and open windows.

"I left your bedroom how it was before. I thought that might be pushing it," Velis says from behind me. "So, yes? No? Still deciding?"

"It's awesome." I turn to offer him all the appreciation in my eyes. "It feels like I'm back home. I love it."

He takes my waist, subzero stare as piercing as ever. "I like granting your wishes, Master. It's fulfilling."

I don't correct him this time because it's like he's saying the title with pride.

"Oh!" He adds, "And I also got you HBO. In case you wanted to watch *Game of Thrones* while I'm out."

Of course, I've already seen it all.

"Thanks, Vel," I say with a laugh. "You did good."

He lifts a brow. "Did I?"

"You did."

Oh no. I hope he can't feel that. Emotions I shouldn't have. Desire I can't control. All leaking out of me as we stand close together, caught in a web we can't escape.

His hair is still blond. He left it that way after last night. After all the gripping and crawling and tasting.

"B-better get a move on, traveler." I tap him on the chest cordially. The sooner the better to get the empath away from my heart.

"Psh, you're the one who has to initiate it," he says, snatching my hand to make light of the tense air. "Unless you can't stand the thought of sending me away?"

He should know better than to bait me like that.

"I wish you'd get out of here."

"It only sticks if you mean it, doll."

This time, I say it for real: "Velis Reilhander, I wish you would go back in time to see whether or not we really have met before, and don't come back until you also figure out how this lock was placed on my soul, got it?"

His eyes flare as the wish hits him. "Ooh," his voice shivers, "so *authoritative*. I'll be back soon with answers. In the meantime, check out your new digs. See if I got it right. Spoiler alert: *I did*."

He stays as long as the wish will allow him before blinking away, leaving me alone for the first time in days.

Good. Great. It's claustrophobic being around the same person day and night. Separation is healthy.

I take a moment to inspect 'the new digs.' It's scary how accurate it is. That means he can see my desires much more vividly than I thought.

That means all the times I've desired him, he's seen all of the nasty details.

And I have to say, it is a little weird, seeing a blanket my mom knitted and my grandpa's favorite chair in my apartment. Creepy? Maybe. But also . . . comforting.

It's cute that he did this for me.

You're an incredible person, Dolly.

You're adorable, Master.

You're a friggen' warrior.

Argh. Stupid genie.

I make my way to the kitchen for a feast of plain saltines, vegetables, and instant gruel, only to find the fridge stocked with fresh farmer's-market-grade food, at least five bottles of delicious, drippy ranch, and two rows of various kinds of pickles. How did he even know I like pickles?

Fuck.

I collapse to my knees, one hand on the refrigerator's handle, the other clutching my disobedient chest. Maybe I was wrong. Maybe separation isn't healthy. I can't get sick of him if we're apart, and the sooner I get sick of him, the less this is all going to hurt.

Next to the sink sits the vase that started it all. The one I may or may not have purposely broken so that I had an excuse to buy something for myself. Now restored to its former glory. I push it into the trash on my way to the bedroom.

Its replacement was the best two-ninety-nine I ever spent.

I assume this isn't going to take long. We haven't met before, so that wish will go nowhere. And then he just has to dip into the single moment when the lock was placed. I expect he won't be gone long at all.

I starfish out over the bed made just the way I left it and breathe in the smell of home.

Silence seems so much more silent now. Has my breathing always been this loud? Has the space around me always felt so vast?

The drawer to the nightstand is open. That's because Velis

went snooping in there the first day we met, while I was on the dirty kitchen floor in a swoon-like state.

What happened to you? Those pictures in your bedroom nightstand are like a completely different person.

He was right.

I kept myself locked away in that drawer, along with those pictures, and only once that drawer was opened did I start to remember who I am and what I want.

Is it pathetic I couldn't get there on my own? Or is it okay to get help from another hurting soul? Maybe these feelings aren't the forbidden L word. Maybe we're trauma bonded. I'm certain a psychologist would frown on this relationship.

My mother would too.

The pictures Velis snooped through aren't the ones I was afraid of. Painful, yes, but not harmful. The true terror lies at the bottom of the drawer in a sealed envelope. Even Velis didn't venture that far.

Those are the pictures from that night. The night it all went to shit. One of our friends had an instant camera, and after they all disowned me, Gabe dropped off an envelope, claiming it contained all the pictures taken of me that night. I don't want to see what I looked like blackout drunk. I don't want to remember what that duplex looked like or what I was wearing or what I was doing. I want it to stay lost forever.

If you were too intoxicated to remember it, then you sure as hell weren't sober enough to be responsible for it.

But you don't remember initiating it.

I'm glad you cheated on him. If that's even what happened.

If that's even what happened.

My hand finds the nightstand, the drawer, the envelope.

God, give me strength. I tug at the paper, not deciding until I'm halfway through whether or not I want to continue. I allow myself an out, but I don't take it, instead choosing to rip the paper the rest of the way and expose the envelope's cursed contents.

I've never met a person with so much restraint.

You aren't a slut, Dolly. You're a little smokeshow, but you aren't a slut.

I know that. I didn't need Velis to tell me. I just needed one other person to believe it.

The first picture is a group shot. We all look happy, save for Gabe's ex, Fallon, who never looks happy. I'm sitting on the edge of the couch in—you guessed it—black leggings and a black shirt, my hair the way it was before I shaved it, long and beachy. There's no drink in my hand.

The next picture is harder to stomach. Gabe's arm is hooked around my neck, his hat on backward, all fratty-like, and a red plastic cup in his hand. The 'chummy' picture the group referenced as evidence. But I don't look chummy; I look *annoyed*.

Yet somewhere between then and the moment before the storm, I know I kissed him. I remember being unable to resist kissing him. *Why*? I never even really liked Gabe. If only James had been there that night. If only . . .

Then I'd have never taken a pledge. I'd have never broken the vase. I'd have never found a genie waiting for me in a magic bottle.

Two more pictures. A selfie of me with a brassy girl named Kate, and another group pic—this time one I'm not even in. There's Gabe, front and center, and his ex, a handful of others, and . . .

"What the hell?!"

There. In the back corner.

I hold the picture up to my face like I might be able to enter the past too.

That's definitely him! I mean, he isn't even wearing a shirt! I press and peer into the reaches of a photograph telling an impossible story:

Velis was there . . . on that night?

There's no way he was there. WHY would he be there? His first time to the human world was four months back, when the contest started. And he can't change the past. Even if he did travel there, people shouldn't be able to see him, let alone photograph him. So how is there a picture of him with BLOND hair standing in the living room of my ex-friend group's duplex nearly a year ago? And why is his shirt off? When he left, he was wearing one.

What the hell is going on?!

I grip the photograph as if I can wring out its secrets.

Velis can't lie to me. Not to mention I saw his face when Mayree claimed we had met before. He was just as confused as me!

So how . . . ?

My soul was locked by a genie, but I don't remember having it locked. The only night I can't remember is *that* night. Velis was there on *that* night. Is that the night my soul was locked? Was HE the one to lock it?

Does this all have something to do with why I have *those* kinds of feelings for him despite my best efforts?

"You had better get your ass back here soon, Velis, or so help me!"

But he doesn't return soon. He doesn't return after an hour has passed. How long can it take to blip in and observe one moment?! I grow fitful the longer he doesn't show, until I'm pacing in my bedroom, chewing at my cuticles, which always get the brunt of my anxiety.

You can call me back to you at any time—you know, if you start to miss me.

Right, that's an option. I can simply wish him back. Would that be desperate? No, I think finding him in a freaking photograph from one of the worst nights of my life constitutes an emergency.

"Velis?" I speak to the corners of my bedroom. "Return to my apartment. I wish you would!"

My heart thuds loud enough to wake the grumpy neighbors, but even after several minutes, I remain alone. Just me and the ghosts of this aged, creaking building.

Shit! Did he get trapped there? Or did he figure out what happened that night and decide to ditch me?

I more than like you, Dolly. I know it's crazy, but I do.

I like you. I wish I could tell you how much.

No. He's harboring the same forbidden feelings I am. I know it. So if he isn't returning at my call, there's a reason for it.

But I don't know shit about how wishes work. He said that time travel was more complicated, and he's only done it twice before. What if I effed up the wording? What if I need to use some special incantation to revoke it?

A quick internet search takes me to old reruns of *I Dream of Jeannie*. Not helpful.

Another hour passes. Oh my god, I'm freaking out. Since when does my blood move this fast?

Since Velis.

Argh! I crumple my head against the desk. I need help from an expert, like Mayree, but she isn't even a wish granter! It's not like I can just summon her the way I did Vel—

An incredibly stupid idea crests the horizon of my mind.

There are three other wish granters bonded to me. Three others I could potentially summon to help me. But none of those three would give help willingly.

But . . . now that they're bonded to me, they have to obey my wishes, don't they? And they can't physically hurt me. And they have to tell me the truth. But I took all of their soul power and transferred it to Velis, so how would they even be able to cast magic to get to me?

Beckham and Arrik both worked as wish granters before all this, so they've got their own savings not tied to the estate.

That's true.

Oh geez. Am I really considering this? Think it through, Dolly Jones. Don't panic. Don't let emotion run you. Think *logically*. By all logic, Velis should be back by now. By all logic, he shouldn't exist in that photograph. By all logic, I need a djinn's help to know how to call him back from the past.

Between Beckham and Arrik, Beckham is probably the more dangerous one, but Arrik seems dangerous for a whole other set of reasons.

Namely, his penchant for *fraternizing* with humans.

But I can wish for him not to touch me, right?

I spend another fifteen minutes deciding, leafing through the photographic evidence from that night, taking a picture of a picture to blow it up on my phone. I'm a thousand percent certain that's Velis.

I try the wish with more specifications. "Velis Reilhander, I wish that you would give up on researching the lock that was placed on my soul and return to me at once!"

My time is all messed up due to hopping between worlds and Velis altering the daylight during yesterday's makeout sesh, but based on the balcony windows, it looks like it's becoming dark. I can't go through the night this way.

It is with the deepest of breaths and greatest of reluctance that I direct my next wish elsewhere. "A-Arrik? If you can hear me, I wish that you would see through the cloaking over me, penetrate the barrier around my apartment, and come to me right now —*alone.* And when you get here, I wish you wouldn't even think about putting your hands on—"

The last part of my wish is cut off by the sudden appearance of a shirtless, tattooed djinn with what looks to be the stick of a sucker protruding from his lips and his right eyebrow lifted higher than the Andes.

"Well, well, well."

CHAPTER 17
Arrik

"Arrik, I wish you wouldn't put your hands on—"

I was right. That is a sucker he's been sucking on, for he's just popped it into my mouth.

"Now, now, kitten. Not so hasty."

Ugh. I loathe the way he's always looking down, his mouth propped open to show a hint of his teeth, waiting at the ready to slide against his bottom lip and drag out the word "fffuck." Every roll of his neck, every bend of his joints, every turn of his lean body is made with hot arrogance. And he's got that voice, all raspy and worn, that makes you wonder what he was up late doing the night before.

I spit out the sucker just as furiously as I throw his grasp from its unwelcome stay around my shoulder. "That was in your mouth," I say, stormy.

"Yeah? Tastes better now, huh?"

This. Bitch.

"Arrik, I wish you wouldn't touch—"

In a flash, he's at my level, clutching my chin in his fingers and giving me a look dark enough to break through his well-crafted façade of fuck-all. "I can find other ways to stop you, Master. How about you tell me why you've invited me here before you go ordering me around? I'll play nice with you if you play nice with me." He gives my cheeks a squeeze before releasing me and popping the sucker back into his mouth with a clatter against his teeth.

"Don't touch me." I glare at him. "That isn't a wish. It's a demand."

"Not even with my mouth?" he asks as he eyes mine.

"Especially not with your mouth. I'll wish it sewed shut if you try."

"Scary," he patronizes, dull. "But the thing is, you can't exactly hurt me now, poppet. The only perk of being bonded to a human I can't even draw from. You've locked us all to you, you know. None of us can seek out new masters to try regaining the power you stole until someone manages to tether you. And the other two? They're less than happy about it." He stops to eye me over through languid, scheming eyes. "You aren't really a magnesium or whatever you said you were, are you?"

If I want his help, I need to explain the situation properly.

"No," I surrender. "But it's true there's a lock on my soul. Velis is off investigating why."

"So that's why he's not around. I thought maybe you'd seen the folly of pursuing him and given up." Arrik cracks his wrists while taking in a hearty helping of our surroundings. "And what happened to your dwelling? Looks like an old person's home in here now."

He isn't wrong.

"None of your business." I sniff.

He bends forward to study me. "Vel did this? Is this place sentimental to you or something?" He answers his own question with a long whistle. "Must have cost him a pretty dirham. Alright, love—" Arrik moves his hand to the zipper of his jeans. "Let's get this over with."

I grab a chair from the shaker table and hold it up like I'm about to enter the ring of a televised wrestling match. "*What*?"

Arrik doesn't seem put off in the least. "That's why I'm here, right? To fuck?"

"Ha! Are you *joking*? First of all, if I wanted to fuck you, why would I have ordered you not to touch me? Second of all, WHY WOULD I WANT TO FUCK YOU?"

He seems genuinely confused as he releases his zipper. "Because humans always want to fuck me. You don't?"

I mean, maybe in a world where I had zero morals.

"No, I don't want to FUCK you! I'm involved with your brother, and I don't even know you! Also, I think you're kind of creepy and gross!"

The sucker makes a clank against his teeth as his mouth falls open. "Creepy and *gross*?" More rise than I've seen from him yet. "I'll have you know I've pleased *many* human women, Master."

My point exactly.

Dumfounded, like the popular guy dumped for the first time, he probes: "You don't think I'm attractive?"

Seriously?

"I think you know you're attractive, Arrik. It isn't your body I find gross."

He stares at me blankly for several seconds before settling into a chair with his hands limp between his knees. "Huh." Looks like he may be questioning the meaning of life.

We don't have time for him to philosophize.

"I'm sorry if that hurts your ego, but it's the truth. I would never have sex with you while having feelings for Velis. I also wouldn't have sex with someone I'm only attracted to physically. Not all humans are the same."

"But they are," he says. "That's why I like them. They're so . . . excitable. Show them a little magic and they do basically whatever you say. They fuck us like we're gods."

Yup, creepy AND gross.

"That is definitely not how all humans are. I assume your vessel chooses those types specifically. There's nothing wrong with it, it just isn't how I roll, okay? So, will you listen, please, to the real reason I called you here? It's for your benefit too. The sooner I get tethered to Velis, the sooner you'll be free of me."

Still looking disillusioned, he clears his dry-sounding throat. "Can I get a glass of water first?"

This situation may be weirder than I expected. "Surrre."

A glass of water for the bad boy, tatted-up, sexed-up genie I probably shouldn't have invited here and probably shouldn't be alone with.

I keep one eye on Arrik from the kitchen as I fill up a glass of metallic water from the ancient tap. He's chewing his cheek, his brows knitted in thought. I can't have been the first human to have ever turned him down, can I?

Leaving ample space between us, I try to hand him the glass of water, but it isn't really a surprise when he snatches my wrist instead. He looks up at me with that artful, piercing stare and swallows. "Are you sure, Master? I want to bed you even more now. You won't be disappointed."

Goddamn, where did these boys get those lips? Full and built to tease. They all have them. Must be from their daddy.

"I'm sure," I tell him quietly. "Take the water or I'm dropping it in your lap."

With a frown, he snatches the tumbler and guzzles it down. "I'm not creepy, Dolly Jones." His expression is flat. "And I'm not gross."

"And I'm not a piece of human meat."

That high eyebrow of his is back. "But you are meaty." Whatever disdain is showing through my expression causes him to back down. "Er, sorry. I'll behave, love. Why am I here if not to pleasure you?" He spreads his arms around the head of the chair like he owns it. He sits like a king, displaying his painted body like a work of art.

In some ways, it is.

"I need your help. Velis went back in time to investigate the lock on my soul, and now I can't seem to call him back to me. I know I did you dirty by wishing all your soul power over to Velis, I know you have little reason to help me, but to be honest, I don't care about the contest right now. I just care about getting him back here ASAP."

"Why?" The leftover stick of the eaten sucker wiggles between his teeth. "Time travel can take a while. Why are you so frantic about it?"

I don't answer.

"Come on, Master. You're right—I have little reason to help you, especially after you called me *creepy* and *gross*. I have even less reason to help if you don't tell me the whole story. So what is it?"

I grimace because I didn't want to pull him in all the way. But even if I wish it out of him, he won't know how to help me if he doesn't know the details.

"Wait here," I tell him, returning to my bedroom to retrieve the forbidden photograph. I check it over to ensure that, yes, that's still Velis, before reluctantly handing it over to Arrik.

"What is this?"

"It's a picture taken over a year ago," I tell him. "Something bad happened to me that night and I can't remember it. Somehow, Velis was there for it."

"He wasn't. He was in school without the ability to travel to the human world." Arrik throws the photograph back at me. "The picture's probably been altered."

But . . .

"You and Jeb followed us to a reader named Mayree, remember?"

"I remember things that happened in the last week, Dolly Jones," he says, deadpan.

I ignore the snark.

"Well, she did a reading on us and told us that we've met before. She said it would 'help us greatly' to recall when. She also told us our arrows are pointing *at* one another instead of being aligned the way masters and wish granters normally are."

And then there's . . .

"The night you found me at that nightclub, Velis was meeting with his great-uncle, who said that the only reason none of you would be able to tether to me is because of a wish previously placed on me. Velis did the math and determined I had to have been the one to wish it, but I don't remember doing so, and the only night I don't remember is the night that picture was taken—and Velis was there? It all seems really suspicious. I didn't discover the picture until after I'd already wished Velis into the past, and after I found it, I tried to wish him back, but he isn't showing, no matter how hard I desire it. I don't know how this all works, and I didn't know who else to turn to. Believe it or not, you're the least sketchy of the options I have. I'm pretty sure Jeb and Beckham would kill me if given the chance."

Arrik says nothing right away, just studies me. Then, "You're more like a djinn than a human, Master. You're shrewd."

"Again, I think that's because of the *type* of humans your vessel is attracting."

"Hmph." He snaps his fingers to materialize a black shirt over his ungodly toned body. "I'll help you. If you agree to transfer all of Velis's soul power to me afterwards."

"I'm not doing that," I tell him firmly. "Velis deserves to win. I'm not taking it away from him."

"How do you know I don't deserve to win?" he says, eyebrow cocked.

"Do *you* think you deserve to win?"

"Um, y—" he starts before being compelled to answer: "*No*." Sourness sets over him as he mutters, "Fucking truth oath."

"Why does it matter anyway, if you all think your dad will revoke the win? Why not let Velis see this through to the end if it really has no consequences?"

Arrik scowls a millisecond before stuffing it down and gazing to the side like someone on the cover of a fashion magazine. "We aren't monsters, Master. We have our own backstories too. You have no idea what it's like to have your entire family snubbed because some pretty half-blood enters the scene and steals your father's affections from your mother. Vel isn't innocent in all this, you know."

So it IS jealousy. I knew it.

"Yes, Vel is. He didn't ask to be born into your family, and he sure as hell didn't ask to be born part nymph. He worked harder than any of you during this contest, and he deserves to win. And deep down, you have to know that."

From thin air, Arrik manifests a lit roll of paper that smells like actual weed this time. "Relax," he says when he sees my reservation. "It won't stain your curtains or set off your smoke alarm. I'm not a hack." He takes a puff and blows it thinly through his exquisite mouth. The line of smoke reacts as if it's hit an invisible wall before dissipating. "If I help you, will you change your mind about me?"

There's something to be said for the power of vanity.

"I could always wish it out of you," I threaten.

"Now, that would just be an abuse of power," he says with a sigh. "A bit *gross* and a bit *creepy*, if you ask me."

He's really stuck on that?!

"Fine." I fold. "If you help me without me needing to wish it out of you, it *may* begin to change my opinion of you. I don't think you care about winning the contest anyway, right? Don't you just want to run around and have fun with your masters? I assume you were just pursuing us to help out your other two brothers. Why not help Velis? He's your brother too. I've heard what it was like growing up for him, and I think it's the least you could do. So do it, and I'll reconsider how I feel about you."

He says nothing to show he agrees. Instead, he pats his knee. "Come here, kitten."

"I'm NOT sitting on your lap." And especially not in my grandpa's favorite armchair. That constitutes as defilement.

He sighs, annoyed. "Do you want my help or not? I need you close to read your active wishes. It helps if we're touching."

I can get a better read on yours if we're touching.

Velis said something like that once too. And Arrik can't lie to me.

I approach like I'm walking up to the highest rollercoaster in the park—but stand at the precipice, eyeing him over.

"Do I need to put on a fucking snowsuit? I'm not going to touch you in that way, I promise. It's no fun if you don't want it too. Proved that with our kiss yesterday." The joint in his mouth dangles. "Sit here. Pretend I'm that fat red guy. He's much creepier and much grosser than me."

I can't help snorting at that one. "Do you mean *Santa*?"

"Whomever the fuck you humans like to sit on. Come on." He scoops an arm around my back and ushers me onto his lap.

Oh, this is so *weird*. And I strongly, *strongly* suspect Velis would not approve. Among other things, Arrik smells like expensive cologne, and he's warm. His arms are long and hold defined veins between the muscles. He's built like a magnet for good girls who want to disappoint their parents.

"Protect your boobies." His joint wags.

"W-what?"

He sighs again. "Cover your chest. I'm going to listen to your soul, and I'm guessing you don't want my face in your breasts."

Cautiously, I cross my arms over myself. One hand to my back, Arrik wastes no time pressing his ear to my ribcage.

Yes, my heartbeat is elevated. Yes, I'm holding my breath. It's not because I'm interested in him. It's because I'm a human being made of sinew and flesh, and I'm sitting on the lap of someone who looks like the drummer for an alternative rock band.

I hope against all hope he doesn't notice.

"Relax," he says, ear to the V of my shirt and smoke from his joint trailing unnaturally away from us. "I'm not going to hurt you."

So long as that's what he thinks it is.

After thirty seconds of silence, he begins rubbing my back like he's consoling a crying friend.

"*Is that necessary*?" I rebuke.

"I'm just trying to calm you down. It's hard to hear your soul behind the sound of your heart." He sits up. "Fuck, I really did a number on you, huh? Er, sorry about that. Want a drag?" He holds the roll of paper between his thumb and pointer like the cool guy behind the building at work.

"I . . . don't smoke anymore."

His brow pops, as it seems to like doing. "Anymore?"

"I gave it up a year ago. I'm fine. I'll calm down. Try again."

I stow my nerves because I have to. I need to figure out what's going on with Velis. Why he's stuck in the past and how all of this is related. I need him here with me.

"Wow, that's . . . You know, before it was based on observation, but now that I'm bonded to you, I can really feel it. You're pretty infatuated with my little brother, aren't you? Must be, to go through all this. It's so . . ." Arrik laughs to himself like he's laughing at a child. "*Pure.* I'm used to tasting desires that are a lot darker."

Why is he talking like that? All subdued and low, with his head cuddled against me like I'm his freaking *mother*?

"It does taste good, though," he continues. "I bet he goes crazy for it, being directed at him. I'm starting to understand this thing between you guys."

"Sh-shut up and tell me about the wish."

"Touchy." He pushes my back to smoosh my chest closer against his cheek. "Well, it's still enacted if that's what you're wondering. He hasn't unshackled it or anything. It's just taking longer than you expected, but he is in the process of carrying it out. Now, as to why you aren't able to break it . . ." He squints as if listening hard. "Mm. What exactly did you say when you made the wish? Do you remember?"

Velis Reilhander, I wish you would go back in time to see whether or not we really have met before, and don't come back until you also figure out how this lock was placed on my soul, got it?

Arrik stiffens before leaning away. "Well, there's your problem. You wished him not to come back under any circumstances without fulfilling it."

"I didn't mean it like that."

"Yeah, but you said it like that. There's this whole hierarchy to wishes, and wording influences which ones take precedence. It was moronic of him to let you word it that way. He's a newb. Hasn't time traveled much. What if it took years for him to figure it out? Then he'd just be stuck there. Dumbass."

"It's not like he really had a choice as to how *I* worded the wish," I defend, grumpy.

"Yeah, but he's supposed to guide you in making the wishes. You don't just let your masters blurt them out. Part of our job is figuring out what you really want and helping you form it. Little bro's not thinking like a wish granter. He's thinking like a *boyfriend*."

Oh. Well, it shouldn't take years to figure out. Maybe hours. If he really is at that party, then maybe he's attending the whole thing? I feel relief for the first time since finding the compromising photo.

Moreover, I didn't realize there was such a science to it all.

"You enjoy being a wish granter, don't you, Arrik," I conclude.

"What's not to like? Freedom, chicks, *magic*." He wiggles his fingers at that last one.

I knew it. He doesn't care about becoming the heir to their estate at all.

"So, ah—" He lifts those temperamental eyebrows of his. "I noticed you're still on my lap. Does that mean you want me to entertain you while your nymph's out?"

I clamber away from him as quickly as I can, desperately feeling around behind me for my glue gun.

"Heh. That was a joke, sweetheart. Shouldn't be too long. The wish feels like it's close to being fulfilled. But someone needs to have a talk with that idiot so that he doesn't get lost in a time hole next time."

Someone. It doesn't seem like Arrik intends it to be himself.

I will never understand why someone would value the way one person is born over another. It's literally the thing we can control least in our entire lives.

Arrik watches me ponder it while fogging up the air around him like a Dust Bowl cloud. "Do you want me to wait with you until he gets back? I can sense you don't want to be alone."

"I'm good."

"Really? Your desires say otherwise." Arrik reaches out and beckons to me impatiently, turning the smoke trail from the blunt between his fingers chaotic. "Let me see that picture one more time before I go."

I hand it over with trepidation. "Can you verify whether or not it was tampered with?"

"Already did." Arrik scans it. "It's legit. Fuck if I know how, though. I'm certain he had no way to enter your realm last year. And I'm certain that time travelers can't be photographed. We can't interact with the past." He hands the picture back to me. "The kid's vessel's weird. Maybe it has something to do with that. Do tell me when you figure it out." He stands in my living room like he's waiting for something. "Well? What do you think? Still gross and creepy?"

"Less," I offer. "*Slightly.*"

His mouth shifts into a coil. "I'll take it. Give me a call after he breaks your heart, yeah? I wouldn't mind being a rebound if it was yours, *Dolly Jones*. I'm not a giver by nature, but I'd make sure you woke up hoarse the next morning."

Ugh. And there it goes. Creepy. And gross.

"Fuck, really?" he says when he senses it. He stops to curl his joint into his fist, making it disappear when he reopens his palm. "Well then, I'll wait to feel our bond break, and once it does, you two are fair game again. We'll be coming for what you stole from us. We may not be able to make deals with you after you're tethered to him, but that doesn't mean we can't use you as leverage."

Something tells me he won't.

"I'm going to tell Velis you helped us," I say.

"Ugh. Don't bother." Arrik waves his hand, and then he's gone. Back to find new prey to devour.

But . . . he might not be as bad as I'd originally pegged him.

And he said the wish was nearly fulfilled. I decide I'll wait up for Velis to return. I make myself a solid meal for the first time in months and settle onto my childhood couch, picking up on a random episode of *Game of Thrones* with my socks kicked out on the coffee table in a way I was never allowed to do back home.

A half hour passes, and I shift into lying down.

Another passes, and I pull a lumpy, woven blanket over myself.

Sometime after that, I wake to my shoulder being shaken as the television asks if I'm still watching.

"Velis?!" I shoot up from the couch to find him crouched over me wearing a different shirt than the one he left in. "You're back!" I throw arms around him, detecting instantly that he isn't returning the embrace.

"Dolly," he breathes. "I'm so sorry."

There's something wrong with his voice. It sounds *broken.*

I push away from him to find his eyes laced with tears. "I'm sorry, Master," he says again, swallowing. "I'm so sorry."

"For . . . what? What did you see in the past?" I notice now that he has the incriminating photograph in his hand, picked up from the edge of the table where I left it.

"Dolly." He sets his forehead to mine, dropping the picture to bring his hand to my cheek. "This is all my fault. Your year of jailing yourself. All the guilt you've shouldered alone." His voice cracks again. "It's true, you did cheat on your boyfriend that night, but it wasn't with that pig Gabe."

I wait for it. An anvil's worth of weight falling at me from the ceiling.

"You cheated on James with me," he confesses like it's his greatest sin, "and I'm the reason you don't remember it."

The anvil hits.

CHAPTER 18

Timeless Travels

VELIS

MAKA, I hope I don't screw this up. I've only done it twice, and she's staring at me like someone who's traveled at least a hundred times before. Doesn't she realize this is the hardest kind of wish to grant? We aren't even allowed to go into the past unless wished there. Why does she have so much confidence in me? Somehow, I've fooled her into thinking I'm a guy worth being looked at like that.

Fuck, she's pretty.

Here it comes. It's getting harder to stand here and withstand the pull of it. *I wish.* Those words are satisfying as hell to hear out of her mouth, but once they're uttered, it's like trying to hold in a sneeze. It's coming, and I can't stop it. One more look at her—this beautiful, grumpy creature who sank her claws into me the first time I felt her lips on my vessel.

Maka, I love her.

Maka, it's getting harder and harder not to tell her so.

This is all friggen' crazy. I'm not seriously considering giving up everything I ever wanted for a child of man, am I? That would be like marrying a pet. I'd be ridiculed even more than I am now, and it would be for something I chose rather than something I was stuck with.

How do I fight this off? There was no lecture on what to do if you develop feelings for your master. Because that doesn't happen to people. Because I'm a nymph posing as a djinn.

And she likes that I am.

The world transmutes into the black abyss between realms and time but doesn't restabilize immediately. Just how friggen' far back did we first meet?! If such a moment even exists. I'm skeptical. Mayree fucked me over once by telling Elastia the truth about my blood. Maybe she's trying to do it again.

Elastia was nothing like Dolly. Elastia was a girl driven by image. And money.

Dolly is driven by justice. And beauty.

Is it too soon to fuck her again? Will she think that's all I'm after if I try?

That's not all I'm after, but it's all I *should* be after.

Okay, we're getting there. Somewhere open and summery. I feel the world forming. Trees drop into place.

I'm standing in a park. But not the one near Dolly's dwelling. The air tastes like a different breed of human, a plumper, warmer breed, with traces of corn.

"WHOA!" a tiny voice rings out. "How'd you do that? You just blinked into the air! Are you an alien?"

Blinked? I spin to find a human child with big brown eyes and long dark hair tangled up in the wind. Her knees are stained from playing in the grass, her fingernails grubbed up with dirt.

"You can see me?" I ask.

"Of course I can see you, duh. You're a person. People can see other people."

Aw, frick! I didn't travel back in time! I traveled . . . somewhere else. I knew I couldn't do this right. I'm going to have to return to her dwelling and start over, and then she'll see what a fake I—

"Dolly?" a voice calls on the wind. "Who are you talking to, honeybuns?"

"An alien, Dad!" the girl squeals. "A teenage alien!"

Teenage? I'm not a friggen' teenager. But more importantly,

did the guy exiting that smelly plastic dwelling just call this child—

"Dolly?" I look down into dark, squirrely eyes. "Dolly Jones?"

"Whoa!" The girl hops in excitement. "The aliens really HAVE been watching me, Dad! I knew it!"

"Wait a minute—YOU'RE Dolly Jones? How old are you?"

"Six."

Meaning I met her in the human realm when I was *four*? Impossible. There's no mini version of me here. And why can she see me? If this is the past, she shouldn't be able to see me. Shit, does that mean her dad can see me too? The 'teenage alien' talking to his unattended child?

The man crouches down to child Dolly's level. "Where is she, honeybuns?"

"Right here, Dad! And he's a *boy*! Don't be rude." She shakes her head at me like she's sorry for her dad's behavior.

"Oh, hi, Mr. Alien," says her dad, sticking his hand in the wrong direction. "Thanks for looking after my daughter while I was in the john. Did you just boop beep down to collect some more data on her? She loves pickles and her feet smell."

The . . . John? He was inside another man within that smelly plastic dwelling?

"Dad!" The girl whaps him in the knee in true Dolly fashion. "They don't." She shakes her head at me assuredly. "But I do like pickles."

I wave my hand in front of her father's face. Not even a flinch. What the hell is going on?

"You can see me . . . but your dad can't?"

"Oh! I can see lots of things other people can't," says child Dolly, matter-of-fact. "Mainly ghosts. Only nice ones. And one scary one."

What the frick? Dolly never mentioned being able to see ghosts. Aren't those departed humans? I didn't know they were real.

But this *is* Dolly, right? Dolly, Dolly? I poke her, and she's solid, giggling in response. She's so bubbly.

This was her before those bastards tried to snuff her out.

"Is he here? No? Here? No? How about here?" Dolly's dad is swooping around me, pretending to try to catch me while Dolly plays along.

She and her dad seem close.

Seemed.

He's dead now. Like my mother. Dolly never mentioned how old she was when it happened.

"Oh!" she cries suddenly and begins to wave at me over her head. "He's going, Dad! Bye, Mr. Alien!"

"Going?" I question.

"You're blinking again!"

She's right. The void opens its mouth to swallow me before I can return her goodbye.

What the hell was that?! It's impossible for time travelers to interact with people in the past. By its very nature, magic can't cross time. I'm not real in the past. I'm just part of the air. So how could she see me?! And how could I touch her?

Last time I traveled, I was in a whole concert full of people, and they all just stepped through me.

But she and I *connected.*

Whatever that was for, it satisfied a sliver of the wish. I feel it ticking away, being fulfilled bit by bit.

The world begins to reform. Grass and gravel drop at my feet, the makings of a small human city swirling into place. I'm out front of a building with a steeple.

A . . . brothel? Leave it to Dolly to send me to a friggen' brothel. There aren't many humans around. A man with his canine. A woman with wheels on her shoes. Automobiles burning.

"Mr. Alien?"

I turn to find a girl in a flowery dress leaning against a tree, holding a whip made of grass tied together. There are those eyes. And that hair. She looks a little older this time. Elementary school?

"Dolly Jones?" I question.

"Mhmm." She nods, running the grass whip through her fingers. "Welcome back to Earth. Are you collecting more data?"

So unaffected by a traveler showing up in front of her.

It's like she was expecting me. Weirdo.

I stuff my hands in my pockets. "Uh, yup. Do you . . . still like pickles?"

"Sure do."

Is it just me, or does she seem kinda down? Before, her mood was bursting, but now . . . it's impossible to get a read on it.

Maybe this is a sad occasion.

Maybe she's trying to hide it.

"What is this place?" I eye that pokey steeple.

"It's a church," she says. "*Obviously*. You don't have church on your planet?"

That attitude.

"No," I laugh. "We don't have church the way you have church."

"Lucky." She kicks the dirt. "I hate church. Mom says we have to go to pray for Dad. But everyone in there, they're stupid. They said if you ask, you'll receive, but I've been asking and asking for months and months, and it hasn't done anything! You can't just wish and make someone better. That's what medicine's for." She folds her arms. "So Mom said I don't have to go inside anymore. I can stay out here as long as I don't talk to strangers."

"I'm not a stranger?"

"Nope. Dad met you, and he liked you."

Apparently, that's all it takes.

"Your Dad's . . . sick?" I already know how this story plays out, but I ask anyway.

Like a jackass.

Her little lips begin to quiver. "Not sick. Dying. So all those idiots in there can stuff their prayers in the garbage!"

Her emotions are as strong here as they are in the present. I double over as it hits me, almost as raw as when I went through it myself.

"I'm so sorry, Dolly. Do you want a hug?"

Her desire for one is rippling out of her, stronger than anything else in this world. Strong enough that I may not be able to wait for permission.

"Yes, please."

Oh, thank Maka. I dip to her and scoop her in and feel my shoulder getting wet. Poor kid.

"You know, my mom got sick when I was about your age, Mast—er, Dolly. It was the worst thing that ever happened to me. I can't promise your dad will get better, but I can promise that whatever happens, you'll survive it, and someday, it won't hurt as bad. Okay?"

I feel her nod against me.

"You're a fighter, Dolly. You just have to keep fighting. And . . . you can still talk to people, you know, even when you can't see them anymore. That's what I do."

"Really?" Her eyes are pearly. She looks like an actual doll.

"Swear. And your mother and your grandfather are here for you too, right?"

I hear her sniffle against my shirt. "Y-yeah." And then, "You're leaving?"

Damn it. I feel the world begin to pull me. But she isn't done grieving! If only I could suck that crap out of her and take it with me.

"Will you visit me again?" Her tears shine. "I like being friends with an alien."

An alien. Little weirdo.

"I promise I will. In the meantime, don't hold that crap in, okay? It isn't good for your soul."

Time hurls me into the abyss.

Geezus, what is this? A list of Dolly's greatest hits? Her wish was for me to figure out the first time we met, so where was my kid self both times? Back in Makaya, that's where. So, is this me altering time? Or was time already altered?

Tch. Dolly freaking Jones. Of course if there was a paradox, it would involve her!

It's been now, what, twenty minutes? Not nearly enough time

to justify missing her. Being alone feels weird, though. Like I'm forgetting something. She's probably glad to be rid of me for a while. She isn't the clingy type.

This turn's taking longer. It must be a wider jump than the last. The darkness lulls until—

Here we go. I feel it settling around me.

An enormous box with high-beamed ceilings pulls into focus, smelling like air that's been stored and recycled. Oh *yeeeah*. I've seen one of these before. It's a gymnasium. Am I in a human school?

The rest of the scene sets: the overhead lights work at a fraction of capacity to create an atmosphere of merriment as repetitious, beating music drones from a folding table at the far end of the room. And dozens of human younglings are . . . dancing?

This isn't a gymnasium. It's a child discotheque. How old are these kids? They look on the verge of puberty, some further along than others, many of their faces gross and greasy. Several of them have metal over their teeth.

This is not a flattering age for humans. And is that really dancing? Why are they standing so far apart? Why do they look like they don't want to touch one another?

"Mr. Alien?!"

Per usual, Dolly finds me before I find her.

Oh my GOD. This is my favorite version of her yet. She's just as awkward as the rest of them! What is that dress? And those bangs? And those *stupid* eyebrows?

She looks like an adorable little nerd.

"Hi, Dolly."

"W-why are you here?! Why are you laughing?! I haven't seen you in years! I didn't know if you were real!"

Oh, I'm real, darling, and I'm *ecstatic* over getting to see you this way.

Her face is the best shade of red. She looks like she's about to die of embarrassment.

I love it.

"People can't see me talking to you here! They're going to

think I'm nuts! Come on!" She grabs my elbow to pull me into a deserted hallway lined with metal rectangles with numbers on them. Ugly decoration.

Humans are so strange.

"Is this a special occasion, Dolly? You got all dolled up."

"Yes! It's my first middle school dance! And I know what I said before, but I changed my mind! I have a date now, so you have to go!"

"Whoa, whoa, whoa, what? What did you say before?"

"Oh." Her face flushes deeper under fake rouge. "I . . . w-we made bottle rockets in science class, and I sent you that message? T-telling you I didn't have a date to the dance?"

Ohh, this is too good. I'm going to *torment* her when I see her in the present.

"You asked me to the dance!" Thank Maka I can lie to this version of her. "Of course I got your message, and of course that's why I'm here. Sorry about the long absence, I had alien stuff to do. Invading planets. You know."

"Yeah, well, you came totally underdressed for a dance! And I don't need you anymore anyway!" She glances behind her like she's being followed. "Dan March invited me to the dance at the last minute because he broke up with his girlfriend, so I didn't have to come alone. I'm sorry. I didn't mean to lead you on."

Lead me *on*?

"Don't you think I'm a little old for you, Dolly?"

She points her toes inward. "Well, I keep growing, and you always stay the same. I figured I'd catch up to you eventually. And, I mean, you keep coming back and visiting me, so it seems like you probably like me."

Well, the logic is there.

"Sorry, not into kids, kiddo." I mess up her ringleted hair. "But you're right. Maybe someday when you catch up." The pull of the void comes faster this time. "Looks like time's up."

"I'll see you next time," she says, hasty, glancing behind her.

"And hey, Dolly? Don't kiss Dan March. Only boys that make you their first pick to the dance deserve your kisses, yeah?"

"O-okay."

That may have been excessive. But I want her to kiss as few people as possible before I make her mine.

. . . Make her *mine*?

Make a human mine.

Argh! Why the hell can't I shake this girl?! I've hung out with tons of human girls over the past few months, so why is this one different? And WHY does she have to be human?

I know it's hypocritical. I realize I'm making her race an issue the same way full-blooded women do to me, but the difference is, I don't have a choice! What kind of life could we have together? Where would we live? And what about our kids? They'd be screwed even worse than I was!

. . . Kids?

Having kids with Dolly would be . . . so fun. Imagine living every day with that cantankerous little turd. Creating a life with someone who looks at beauty the way she does.

Ugh. She would freak out if she knew the things I think about her. I'm sure she doesn't want any of that. If she did, she wouldn't be working so hard to help me win this contest. Winning this contest means an end to our time together.

Ow.

The last time I experienced emotional pain that turned into physical pain was when Mom died.

That's what loss feels like.

I don't want to lose her.

The blackness begins to ripple. We're coming in for another landing. Hopefully this time she's of age. I'm not used to girls I'm in love with flirting with me in teenage form.

This time I drop into the center of what looks to be a lecture room with crappy paintings and drawings all over the walls. Thirty little heads bend over thirty little desks, scribbling. They're drawing? And the woman in the front has frizzy hair, dangly earrings, and a long skirt.

A witch!

No, not a witch. This is an art class.

Dolly's right in front of me, but she doesn't sense me. Meaning a chance to catch her in the act and see what her face looks like when she's drawing. Ha, that's about what I expected.

Her sketchpad shows a festival with a big wheel-shaped ride and food carts and strings of bulbed light.

"You're an incredible artist, Dolly."

Dolly, who looks a couple of years older now, starts and then slowly turns to me with eyes like saucers while the rest of the kids carry on, not knowing there's an *alien* in their midst.

She shoots up in her seat, hand raised beside her face. "Bathroom?"

Because it's abnormal for humans to converse with beings no one else can see.

"Again, Miss Jones?" the frizzled teacher scolds. "You just went."

Young Dolly narrows her eyes the way she still does. "I'm on my period." She grips the corner of my shirt and storms out of the room, paying no mind to the giggles of those around her. In the freedom of a hallway marked by those same rows of metal rectangles, she releases me, face the color of a berry. "I-I'm not really on my period."

I eye her over. Well, she's starting to look slightly less awkward. But why do humans have such an unfortunate growth process? "I'm glad you grew out your bangs. They weren't a good look," I tell her.

"I-I-I know."

A stutter? She's so nervous this time.

"How old are you now, Dolly?"

"Fifteen." She doesn't meet my eyes. "Look, Mr. Alien. I know why you're here, and I don't know what to tell you. I know you like me, but I can't just wait around forever!"

'Like' a fifteen year old? Yikes. Not my style.

"What are you talking about, Dolly? I'm only here to see if you still like pickles."

"Why do you guys care about that anyway?" she grumbles, fidgeting, still refusing to meet my eyes.

"Oh, it's *very* important to us," I lie. "The day you stop liking pickles is the day the asteroid hits."

"WHAT?!" This time she looks at me directly.

"Kidding." Though it is fun lying to her without being forced to tell the truth afterward. Man, if this truth oath ever breaks, I'm going to mess with her so hard.

I love messing with her. The adult her.

I love.

"You really don't know?" Dolly says, inspecting me until she decides I'm telling the truth: "I . . . have a boyfriend now."

Ha!

"That's okay, Dolly," I say with a laugh. "You're young. You should be having fun. But not *too* much fun, yeah? And remember what I said about boys who pick you second. Not worth your time."

"Okay, DAD."

Nope. Don't like being called THAT.

"I should . . . I should probably go back now. My teacher might send someone to check on me." Beet-faced, she fidgets and plays with her hair.

It's like she's *smitten.*

Delightful. I'm going to give her so much crap for this when I return to the present.

"Before you go, I meant what I said about your drawing, Dolly. You're an incredible artist. Don't let anyone tell you otherwise, okay?"

Looks like I'm the one leaving first. The cosmos zippers me into the abyss before she so much as turns away.

So that was fifteen-year-old Dolly. Dolly is twenty-four now. We've got a lot of ground to cover before we make it back to the present. I hope to Maka I'm not fucking up the timeline by talking to her.

Before I left the present, she didn't seem to remember any of these conversations. So what happens when I go back?

This shit is complicated.

It's taking even longer this time, passing through years. Too much time alone in my head obsessing over a human woman. That pale skin from being inside all year, those deep brown eyes that seem to go on forever, and that body you could just pin down and destroy.

Goddamn, I crave her like she's sugar.

I wonder when her boobs show up? Seems like she was a late bloomer.

Here it is. The walls are filling in. Whatever this room is, it's small and cluttered, with two beds pushed up to the ceiling on posts. I've never been in a place like this before. Is this like where monks sleep? There are bras and shirts flung over a built-in desk and shoes and books piled up on the floor.

"Dolly?"

No answer. There's no one else in this room. Did I get the jump wrong?

In the reaches of my mind, I hear a voice:

"Velis? Return to my apartment. I wish you would!"

Dolly! The *real* Dolly. She's calling for me?

But I can't return to her. I'm still under obligation to the first wish, and she said that part so *sternly*.

A shiver hits the back of my neck in remembrance.

Why do I love being bossed around by her so much? I've never been the masochistic type. Only when it's her, apparently. She thinks I'm joking, but imagine what she'd look like in dominatrix getup. She's a friggen' fox. Maybe I was wrong before. Maybe I want her to be the one doing the pinning.

Fuck, she's a good lay.

But she's also good at . . .

I'm Team Velis. I'll do whatever I can to help you beat them, okay?

Well, I think it's wack. I don't see any difference between you and any other djinn we've met.

Tell Beckham to fuck off. You're going to win this, Velis. And I'm going to help you.

Because your dad clearly loved your mother so much. And still does by the looks of it.

You can't force that kind of loyalty. It comes to those who deserve it.

And for the record, screw your ex. Racist bitch.

She's so sexy, so dorky, and so . . . encouraging. It feels like a trick. It feels like someone created her for me, and they're waiting until the end for the big ha-ha to reveal she's all smoke and mirrors.

But I know that's not true. I know that, in the end, I'm going to be the one that ruins it. I need to figure out her heart's true desire before then and give it to her, free of charge. It's the best and least I can do for her.

Just as soon as we get her soul unlocked.

The knob clicks, and a woman enters, pushing the door with her ass, an iced beverage in one hand and a stack of books in the other.

I know that ass.

And I know that fragrance.

"Hello, Dolly Jones."

The books thunder to the floor in a mess, but the iced beverage is saved, barely, as she whirls around to see me.

Okay, she's definitely a woman this time, breasts and all. Though she still looks younger than the current version of herself. Her face is slimmer, and her eyes a bit brighter.

"Y-you!" she stutters. "You're real?!"

Geez, does she always convince herself I'm not between these visits?

"I'm real, babe. What is this place?"

"It's my dorm room."

Dorm room? I've heard of those. She's in college.

Wonder if she's with that dick *James* yet.

"Have you transferred already?" I ask.

She's still blinking at me like she doesn't believe I exist. "Er, transferred? No, I'm planning to move to the west coast next year for an art program. But how do you know about that?"

She's not with him yet. She's still at her first college. I should tell her to stay here. I should tell her to keep pursuing art right here at home, where her family is, away from that noxious group of friends. It's probably best for both of us that we never meet.

But I'm not nearly selfless enough to do something like that. She needs to go to that other school so that she can meet that prick so that she can start her pledge so that she can come find my vessel out of desperation. I need to meet her for real. I need to have these memories of our time together.

I'm not willing to give them up for either of our sakes.

"Why are you looking at me like that?" she asks slowly.

Because I'm in love with you.

"Because you have shit on your face."

Embarrassed, she hurries to wipe the nonexistent smudge away. "Why are you here?" she says after, setting down her drink and coming a few steps closer. "I haven't seen you in four years. You aren't really an alien, right?"

Fuck. She really is a woman now, and she looks damn cute. Are those overalls? Did she purposely make her hair look like she's been studying?

"I'm your guardian angel," I lie.

"Pffft!" Mist from her mouth sprays the room.

Why is it so hard to believe I could be an angel?!

"You are not," she says. "I mean, I told you when I was little that I hated church, and you said squat against it."

Oh. True.

"Speaking of which . . ." Her eyelashes fall over her eyes. "I always told myself that if I ever saw you again, I would thank you for what you did back then. Your advice helped me get through a really tough time, with my dad's passing and all. You always seem to pop up when I need a little support. I guess that's why I created you. I should probably find a shrink, right?"

She thinks she created me?

"I'm real, Dolly. You didn't make me up. I can't explain the details now, but I'm glad you see me that way. It's the least I can do after all the help you've given me."

She tips her head cutely. "How have I helped you?"

"You just have."

"Oh." She's closer now, close enough that I can feel her breath. "Then . . . can I have a reward?" Her hands begin to move up my chest.

Since when is Dolly this forward?!

Keep your cool, keep your cool, keep your cool.

"You really think you deserve one?" I manage.

"I do." She moves her dainty little fingers to the back of my head to pull me to her level. "I've been wanting to do this for a very, very long time, Mr. Alien."

Oh shit. Is this cheating? Is it possible to cheat on your girlfriend with a past version of your girlfriend?

Her mouth finds me but not in the place I expect.

What is with this girl and necks?!

"So warm," she coos. "You smell like a real boy."

There it is, that desire *dangling* in front of me, promising release if I would just—

Fuck it.

I take her waist and kiss her where I really want to.

On that cunning little mouth.

Man, she is not a good kisser yet. But she tastes the same as ever.

By my calculation, she's nineteen here. Three years younger than me. It's kinda hot to be older than her for once.

The things I'd like to teach you, Dolly Jones. But you're going to learn them from other men.

That's okay. I'll be waiting.

"Thanks for stopping by," she says, resting her head against me. "I'm super stressed out with midterms. Like I said, you always seem to show up when I need you most. You're the reason I kept practicing art and the reason I don't let jerks kiss me. And with Dad . . . I kept thinking about how you said it would get better, and how an alien Dad liked was keeping watch on me from the stars. I've thought about you a lot over the years." She sets her hands to my chest to push me away. "Leave it to me to create the world's hottest coping mechanism."

Aw, she thinks I'm hot.

"You're going to be okay, Dolly Jones." I take hold of her chin. "Things are going to get hard for you, but you're going to push through them like you always do. You're smart and strong and capable. I'll be waiting for you at the end of it." I kiss her forehead as time mercilessly rips me away.

That one was harder than the rest. She's becoming more and more like herself, and we're getting closer and closer to the present.

It's hard to say goodbye to even a version of her I've known for five minutes. How am I supposed to say goodbye to the version I know best?

How is it possible to feel like you've known someone their whole life after only knowing them a week?

I guess, because in a roundabout way, I have.

Through the swirling darkness, a command strikes me:

"Velis Reilhander, I wish that you would give up on researching the lock that was placed on my soul and return to me at once!"

Oh crap. She's still calling for me again? With my FULL name now? How long have I been gone? And why does she sound so *spazzy*?

I wouldn't have left her alone if I wasn't sure she was safe. So there's no reason for me to be this worried. Argh! Let's get this over with. Come on.

Come ON!

I wait for the years to pass, and when the world returns to its senses, I'm in a . . .

Goblin's hovel?

A disorienting place with too many people, a film of smoke, and garbage human music cranked up too high. It reminds me of Arrik's bedroom.

And through it all, I hear:

"Dolly-kins, Gabe, get together for a photo!"

The rest of our friends went to a local music festival and then to a party at a duplex a few of them rent. That place was so gawdy. Decorated with all kinds of shit they stole from hotels and restau-

rants, and crap they picked up at flea markets. It was the perfect place to just chill out. No expectations.

Oh no.

This is that place, with strings of lights over doors and windows, with mismatched furniture that looks sunken in.

Is this that night?

The night Dolly was assaulted?

CHAPTER 19

That Night

VELIS

IF THIS IS THAT NIGHT, time can't expect me to just stand back and let it happen! There she is, lost in a sea of fools, looking catty as ever in her usual getup. And that obnoxious guy with the backwards hat and his arm around her must be—

"Gabe, get the fuck off me!"

Dolly throws his arm from her neck as soon as the flash from a camera device ends, calling into the crowd:

"Fallon, come get your boyfriend, he's drunk and he smells!"

"Don't do it, Dolly," the punk sloshes. "She's being mean to me. Let's go hang out somewhere."

"Touch me again, Gabe, and I'll break your fingers."

Atta girl.

Dolly looks annoyed to be here, getting jostled and wrung around the neck. She's not as pale as she is in the present, and her hair's longer, but that's her. Feisty and fine.

This was one year ago.

"Dolly!" I call for her, but she doesn't hear me over the clatter of party guests. I make my way through them, unable to push them out of the way, like I'm a motherfucking phantom. "Dolly Jones!" I jog to her, glancing over heads and under raised cups to reach her, extending a hand to her shoulder—

"Master!"

She spins around and at the same time is knocked into from behind by a girl with an annoying voice and a floppy hat.

The cup of water in Dolly's hand hits me in the chest.

I shouldn't be able to interact with objects here.

And yet, here I stand, soaking wet.

"Mr. Alien?!" Her wide-eyed stare gives way to understanding. "Aw, hell. Am I having a mental break?"

She looks so much like herself, it's hard to remember she doesn't really know who I am.

"How many times do I have to tell you, *I'm real*." I peel my wet shirt away from my skin.

"Goddamn it, it's been, like, four years! I thought I had all my issues sorted out!" She's grumbling. "Yes, I still like pickles. No, my feet don't stink. Come on, let's go dry you off." She takes my wrist and marches us through the party to a dim, musty toilet room where she hands me a towel.

That was a full glass of water. I disrobe.

"H-holy—!" she gasps.

She's staring at my body. I look down to see what she sees, and when I look back up, she's holding her forehead.

"*Why* did I have to make my imaginary friend so hot? This isn't normal."

Lusty little thing.

"Dolly," I say with a laugh, "I'm *real*. Feel me." I take her hand and set it to my chest, where it soon comes alive and runs over my skin.

Because even though she doesn't really know me, she already *yearns* for me. I can feel it spilling out of her, all fragrant and enticing, sending shivers up my spine. I take her waist because it's the only way to stop myself from what I'd really like to do.

"Hellooo!" The waves of desire are interrupted by the door to the toilet room flinging open. "Oops, sorry DOLLface. I have to pee." The annoying girl with the floppy hat stumbles in and fwomps herself onto the basin.

Yup, that's the sound of pissing.

"Hey, Kate?" Dolly questions, hand now hidden behind her back. "Is there a . . . guy in here with us?"

"Where? Like, behind the shower curtain?" the hatted girl asks.

"Just what I thought," Dolly mutters, crabby.

"I'm *real*," I insist.

"Oh yeah? Then why can't anyone else see you, *alien boy*?"

Kate flushes. "Um, who are you talking to?"

Dolly eyes me over. "Myself, I guess."

"By the way," Kate says, struggling to rearrange her skirt, "Fallon is pissed at you. She says you've been flirting with Gabe all night."

"Ugh! *Flirting*? That guy won't keep his hands off me! She's delusional."

"Yeah, well, she's got a big mouth and she's jealous AF, so be careful you don't give off the wrong impression." Overtly loud Kate takes up residence in front of the mirror.

"I'm literally not," says Dolly.

"I don't know," says Kate, pushing at eyelashes that look to be . . . glued on? Do humans glue hair from their heads onto their eyes?! "Don't you think maybe your body's a little too *juicy* for that outfit, Dolly? People notice that stuff."

What a *bitch*.

"I wear these because they're comfortable, not because I'm trying to get any," Dolly retorts, flicking her eyes to me.

"Mmkay. Here, take some pics, would you?" The hatted girl throws a camera device at Dolly. "I'm too drunk."

"Come on," Dolly whispers at me, taking my hand to lead me away from a girl now drawing crooked lines out from the corners of her eyes.

These people are a mess. All but—

"You aren't drunk," I realize, speaking of the best of the humans here.

"No," Dolly confirms, "why would I be? I'm sure you already know this, being part of my subconscious, but I get . . . frisky when

I drink, and my boyfriend is out of town. I don't like to drink alone in settings like this anymore."

But if she isn't drunk, then how does she end up screwing *that*? The Gabe guy is now shot-gunning consumables in the center of a group of other similar animals, their heat and stench rising above them like something from prehistoric times.

Dolly is a gem amongst beasts.

"Wait here," she says. "I need to go do damage control."

As she moves away, wiggling the camera device, I remember: "Crap, I forgot my shirt." But the toilet room door is now securely closed, and there are retching sounds coming from within.

Dolly displays an evil little smile from over her shoulder. "You don't need that."

Lusty little thing.

She winks at me before scurrying away to the other side of the room. "Gabe, Fallon, get together for a picture!"

The spark of a flash goes off.

"Good. Now *stay together*," she barks, loud enough for me to hear. "Don't let him out of your sight, Fallon. He's wasted."

Dolly returns to where she left me, beside a coatrack overflowing with raincoats. "You heard that, right? Everyone heard me tell those two to stay together?" The photograph she just took is wafting through the air in her hand.

"Yes, I heard it. Are you okay, Ma—Dolly? You seem really stressed out."

"I shouldn't have come to this party. I'm guessing that's why my brain spit you out. These guys get too fired up, and it's hard to be alone in a cloud of idiocy."

"You're too good for this, Dolly." I mean it. "Why are you friends with these people?"

"That IS something my conscience would say, isn't it," she speculates. "I'm friends with them because it's better than being alone out here without my family. And they aren't all bad. Not all the time."

She distracts herself with the photograph, which is taking its time revealing its secrets. Clicking a device and creating an image of what you see? Humans are capable of magic too, but they never seem to see it.

Whatever the picture reveals causes Dolly to jolt forward and those dark eyebrows of hers to scrunch. "Wait, what?" She looks at me suspiciously before shoving the picture in the face of a random party guest mixing beverages for other humans. "How many people are in this picture?"

"Six," the partygoer responds.

Dolly exhales out of what appears to be relief, until—

"Oh, wait. Seven. I didn't notice the shirtless guy in the back."

She twists to face me, confused as I've ever seen her. "*You* showed up in it? How is that possible?"

It's not.

I snatch it from her to confirm.

What? Is it because she was the one to take the photograph? Is that how the device's magic works?

"You . . . aren't in my head?" She looks at me with new definition. She's softer and, at the same time, more guarded.

We've been through all this before.

"Come with me, Dolly." This time, I'm the one to take her hand, leading her to a closed-off bedroom at the back of the party, shutting the door to dull the horrible music concocted by a race that doesn't know anything about music.

On the edge of an unmade bed, Dolly is wearing a look that says she doesn't trust me for the first time since meeting me in the past.

I preferred when she thought I was an alien.

Things aren't adding up, here. How does it come to pass that she blacks out and cheats on her boyfriend if she isn't even drinking?

"What are you?" she says, defenses up. "The truth."

"I'm a time traveler."

She narrows her eyes at me. "I said the truth."

"That is the truth! I'm a time traveler, but you aren't supposed to be able to see me. No one is. And I'm also a djinn. Er, genie. And . . . your boyfriend, I think."

Her blinks become profuse. Why is she always blinking like that?! Makes me fucking nervous for what's to follow.

"You're my time-traveling genie boyfriend from the future?" she repeats with slow intention. Then, for the first time all night, she laughs. "Well, that's a story." A story that puts her at ease, apparently. Her posture shifts. "So, what year are you from, Mr. Time Traveler?"

"Next year."

"Oh, okay, sure." She sounds like she's merely playing along. "But I already have a boyfriend. His name is—"

"James. Yeah, I've heard about him. He sounds like a tool. I thought you promised not to kiss jerks?"

She's clearly surprised that I know his name. She looks away. "It's complicated."

I don't know what to do here. I should be incapable of effing up the timeline, so how much do I tell her? And why am I even here? Is this the night her lock was placed?

"Dolly, I know you don't believe me, and I don't have time to convince you, but I'm here for an important reason. I need to look inside your mouth."

Getting access turns out to be easier than I expect.

"Why not." She shrugs. "I mean, my psyche has clearly broken, so why not let the time-traveling genie boyfriend take a peek inside my mouth. Just to warn you, I ate some nachos earlier."

She leans back on her hands and opens wide.

I can work with this. Letting her think she's gone crazy will be easier than getting her on board for real.

I grab hold of her chin to tip her back a little farther and peer through her aura into the holding cell of her soul.

It looks the same as it does in present day.

The lock was already placed?! When? Did I miss it during one of those jumps? Shit! I should have been checking her all along to pinpoint when it happened! She wasn't *born* this way, was she?

I release her mouth. "Dolly, have you met another djinn before?"

"Do they all look like you? Definitely not."

"No one has ever come into your life and, like, cast a spell over you? They would have had to tell you they were doing it. They may have even asked you to wish for it."

Her brow furrows. "You mean besides you?"

What? *What*? "What?"

Music pulses against the door like it wants to burst in.

"You're the only one who has ever done something like that. I was pretty young, so I don't remember it clearly, but I do remember you showing up and putting this blue light around me. It's pretty much the first memory I have."

"You mean before we met in the park with your dad?"

"Oh yeah, way before that. I thought it was a dream until you showed up again in that park."

A memory I haven't jumped to yet? But why would I do that? And why doesn't present Dolly remember any of this? She doesn't remember the lock or meeting me or any of this night.

This time, music isn't the only thing pushing against the door. The knob turns, and in stumbles a drunk partygoer with a backwards hat.

Ugh, the worst of the humans. Motherfucking Gabe.

"What the hell, Gabe?" Dolly hops up from the bed. "Can't you see I'm having a conversation in here?"

But from what he can tell, Dolly is alone. "With yourself?" Gabe shuts the door behind him. "Are you sure you weren't waiting for me in here, Doll-lectable?"

"I told you not to call me that." She folds her arms. "And I definitely wasn't waiting for you. Get out of here. Go back to Fallon. I told her to keep an eye on you."

"Come here, Dolly." Gabe takes her wrist to pull her down onto the bed beside him. "Let's hang out."

"Dude, back off! She's not interested." But he can't hear me. He's a big guy, and he smells stale. And I know where this night is headed. "Dolly, you should get out of here."

She meets my eyes and nods, but even after she stands, Gabe refuses to release her wrist. "You know James is off boning that redhead he works with. Why can't we have a little fun together?"

"He's not, Gabe. Stop spreading shit."

"Dolly, he literally sent me a photo of her in his hotel bed like twenty minutes ago. I'm not supposed to tell you, obviously, but I'm a nice guy. I can't stand by and watch you be treated like that. So, come on, let's hang out tonight."

"NO, Gabe." Dolly struggles to free her wrist. "And what about Fallon?"

"We're done. I told her so a hundred times, and she refuses to accept it. Maybe she finally will if you and I . . ."

Dolly responds with fire in her eyes, clenching her teeth to rip her wrist from him, but the beast holds tight.

"Dude, let her go!" I jump in and take hold of Dolly's arm to help her pull, but because I can't do shit to touch Gabe, all it does is hurt her wrist.

Fuck! I wish I could put hands on this jackoff!

"I know you want me, Dolly. You've wanted me ever since we went on that date sophomore year. I've seen the way you get when you drink. I'm not blind."

"Why do you think I'm NOT drinking, Gabe? I swear to god, if you don't let go of my arm, I'm going to rip your face off. FALLON!" But the closed door and music stand in the way of her calls. "FALLON, GET IN HERE!"

Gabe uses his free hand to cover her mouth.

I boil.

"WHO THE FUCK DO YOU THINK YOU ARE? LET HER GO RIGHT NOW, YOU COCKSUCKER!"

I hold Dolly from behind to help pull her away, but this fucker is fueled with animalistic aggression, and he uses it to throw her back onto the bed. Trying to get between the two of them does jack too, because I can only interact with one of them.

FUCK! This is that moment! The moment Dolly thinks is her fault. I knew it! I knew she had nothing to do with it! Who cares if she gets flirty when she drinks? Who cares if she wears pants that make her ass sing? Who cares if they went on a date three years ago? That doesn't give this shithead the right to—

"GET OFF HER!"

She's fighting hard, and I feel like a helpless piece of shit. Why am I here for this? Why do I have to see this?!

"Dolly! Fuck, fuck, fuck, what do I do?!"

She yells against his moist hand as he works to position her into compliance in a messy bedroom on top of sheets that smell like some other person's sweat.

I try to grab a skinny club-shaped object from the ground, and my fingers slip through it. I tackle his head to punch off his hat, but my fist flies right past.

"Dolly, I'm right here. It's going to be okay. I'll think of something!"

Those are sobs coming out of her, being choked out behind the hand clamped over her mouth. He's got both her wrists down now in his other hand and is glancing at the door to make sure it's secure.

I lasso my arms around her waist to pull her out from under him—asinine, because she's being held down by weight I can't feel!

I don't cry often, but this fucking sucks!

I'm not giving up. We still have time. I search the room for a solution. "ARGH! I wish I could lay hands on this guy!"

The world freezes as invisible ripples fluctuate in the air, the way they do whenever a wish is cast, the unseen pull of compulsion raging through me. I can't stop it. I can't fight it. My eyes burn hot with Maka's energy because wishing words were spoken.

But my master wasn't the one to speak them.

My body moves on its own as I become a physical being in a time that isn't mine, taking hold of the mongrel's shoulders and wrenching him away from Dolly.

"Who the flip are you?" Gabe asks as our eyes connect.

"I'm her boyfriend, you rapist fuck!" I throw him to the ground, feeling that same animalistic aggression as I throw all of my weight behind a punch to his ugly face, causing a spray of blood the color humans bleed before pulling back and doing it all over again until his nose is dripping and his eyes are closed.

"Pig." I give him one final pitch against a scratched-up armoire before rushing to Dolly, whose eyes are wet and wide as she clutches herself in the center of the destroyed bed. I put my hands out but worry she may not want to be touched. "Maka, I felt so defenseless watching that! Are you okay, babe? I wish I could have jumped in sooner."

I wish.

How the hell am I granting my own wishes now?

"Thank . . . you." Her stare is deep and welling. So easy to get lost in there.

What does she want? What does she want? Focus.

I can sense that she wants to be held but that my bare skin is throwing her off.

"I wish I was wearing a shirt for you."

A second time, compulsion rushes through my veins as I'm forced to concoct a shirt for myself. I shouldn't be able to cast magic in the past. I shouldn't be able to grant wishes in the past. I shouldn't be able to grant my own wishes *ever*. Is this all her doing?

Dolly clenches her fingertips into the fresh shirt painted over my body and leans against me to bury her face in the fabric. I made sure it smells good for her. She likes the smell of lilacs, even if she's never told me so. She says nothing, but I feel her shaking. I wait for that shaking to let up before setting a hand onto her back. "Is this okay?"

She nods.

Being an empath, I can *feel* her pain and embarrassment like it's my own. She has nothing to be embarrassed about. I tell her so.

She isn't drunk. She's going to remember all this. How scared she was, how he smelled and the weight of him trying to hold her down.

But if I can use magic here, I must be the one that erases her memory of it. Maybe I do it to maintain the timeline. Or maybe I do it so that she won't revisit this moment whenever she's alone. I don't ever want her to relive it. I don't ever want her to feel that way again.

I can consider it practice for when I have to erase her memory for real.

"For the record, you did nothing to deserve that," I tell her. "That guy's a cockroach. You made it clear you weren't interested."

"I know." She sits up. "I know it's not my fault."

Erasing her memory is going to make her think it is. The guilt I feel—that's my own this time.

Dolly never looks this fragile. I'm afraid that if I touch her, I might break her, but she isn't afraid of touching me. She uses her fingers to brush the hair from my forehead, a new wish forming in her, small. I wait for it to manifest.

"I don't know what you are," she whispers, "but I don't care. You've always been around when I needed you most. Before you disappear again, I have to tell you something." Her endless gaze sucks me in. "I think I fell in love with you a long, long time ago."

It feels like a dart to the chest.

This Dolly . . . loves me?

I can feel it sparkling through her other emotions just as surely as I can feel something moving in my own.

I can't hold it down. It's been getting harder and harder to keep it down. "I love you too, Dolly," I admit to her. "It hit me so fast I couldn't stop it. And I'm dreading the moment I have to tell you goodbye. It gets darker every hour we get closer."

Desire pulses in her. I feel that she wants to kiss me, but she feels dirty about wanting to kiss me after what just happened to her.

"It's okay, Dolly. There are no rules for how you're supposed to feel."

I let her take what she wants. It's nothing much. Just a peck. Just enough for her to feel safe and loved and in control. I keep my hands to my sides and wait for her to feel all those things, and when she does, that's the moment I do it.

I touch my fingertips to the side of her head and remove all her memories of me. The park, the church, the gymnasium dance, the art classroom, the dorm dwelling, this horrible night, and the one I haven't visited yet. The one where I lock away her soul. I pull the memories out of her, absorb them into the pads of my fingers, and when it's over, her body hardens because a strange dude is kissing her in a room that isn't hers.

She pushes me away with coldness I've never seen from her before. "Who the hell are you, pretty boy?"

The sparkling I felt from her is gone. Her love for me is gone. She has no idea who I am.

Ouch.

She's looking at me like I'm a stranger. Just another guy trying to make moves on her.

Ouch.

I've smeared clean plenty of memories over the last few months. None of them felt like this. It hurts to see no recognition in her big, beautiful eyes.

"I don't know you," she says like an accusation. "Why are we in bed together? Are you *crying*?"

I can't stand it. I tap her forehead and send her to sleep.

She won't remember this night. She'll lose all her friends and harbor consuming guilt all alone for one year because of what I just did.

But what else am I supposed to do? I couldn't let her remember the trauma of what just happened!

But . . . maybe it should have been her choice.

FRICK. It definitely should have been her choice! What am I doing? I shouldn't be making decisions for her!

My feelings for her are screwing with my judgment.

With the weight of what I've just done setting in, I deal with the crumpled dickhead in the corner, sealing his wounds and pushing him into even deeper sleep that ensures he'll wake up after Dolly.

And then, because I've fulfilled what I was sent here to do, time slings its lasso and tears me from reality.

In the darkness between time and space, I squat, wiping my

face on the bottom of the shirt I made for Dolly. I thought I had the strength to remove her memory. But to be looked at like that by her? To feel the things I've felt brewing in her cut off like they never existed? I don't know if I can do it again.

What am I going to do? It's like I've fallen in love with her twice.

I crouch and compose myself and wait for my final destination.

It takes longest of all this time, and when the darkness melts, I'm in a living room that looks just like the one I made for Dolly's dwelling. An old television cube against the wall plays a cartoon about . . . aliens? A toddler sits on the floor in a patch of sunlight, pushing around a long red toy automobile. Isn't that a toy for boys? Dolly seems the type to like boy toys.

Her eyes are even bigger in that small head. She's always been cute.

From an adjacent room, a man sings a song: "Foll-y. Loll-y. Love my baby Doll-y."

Dolly's dad is a dork, like her.

When she sees me, toddler Dolly reaches her arms up like she wants to be held. She looks like I could poke a finger into her stomach and it would get lost there. She's so . . . squishy. I pick her up and find that she feels as squishy as she looks. Is she old enough to talk? I don't know how humans work.

"Can you show me your tongue?" I ask.

A very uncomfortable thing to ask a toddler human, but she complies, opening her mouth wide. She tries to lick me.

"No nonsense now, little one." I tip her chin to get a better look and can't help but gasp.

It's . . . stunning. Dolly's soul is *stunning*. The warmth of a thousand sunny days meets my cheeks as I peer down the glowing throat of a tiny human. It's so *bright*, the taste of it deeply quenching and close enough to draw saliva. If only I could sink teeth into a soul like that.

But where is her heart's greatest desire? I don't see one. It's like she didn't come built with one. She's like an unpainted canvas, waiting to be marked. Dolly's soul is nothing like the souls I've farmed so far. It's—

Shit, if any other djinn got a whiff of this soul . . .

"Dolly, I'm putting a protective spell on you. It's going to take a hefty amount of the power I have, but no djinn will be able to siphon your soul until I show you our forgotten past. And after you find out the truth, you can decide whether or not you want to be tethered to me."

Blue light funnels around her as I set my mouth protectively to her forehead, imbuing her with a lock no djinn, myself included, will be able to remove until the moment I admit I'm the reason she lost so much.

She's going to hate me.

I love her, and she's going to hate me. I fight the emotion pushing at me as I set down the toddler version of Dolly and let myself be ripped one last time into the abyss.

CHAPTER 20

The Symphony of Truth

"You cheated on him with me," Velis has just confessed like it's his greatest sin, "and I'm the reason you don't remember it."

What the hell is that supposed to mean? Moreover, what happened back there? He looks like he's been through a battle. And, well, I already know he was at that party. There's photographic evidence of it. But—

"You're saying the person I slept with last year at that party was *you*," I say slowly.

"Oh! No, you didn't sleep with anyone, but you did kiss me. And while that was technically cheating, your boyfriend was also cheating on you. And you didn't fully believe I was real? And . . . there are so many other things you should know. You weren't even drunk that night," he says.

"So then . . ." I put the pieces together. "You're the one that stole my memory of that night. You traveled back in time, kissed me and then erased my memory of it, leaving me passed out and alone with some other guy." Uh oh. I feel it building. "Does that about sum it up, Vel?"

"Yes, but not entire—"

And here it comes crashing:

"You ruined my life, Velis! And you lied! You told me you

couldn't interact with the past! You told me you'd never erased my memory! You told me we had never met before! You've been lying to me this whole time! What kind of game are you playing with me? Arrik said you couldn't manipulate the past, but you clearly can! Is it because you're a nymph?"

I've struck a nerve.

"Because I'm a *nymph*?" His face turns haughty. "And when the hell did you talk to Arrik? Did you . . ." He sniffs the air like he can still smell the marijuana. "*Invite* him here? While I was gone?! What the hell, Dolly!"

"Well, what was I supposed to do when I find a freaking picture of you from the worst night of my life? And then you weren't answering my wishes and coming back to me! I had no one else to ask!"

"But ARRIK? He's the slimiest one of the bunch! Why would you invite him here after what happened to you?!"

Lord help me.

"After what *happened* to me?" I lash. "So, you really do just see me as a victim. Even more now that you've experienced it, I guess."

"Argh! NO. Why is this so hard! Why can't you just stop and listen for a minute! Why did I have to fall in love with such a challenging, temperamental girl?!" His head falls. "Maka, we fight like we fuck."

I freeze. Did he just say . . .

"Velis . . . you're in love with me?" Like waves overtaking a shore, the pound of my pulse rises from my chest to my ears as I wait for him to repeat it.

"Oh." His eyes crawl up from the ground. "I didn't mean to say that. I should—"

He extends a hand to me, and I flinch.

"Please don't." I bare myself. "I want to remember it. I want to remember that you love me."

His hand falls along with his brow. "Geezus, Dolly, I'm not going to erase your memory. It was hard enough the first time."

He stares at me with that untraceable, unreadable, unflinching stare of crystalline ice.

He's in love with me.

But he doesn't want to be. Just like I don't want to be in love with him. Because love means that the end of this will be so much harder, so much more painful.

His throat betrays a swallow. "I was going to say that I should return your memories. There's a lot you don't know. We have met before, and it wasn't only the night of that party. I . . . I don't know how any of this is possible, but I know what happened. I know how the lock got on your soul, and I know how to remove it. We'll talk after your memory is restored, yeah?"

He extends his fingers to my temple, and this time, I don't flinch but keep my eyes securely on his.

He loves me.

My genie loves me.

And I . . . ?

Velis's fingertips graze me while he produces a soft voice to mirror an even softer expression. "Something did happen that night with Gabe. Or at least he tried to make it happen. I'm going to try to cut around that part so you don't have to see it, okay? I'll keep that memory for you if you're okay with it."

I'm scared.

"Show me the rest of it first and then I'll decide," I say.

He agrees with a bob of his head. "And Dolly, I only want you to tether to me if that's what you still want after you see all this."

His fingertips make full contact with my temple, and it comes rushing back to me like snowflakes hitting the dashboard of a speeding car.

My first memory, my favorite park, the day before my dad died, my first middle school dance, the day I drew my first award-winning picture, my first college midterms, and . . . that night. The night Velis saved me. The night I was forced to leave a toxic relationship and group of friends. The night he first told me he loved me. And I him.

It's seconds, but it feels like hours.

When he removes his fingers, my cheeks have become stained with salty evidence of the lump in my throat.

I don't want to see it. I don't want to see the parts he blurred over, and I don't care if that makes me a coward. I'm not a slut. I was never a slut. And it doesn't matter how the rest of them perceive me because I know the truth. I know who I am, and I am done apologizing for it. Fuck Gabe, fuck Fallon, fuck Kate—and most of all, fuck James.

Velis was the only one there for me that night.

I understand now, why it was so easy to fall in love with him. I've known him my whole life.

My chin shakes my teeth too vigorously to control. "You're Mr. Alien."

The corner of his mouth ticks momentarily before he buries his hands into my hair on either side of my face. "Oh Dolly, I've been trying so friggen' hard not to fall in love with you, but it's pointless. I don't understand it, but me going back, it wasn't changing anything. It was just fulfilling what was already there. It's like what happened between us was always meant to happen. I love you, and I think I was always supposed to."

Behind him, the 'television cube' gives up and turns off, darkening the room. Outside, night wind brushes branches against grumpy, brittle trees.

There's no use denying it.

"I love you too, Vel. So where does that put us?"

Wherever it puts us, our impulses take precedence.

Velis lunges to scoop me to him, burying his face in my unkempt hair and putting the full warmth of his chest against mine until it feels like my skin is dripping from my body and my soul is melting.

Wait, is my soul actually melting?!

Something feels different inside. Tingling. Lightness. Liberation?

"You have an incredible soul," Velis whispers as he holds me. "I can tell it's expensive from just one glimpse. And I don't want to take it from you. For a while, it was hard to distinguish between the two, but . . . I don't want your soul. I want *you*."

And I want him. Bad.

"At least take a little." I offer myself to a ravaging beast. "So that we can be tethered. So that your brothers' bonds with me will be broken."

"You still want that?" He pulls away to get a look at my face. "Knowing what I did?"

"Especially because of what you did."

Delight begins to lift his features. "Make a wish."

The only thing I want right now is—

His finger is to my mouth before I can ask for it. "You don't ever have to wish for a thing like that." He kisses me deeply, sincerely, like he's treasuring the experience, like he feels lucky to do so.

Quite an ego boost to be kissed that way by someone who looks like him.

After a hearty helping, he skates his hand to my chest, breathing, "I can feel that desire in there, Master, *throbbing*." He shivers over the feel of it being directed at him. "We'll get to that soon. But first, make a wish."

I wish that Gabe would lose his erectile power.

Velis snorts when he senses it. "You aren't supposed to make wishes that hurt people, and I'm not supposed to be able to allow them, but I may be able to morph it. Say it out loud."

I do, if only to see his eyes flash their signature blaze of blue.

He makes a twisting motion in the air with his hands before screwing up his face in concentration and shaking his head. "Well, that didn't work. How about this?" He pivots his hand in the other direction this time, smiling, satisfied, in the aftermath. "Yeah, that worked. Your boy Gabe won't be able to get hard without first singing an annoying song I heard on the inner nets about loving cats."

Again, I think he means *internet*.

And I think I know the song. Brilliant.

I throw my arms around his neck. "Did it *work* work, though? Are we tethered?"

He rubs his fingers together as if massaging a substance I can't see before letting out the shakiest of exhales. "Oh, it worked." He draws air through his teeth. "And I'm going to show you just how good it feels. Prepare yourself, Dolly Jones."

His expression is dangerous enough that my instincts tell me to back away. But if I'm a little mouse, I'm one that's easy to catch. He crawls over me, peeling off his shirt as he comes for me, maneuvering his way between my knees.

Well, look at you, you little multitasker.

For someone that teases me about liking necks, he's sure going hard on mine, burying his face, nibbling, tugging.

I curl my toes because it tickles.

It's hard to believe this is real. Hard to believe alien boy is Velis. Hard to believe he's mine. Man, I crushed on him so hard when I was a kid. And that kiss in my dorm room? I spent the next year trying to find a comparable one.

But there's nothing like him. Nothing feels as good as him. Nothing pulls me in with so much force.

He kisses my collarbone, making me feel thin and pretty as his teeth sink into me with care. He wants his bite to hurt, but only a little. Only enough to feel good.

It all feels good. Even better now that he's admitted that he's in love with me, but . . .

What does that mean for us?

Our relationship is supposed to have an expiration date. Based on what I've seen of his world, my race is a deal breaker. And what happens to a genie that refuses to siphon his master's soul? Does our bond just stay intact forever? Can he never find a new master?

But he doesn't want to be a wish granter anyway. He wants to be a healer.

"Dolly?" The word is full of the sound of his mouth on my skin. "You're distracted." His lips travel up my arm to my shoulder to try to pull me back to him.

It works.

I slide my hand over the center of his sweatpants, magically conjured to allow for easier access, I assume. I want to lick him, suck him, make him throw his head back and cry out at the feel of me. He senses the things I desire dripping out of me and succumbs to a boyish whimper. "You can't tease me like that, Dolly Jones. You'll be the death of me."

I can tease him like that, and I will. I'll tease him and tease him and tease him until he can't stand it anymore.

Passion like this only exists in movies and raunchy books with unassuming illustrations on the cover.

I slide my hand beneath his elastic waistband and watch him tense in pleasure, never looking away, keeping his breath even with mine.

"I love you, Master."

I lift an eyebrow the way genies like to do. "I love you too, doll."

"Cute," he says.

"Am I?" I tighten my hand around him, and he pushes back against me, soft and warm. And sizeable.

"You have no idea," he says.

It's the spark that sets off the dynamite. He takes charge of the situation, tearing down my leggings to reveal underwear formerly stowed at the furthest reaches of the drawer. He mingles his tongue with mine, beginning a motion with his hips that we both know well, pushing against me like the opening movement to a long concert. I wrap my legs around him in compliance, to pull him closer, to ready for what comes next—

"Velis Reilhander, you're wanted at your father's estate at once!"

The symphony of it all comes to a violinist's shrieking halt as a blue-haired man in a formal suit manifests in my living room between my mother's knitting basket and my grandfather's favorite chair.

Velis stops, midway through his teeth pulling at my lip, his hand cupping my nipple, while I scramble to dissolve myself into the crack of the couch. "*What the hell*?!" I hiss, tucking my knees into my chest and covering my face.

Velis shifts his body to hide me from view. "Evaris." He reveals the man's name with tundra dryness. "*Great* timing. What are you doing here? We still have over a week left."

"Your father has called an end to the contest. You are to return to him at once. I suspect it may have something to do with whatever's happening here. Is that a human hiding behind you? I see you're following in your brother's footsteps."

"I'm nothing like Arrik!" Velis charges with bravado. "Piss off. Tell Father I'll be home in a week."

I take the moment to use Velis as a shield and pull my leggings back over my hips—all the way up past the belly button where they belong—before I peek over my genie boyfriend's shoulder to get a better look at the djinn intruder.

The man named Evaris is likely in his forties and completes his getup with a pair of light blue gloves and matching neckpiece that looks more like a gaudy, six-looped gift bow than a traditional bowtie. His hair is short in the back with a large curl in the bang, like he might be the doorman at a swanky mansion party.

Not that I've ever been to or will ever be invited to a swanky mansion party.

"You have ten minutes to come home willfully, or I'll return with the guards. Clean up, and leave the human." Without allowing time for rebuttal, Evaris exits the scene with a double snap of both hands like he's applauding a spoken word piece.

After, Velis lets out a groan. "Fuuuuck. Sorry about that, Master." He shifts over to stroke my collar. "Ten minutes isn't enough time for what I want to do to you."

"An end to the contest?" I sit up, hair askew, like it was caught in a wind turbine. "What does that mean for us?"

He eyes me over piercingly. "I'm . . . not sure. But I am sure that I don't want your dwelling crawling with guards from our estate. I'll dip back to Makaya, see what's going on, and then be right back."

But only wish granters or those with 'special permission' are allowed to hop between realms. Will he no longer be considered a wish granter after the contest ends?

"What if you aren't allowed back?" I try not to show my desperation.

The question is enough to make him reconsider. He transitions to the edge of the couch, elbows to his knees, and rubs his face with both hands, thinking through the outcomes of being called home early.

"Whatever happens, they'll want me to come back here to erase your memory. They won't let you go on with everything you know." He looks up at me. "Don't worry, I'm not going to erase your memory. It nearly killed me the first time."

But to me, this all feels so final, like gray clouds are rolling in over the ceiling of my 'dwelling.'

"They wouldn't send someone else back to do that?" I question.

"Shit." This time it's his mouth he holds in contemplation. "I don't know what to do. What I know is that I love you and I can't let you go. I also know that choosing to be with you would mean giving up everything—my family legacy, my place in society, and that's a hard decision to make. I'm not saying you aren't worth all that, I just . . . I need more time."

I get it. It's asking a lot. And while I do love him back, I have no idea what I want my future to be like either. I was so focused on making it through the last two weeks of that year-long hell that I wouldn't even allow myself to look beyond it.

What do I want?

Do I want to . . . marry him? Marry a genie? Live in a fucked-up, socially imbalanced fantasy world? It's all so unfathomable and ridiculous, but . . . I want more time with him. I've loved him for so long, even if I've only just remembered it. But love can break, love can change. People can change.

I need more time too.

"Come with me," says Velis, reaching a hasty decision. "I'll make you invisible again. It's a stupid idea, and I'm sure we'll get caught, but just . . . come with me. I want the person on my side *at* my side for once."

That's what I want too. "Can I change quick first?"

I feel like I've been camping in the wilderness for a week.

"As long as you don't change into that hideous sweater," he jokes.

No. I'll be burning that hideous sweater, along with the pictures from that night. I'll make a ritual out of it.

By the time I return to my genie, freshened up, his hair has reverted to that fake dusk blue, and he's dressed fancier than I've seen him this whole time. Are those *slacks*?

"I thought you said you were going to change?" he says.

"I did." Fresh black leggings. Fresh black shirt.

He can't stop the grin from invading as he shakes his head and extends his hand to me. "All right, baby doll. I'm taking you home."

CHAPTER 21
All the Love

We transport into a white study with marble floors and golden trim and windows backing up to a multi-colored garden of hedges, standing polite and tidy as soldiers. The man called Evaris is standing beside the door, equally tidy, equally soldier-like. And behind a grand dark-wood desk sits a man, Velis's dad presumably.

But ohh lordy. Velis's dad is a *daddy*.

I suppose I should have expected him to be, having housed the seed responsible for the specimens that are Velis and his older triplet brothers. His eyes are that signature pale blue, his hair the darkest cobalt peppered with flakes of gray and white. His bone structure must be what laid the pattern for all the blessed male children after him.

He wears a white business suit similar to those found in the human world on only the richest, swaggiest men.

Velis stands before him, fingers woven through my invisible ones.

"Hello, youngest son."

"Hello, Father."

Velis was right. His father won't look at him; he merely scribbles with a quill as if it's far more important than Velis. His demeanor is cold and distant, his chin stern.

No wonder Velis feels unloved by him. And yet, over the fireplace mantle is a great portrait like the one in the library. A carefully decorated depiction of Velis's beautiful mother, shimmering golden hair tied back in an elegant knot and eyes that seem to jump at you from the frame. Eyes that are a shape unique to Velis. None of his brothers have the same.

How can a father love a mother so deeply but feel nothing for their son? I don't believe it. The only thing strong enough to create a rift that vast is pain.

"Set your vessel on the table, Velis," his father instructs.

Velis's grip tightens around my invisible palm. "Why?"

"Set your vessel on the table, or Evaris will do it for you."

Showing his teeth, Velis begrudgingly retrieves his shrunken vessel from his pocket and restores it to its full size.

Come to think of it, Velis mentioned that the vessels were made of a substance no longer mined. His looks so antique and glassy, while his brothers' are modern and metallic. Is it a *magical* substance capable of being formed into different appearances?

"I hear you've been having fun, Velis," says his father, never looking up, words unflinching. "Stealing power from your brothers, visiting your great-uncle, traveling to the past without filing the paperwork properly—"

"I didn't know how many stops I was going to make at the time—"

"I'm not finished," his father cuts him off, sharp as jagged glass. "Granting your own wishes, using wishes to physically injure a human boy—"

"He deserved it, Father! He was going to—"

"*I'm not finished,*" Velis's father snaps, and suddenly, Velis's lips are no longer able to part.

"What the heck? Your father's a jerk!" I say to the only one that can hear me. "I'm right here, Vel. We'll get through this."

His jerk of a dad is rambling: "Then further altering that boy's fate by sticking him with an ailment that will change the trajectory of his life."

The erection song. Oops.

"And, last but not least, your human pet, whom you've confided in, told djinn secrets, brought to the djinn realm more than once, had intercourse with, and have confessed your love for. Now, I assume all of that was a disarming technique? I'm told by your brothers she has an impenetrable soul."

Velis says nothing.

"You may speak," his father allows, without yet showing his son the respect of eye contact.

Velis looks at me with contagious sadness because he knows our fate is sealed. And it's come sooner than either of us hoped it would.

"It's okay," I tell him. "You can lie to him. Tell him I don't mean anything to you. Tell him it was all a trick to get my soul."

"No," he says, gentle and broken. "It wasn't disarming. I did all of that because I love her. I love her a lot. In fact—" The next part he utters to me and me alone: "There isn't enough love in the world."

It zings through me like electricity, forcing the hairs away from my neck and arms.

He's just quoted my hidden tattoo.

Velis's father stands, hands behind his back. "I see. Go on then. Reveal her. We know you've brought her with you, though Evaris explicitly ordered you not to."

Fear overtakes my genie, enough to burst through his eyes. "*I'm going to send you back, Master*!" he hushes, frantic. "*I'm sorry, it's all I can do for you*!"

But when he gives my hand a squeeze to enact the spell, nothing happens. His efforts have been blocked by someone with far more stockpiled soul juice than anything he could have ever amassed.

"Fine then," says Velis's father, approaching from behind the desk. "You do it, Evaris."

The bow-tied minion is on us in a flash, setting a hand to my head, and after, it seems I've become visible to the rest of them. Anxiety building, Velis tries to sneak another spell to send me back to the human realm, but again, his efforts come up dry. Not one to give up, he swears under his breath before twisting his hands in another direction and beginning another approach.

"Don't strain yourself, Velis," his father says, having no trouble locking eyes with me. "The room is cloaked against your magic. Your power is sealed."

Velis is breathing heavier now, his expression showing traces of that darkness hiding beneath the surface. "*What are you going to do to her*?"

"Me?" says his father. "I'm not going to do anything. That's your responsibility."

Evaris moves his hand to my shoulder to pull me away from Velis.

"You've yet to steal her soul and erase her memory, though it seems you've managed to tether. Go ahead. Finish it. We'll wait," his father orders.

The way he speaks is without any shred of emotion. He's as flatlined and hard as the wood forming the furniture in this cold, pristine, *cold* room.

I prefer bohemian love nests.

"No," says Velis.

"No?" says his father.

"No, I don't want Dolly's soul, and I'm not erasing her memory."

"Very well," says Velis's father. "Put her to permanent sleep, Evaris. Make the decision easier for my wayward son."

"NO!" At that, Velis leaps forward and captures me in his arms, ripping me from Evaris and pushing me into the corner behind his back like a mother bear guarding her cubs.

I don't know what to say. I don't know what to do. I feel helpless.

"I don't know why you're protesting so hard, Velis. You've won the contest. I called it early because it's statistically impossible for your brothers to catch up to you in the remaining days. You've won. The estate is yours. All you must do is tie up this loose end."

Velis's fists are tight as knots, his teeth throwing snarls.

"I know that's a lie, Father! I know you'll never give the estate to a half-blood like me! I won't give up Dolly! Let me send her back with her soul and her memory."

His father's tone doesn't shift. "I would never lie to you, Velis. The estate is yours. Evaris already has the deed drawn." At long last, Velis's father lets his eyes meet his son's. "I swear it on your mother."

Magic words. It's as if one breath moves through Velis as he finally believes his father. His fists unclench and his shoulders straighten. "The estate is mine?"

"You must allow your brothers to remain lairds of it, but yes, you will be named laird-in-waiting. You will act as my proxy until I can no longer maintain affairs, at which point they will transfer to you. You may continue your healership studies in the meantime."

It's everything he wants. To become a healer and to win the estate.

"But . . . I have to give up Dolly to get it," Velis says, voice cracking.

Sweet.

But this shouldn't be a choice he has to make. This can't be a choice he has to make. This path is a guarantee, and our future is not. Relationships swell and fall, and even though I want him, and even though I know I love him, I can't allow him to make this choice. It's for both our sakes.

If he chooses me, he'll eventually resent me for it. And I will feel guilt worse than the guilt I've faced the last fifty weeks.

If he doesn't choose me, I'll feel heartbroken.

I need to be the one to do it.

"I can't let you make this choice, Vel." I come out from hiding behind him. "This is everything you want, everything you've worked so hard for, everything you deserve." Hell, here it comes. Why am I always crying around this boy? "I love you, and I want to be with you, but I can't ask you to give all of this up when we don't even know what a future together would be like. You need to do it. You need to accept his offer and wipe my memory. I'll be fine." My breaking voice is doing little to convince either of us. I force it down. "You know I don't need some *guy* to make me happy."

"Dolly." He can barely get my name out as he shows me all the anguish in his eyes. He gathers my cheeks and tries to form something else.

I know this is hard for him. It makes me feel so warm that it's hard for him. I'm nearly as important to him as all of this. As a mansion and a title and a future and everything he's ever wanted.

"Thank you." Eyes wet, he finds my forehead and kisses me the way he did back at Mayree's. Even then I knew. I knew there was something more between us, something neither of us could resist or control. Whatever it is, it doesn't have a name, but it's there. "I love you," he whispers. "I'll miss you."

"I won't," I joke because I'll have no memory of him.

Tasteless.

"But don't make me be the one to do it, Father." Velis looks up. "Please. I have plenty of soul balance. I don't need hers. Please let her keep it."

"Very well," says Velis's father, observing us like a stone statue. "Evaris will wipe her memory and bring her back to the human realm. After, we will unregister your wish granting license, and it will break her tether to you. Her soul will remain intact, save for the small amount you've already drawn from her. That can be your consolation prize."

Consolation prize.

Heartless.

Velis nods in solemn acceptance. "Okay. I'm sorry, Master. You're going to forget what really happened that night, and your guilt is going to come back."

"It's okay. I was just about ready to move on with my life, and I know now it was for the best that I got exiled from that group of people."

"And your dwelling will need to revert to the way it was before," he says.

"You know I have plenty of money to spruce it up on my own." I force a smile that's too weak to make impact.

The invisible elastic connecting us stretches as Evaris coaxes me away from Velis, who stays in the corner, face tight and suppressed. It hurts. But I'm going to be okay. I've survived worse. I am smart, and I am strong, and I am capable.

But . . . who was the first person who ever told me that?

Things are going to get hard for you, but you're going to push through them like you always do. You're smart and strong and capable.

I could feel how badly you wanted one of these. It's on the house.

I like the way you look at beauty. Most people just look. You absorb.

You're a good person, Master. You deserve a break.

What can I say? You're a spunky, unapologetic little dork who isn't afraid to stand up for herself and call others out on their bullshit.

I was really close with my grandfather too!

Oh, you're gonna like my flavor, Dolly Jones. I guarantee it.

Humans have bugs living in their beds?!

I'm her boyfriend, you rapist fuck!

You are something else, Dolly fucking Jones.

A myriad of memories come swarming over me like gnats on a baseball field. I don't need to remember all of this right now. I don't need to remember why I fell for him.

The face he wears is like someone stretching to reach a lost balloon over a great chasm. Is he experiencing the same trip through our time together as I am?

You're worthy of winning, Velis. And everyone knows it.

I have a very steady hand. You have three seconds to get out of here or I'll shoot!

Oh my god, don't talk about touching tips in front of me right now.

I showed you a beautiful place. This place is just as beautiful.

There's blatant discrimination going on! How can you stand it? I want to punch that girl in the throat!

Any human film will tell you that you're the kind of character that deserves to win.

What the fuck is this?! An adult onesie?!

Just your neck, Velis. Just yours.

Arrik, Jeb, Beckham! I wish you would transfer all of the soul power you've won during this contest into Velis's balance!

I've been wanting to do this for a very, very long time, Mr. Alien.

Yeah, memories are swirling around him too. I don't hate it. I don't hate how hard this is for him. It means his feelings for me are real and deep and raw. God, I can't believe he's been a part of my life for so long. I can't believe my imaginary alien friend turned out to be a hot, sweet, magical being that loves me back.

It's . . .

It sucks.

Love fucking sucks. I should have a say in this. I should have a say over when and how I get to fall in love. I didn't want this. I fought against it with all my might, and yet here we are, standing in the pretentious office of a pretentious manor in a pretentious other world.

And my heart is beating at him. It's going to take only a measly second, and then it will be over, and I'll forget I ever knew or cared about a genie named Velis.

I'm living through the pain of it all at once.

Evaris places his hand atop my head. It feels like I'm rolling up the creaking rails at the top of a giant rollercoaster, looking down at the ant-like world before the outcome of the choices I've made pushes me over the edge. I'm about to plummet. He's so close and yet so far, breathing as short and fast as I am. We're climaxing together but in a way neither of us ever wanted. I can't will my voice to show, so instead, I mouth the thing I want to say to him:

Knock 'em dead, doll.

"STOP!" Velis lurches forward, fine-ass arm outstretched. "Evaris, stop!"

"V-Vel?" I stammer through thick anticipation.

He ignores me to desperately petition his father, who is standing still as an unshakable pillar. "I changed my mind, Father. I want Dolly. I choose Dolly!"

That's stupid. We both know it's the wrong choice.

And yet my heart is reacting with fervor, pulsating so hard that it feels like it might come bursting out of my ribs and hit Velis in the face.

Wait, that isn't an exaggeration. Something's wrong. My heart is racing way faster than it should be! I'm having a heart attack? I fall to the ground, gripping my shirt and letting out a sick frog-like croak, and notice that Velis is across the room doing the same.

What is this? What's happening to us?!

We're dying. Velis's father is killing us because of our love.

The sound of a thud lets me know that my back has hit the unforgiving marble ground as the world around us goes dark.

"Open your mouth, human."

That isn't Velis. It's that Evaris guy, and his silky gloves are gripping my face. The world remains dark; my eyelids refuse to open.

"Open your mouth, Dolly Jones," the butler says again.

I comply because I don't have the will to disobey.

"Well?" says a second voice from above. Velis's father.

"It's there, Sir," says Evaris. "Just like yours was."

"And my son's?" says the man made of stone.

"His has manifested as well."

"Thank Maka." These are the last words I hear out of the mouth of a cold, stern daddy djinn before the world returns to silence.

CHAPTER 22
My Grandfather's Vessel

I'M SLEEPING in a heap of flower petals overrunning the streets like an Easter curse. The parasites coat me, my arms and beneath my back, finding their way into my *crevices*. My mouth is full of them. My armpits too. I cough them out and open my eyes to a strip of daylight creeping through long drapes fancier than any I own.

The softness I feel isn't due to the deceased petals of flowers that have overstayed their welcome on brittle branches. It's due to a bed with soft overflowing blankets of purest white and a mattress built to suck you in.

This bed was made for kings. And, oh look, it's suspended from the ceiling, hanging off the ground by inches.

I'm not alone in it. Through the cloudlike folds, two arms stretch out and latch onto me, forcing me close.

I smell him before I see him.

"Velis?" I whisper, afraid to shatter whatever dream this is.

He releases a sleepy groan.

"*Velis*!" I hiss, harsher this time, waking fully and shaking at him to do the same. "*Get up*! *Where are we*?!"

He looks like someone in the middle of the softest dream as he flutters his eyes open like a princess. "Hey, baby. Morning. Come get your sugar."

"*No*!" I swat at him. "Wake up, you moron! Where are we?!"

At last, it hits him, and he remembers what went down in his father's office. He blasts into a state of waking like someone jumping into an ice bath. "Dolly!" He clutches me to himself. "I'm so sorry, I almost—I can't lose you. I tried to convince myself I could, but I can't."

I know. I smile at him. The freaking dumbass chose me.

And I love him even more for it.

But still—"Where are we? What's going on? I felt like I was having a heart attack and then . . ."

"This is the manor," he says, shuffling into sitting up. "This is one of the rooms reserved for foreign lairds."

Must be why it looks extra fancy. With a huge walkout balcony, windows open to flirt with the curtains, and furniture that looks like something out of a period drama featuring royalty. Is that a flipping *chandelier* hanging from the ceiling like something you'd drop on a villain in an action comedy?

"I felt it too," he says, rubbing his chest. "I thought my father was ripping me open from the inside for defying him."

No. That isn't the case.

"I think . . . I think he wanted that to happen," I say slowly, as I remember. "After it did, that Evaris guy looked inside my mouth and saw something and said you had the same thing, and your dad sounded relieved."

"Really?" says Velis. "Mind if I take a look?"

I part my lips for him, and he takes my chin the way he always does, but before prodding me open, he leans forward and gives me his breath and warmth through a kiss that seems to be verifying that I'm real.

Is it possible that my feelings for him have reached new heights?

Yes.

I resist all urges and instincts to pummel him into the mattress and make up for the scare of thinking I'd never see him again, and instead push him away to open my slumber-scented mouth.

I'm sure it smells not great.

He tips me with authority and peers inward with those special djinn eyes, letting out a gasp at what he sees in the chasms of my soul. "Dolly! It's there!"

"It?" I slobber with my mouth still hung open.

"Your heart's greatest desire! Most people are born with them, but even before the lock was placed, I couldn't see one in you. I, er, checked for it when you were a baby."

Awkward.

"But it's there!" he continues, excited. "I'm trying to read it, but it's a little harder for me to see because my eyes aren't full djinn. Shit. What is it? It's like it's . . ."

He releases my mouth. And stares at me dumbly. Yes, that's the look. He looks positively stupid.

"*Velis?*"

"Dolly . . . it's me. Your heart's greatest desire. It's me."

"What?" I fan him away. "I mean, of course I like you, but I wouldn't say you're my heart's *greatest* des—*Why are you looking at me like that?*"

Gooniness doesn't suit him.

"Aw, Master," he says in a 'gee, shucks' kind of way. "You love me sooo much." He pounces to smother me into mountains of blankets white enough to show one drop of stain.

"I do not! Stop it! Your sex factor is dwindling before my eyes!"

But it isn't. His is a sex factor incapable of dwindling. He could be wearing a clown costume, complete with rainbow hair and a squeaking red nose, and I'd still want to bang him.

"Well, Evaris said you have one too!" I argue, feeling my face redden against my will. "So stop acting like it's just me."

Velis stops. "But I'm a djinn."

Djinn don't have heart's desires?

There's a knock at the door. Ugh. *Evaris.* Here to ruin some perfectly pleasant flirtery. But Velis is in danger mode. He pulls me to his defined body and lowers his chin darkly, in a way that makes me feel small and damsel-like, as if he's the hero in this story.

Evaris doesn't look to be attacking us, though. "Are you naked?" he asks, head popped through the opening between door and frame, covering his eyes with his gloved hand.

"No, we aren't naked," says Velis, dry. "We can be alone together without fucking."

"I'm just going based off what I've seen," says Evaris, refusing to uncover his eyes. "If you are naked, get dressed and meet your father in the visiting lairds' drawing room." He snaps, and two white robes fall into the bed with us. One of those 'special permission' cases, apparently.

"I am not wearing that," I say after Evaris shuts the door. "I'll look like a polar bear."

Based on Velis's creased forehead, he has no idea what a polar bear is. Or he's giving me shit. There's really no way of knowing with this one.

He hops out of bed and moves to the balcony, giving his fingers a snap along the way to drop a lilac in my lap. "My magic is working again," he says.

How does he know I love lilacs?

"What is this, Velis?" I take a moment to brush my thumb over the intricate beauty of the flower he's produced. "Should we be worried?"

"I don't think so. I don't know what's going on, but my father wouldn't have had us brought here—alone together and with working magic—if he meant to harm us. I think he did that as a show of faith. I'm going to go see what he wants. You stay here. I'll be back for you."

But he should know I'm not the sort of woman that stays behind and hides.

He does know it.

Without me saying a word, he pauses at the door. "Fine, Master. *Be that way*." He turns to give me a smirk. "Come on."

"You aren't wearing the *robe*?" I force.

"I am not." The smirk he's wearing swells but soon gives way to focus. He *is* worried. At least a little. His hand finds mine like it's second nature. This time when he holds it, he holds it like he never plans to let go.

The sweat will make him forfeit that ambition, though. I'm sure of it.

Through a hallway that looks like it belongs in a castle, Velis leads me past door after door, each carved with ornate decoration, each hiding rooms as lavish as the one we woke up in, each barring the way to places no human should see, until at the furthest end, we reach one that's open.

The drawing room, by the looks of it. To be honest, I don't actually know the purpose of a drawing room. Is it really a place for people to draw in? I doubt it. But then, I'm an uncultured swine in a setting like this.

Human? Check.

Lower middle class? Check.

Tomboyish, squishy, and crass? Check, check, checkity check.

This manor is no place for a person like me.

Inside the room are two uncomfortable looking . . . settees? I don't know what constitutes a settee; all I know is that these objects are much classier than your standard sofa. Velis's daddy dad sits in the center of one while the Evaris chap stands behind him, proper-like.

Velis's father gestures to the opposite settee.

This room has a portrait of Velis's mother in it too, in a different dress, in a different position. This time, she's in a woodland setting, glancing down over her shoulder to show off luxuriously long eyelashes that look to be masking a hundred secrets.

Velis glances up at it with a flicker of emotion on his way to the fancy *settee*.

A low ovular table stands to separate us from his father, boasting a . . . hookah? For some reason, I expected tea. And I expected jeeves over there to speak nasally while offering us some.

Instead, Velis's daddy brings the hookah cord to his mouth, causing the water in the glass body to bubble with a lovely swampy sound. He shoots a ring of pink smoke from his lips before offering the spout to Velis.

Not what I expected.

Velis follows suit, blowing two rings before handing off the nozzle to me. "Only if you want to," he says. "It won't get you high."

I mean, is it rude not to? The last two times I inhaled smoke, it was soiled with Arrik's breath. Whatever. Might as well try the genie hookah. Just another day in the life of Dolly Jones. I take a pull and expect to cough. But it's smoother than any hookah I've ever tasted. It may not make me high, but it has a soothing effect. I feel ten times calmer as I exhale a ring, to Velis's clear surprise.

Yeah, homeboy. I got tricks too. Told you so.

Even in the presence of his father and weird butler, it's hard not to get caught up in the signals we transmit to one another through the shadows and bends of our faces.

I offer the cord back to Velis's father, but he declines with a shake of his head, instead beckoning over his shoulder for Evaris to bring something forth.

It's Velis's vessel, as mysterious and murky as the first time it caught my eye in that thrift store with a two-ninety-nine sticker cemented to the bottom and sandwiched between rejected home-made pottery and Christmas plates. Velis should know what a polar bear is. He was surrounded by them.

Evaris sets the vessel onto the table with a heavy *thunk* before returning to his post behind Velis's father.

Father djinn looks his son in the eye, though it seems to be taking a great deal of effort to do so. "It was your mother's last wish that you be given a chance to use your grandfather's vessel at all costs," he says. "It is an extraordinary vessel, Velis, with a purpose that is held secret by your djinn line on your mother's side. While your vessel is crafted of Drake Rock, the same matter as all vessels, it is also imbued with another substance known as Aphrode's Blood."

"Blood?" Velis questions, leaning forward to study his vessel with new wonder.

"It is not blood from a living being but rather from a moonstone fallen to Makaya many millennia ago. Drake Rock gives it the properties to hunt and farm human souls."

Velis flicks his gaze my way, ready to do damage control over the wording of 'hunt and farm,' but I let it pass. Not worth the fight. And certainly not in Daddy's presence.

The daddy in question continues, "But the Aphrode's Blood gives it another quality: the ability to locate the heart's desire of the one who uses it."

"*My* heart's desire?" Velis asks, like it's funny. "But I'm djinn."

"All living beings have a heart's desire, Velis. Humans are merely the only ones that wear it on the outside of their souls, being the most indulgent race of all."

Indulgent, he says. Has he seen where he lives?! And is it weird that he hasn't, like, introduced himself yet? Or am I supposed to do that? Or is he still planning on wiping my memory, so social niceties won't matter in the end?

"Your vessel bends the rules of what should be possible for a wish granter, for it has another objective that takes precedence over the rules of djinn." This time the silver fox slips his gleaming eyes to me. "And that is to find the person that is your heart's desire."

"The . . . person?" Velis repeats, also looking at me. He's looking at me, his daddy's looking at me, the freaking BUTLER is looking at me. I have an urge to wave, but I refrain, reaching instead for another shot of that hookah haze.

"Your djinn grandfather used the vessel to find your nymph grandmother. Your mother used the vessel to find me. I was hoping against all else that the vessel would lead you to a djinn woman, but that is not how fate was written on the scroll."

Velis's perfect face crooks in confusion. "Mother used it to find you . . . when you were already married?"

"No." Velis's father looks to the portrait hanging over the mantle. "It led her to me while I was young and free, and I courted her, in secret, for the better part of a year. But unlike you, I made my choice based on expectation. I loved her, but I didn't have the courage to defy my own ambitions. It was only after I wed another and made heirs by her that I realized the error I had made. I worked quickly to rectify it, making your mother lady of the estate, despite the nymph in her blood. But she grew ill shortly after." His voice begins to trail. "I regret the time lost during our time apart. If I had known she would be taken early . . ." Velis's dad shows little emotion, but it's definitely there, hidden behind the stone.

"The pain you felt in my study was the burgeoning of your heart's desire. Both of your hearts' desires. Evaris and I put the choice before you to force it out of you, for this human's will resonates as stubbornly as yours does, Velis, and I feared that left to your devices, you would succeed in suppressing your own desires. Alas, I did not want you to make the same mistake I made. You are arrow-pointed lovers, and it is the will of the scroll that you be by each other's side."

It's a lot to hear, and here I am in the middle of some serious family revelations, toking away on magical hookah, the clear outsider. But at some point, Velis's arm has found its way around my shoulder. At some point, he's scooted closer to me. At some point, he's begun caressing my upper arm.

He's got it bad. As I've got it bad. Because we're *arrow-pointed* lovers, don't you know?

"Why would you help us, Father? I know I'm a disappointment as a son."

"You are far from a disappointment, youngest son."

I feel Velis's body react with disbelief. I suppose a similar situation would be hearing my loving mother say she hated me out of the blue.

Velis's father looks past him. "I understand why you think it, and that is my error. I have tried very hard not to favor you over your brothers, for I know the streak of darkness bred in them, and also . . ." He looks again to the portrait. "Your mother is a wound I have not managed to heal. When I look at you, I am reminded of the guilt I feel. For it is you who should have been born first son, Velis. And you would have been, had I not failed to acknowledge her as my first mate." He beckons again to dull-faced Evaris, yet standing behind him. "And that is why I meant what I said. You have won this contest, Velis. The estate will be yours, and you do not need to give up your human to accept it."

Velis lurches forward, forgetting his arm is still wrapped around me. "What?!"

"Your struggles have made you into an extraordinary empath and suitable heir to our family's legacy. You will be laird-in-waiting, and this human, should you so choose her, shall be lady of our estate—though I *strongly* suggest you use a surrogate for the bearing of any heirs."

Evaris, summoned from around the settee, sets down a scroll penned in glowing blue ink and written in a language I can't read. Velis snatches it up with hunger and consumes it at speed-reader's pace. Whatever the document is, it is official and binding enough to make Velis affirm: "It's . . . not a joke."

"It is not a joke," says the father that looks incapable of joking.

I suppose Vel's is the look of someone who's just had all their dreams come true, and all I can do is smile weakly, overtaken by the calming push of pink hookah smoke.

I . . . may have overdone it.

Velis turns to show me his joy, which falls flat when he sees the state I'm in.

Well, this is embarrassing.

"It seems the human has become *inebriated*," butler Evaris notes to the daddy djinn's displeasure.

Crap! They're talking about making me lady of their estate, and it feels like if I open my mouth I might start drooling. Why didn't anyone stop me?! I thought this was just a little chillaxing hookah, not a knock-you-on-your-ass hookah. Velis shows no embarrassment or disappointment, just wicked amusement that I've gotten myself into this mess. He clicks his tongue, saying quietly, "Dolly, Dolly, Dolly, I can't take you anywhere."

"Amusing," says his father, not at all amused.

"I will take care of her, Father," Velis comes to my defense.

"You will need to," says his father. "It is unheard of for a human to hold a title in our world. She will need to be . . . *tamed* before she can be accepted as lady-in-waiting of the estate."

Tamed? I, Dolly Jones, will never be tamed. Velis knows it too. He casts me an uneasy glance.

His father doesn't seem to notice. "And if you wish to wed, you will also need to gain the blessing of the leaders of your nymph bloodline, meaning you will need to make the nymphean pilgrimage as your mother and I did, and as your grandfather and grandmother did before us. It will not be an easy journey, one ridden with conflict, but it should be manageable for arrow-pointed lovers such as yourselves."

More uneasy glances from Velis coming my way. After all, his father hasn't seen us *fight*.

"Also, you will be met with opposition from the community. And I expect your brothers will stand to get in your way. They will not be pleased when they find out you have been made laird-in-waiting. I will do what I can to aid you behind the scenes, but this is your battle to fight with the help of your . . . human." He says the word 'human' like it tastes gross.

I expect I've surpassed all of his expectations in the most negative way possible.

"I understand, Father," Velis says, rising to bow low like he's showing respect to the emperor. "Thank you. I can do this. I'll make the pilgrimage, I'll . . . t-tame my human, and I'll prove myself a suitable proxy. I'll make you and Mother proud. Come on, Dolly." He hurries to hoist me, still mid-bow, crutching my drunk-ass self all the way out the door before I can embarrass us further. As we leave, I hear one of the men left in the room muttering:

"Maka, help us."

"Oh my god." I lie sprawled out over a rug that probably costs more than my college tuition, groaning, "Oh my GOD."

Velis, the devil, finds it hilarious. "That was amazing," he coos, crouched at my side and wearing a demonic smile.

"Amazing isn't the word I'd use, but I'm glad you're amused. What the hell was in that stuff?! You said I wouldn't get high!"

"Yeah, well, to be fair, you didn't get high, you got low. And I didn't expect you to turn into a chimney!"

I roll to face him. "And what's all this bull about taming me? You aren't planning to turn me into some hoity-toity, floofy-doofy wifey, are you?"

"Absolutely not. That would take away most of what I like about you."

Oh.

Cute.

"But . . . we may have to play the part a little bit. And speaking of wifey . . ." He glances down at me. "I know this is a lot. I know you don't really believe in the scroll and arrows, and I know that before a week ago, I was just some mysterious alien visitor to you, but . . ." His eyes are shifty. "Is . . ." He's having a hard time getting it out. "Is that in the realm of something you'd be interested in?"

The world's shittiest marriage proposal.

He's right. It is a lot. A whirlwind love forced upon us by . . . what? Fate? Destiny? *Maka*? Whatever the heck that is.

I'm not sure of a lot, but I am sure that I love him. I am sure that I want to spend as much time as possible with him. I am sure that my life has been worlds more exciting in the last week than it has ever been before. I'm sure that I don't have a lot going for me back in the human realm. I'm sure that I'm not *opposed* to the idea of marrying someone like him . . . eventually.

"Tentatively, yes," I say. "Tentatively, I'll take a shot at becoming your fakely tamed, lady-of-the-estate-in-waiting, arrow-pointed, human bride."

If I thought all of his dreams had come true before, it's nothing compared to the look that splatters onto his face now. But that look is quickly consumed with darkness. "Consummate it." He pushes my shoulders to the ground.

"But that happens after you get married—"

"Consummate it," he says again, kissing a spot on my neck that he knows makes me cry out.

"Ugh, fine, you horny genie," I succumb.

But he's leering like that because he knows I'm equally as horny. He goes in for seconds on my neck, ready to feast, but stops himself at the last minute:

"Hey . . ." His aura fades to one of earnestness, compelling me to take his cheek.

"Vel?"

"You don't have to put any stock in all that arrow and heart's desire stuff if you don't want to, Dolly. I know it's not part of your culture." He takes a breath to help propel him forward. "What I mean is, you aren't stuck here. You have an out any time you want one, okay? I love you, and I want you around, and I meant it when I picked you over the estate. For me, I do want things to get serious. Nothing would make me happier than to take this all the way with you by my side, but . . . I know you've been through a lot. This isn't all about me, so keep me honest, okay? Make sure you tell me if you're having doubts. I'm on your side too."

I'm not having doubts. And it scares me that I'm not. I feel like I should be having more doubts than I am.

It's okay, Dolly. There are no rules for how you're supposed to feel.

He's the one that told me that in what feels like another life. He's already helped me through so much with such little effort. Maybe we really are built to complement one another. I'm not sure of a lot, but I am sure of one thing above all else:

"I'm in, doll. When do we leave for the land of the nymphs?"

Acknowledgments

I can't very well publish a book without thanking the two people who get to see all the dirty, behind-the-scenes footage, who constantly get the brunt of my insecurity, and who encourage me to keep going all the same: my fierce mother, Katherine, and my devoted life partner, Kent. I love you both more than words, and I wouldn't have made it through without you. To my editor, Meg, thanks for helping me get this sucker ready to see the light of day. It is with your feedback that I have the confidence to move forward. To Brooke and family, my constant pluggers and unwavering believers in my craft, thank you for your unconditional support and for flooding Facebook with my posts. To Jenna and Kara, fangirls after my own heart, thank you for motivating me to create a male love interest better (worse?) than Ardette. It's a high mountain to climb, but let's see if Vel tops him. To the rest of my family and friends, you know I love ya! Thanks for checking in and making sure I carve out time for fun. And to Liz of Quirky Cat's Fat Stacks, your passion for books and support of the little guys doesn't go unnoticed. Thanks for all your support!

To my readers who have been with me since the beginning or who are just joining anew, YOU are the reason I do this. I wrote this book as a reflection of a personal experience I went through that tarnished my image and made me question my identity. If you've gone through something similar, I hope you find comfort in Dolly's journey and acceptance of herself and all her flaws. We're only human.

Last but definitely not least—an enormous THANK YOU to my publisher, Midnight Tide Publishing, for welcoming me into your fabulous group of authors and helping me find a home for Come True. Our fearless leader, Elle, has been such a champion for me and the rest of us, and the friendships and support and resources I've found within this organization have been priceless. I'm proud to have an MTP stamp on this book!

For anyone struggling through the first (or fiftieth) draft of their first novel, keep going. It's so worth it!

Xoxo,

Brindi

About Brindi Quinn

Brindi Quinn is a fangirling fantasy author from Minnesota specializing in world-building and romance. She is an advocate of quirky love and firmly believes that banter makes the heart grow fonder. Her main ingredients for a great read are sparkle, steam, and SWOON. Since 2011, Brindi has written over a dozen young adult and new adult novels beginning with her debut epic fantasy series, *Heart of Farellah*. Her works often blur the lines between paranormal romance, science fiction, and fantasy, and her series have been hailed as unique, addictive reads by reviewers. Brindi is an IT Project Manager by day and has a bachelor's in communication-based studies from Southern New Hampshire University. She lives in suburban Minnesota where she likes to bike, indulge in video game lore, and spend time with her life partner, Kent, the world's cutest pup, Burton, and the fluffle of cantankerous rabbits that hop around her house. Brindi is published through Never & Ever Publishing and Midnight Tide Publishing.

Find out more at: www.brindiful.com

facebook.com/brindiful
instagram.com/brindiful
tiktok.com/@brindiful
goodreads.com/brindiful
bookbub.com/authors/brindi-quinn

Books by Brindi Quinn

The Come True Series

Come True: A Bomb-Ass Genie Romance (2022)

Granted: A Bomb-Ass Genie Sequel (2022)

Dreams Really Do: A Bomb-Ass Genie Wedding (2023)

The Echoes Series

A Crown of Echoes (2020)

A Crown of Reveries (2020)

A Crown of Felling (2021)

A Crown of Dawn (2021)

The Crown Saga (2021)

The Bexley Chronicles

Lightborne (2016)

Nightborne (2018)

The Eternity Duet

EverDare (2013)

NeverSleep (2014)

The Eternity Duet (2016)

The Heart of Farellah Series

Heart of Farellah (2011)

Moon of Farellah (2011)

Fate of Farellah (2011)

Atto's Tale (2013)

Farellah: The Complete Series (2017)

Standalones

Seconds: The Shared Soul Chronicles (2012)

Sil in a Dark World: A Paranormal Love-Hate Story (2012)

The World Remains (2013)

The Death and Romancing of Marley Craw (2014)

The Pursuit of Zillow Stone (2017)

More by Midnight Tide Publishing

See the full catalog at: www.midnighttidepublishing.com

Tin by Candace Robinson & Amber R. Duell

A curse to break . . .

Tin is the most famous fae in Oz for all the wrong reasons. Cursed with a stone heart, he is the perfect assassin: ruthless, efficient, and merciless with thousands of kills to his name. When his old friend, Lion, offers him a small fortune to deliver Dorothy to the South for his lover to wear the girl's head as her own, Tin doesn't hesitate to accept the unsavory deal.

Dorothy Gale lost everything—her family to illness, her dog to age, and now her farm to foreclosure. The entire town thought she was crazy for believing in a faerie world called Oz, but even after ten years have passed, she can't help knowing she was right. So when an emerald green portal opens in her wheat field, she jumps at the opportunity to return to the only place she ever felt like she belonged.

Tin wasn't expecting a grown woman to step through the portal, just as Dorothy wasn't expecting Tin to have his stone heart back, but Oz holds more unexpected things than either could have imagined. Magic has hidden dangerous lies behind glamour, trapped innocents in curses, and left the land of Oz in turmoil—none more so than the South. As Tin and Dorothy travel together for the second time in a decade, their lives begin to make sense again. Soon, they must decide who to give their loyalties to before Lion takes Dorothy's head and Tin's cursed heart is forever doomed.

A Cursed Kiss by Jenny Hickman

Living on an island plagued by magic and mythical monsters isn't a fairy tale . . . it's a nightmare.

After Keelynn witnesses her sister's murder at the hands of the legendary Gancanagh, an immortal creature who seduces women and kills them with a cursed kiss, she realizes there's nothing she wouldn't do to get her back. With the help of a vengeful witch, she's given everything she needs to resurrect the person she loves most. But first, she must slay the Gancanagh.

Tadhg, a devilishly handsome half-fae who has no patience for high society—or propriety—would rather spend his time in the company of loose women and dark creatures than help a human kill one of his own. That is until Keelynn makes him an offer he can't refuse.

Together, they embark on a cross-country curse-breaking mission that promises life but ends in death.

The Stars Forgot Us by R.J. Garcia

Fifteen-year-old Jacob Kelly would love to go back to simpler times. Before his parents' divorce and the onset of his older brother's schizophrenia. But when he returns to his hometown, things feel off. After a series of strange occurrences in his new house, Jacob fears the house is haunted, or even worse, he is losing his mind.

To his surprise, Jacob discovers a mysterious teenage runaway, Sanctuary Daniels, living in the house. She reveals she has been kept by a figure known only as Mother, in a place where downstairs children are languishing prisoners, and upstairs children do Mother's bidding.

Both Jacob's investigation into Sanctuary's allegations and their budding romance are cut short when she is reclaimed by evil beings. Beings who unleash terror upon Jacob and his family. Now he must journey to a real haunted house to save his first love and fight for his life.